THE
YOKE

MARK CALLENDER

THE YOKE

iUniverse books may be ordered through booksellers or by contacting:

iUniverse
1663 Liberty Drive
Bloomington, IN 47403
www.iuniverse.com
844-349-9409

ISBN: 978-1-6632-2911-3 (sc)
ISBN: 978-1-6632-3094-2 (e)

Print information available on the last page.

iUniverse rev. date: 10/21/2021

CONTENTS

1

CHAPTER

"WHAT THE HELL are you waiting for?"

"Throw the damn dice; can't you see we're all waiting to hit it big today? Come on, roll the dice!"

This had to be loud mouthed Arnie, a burly, big mouthed youngster who wanted to see action. The overly enthusiastic group anticipated that this inaugural game was the first in the birth of a new and successful underground gambling enterprise.

Andy Cole looked around at this gathering of the greatest minds in the business, all under 14 years old! It was easy to see we had a great future ahead, thinking, I was able to assemble the smartest on our side of town.

Who cared whether or not it was raining? We were in the planned meeting place we had determined a month ago to be the safest. The venue for this gambling experience was under the bridge at the junction of the Highway 28 and Highway 95 in the city of Amalta.

For weeks myself (Andy), Arnie, Chris and a few others had worked out the plans. So, it was not a surprise that in spite of the rain, you could see us youngsters finding excuses to leave our homes for this destination. There was no dithering or contemplation. The plan was set; we would meet on Saturday mornings regardless of weather conditions. We knew that our highway police never liked working whenever it rained, so today our plan was safe.

Today's gathering at this location in the middle of the thunderstorm was the launching of our inaugural game. 'Yes," said Chris, "start the game." He had sensed the mood of the gathering and wanted to warn me of their growing frustration. They were excited and extremely anxious for the grand start of the game.

I hated when Chris opened his mouth. He had this compelling, even voice which caused everybody to listen and to agree with everything he said. "Are you sure you know what you are doing?" This was my call; I needed to be the one to initiate the process and show that I had some knowledge of the game. Although I resented some of what he said and did, Chris was my close friend.

From someone else who was just stepping in there was a loud outburst. "Yes, start the game; no messing around; let's go." This was big Nick, and when he spoke, you had better listen. His fist could open your mouth with one punch, disconnecting each nerve, forcing his thoughts down your throat as well as into your ears.

As we kept silent, the atmosphere was eerie. Thoughts that our future gambling empire was ending before it was started could be felt. We had big dreams of one day having a large gambling casino and employing pretty girls in T-shirts, with dice and money printed on them.

We felt knowledgeable and like experts from our observations of the inner workings of the game that we saw at the Red Roaster, a local gambling joint. Being too young to enter that establishment, a small delegation of us had climbed on the roof a couple of weeks ago and observed the true activities of what gambling was all about, or so we thought. We knew right away we could master this amongst ourselves.

As Andy held the dice nervously in one hand, swirling them gently but carefully moving them to a double palm shake, shaking them harder but unable to separate his hands, the uncertainty of the outcome undermined his confidence to let them go from his palm.

The raindrops pounding on the overhead highway could not undo the sounds of a restless and nervous crowd.

Andy continued shaking, copying the motions as seen from the roof of the Red Roaster club on the spying expedition some weeks earlier. As he was about to release the dice, Frank, our "lookout" man, signaled that the squad car was slowing down overhead. We all stood quietly as "Big Nick" raised his hand to command silence. This calmed the "gang." Frank knew that because of the incessant rain, slowing down was as far as the cops would go. Getting wet was never a part of their job. This knowledge also gave me some relief. I was able to gather my composure and now with some confidence faced the action. I took a deep breath and felt the relief.

Frank, the lookout person and the smallest in our group, knew his job and did it well. He was smart, very observant and dependable. "They are gone." He looked at the group with a fear never seen on his face before. I guess he had never participated in anything illegal for which he could be seen as an accomplice. With a sigh of relief, he repeated, "They are moving. Thank God, they are gone." Then the burden was lifted off him, the one with the responsibility to warn the group of the outside world.

"They do not know we are here, so don't worry," Nick said with an air of excitement as he waited to restart the game. "Let's start the game." He was so happy to restart the game, feeling his odds were so good he would be able to buy himself the double king size lunch on Friday. All Nick thought about, apart from fighting, was his stomach. Guess this is why he was twice the average size of all other kids his age.

All attention was now once again on the game. I held the dice in both hands and the shaking in the legs was not as intense as the first shake, but while the guys thought my hands were more comfortable shaking the dice, they would never know that both hands were trembling as the shaking of the dice became more intense. I could not separate them; they were clasped together for fear of the unknown.

Then the thoughts came tumbling. What will happen when I release them onto the table? This experience being new, did I know what my next step would be?. What will be the outcome? The small droplets on my forehead started to coalesce. I had better throw before they became a stream. I could not show fear, so I tried to keep my composure and, in an instant, I released the dice from my hand. The sweat from my palm allowed them to slide effortlessly from my fingertips. I just simply released them onto the ground.

In slow motion the first die spun until it stopped, showing the three. The second stopped again, showing another three while the last die kept spinning and lodged right under the crotch of big Nick. He could not turn in time to clear out of the way before it stopped. There was complete silence as we stared in amazement and wonder. Although we wanted to know the number on the face of the die, no one was willing to move the part of the pants overlapping the face of the die.

As Nick gradually moved his clothing and withdrew from his comfortable seating position, he revealed that the die had another three dots and we all looked at each other expectantly. Nick was about to open his mouth, and I braced myself for the expletives.

Before he could utter a word, Jerry, the troublemaker in the group, quietly said, "I think Nick and Andy are working together."

I didn't know if he was joking or serious. All I knew was Nick jumped from his seating position to physically lift Jerry in one upward movement. He was about to flatten him. I knew that I was here for a game and to experience gambling, not for this. Before the first fist was thrown, I tried to explain what was happening.

"Stop, hold up a minute!" I shouted while also rising to my feet. "We have bets in place above nine and lower than nine, but we don't have rules for exactly nine," I quickly said. "When we were on the Red Roaster roof, there was nothing like this; it was always lower or higher." This helped in calming all the voices and as Nick lowered Jerry, I knew I had cooled the tempers. At this point, I don't know if I wanted to repeat the game or keep it as is. If I kept it as is, then the winnings were all mine.

As I remembered, from the roof of the Red Roaster the one shaking the cup was always collecting the winnings. I liked his job, not to mention the girls in the short skirts and pom-poms on their derrieres.

On the ground was a fortune. I could easily make a bucket of money. As the reality of the situation struck me, I realized all eighteen eyes were on me. I felt my stomach churning, and I now had to find an explanation because these ten-cent bets grossed the large amount of ninety cents. This was a fortune. Do you know that with ninety cents per game after a couple of games, I would hit the jack pot? I would be able to make a deposit on that new bicycle in the showcase at Willie's Cycle Works. I pictured myself riding into school and Molly Jones looking at me with new love and respect in her eyes. Then someone shouted, "What the shit is happening here?" bringing me back to reality.

Quickly forgetting the dream, I thought to myself, I could do only one thing, so I said, "I will do it over." You could see all the heads nodding with approval. Thank goodness I had saved the day, and my hide.

As I collected the dice, Nick refused to sit close to me. He preferred standing away from the line of throw. I once again placed them between the palms of my hands and started shaking, now confident with my throw. I released these three dice, squashing the odds that it could never happen again. The first die spun towards the middle of the charred area showing a "four" then the second stopped showing a "one." The third die spun on its axis and just as it was about to stop, it showed a "four." What the hell is happening? If the last die lands on a "four," I would be flattened and who knows may even die. If I died, I would never see heaven because this is gambling and my mother always said, "No gamblers live in heaven, and the odds are always against them." It seemed like forever for that last die to settle, but as soon as it was about to end on the "four," it made a last spin and showed a "two." What a relief!

I now had another burden to face – the paying out of winnings. Fortunately, only two bets were for under nine. I had to double their bets, but a profit of thirty cents from my first game was enough for me to know there is something worthwhile to gambling. Furthermore, being the banker increased my chances to get rich quickly.

Over the next couple of weeks, every Saturday whether rain or shine, we met under the highway. This was the meeting place. We had grown not only in number but gaming supplies. We now had a table and cup to place the dice in. We still preferred to play when it rained as the rain made us feel more secure and protected. I was called the Prince of Swindle, a name I cherished.

I had devised a scheme to make my own die with lead fillings in the dots under the paint, so that when I rolled the dice a short distance, the weight would give them the time to settle, hopefully showing the large number and thus improving my odds when most of the bets were under nine. This was a skill learned over time. You had to know when you do a long throw or a short throw depending on the bets. Throwing them further towards the edge of the table increased the odds of the large numbers settling at the bottom, improving the odds of over nine coming up.

2

CHAPTER

I LOVED THIS area of my life, and each week I played out all or nearly all my weekly allowance. I enjoyed the feeling of rolling the dice, and I have never forgotten that first experience of getting into the field, over time, and earning my Prince of Swindle title.

Our new activity had introduced us to the relationship of chance and the understanding of and appreciation for permutation and combinations, which helped me in later years with statistics courses in college. I was successful in earning my degree in Business Administration and then an MBA. My thesis was titled, "Benefits of Gambling in an Open Economy."

Frank and I maintained our friendship through the years; he also got a business degree and an MBA. These early experiences prepared me, or so I thought, for a career in the lottery business and after five years at the company, I had become Chief Executive Officer of the Amalta City Lottery. At this point I encouraged Frank to apply for a job in the same company, and he headed the Finance and Accounts Department.

This was not a local government run department but rather a pseudo agency which financed itself and gave the state sixty percent of its earnings. The main proceeds were used for education assistance through grants to final year high school students with a GPA of 4.0. This program had a great impact over the years and helped students to strive to maintain good scores throughout their high school years. As a result, many students were motivated to stay in high school and still move on to higher education, even if they did not get any grant money, as with that expectation, their grades were high enough to qualify them for college.

This profession had allowed me the splendors of a wonderful life. Unfortunately, and sadly, I lost my wife during a robbery fourteen years ago. She stuck with me through the early years of the lottery business, seeing me through the good as well as the bad years, and believe me, we had a lot of the latter. Fortunately, however, she had given me three of the most beautiful and smart children, and this week I was celebrating this fact. I was especially happy, unable to hold back the smiles as witness to the fact that I was feeling so excited and happy.

My oldest child and only daughter Nadia was starting her last year in college. She chose to pursue her college degree in the state of California. Nadia is all a father could ask of a daughter. She played her part in raising her younger twin brothers, Mark and David. Both boys looked up to their sister and adored her. Thinking of my three children with their distinct personalities, I could not help wondering where these personality traits came from. These kids were brought up in the same environment and had the same type of gifts and inspiration, yet their personalities were all different. I wondered if the personalities of some past forbearers had waited to embrace a new body, like in the form of reincarnation, as I certainly could not take credit. I felt complete, however, as the three children, though so different in their personalities, were good kids. I prayed their inherited traits of goodness would stay with them and bless them throughout their lives.

It was a gorgeous Saturday morning, and I saw this as my last trip to see Nadia off at the airport, this being her final semester. The boys accompanied us, sitting quietly in the back seat. As we arrived at the airport, I felt a new pride in her achievements. Those achievements were countless, and I felt proud to be her dad.

"I am proud of you and I love you so much," I said in a voice that betrayed my emotion. She looked at me with that smile she carried with her from childhood, barely opening her mouth while affixing her eyes straight on mine. You could see the appreciation and pleasure on her face. I felt the joy of having her as my daughter and she knew it.

All these years I had endeavored to treat all my children with the best nurturing and guidance I knew. We exited the car at the thirty-minute drop off site and moved towards the departure desk. I felt proud of my little family, the four of us standing together with pride and honor – not bad for a guy who toiled mostly single-handedly to bring the family together and to this point. The boys were also well grounded and maturing, good at sports and schoolwork. Their friends also met my approval. I felt as proud as hell, man, and I was wearing a smile all day today; this was my day!

Suddenly from the other side of the wide walkway, I heard someone calling my name. "Andrew, hello Andrew Cole," the calm voice greeted, and as I glanced to the right, I saw a short, almost pleasant looking, ruddy-faced, elderly gentleman. I focused, and recognized the face. The person was now closer as he repeated, "Hi Andrew." It was Michael Orrett, the mayor of our great city, and he was saying hello to me.

We have had meetings in the past but have never met outside of the workplace. I was always present at the meetings; however, any meetings we had were with the chairman, whose role was that of a spokesperson. I must say I was pleasantly surprised that he knew who I was.

"Hello, sir. How are you?" I responded in a very subdued voice. Then I remembered I had my kids with me and they were watching. I smiled and with a voice of authority, I said, "Hello, Mr. Mayor. Nice seeing you."

We shook hands vigorously like old friends. Then I said, "My daughter is leaving for her final semester at the University of California." I don't know why I said that, but I guess it was a result of my happiness surrounding the event. I must have been crazy. I needed to first ask him or comment on something pertaining to work, but who cares? I was with my family and for this moment, I didn't care what I said; I said it with pride.

"Congrats!" he replied. "My son also is returning to school in New York. Let's hope that they will both be able survive 'out there.'"

We continued to talk, and with the growing ease of the situation, I became more relaxed. With little else said, we gave each other farewell smiles and as both groups wished each other well, we started to go in different directions.

The mayor hesitated, then turned and said, "One thing, Andrew…" he moved towards my direction, and the feeling I had is that he wanted to move away from each of our groups to talk privately. By this time I felt so encouraged and excited that the mayor wanted to compliment me; my smile got wider.

Suddenly the expression on his face changed to the one I was used to (sour and unpleasant) and he said, "Can we do something about your numbers? The city needs to increase the profits from the lottery."

The voice had now changed back to the one I was used to in the workplace setting. Being caught off guard, the best reply I could muster was, "OK, sir."

In a split second an engaging, but to me an obviously false smile, settled in place to impress the people who, having recognized him, crowded around. This was my chance to escape this unnerving encounter, which had sent chills through my body, and return to the pleasant experience at hand – my children.

As we continued to move towards the counter, Nadia said with admiration in her voice, "I did not know you knew the mayor that well, dad." I responded with a matter of fact smile which belied my feelings. The need for my family unit to succeed was uppermost in my mind. Her expressed pride in my association with the mayor blunted the feelings associated with what he had said to me privately and the ominous implications of those few words. I thought, what price would I have to pay to satisfy the greedy bastard?!

Nadia said, "Anyway, here we are and the line is quite long. I am glad we are early." This brought me back to the pleasant activity of the day.

"Is the plane on time?" she questioned the clerk at the counter.

"Yes, madam." After processing her ticket, he directed her to Gate 14 on Concourse B and wished her a safe trip. She had another thirty minutes to start boarding. I was again preoccupied with my encounter with the mayor. Nadia had to get my attention. "Come on, dad, wake up. I had better go straight to the gate."

We all walked to the security point then embraced, and as father and daughter, we shared parting messages. For each brother she whispered a message not meant for my ears, true to the bond they shared which I admired. Soon she was on her way promising to call when she arrived.

With Nadia gone I would again be able to try to understand the implications of the conversation with the mayor. There was a lot of significance to what was said. I thought this must be a result of post meetings and conversations that identified me as the key person involved in the running of a lottery that was not meeting their expectations. As I returned to the car, I realized had I had overstayed the half an hour limit and there was the parking attendant writing a ticket. The three of us ran towards the car, hoping to stop her, my embarrassment at the indignity being made worse by the mayor commenting as I ran past him towards the attendant.

"Andrew, they are pulling those taxes out of you." He was parked close by in the area designated for city officials. He followed the earlier comment, now addressing the attendant, giving her the usual official smile. "This is one of our officials, and we were here on business." She, in turn, did as was implied, disappointment at having written one less ticket shown all over her face.

The mayor then beckoned Andrew to come closer and quietly said, "There must be a message in these chance meetings." His conversation quickly returned to lottery matters. I told the boys to wait by the car, not wanting them to hear the conversation and also for them to know when the boss calls, one complies without hesitation. The conversation quickly picked up pace.

The mayor stated, "As you know, we rely on the revenue from the lottery to meet the shortfalls in our budget. We are way below expectations. Do something about it. We need to have people winning bigger prizes as it also increases revenue returns. More people need to be buying. That is the bottom line; you need to start a new strategy."

This was a command not a question. My brain up to this time was in weekend mode, but as he added, "Let us meet in my office on Monday. Arrange the time with my secretary," the brain was out of weekend mode. What would my new strategy entail?!

While driving, I thought of the possibility of a four number pick rather than the current six number pick, thus fooling people into thinking the odds were in their favor. What if I added a scratch off option or a special draw at the end of each month? Then suddenly it occurred to me that the Marketing Department needed to be involved and that this was not a one man job. I needed Frank. I immediately called him.

"Hello!" he answered, sounding as if I had awakened him from the best dream of his life.

"Wake up, man. This is no time to be sleeping."

Seemingly shaken out of his sleep by the realization that I was calling on a Saturday, he replied, "Something must have happened for you to call me on the weekend."

"Yes" I replied urgently. "I just saw the mayor at the airport and he expressed his concerns about the lottery. He gave me a mandate. I need your help. You and your staff have to prepare for a meeting on Monday evening. In the meantime, I have to meet with you to plan the approach." I asked if Frank could get his staff together for an emergency Sunday morning meeting using any means possible. They all had to be there and his assistant Consuela was assigned the task to have everyone in attendance. She has to immediately get to work.

I, on the other hand, retreated to my back patio, sipping a double scotch. I knew, although I could not identify what it was that had gone awry, some reorganization had to take place in order to increase the revenue which included increasing the customer base. The back patio always provided the atmosphere I needed regardless of the need. Today, however, was the exception. I needed to concentrate and plan, but even sitting still was impossible.

I felt lonely and alone, having laid the groundwork and built the organization over a twenty year span. Indeed, I was dubbed the CEO of the lottery operations in Amalta. I had put my experience as the Operation Director in Vegas to good use and with Frank as the marketing manager, I knew I had made the current lottery operations solvent. Now they needed me to make it more profitable to buffer the shortfalls in city revenue, partly due to the economic downfall. I felt as if it was all mine to solve, knowing full well many of the issues and solutions needed to be addressed by the marketing department. Marketing was not my forte, albeit my MBA and thesis on "Benefits of Gambling in an Open Economy" was certainly a benefit.

I had excelled in my first job at Libbin and Lebrun, an actuarial company dedicated to the gambling industry. The company prospered and the experience gained there was invaluable, but it did not include marketing and sales.

Such thoughts were interrupted by the ringing phone. It was Nadia. "Hi, dad. Just calling to say I am home and made it safely. How are you?"

I replied, "We are all well. I am preparing work for the coming week." Her comments indicated she sensed this Saturday work stemmed from the airport encounter earlier in the day.

The boys who realized their sister was on the line asked to speak with her, and as I turned to hand them the phone, I realized the dog was lapping up the last of the double scotch.

This was a welcome interruption, more pleasurable than the thoughts of work, which were constantly changing and evolving since today's encounter. The rest of the evening was spent tossing ideas around, but none seemed to come near to a solution.

Nadia called again. "I know you are concerned about the job." That was her way of telling me she figured out something was up. I spent the next couple of minutes giving Nadia an overview without too much details. I did not like to bring work home. I prided myself on being able to separate the tasks of home and work but today proved the exception. We both wished each other "an exciting week" and ended the call.

After hanging up, Nadia said to her roommate Vern, "There is something happening with my dad. After the encounter with the mayor yesterday, his voice and demeanor are different."

Nadia and Vern had been best friends from high school and pledged to go to the same college. Now as roommates in their final year, they continued to share thoughts. "Your dad certainly gets caught up in his job. That's why, as you say, he has done so well," replied Vern.

It was 8 am Sunday morning. No other living thing in that house stirred, as the dog was suffering from a hangover. Such a restless night, Andrew reflected as he grabbed and looked over a mass of papers. There was nothing new to record, no new ideas or solutions to address the current lottery issue. He was as good as dumping them and waiting to see what "the experts" from the marketing department would have to offer.

Andrew became more anxious as the minutes passed, but he made it to the office for the mandatory 10 am meeting. He was large in stature with a voice and persuasive ability that matched his size, and with a quick glance, he could see all were in attendance. His precise and accurate use of language had all nodding in agreement to his greeting and the purpose for their getting together. "I trust you all know what we need to achieve today, so let's begin."

The air was tense, even the breeze from the air conditioner vents seemed quieter than usual. Andrew took his place at the head of the table, hearing the proposals offered which seemed no different from previous ones, despite a few added ideas which did not leave him impressed and only added to his frustration.

"Please remember, we have a responsibility to better the lives of our customers, so that win or lose, the game is enjoyable to the point where losers never lose their hope that one day they will win. On one hand, we have the obsessive gambler who makes up 6% of our lottery customer base, on the other hand, we need to get other people interested and increase the number of customers."

He paused for a while realizing that he could not even convince himself to go on and complete the comparison not knowing what else to say, so he prayed that no one was paying close enough attention as he switched course and proceeded to give the history of the game including some trivia to pique their interest.

"Gambling dated back to the days when Nero, the Emperor of Rome in 54 AD, used lotteries as prizes at his parties. The Great Wall of China in the 7th century BC-1878 BC was financed at some stages by a lottery. In the 15th and 16th centuries some countries in Europe used lotteries to finance their public works. Another notable lottery funded scheme was the British Museum in 1753. Public scandals and criminal infiltration closed the practice down in 1699. In 1995 worldwide returns from lotteries were in excess of $95 billion.

"Those who oppose the practice cited easy money, destruction of ethical values, and crime escalation without acknowledging the enjoyment factor and the good use the proceeds can provide. We need to share these positive aspects and highlight the benefits with the general public in innovative ways."

Andrew gained more confidence as he spoke, seemingly convincing himself as well as his listeners. With new found inspiration Andrew continued, "For the lottery to be successful the following areas need to be addressed: the tickets need to be affordable for all, the prizes need to be attractive, and there needs to be more weekly drawings, with increased and effective advertising, to name a few." Now that he had given them this briefing they recessed for a one- hour break. Their task of returning at 2 pm was to pool ideas for an immediate action plan.

Frank seemed nonplussed in response to Andrew's questions: "Why can't we find the change we need, something revolutionary? Why can't we find it?" This only served to disgust Andrew more as it dawned on him that any break in this impasse would have to be his personal doing. This realization was confirmed when they reconvened and after two hours of haggling and nothing substantial was achieved.

Disappointed, tired, and totally frustrated, Andrew stood up and in a quiet carefully modulated voice stated, "I am totally disappointed with this outcome. You represent the best with your education and degrees in marketing and sales, but initiative, flexibility and performance are lacking. This cannot continue as our jobs are all in jeopardy. I will meet with the mayor tomorrow to ask for a two-month strategy planning period during which time a plan to successfully improve lottery earnings will have to be ready for implementation."

It took all he could muster to keep up appearances and hide his disgust.

Reaching home, Andrew went to his favorite room and as he settled into his favorite chair the phone rang, and it was his favorite daughter. "How is my darling?" he asked.

"Relaxing and getting ready for classes starting tomorrow," she replied, then added, "Any new development in your job? You know this is one of the few times we have discussed your job. I feel honored." Andrew explained that he never wanted to burden them with those discussions, instead, wanting them to concentrate on school work and other things appropriate for their age.

"You are a good daughter, Nadia. For now just concentrate on your school work. I will find a way out." They continued talking for a while, then expressed their usual parting father daughter sentiments.

"There is something different about my dad. His voice is different, all starting with that encounter with the mayor yesterday. I don't know what they were talking about, and it seemed more than pleasantries." She again expressed her concerns to her roommate.

Vern seemed impressed that the mayor knew her friend's father enough to hold a conversation with him at the airport and joked, "I knew one day I would be in the company of royalty." This lightened the atmosphere and transported them to a happier mood.

The University of California located on the coast boasted of summers beautiful sunrises and sunsets while being cooled by sea breezes. The two roommates walked to classes on another beautiful morning expressing their appreciation for the natural unspoiled beauty with little concern for the time. Reality set in, and realizing classes were about to begin they went their separate ways.

Nadia scrambled to the only available seat beside a guy who acknowledged her presence with a smile. She responded only enough so as not to be labeled rude, thinking that he must be new since she had never seen him on campus before. Being accepted for Professor Wassenberg's class in Economics of International Law was the highlight of her college career. It indicated that her GPA of 4.5 had earned her a place in the "Wassenberg clan."

The class proved interesting as was the attention of the person sitting next to her who at some stage mumbled a "Hi." She could sense a new phase in her college life. She wondered if this unfamiliar feeling was anxiety or excitement. Whatever it was, she could not afford to have anything interfere with her studies, so she did her utmost to concentrate on the class.

At the end of the class, she made eye contact and then asked with as much distress in her voice as she could muster, "Why did you keep staring at me? Why did you do that?"

He smiled and said, "I promised myself that I would get your attention if ever you sat near me in class, and so I did." Then Nigel introduced himself.

Nadia summoned all she had learned from the novels she read and skillfully, or so she thought, kept her composure. He had, however, piqued her interest, and she tried to identify why he seemed different from all the others who made passes at her.

What was it? she questioned. Was it his looks, shyness, approach? No ready answers came, but she knew he certainly had her interest. As they chatted for a while, they realized The Ethics of Law was another class they shared. She thought heading all the way to the next classroom until they seated themselves seemed so easy and comfortable, and then Nigel echoed her thoughts.

After class, Nigel invited her for lunch in the cafeteria. She replied, "Do you think that after two classes I would welcome more of your company?" deflating his current euphoric mood. Then with a coy smile, she quickly replied, while winking at him, "Yes, come on. You seem harmless."

Lunchtime sped by as they ate and talked about campus life and studies. Nigel sought to extend their time together, risking being late for his class while offering to accompany her to hers although in a different location.

"Do you think I would get lost on the way?" she responded, at which point they both hesitated, looked at each other and laughed with realization that something different was evolving. Both continued laughing as he walked her to the building before going off to his class.

With classes over, Nadia's thoughts returned to the morning's exciting events. She took a deep breath, recalling the conversations. Not wanting to be laughed at in case things "fizzled," she resolved to be calm and not anticipate or put meaning to anything that was said. The recollections, however, filled her with excitement.

Reaching her apartment door, she took one more deep breath and opening the door blurting out, "I feel so damn good. It's a feeling I never had before," forgetting her resolve to stay calm.

Vern, who was hunched over her books reading over the day's classwork, immediately sensed the mood and urged her on.

Nadia replied, "I met the man of my dreams." Vern echoed Nadia's earlier thoughts and cautioned her similarly, while experiencing a tinge of jealousy. She sensed Nadia's controlled excitement as she proceeded to recount the morning's events.

"Something has certainly changed for you today," Vern commented while sharing a long evening of girl talk.

3

CHAPTER

IT WAS AN exceptionally beautiful Monday morning back at home. As Andrew expected, the mayor's secretary called to arrange a meeting for the afternoon. Later that day, as Andrew made it to the mayor's office for the meeting, with each step he calculated what he needed to say to sell them on the idea of implementing a strategy to double lottery sales over the next two months!

Success! He sold them on the idea that a plan was evolving although no specific formulated plan was outlined, not unlike Sunday's meeting. The serious faced mayor detained him post meeting, and Andrew listened intently as the mayor stated, "You have to be creative, revolutionary, take chances on this issue." The mayor also warned, "I need to get the votes to keep this job. Your job depends on this also."

The mayor remained serious as he walked Andrew to the door. Andrew knew success or failure of this venture would be his legacy. He wished he had brought Frank along to take some of the "heat." Tuesday he would start the planning in earnest.

On Tuesday morning all the members of the marketing team gathered in the conference room adjoining Andrew's office. All had assembled early, hoping to have a few minutes' discussion before Andrew arrived. Surprise! Andrew arrived earlier than expected.

He greeted them in one breath with, "All present; let's get started." The lottery project was all his responsibility, and with his usual eloquence, he added, "Consider this to be the starting point; the past is buried."

The meeting got off to a slow start. Andrew thought he would spur a discussion by inviting an open forum where all scenarios and suggestions would be entertained. Frank took this to be his cue and started to present his first scenario. There were three to be proposed.

The first he said could be the introduction of a new game. Andrew quickly countered, adding a new game would compete with the old game, instead adding new dimensions and adding incentives to the old game would be a better option. This got the attention of everybody in the room as they waited for more proposals. Andrew reveled in the moment, keeping quiet as he waited for the other ideas to be expressed. The moments ticked away with no one speaking until Jason asked, "What do you want? Do you want us to be dishonest and illegal?" This response was totally out of character for him.

Jason, up to this point in the company, had remained quiet and insignificant. He was seen as a fitness freak and a computer wiz, never making any waves. Andrew was taken aback on two accounts – the source of this comment and the fact that no one in this company had ever back-talked him.

Sarcastically, Andrew replied, "At least that is a better alternative to the nothing you have all offered." He then proceeded to outline how even with their combined degrees and know-how, they had no new proposals. "The fat salaries up to this point only resulted in losses for the lottery scheme without the balance of adequate sales. For more effect," he added, "thanks for your ninety minutes of nothing."

Frank was not offered the chance to introduce his other two scenarios as Andrew abruptly ended the session, hoping that by doing it this way he would get them to produce and come up with new ideas.

The morning's trip to the office and subsequent meeting frustrated Andrew. His staff's inability to come up with a reasonable plan made him feel like a failure. Frank, who he thought would have proposed something tangible, proposed a plan that seemed totally ineffective. This was a disappointing start to the day, and the slow traffic was not cooperating either which gave him time to think about and mull over the morning's events. Frank was intrigued by and wondered what Jason's comments meant.

Arriving at the lottery building, Andrew took the long walk from the parking lot to the elevator and up to his office. He passed no one on his way; this he figured was confirmation that all were avoiding him. Needing someone to bounce things off of, he asked Frank's secretary to have Frank come to his office. Morning pleasantries were exchanged in a more meaningful way as Andrew tried to put him at ease and dispel the obvious awkwardness left over from the earlier meeting. Andrew needed Frank to motivate and exert pressure, whatever it took, on his department to come up with tangible ways to get the job done and make the lottery increase in profitability. Andrew wondered what strategy he could use to get him motivated, so he could, in turn, pass it on to the rest of the staff.

Frank entered. "What is the salary budget for your department?" Andrew asked.

"$800,000 to one million with bonuses," he replied. Frank anticipated the next question and with his affirmative answer set the stage for Andrew to start his tirade in a quiet, well modulated tone. Frank sat quietly as Andrew blamed, berated, and credited every failure to Frank's inability to have his marketing department salvage the lottery's failures and make it profitable. In addition, Andrew made it known his successful image was being tarnished (not that he himself had any solutions or anything to offer). Eventually they both looked at each other with the realization that their mutual, longtime friendship and regard for each other was being threatened by this situation. Neither had a solution for the problem, nor did it seem one would be forthcoming during the two months that their ultimatum stated.

"Who is that youngster that interrupted our meeting this morning?" Andrew asked, a welcomed diversion for Frank. His name is Jason

Paye. Everyone calls him Slims," Frank replied. Usually, Andrew did not show interest in staffing matters that his managers could handle; today seemed different. Frank replied that Jason was the son of a former employee, who had asked that he be allowed to prove himself with no special favors granted as a result of being related to her. Frank went on to explain that Jason had proved himself to be a very proficient computer genius though "scattered in the brain" for other things.

Andrew's reply questioned whether this added to the poor functioning of the department, but Frank, who was not sure if he was joking or serious, ignored the comment. Andrew requested to have Jason come see him, so they could talk and probably find out the reasoning behind Jason's comment.

Frank in parting remarked to Andrew that wanting to listen seriously to options from a youngster was a sure sign of aging. He also thought about what could result career-wise for him if Jason was able to offer solutions that he had not thought of.

The phone rang as Frank leaving Andrew's office. It was Nadia.

With an instant change of countenance, Andrew answered, "Hi, my little sparrow." This was his usual morning greeting as she walked into the kitchen while he made breakfast.

"Dad," she replied, "I hope you are not allowing things to rest in that brain of yours and that you are doing well."

Andrew reassured her that things would be sorted out soon at the job and hastened to ask her how things were with her. He sensed the excitement in her voice as she replied, "Wonderful and exciting. I can't wait for the semester to end, so I can make my next move. In the meantime, I have something to discuss with you." Feeling important as a consultant, Andrew wished the tables were turned and he could seek guidance from someone else regarding his work issues.

Nadia outlined her plans to apply for a one-year fellowship in France at the International Court, all to do with her goal to pursue graduate studies in international law. Andrew endorsed the plan as soon as she had outlined it

"I am all for it," he replied.

Nadia then went on to explain that the course started soon after graduation, so he would not be seeing her for a year. Without hesitation he repeated his approval and gave his blessings.

Their conversation was about to end when Andrew answered the knock at the door and after the usual parting pleasantries, welcomed Jason in, beckoning him to take a seat.

"So, you are Jason Paye," Andrew greeted Jason, whose hair was pulled back in a pony tail. He had replaced the usual workday white shirt and tie with short pants to the knees and a T-shirt, and he was wearing track shoes.

Andrew commented, referring to Jason's attire, "I can see you are quite comfortable."

It took a while for Jason to figure this out, but having done so, he replied, "Oh, you mean this cool way of dressing?! I would have worn a tie and shirt if I knew I would be coming to see you."

Andrew, trying to clear the air, commented, "I guess the tie would have been blue to go with the red pants."

Jason replied, "No, pink." They both laughed as each experienced a mutual connection in spite of the age difference.

Andrew, not wanting to waste time, asked, "What did you mean when you commented on thinking too much within the box?"

Jason's reply was forthright. "It's time to stop playing the game of roulette and chance. Things need to be structured, so the outcome is predictable. I am not suggesting anything dishonest. I just like to be different."

To this Andrew replied, "I know exactly what you mean and technology can be used to manipulate the desired outcome."

Both men not knowing exactly what was expected from the other did not state or offer any specifics at this point besides agreeing that technology would be necessary to influence the future of the game. Without further commitment the session came to an end, with each sensing the other's piqued interest and anticipation of more to come. As Jason prepared to leave, Andrew warned, "Everything we discuss here remains in this room."

Jason replied, "Yes, sir."

Andrew had sensed Jason's enthusiasm for a new venture, so it was no surprise that later in the day Jason returned. As if speaking in parables, Jason said, "This is an idea that needs to be developed, but it leads to the outcome of what is to be achieved." Andrew was taken aback and asked Jason to explain what he just said. Jason continued, "I cannot provide the steps until you fill in the blanks."

Jason got bolder, sensing that Andrew was reluctant to state the details but knowing just what he wanted. Jason continued, "Customers stop their betting ten minutes before the actual draw. It needs to be changed to an hour, which gives me enough time to go on line and gather all the information we need in terms of the numbers played for that game."

He stopped for a while to gauge Andrew's reaction, acceptance, understanding and whatever he needed to go on. "Are you following me?" Jason asked. Andrew nodded in agreement. "Other information needed will be extracted from computer data as in the frequency of numbers played and the actual numbers to avoid."

They stared at each other in complete silence. Jason, as if coming out of a trance, then said, "That's it." Andrew laughed out-loud as Jason continued with a serious face, "You now have to do your part in getting those numbers to play. I have done my part."

A longer silence ensued after which Andrew remarked, "How could we ensure that the actual numbers which they need to play would be at their disposal? We may know the numbers played, but there is no way to effect the desired outcome without physically manipulating what goes in."

Repeating his earlier statement of having done his part, Jason walked towards the door. Blocking his exit, Andrew started to recount the history of the lottery scheme from its alleged beginning in Roman times. He stated that over the years the game has had to prove profitable for players and management both on opposite ends of the spectrum in order for it to gain a foothold and achieve popularity. He continued to explain that in order to boost its appeal, the profits needed to be used for worthy efforts like education, improving infrastructure, and healthcare delivery.

As the conversation continued, Andrew managed to complete his analysis of the current system explain the need for increasing profits. This also included a brief discussion as to how to make the marketing attractive, so more people would participate delving into some areas that were outside of his supposed expertise. As he did so, he commented on the inherent risk of their scheme being detected and the inevitable punishment of jail, so Andrew warned that the plans had to be kept secret.

Continuing his commentary, Andrew outlined that with the current "low level profits" the goal of using the lottery for education and other identified projects would never be realized. Having been made aware of Andrew's private thoughts, Jason sensed in him a commitment and sincerity towards a greater good, thus justifying the means.

In parting Jason said to Andrew, "I have always admired you and our meeting has made me more respectful of you." He paused and added, "You are truly a good person to work for. Thanks."

The parting sentiment evoked a sense of renewed commitment and approach to elevating the lottery game to a successful and profitable venture.

4

CHAPTER

AFTER THE EVENING'S conversation with Jason, Andrew saw an exact replica of his youthful days in the young man's energy and enthusiasm. Thoughts of Nadia vied for equal attention. Andrew thought of how Nadia made him proud and recalled the night coming from the theatre when her mother in the robbery attempt took the bullet that was intended for him. He always felt that the hold-up was not robbery related. However, there was no way to prove that as the two perpetrators were never caught. He felt sure there were three assailants because as they made their escape, he glimpsed a third person hiding in the shadows. Nadia, a middle schooler at that time, never lost her free spiritedness, and she with her two brothers gave him the will to go on. His reverie continued until late in the evening.

While Andrew sat in his office considering the blanks to be filled in both his family and career endeavors, his daughter Nadia was embarking on a new experience.

The invitation was a surprise to Nigel. He wanted to get closer, and this might be his chance to show her what he really thought of her. As she unlocked the door, Nadia held it open for him to enter. With the door closed, Nigel held out his arms for and gently drew Nadia closer into a beautiful embrace. She felt heavenly, a great feeling that he has it all were her immediate thoughts.

They both looked into each other's eyes and gently pressed their lips together; it felt good. She thought this was enough to consummate their first contact, but he only slightly released his grasp and drew her back even tighter, mouths opening simultaneously – their first kiss. Nadia felt the rush of blood to her upper body, leaving her weak in the lower extremities. It felt heavenly, she thought.

At that moment Vern walked into the living room. "Forgive me. I apologize. I didn't know you had company." They both quickly backed off in embarrassment, all three looking at each other. Then the atmosphere somewhat cleared.

Nadia, not totally back to earth, said, "Vern, this is Nigel." Then looking at Nigel with glitter in her eyes, she said with a childish giggle, "Nigel, meet Vern." It felt like they were children being surprised by their mother. They all laughed as they showed Nigel into the living room.

"Well, Vern, it's a pleasure meeting you. I've heard so much about you," said Nigel.

"I hope that these were all good things," said Vern.

"Oh, yes. You are the best friend and roommate anyone could ask for," replied Nigel.

That evening the three sat on the rug in the living room and enjoyed a wonderful conversation ranging from the university to public affairs. As soon as Nigel left, Nadia got the initial nod of suspicious acceptance and affirmation from Vern, then an evening of girl talk followed.

Back at the workplace, Andrew was having a late evening as he tried to fill in the blanks from his recent meeting with Jason. They both would eventually leave work and head in totally different directions while sharing a common concern. Andrew headed to the upper suburbs, while Jason headed towards downtown with the excitement of night life and neon lights. They both had thoughts on their minds of ways to take their ideas to the next level, and it would be a long evening for each of them as they thought of workable solutions.

Andrew took the challenge very seriously. Reaching home he retired to his favorite thinking place, his study, where there would be no television interruption tonight. He could sit in his recliner and watch his beautiful aquarium while falling fast asleep.

At three o'clock he awoke, as he looked at all the crumpled pieces of paper scattered on the ground which had all the ideas, thoughts, and possibilities of how to help formulate a business plan. Unfortunately, nothing was flowing, the ideas did not come together, and he could not take the plan in a direction to get the results he wanted. He was a little nervous; it was after three o'clock in the morning and nothing was flowing.

So, he got up and decided to feed the fish, that being the only constructive thing he could find to do. He absent-mindedly kept pouring the flakes of fish food into the water. The fish were very excited about their early morning snack. He moved back into his recliner determined to write an idea down but nothing was coming. So, he sat sprawled in the recliner; he had nothing else to do but stare at the aquarium. How beautiful, he thought, I wish I were a fish. I would swim, eat, and chase the female fish, nothing else.

Suddenly the realization that he had thrown too much food in the water hit him. He was about to get up from the recliner when it dawned on him that of the food that was thrown into the water, the larger particles settled to the bottom and the lighter flakes were still on top. The idea instantaneously hit him like a cannon. He did not move from his inclined position and he just lay back while the wheels turned in his head as he made the association.

That's it, he thought, and he shouted, "YES!"

He could not sleep for the remainder of the night. He improved on his thoughts by the minute, all the way through to six o'clock in the morning.

He had a shower and got dressed for work, forgetting that the boys had to have breakfast and they had to go to school. This was all set straight when the boys heard the garage doors being raised. They rushed downstairs, thinking they were late for school.

His reverie was interrupted by them both shouting, "Dad, we are not ready."

Andrew then realized what had happened; he had absentmindedly concentrated only on his new idea and had forgotten all about the boys.

He then gathered and corrected his thoughts in a minute and fell back into the normal routine. The boys for once were extremely early for school as Andrew maneuvered through the traffic and speeded off to work.

That morning Andrew reached the office in the best of spirits, the guards at the gate were amazed as he entered the building with smiles and the kind of greeting that was missing over the past couple of weeks. As he passed the receptionist, he left a message: "I must see Jason Paye before he goes to his department" and he then placed a "Do Not Disturb" sign on his office door. Andrew waited anxiously in his office like a child with a note from the teacher waiting for his parents to arrive.

There was a knock on the door, and Jason walked straight to his assigned chair. Andrew, although bursting at the seams wanting to talk, did not say a word. They both sat staring at each other, with Andrew smiling.

Jason broke the silence. "Good morning. What's wrong?" asked Jason.

"Are you comfortable in your seat? Are you ready for this?" asked Andrew. By now Jason was uncomfortable, yet excited to hear. "This morning," continued Andrew shaking his head with eyes centered on Jason, "this morning while I was feeding the fish, I realized something about the flakes floating on top of the water in the aquarium."

Jason, in amazement sensing an answer was required, shook his head in agreement and replied, "You want to do the draw in a fish bowl?"

"Yes, ass," said Andrew. "No, if we were to get some balls floating, then those would not sink into the receiver, and then we could predetermine which balls fall into the receiver and control the numbers played. Do you understand?" Andrew asked Jason, who by now had his eyes affixed on Andrew and in a very attentive way.

With a serious face, he said, "No."

That broke the seriousness of the moment. Andrew smiled. "Ok, I will explain. If somehow we were to make the combination of numbers that were not played made heavier than the others, then they would fall toward the receptor while regulating the air just right for the other numbers played to float, never to fall into the receptor. Now do you get where I am going?" he asked Jason.

"Somewhat," replied Jason.

"Look at it this way," said Andrew. "If I had two balls in the air rotating in a bin, the lighter ball will never reach the bottom as you regulate the air to suit it.

At that point Jason started to get the picture but still needed clarification. "If the lighter ball," he asked, "was kept at the higher level in the air rotating throw, how would you get some heavier than the others?" he asked.

"Good question," replied Andrew. Then he remembered as a boy when he wanted the dice to roll, he would just do a paint job on the three. "I know a way!" he shouted towards Jason as he recalled the strategy with the dice game as a teenager.

Andrew went towards the vault in his office where after each draw the case with the balls was locked. Andrew unlocked the vault and pulled out the mobile tray with the balls. In an effort to demonstrate, Andrew proceeded to take out the #12 ball and wrap it with cello tape. "If we were to –"

Jason enthusiastically interrupted. "What do you mean! What do you mean? I may have the idea, but why are you including me into what we are going to do?"

Andrew smiled and reaffirmed, "We are working together and don't forget it. Everything from now on will be us working together and no one else, do you understand?"

Jason reluctantly shook his head in agreement. "OK."

"Let's continue. We are going to wrap the cello tape around ball #12 and place it on the case with all the other regular balls."

As they did this, Andrew then turned on the machine and, as anticipated, the lighter balls floated in the rotating area while the #12 ball being heavier than the rest, after floating briefly, fell into the slot. They were both shocked; they could not believe it had happened as planned. Continuing the explanation, the more excited they became.

"I love it," said Jason. "Let's place all the balls in the case again and wrap the #3, the #6, and the #12 and see what happens. This was done. After turning on the machine and increasing the air flow, the three heavier balls, #3, 6, and 12 fell into the slot, while the others kept floating.

Both were unspeakably amazed. "This is scary," whispered Andrew.

"I know," said Jason. They were both elated at this breakthrough in this high stake gambling scheme, being able to manipulate the game.

"Let's break here," said Andrew, "so we can absorb what has just happened and we can develop the idea later this afternoon."

Both basked in high spirits, knowing the possibilities of what they had just discovered. As Jason left, he commented to Andrew, "Seems as if you are the one filling in the blanks. Just come with the ideas, and I'll be there with you." They both could not wait for the next meeting.

It was a wonderful morning for a good lecture, and the weather was cool as students filtered in Dr. Wassenburg's class. Nigel and Nadia entered smiling and chatting with each other, sharing so much together. The presence of others made little difference to them as they found seats next to each other. They both could feel the admiration and love growing for each other.

After classes their eating place was the lawns near the Arts Center, where they felt comfortable away from the crowds. Here they could discuss the lecture with talk, inevitably ending each expressing how their love and their feelings for each other kept growing.

"Why are you thinking of going to Paris?" asked Nigel. "I believe I am going to miss you."

Nadia smiled and she knew she might want to change her mind. "Firstly, I have always wanted to learn the French language although English so far is the international language. French is spoken in other countries worldwide." She paused. "Also, its culture and close access to other European countries can help to broaden my outlook." Then she added, "Why don't you apply for your dissertation in France?"

Nigel replied, "I don't know. Because I have my eyes on the private sector and to start a family, not necessarily in that order, but if it works that way, then so be it." He looked affectionately at Nadia. Both knew what they wanted, including allowing each other to pursue their dreams.

In the office of the lottery headquarters, Jason and Andrew had their brilliant idea which failed to develop any further. They met regularly during the next few days, still not finding a way to proceed to the next step.

"What is preventing us from finding a way to weight these balls?" Andrew asked Jason, who was sitting with his chair turned around with his arms folded over the back of the chair.

"How easy is it for you to get another set of balls?" Jason inquired.

"Every now and then we order a new supply. Why?" he said to Jason.

"I think it's time," Jason replied.

Immediately Andrew placed an order with next day delivery. They met again when the balls arrived. Jason had made some inquiries on his own and upon getting the new balls, he measured each number and thought he would use the tape to add some weight, to which Andrew countered, "Don't go there because if the tape separates at any stage of the process, all hell will break loose. I don't like the idea of the tape. Why can't we just coat the ball with transparent coating which will make it heavier than the other balls?"

With a simple nod Jason showed his agreement.

Knowing Jason's technical ability, Andrew assigned him the responsibility to get the transparent coating, adding that it had to be water soluble so that it could be wiped off at the end of each drawing to prevent any detection. With that Jason promised to pass by the hardware store after work. Friday evenings he spent with his friends, but not this Friday. He was on a mission.

Andrew asked, "Can we meet in the morning?"

Jason turned around half intending to refuse, but remembering Andrew was the boss and seeing his facial expression, Jason agreed to meet him.

5

CHAPTER

THAT WEEK THE growing closeness of Nigel and Nadia had developed into a deep passion that was inseparable and full of love. As usual each Friday to break the monotony of study, they went off campus for dinner at their favorite intimate corner restaurant, "The Chateau." Then they would take a stroll along the boardwalk before taking a taxi back to Nadia's apartment usually all this by one o'clock.

Nigel always walked her to the door then left, but that night as he opened the door, he held her closely. They kissed passionately, a very special feel; then, he lifted her and carried her straight through the living room into her bedroom, opened the door quietly, and took her inside. They both knew this was going to be a special night. He laid her gently onto the twin bed, and he bent over and kissed her gently on the lips, then moved his tongue down her neck tickling the sweetness, gently exciting her. Then he kissed her thighs while playing with her toes. It tingled and caused shivers throughout her body as she lay there, tears of pleasure smarting her eyes while he moved upward still touching and kissing. He moved her skirt upwards, revealing the beauty of her body. She felt him kissing her between her legs and she experienced a feeling never felt before in her life; it was good.

Vern always waited for Nadia to come home, to share the highlights as all best friends do. This time she found it odd as she approached the room that the light remained off, she definitely heard the front door open so she quietly arose from her bed and looked towards Nadia's room. Innocently, she wanted to know if she was hearing things, so she quietly tiptoed to Nadia's door. She was between two thoughts – if she was not there, then she must be hearing things, but if she is there, all she would have to do is go quickly back to her room.

As she approached the door and peeped through the crack of the door, it was embarrassing to look, but as she turned to move away, she found it stimulating and exciting. As Vern watched, Nadia's body shivered in pleasurable excitement, Nigel moving his tongue over nipples. Vern continued to watch as he took her to the height of excitement. Vern placed her hands in her own underwear as she joined the excitement from a distance but had to withdraw as the pressure of arousal reached that unbearable point. She quietly made it back to her room to complete the unfinished task.

Nigel moving slowly removed Nadia's blouse and stripped off her bra, revealing the most beautiful upper body, kissing her breast and gently licking the nipples. Nadia reeled with pleasure, her body moving to the rhythm of ecstasy and pleasure as they embraced, the feeling of love binding them together. Love is instinctive because she found herself removing his pants. He also assisted by taking off his shirt. What a body, she thought; from his chest to his knees there lay a beautiful specimen of a man. She loved him and wanted the moment to happen with him. Unable to hold back, she shouted, "Wow."

He placed his hand gently over her mouth as he responded to her excitement and passion. He held nothing back as his body tightened. So, she thought, this is how love was consummated. As they held each other tightly, the sweat poured over them, both unable to move, exhausted and tired with pleasure.

As their heavy breathing gradually settled back to its regular rhythm, not a word could be exchanged, so they embraced tightly and passionately kissed, repeatedly looking into each other's eyes. What the hell just happened? She liked the fact Nigel took control of the experience; she gave all of herself to him. It was the greatest feeling she had ever experienced. What a Friday night to remember. Daddy's little girl had become a woman.

At that moment, Vern, now back in her bed, experienced her moment as she could vaguely hear the noises in the other room. She, too, was satisfied with pleasure. What an experience this was, she thought. How I wish I could have taken Nigel's place.

That Friday night Jason could not wait to get started with his search. He found a range of water-based inks, glues, spray paints, and epoxy resins and bought samples of all the coating substances he could find. Saturday morning Andrew's office had the smell of a chemical factory. The job was done again on the #12 ball, hoping for the best undetectable substance. Each time the coating was applied it had to be washed off and another substance applied. Using the new balls and the #12 only, it was decided that 2Y Aceatic Spray gave the best coating. It gave better coverage; it was the heaviest of all the substances and the clearest generating no suspicion. It also washed off with water even after it dried. Each time the #12 ball was added in a trial run, it was always selected with the air control knob turned to volume 6, thus floating the other balls. Jason and Andrew were happy with their accomplishment.

"Remember, as the saying goes, risk is the price you pay for opportunity," said Andrew. "The next step we will be to try all five numbers, so we can set the game." There was silence as this decision was clearly taking them down the road of dishonesty, a frightening path they both knew, and they were scared as they had mixed emotions.

As they broke for the weekend, they both could not wait for the following week to come. The week went quickly. That Thursday afternoon, Jason came rushing into Andrew's office, not realizing a meeting was in progress with Frank and a third person from sales. Andrew shouted, "Come in, Jason." The meeting came to an abrupt halt as Andrew asked the other two, "Let's meet at another time. Is that OK with you?"

The parties were in agreement to break until another time, maybe tomorrow. This raised some concern with Frank and he wondered how a junior in the IT Department could have first preference over his meeting. He thought this was absurd and that he should look into it. Something seemed "fishy." As both individuals left, Jason took his seat excitedly.

He said, trying to catch his breath, "I have come up with the missing blanks. Since the game has a cut off time of one hour before the draw, you don't roll out the balls to the conference room until a half an hour before the draw actually takes place. During this time, I could cross reference from all the retail outlets of the numbers played, and I should be able to supply these numbers within this half an hour window."

Excited, he continued, "You can then find the combination of the five numbers that were not played. If these numbers come up drawn, then you would not have a winner and this is what we are trying to achieve." You could hear the sigh; a weight was lifted from both of their shoulders.

Then there was a big shout from Andrew which could be heard by his secretary who came running in the office only to see Andrew hugging Jason and jumping for joy. This stopped her in her tracks. She didn't know what to do since she knew of the rumors surrounding Jason's after work practices.

"What's happening?" she asked.

This brought quietness to the room. "We just got good news," said Andrew.

Both men looked at each other and laughed. Then Jason immediately started walking out of the office. Andrew shouted to him, "Tomorrow, this Saturday will be the day." Jason nodded in confirmation.

Andrew's secretary looked puzzled. Andrew could not believe the good fortune if this could be achieved and slow down the constant winners. In this way the jackpot would continue to build, creating the excitement for the game. It could be the beginning to other versions of the game. He jumped for joy, grabbing his secretary and proceeding to dance with her in circles, then remembering he was at work, and with Frank entering the room and seeing the dance, Andrew regained his composure.

The waltz stopped and Andrew looked at Frank. "When will this meeting that you ended so abruptly be rescheduled?" Frank asked.

"Monday morning at 9:00 am," Andrew replied.

On Saturday nights it was Andrew's usual responsibility to take the balls out of the vault and present them to the auditors, who would then inspect them and certify the proper running of the game. That Saturday night Andrew as usual was present in his office; surprisingly, Jason was in the computer department seemingly monitoring the event.

The prize this week was considered low against the market comparison, but the regular customers waged against the odds and per usual made their bets by cut off time at 8 o'clock. At eight o'clock as the retailers closed down further betting, Jason began collecting the information by downloading all the numbers played. As Jason cross-referenced these numbers, he realized there was a problem although he had all the numbers played. He could not find five numbers that were not played. Jason continued to cross-reference but time was going, and it was now fifteen minutes and he was typing away but could not find a possible combination.

He started to sweat, and Andrew sensed that something was wrong. Not seeing Jason and knowing time was running out, he hurried out of his office and rushed into Jason's office. "Why aren't you reading what's happening? Twenty minutes have already gone! What's up?" he asked realizing something was holding up the flow. Although worried, Andrew tried not to show his displeasure, consciously not wanting to create excitement with the staff.

"Coming up, soon be with you, the balls are ready," Jason said in desperation. Then, it hit him that it was not necessary for all five numbers to be found if one or two numbers were never played. Two numbers 28 and 15 were never together, so he rushed into Andrew's office with only a few minutes to spare. He shouted to Andrew, "Spray number 28 and number 15. I'll take care of those out of the bin."

Andrew started spraying, but when doing it in the office in the trial run, they had time for the balls to dry properly. This time the spray seemed as if it could not dry in the time allotted. Andrew called to Jason to take the fan from the secretary's desk. Jason rushed and brought the fan, plugged it in, and the process was completed by the 28th minute. Both hearts were pounding with fright, but as they placed them in the bin, there was a knock on the door. It was the auditors. Andrew found that last exertion of energy to push the mobile bin to the door, and he delivered it to the auditors.

As they pushed it down the corridor towards the conference room, there was a sigh of relief as Andrew slumped into his chair looking at Jason, who was already seated. The room was quiet with not a sound heard as they now awaited the draw. Andrew turned on the television to watch the draw. He was so nervous that he could not make it to the conference room.

While watching you could see the number 28 and the number 15 initially slightly holding on to the balls around them, but thankfully when the fans were turned on to lift the balls, they made the balls separate, drying naturally as the game went on.

The numbers played for the game were 2, 8, 15, 28 and 7 – a ticket no one would have played. Jason looked at Andrew, who by now was stiffly still with a little tear leaving his eye, although it was a joyous moment neither of them could celebrate. The whole length of the game took a maximum of ten minutes for the presentation, but for Andrew and Jason, it was the longest ten minutes they had ever lived.

Andrew whispered to Jason, "I think we did it but don't count your chickens too early." The bin was rolled back into the vault with the balls in their receptors; everything went well. After the auditors left, Andrew, with Jason's help, wiped the coating off with water and dried them replacing the numbers 28 and 15 with the original balls.

There were few words exchanged throughout the entire process. They just wanted everything to finish and their anxiety level to abate. They then shook hands and hugged each other as they parted in silence. Jason went straight back to his computer as he felt unfinished and pulled up the program he had developed for the process, which would always find the two numbers that were never played together. He called the program NOSOJ #12.

While Andrew was passing Jason's office, he saw the lights on and he pushed his head inside and said, "Well done." Jason smiled and winked at him which was enough to acknowledge the understanding and bond between them. Andrew closed the door and went on his way without another word. Jason's office light never went out that night; he fell asleep at the desk.

6

CHAPTER

THE MONDAY MORNING meeting usually revealed the winners from the previous Saturday's draw. For once there would be no winners this weekend. The entire team had nothing to do but make plans for the upcoming draw. There was a strange feeling as Andrew instructed the team to double the advertising and marketing expenditure for the following week.

After the meeting, Andrew met with Jason in his office. "Do you have any new ideas for the draw on this coming Saturday?"

"Yes, you have to take out the second set of balls and coat all of them, keeping them separate from the original set."

Andrew wondered why Jason wanted this, so he asked, "Why?"

Jason turned to him and said, "Saturday night had too many anxious moments. If you had the balls coated and waiting to be transferred or exchanged, then the job of coating and washing would not be necessary." Andrew understood and agreed with him.

Later that week, Andrew coated the entire set of new balls and he had them ready for the word from Jason. They spent the week fine-tuning the process. It was a relaxing week for both Andrew and Jason while the market showed a positive attraction by the customers.

Nadia and Nigel always walked to class holding hands, and their conversations were always stimulating and helpful as they expressed their ideas and different points of view in an open-minded way. This approach also helped in improving both their grades as the discussions helped to clarify issues and how they were expressed. It was a great combination and of mutual benefit.

"What do you think of Dr. Wassenburg's point on the Palestine attempt to find a common understanding when Arafat and Rubin meet with Clinton?" asked Nigel.

"It was not explained like that. The conclusion I got from it is that Arafat was the one backing off of the arrangements and not resolving the issues," replied Nadia. "Which class were you in? I certainly didn't understand it that way," she said in the usual assertive tone.

These debates always had an impartial resolution ending with them smiling at each other.

Classes ended earlier that afternoon, so they were sitting under their favorite tree talking. As they sat, Nigel told her about life in the South comparing hers with his. He told her, "My childhood days were involved in hunting small animals with our rifles. That's what boys like."

"I know," she replied, "but guns are dangerous and should be outlawed. There is no place in our modern society for creatures to be hunted by others," she said adamantly.

"Hunting... you don't know how dangerous hunting was in the South during the early days," he said cautiously. "Do you know that people were hunted as game in the South?"

Nadia knew she did not want him to go there as she thought he might want to make up stories, so she laughed and urged him, "Shut up and do not go making up stories."

Nigel got very serious, and he knew he should shut up because these were things never to be spoken about, but he also did not want her to think he would lie. "When I was a little boy, my grandfather told me people would kidnap black individuals from any random area and take them deep into the forest. They would place a locked iron yoke around the neck which had little bells on it. Then they would release him into the forest and hunt him down using hounds."

At this point, Nadia wanted him to stop the conversation which was becoming too sensitive for her. She raised her hand for him to stop.

Nigel said, "They would drink and make themselves merry after letting their prey get a head start. Preparation for these plans were drawn up during the week and the hunting would start on a Friday night. They would set the hound dogs loose and, armed with their rifles, the hunt would begin. The black slaves would have difficulty in running fast with the weight of the yoke around their necks. With the hound dogs on their trail in the dark, they would fall, only to get up again and just keep running. Some even crossed the river only to realize they could not climb the steep cliff on the other side. Some even swam downstream which was worse, the river took them back to where the hunt started. The dogs in the meantime picking up their scent stayed on their trail. No one ever escaped alive." Nigel continued, "At the end their bodies were burnt and buried. The trophy was won by whomever used the yoke most."

Nadia shouted, "Stop! I can't take it anymore. This cannot be true. Such brutality."

Nigel repeated, "It happened. It actually took place. The gangs were called Yokers, and it may still be taking place today."

He looked at Nadia, who responded, "With the education and lowering of racial barriers, it could never be happening in this day and age."

Nigel smiled and concluded, "Stupid people still exist." They hugged and for a moment it was as if they were observing a moment of silence for all the blacks who passed from the brutality of yoking.

It was time to go home, and as they entered the apartment, it was such a depressing conversation that Nadia wanted to be alone. As she got comfortable, her phone rang, and she reluctantly answered.

"How is my little darling and why do you sound so down?"

She looked over to Nigel, who was indicating he was about to leave. He, too, was a little quieter as he reflected on what they had just spoken about, empathizing with Nadia's new knowledge of the experience of yoking. They kissed and he walked back down the steps.

"Dad, I was just going through some old stories and was deep in reflection," she replied, asking, "How are you and my two troublesome brothers?"

Andrew smiled, wondering about the story and knowing there had to be a reason for her tone. "The boys are okay, doing well in school but eating the house down. I can't wait to see the backs of them leaving for college," Andrew replied.

Nadia asked, "How is the lottery company doing? I can feel your more positive reaction recently. It must be doing better," Nadia commented.

"I cannot complain," Andrew responded. "One day I may be upgrading the business structure of the organization and will need an assistant." He surprised her because all her life all she heard about was the lottery. "Since this semester will end soon, do you know anyone who will be interested in such a great opportunity?"

Nadia immediately thought of Nigel, who would be a perfect candidate. He is a little strong headed, but it might just work, were her first thoughts, but up to now she had never told her father of her love interest. She thought how this must be gently released to her dad, the protector of the family, she being his only daughter. Excitedly a plan already forming in her mind, she said, "I will look around and recommend someone for you. Say hello to the boys. Love you."

"Bye," said Andrew who wondered why the abrupt ending. It must be her studies, he thought. She must have to go back to her studies.

Before she could have ended the conversation, she ran from the apartment towards the main steps, shouting to Nigel in the distance, beckoning for him to come back to the apartment. Nigel hurried back up the steps. He could not understand what was happening since earlier Nadia was in distress.

Now she was excited; he could not understand. She hugged him when he reached the top of the steps, and she said, "If you got an executive job right after graduation, would you take it? If the job was near me, would you take it?" She was so excited she could not contain herself,

"Yes, yes," he replied. "What is happening?" he asked.

"Well," Nadia said, "my dad just called and asked me to identify an assistant for him, and I thought of you."

This surprised Nigel because he thought of inviting Nadia to the South before she went off to France, but this might be a great opportunity. "Yes," he repeated as he cleared his mind. "Absolutely."

"Things could work out so wonderfully for us; it would give us the time to start our careers, while building our relationship and you getting to know my family." She had it all planned for Nigel. He saw through this and wondered.

"What do you think?" she asked. "I can see it working perfectly for us. You don't even have to consider it. I will make it happen."

Nadia knew that her dad would consider her decision definitive and accurate. They both hugged and jumped for joy as their lives seemed to be on track with destinations crossing at the right place. By the end of the evening, they were making plans to settle in Amalta. They spent the entire night together wrapped in love, true love.

The non-winning trend continued for some time while the jackpot grew in excess of $15,000,000. Jason and Andrew decided to allow the draw to flow without manipulation. The fever throughout the town was wild; betting had doubled each week. These increases meant more work for Jason, who had to tweak his program to accommodate the increased customers.

New computers and auxiliary equipment had to be purchased to meet demands. Things were on the up for the company. By now Jason was regarded as the technical person in charge and was elevated to a respectable height in the company, and Andrew knew his value. Each Saturday he was able to cross- reference numbers faster and faster, presenting all four or five numbers within fifteen minutes of the closing at the outlets.

The game grew in popularity with earnings over the following months sky-rocketed, while generating unbelievable profits. Customers grew from eighty thousand to over a half million. Andrew was invited to the city manager board meeting, where he was congratulated on his achievements, making him one of the highly acclaimed persons in the city governance.

The drawing became the talk of the town. Every citizen throughout the state wanted to be involved in the growing lottery, taking a chance playing their favorite numbers – the age of the children, their birthdays, even the numbers they saw on the road while driving. Winning numbers appeared even in swirls in their soup all written down for the bet. Any unusual sighting of a number was significant. Little did the customers know that the odds of winning were so low, more than a matter of chance.

The bug was felt through the company, an excitement anticipating chaos. Andrew called Jason into his office and with a worried look said, "I think that this week will need a winner. The game will soon pop at the seams; it's growing too fast. I have asked Frank to come into a meeting with us; just be careful of what you say, before he comes in. I am worried about someone using our formula to place the numbers you have pulled out to possibly purchase a ticket, leaving the funds in the company to use for future growth. This is a serious situation for us to think about."

At that moment, Frank knocked on the door and entered into Andrew's office. He was feeling better being invited into discussions about the game since lately he had felt a little left out of discussions.

"Hi, Frank. Have a seat. I think the game is doing so well. It is bringing pressure on the sales and the accounting department, so we need to make some plans for the future."

This statement and to be part of the planning meeting was all it took for Frank to feel accepted again. He stated, "We have to expand our sales territory. Why not move the game throughout the State of Indiana?"

Andrew interrupted, "How will the game benefit from this experience and added investment for machines and supplies? The state laws they have will have to be rewritten."

Frank countered, "The opportunity cost will be low if the jackpot continues to increase."

At that point, Jason looked at Andrew; their eyes did all the talking.

Permission was needed for the expansion through the offices of the mayor of Amalta. This permission was granted on December 12th through a subsequent conversation with the mayor. A call from the mayor's office to Andrew started with, "Things have shaped up beautifully. You see, my idea of broadening the base has worked."

Andrew looked dumbstruck but agreed, knowing very well who he was dealing with, a true politician. Then Andrew added, "Our game has been expanded statewide. We have been getting inquiries from the state of Indiana. Can you look into the possibility of further expansion?"

The mayor was very interested. "That's great news. I will look into it immediately."

Andrew kept both Frank and Jason abreast with all communications regarding the game. The three were always in discussion when it came to the administration of the game, but the technology and actual physical hands-on implementation of how the game ran was left to Andrew and Jason. Frank knew where his boundary was and was never interested in expanding it. He preferred the marketing and sales of the game, and although he never questioned their activities, he wondered, how they had it put it together.

The draw for that Saturday was $44,000,000 in prize money and growing, an amount never yet seen while customers of thirty million throughout the State of Indiana, the game had grown exponentially.

Suddenly, Jason's phone rang. It was his mother who lived in Illinois. "How are you doing?" she asked.

"Very well," Jason replied. "I have grown to love this job. It is consuming my being, but the self-gratification is comforting. But I will have to call you back. I am at work and they need me here on Saturdays to help with the game."

In amazement she said, "You are at work at this time? What a change, such dedication. Anyway, I know it's late. We will speak another time."

Then Jason asked, "What time is it there?"

"It's eight o'clock," she replied. "Anyway, we will talk later."

In an instant Jason could not put everything together. He could not decipher all the information because he was preparing to give Andrew the numbers, but he knew there was something in what she said with the time. It was out of whack and not in place. Give me some time and I will figure it out, he thought.

It was clear Andrew and Jason had manipulated the game, making it perform satisfactorily, and now it worked to benefit all participants.

At that Monday morning meeting they all congratulated each other emphasizing how each department without exception had performed well under pressure. The marketing and sales department under Andrew showed how their strong advertising through television, billboards, and newspaper presence had brought the turnaround. The IT Department showed how they kept up with receiving all numbers ready for the draw.

Andrew congratulated all departments for their participation and asked them to keep up the good work. On completion of the meeting Andrew looked at Jason with a roll of the eyes and smiled. They both knew that little would the staff know it was their effort who had saved the day. Before the meeting ended, Andrew relayed a message from the mayor's office: "As of January 1, we will be opening in the State of Kentucky." Jason smiled. Frank left the meeting elated but still could not understand the strange relationship between Jason and Andrew, and he sometimes felt left "out of the loop" as Jason was always in Andrews's office.

With so many more entering the game Andrew made the decision to manipulate the game into the new year, making the entry of the new customers a way to provide a well needed big bang.

After leaving work that Friday night, Jason met with his group of friends at their favorite watering hole to have drinks. They met every Friday for the past several months where they always had a good time. The guys had sensed a growing happiness in Jason's demeanor which meant he was happy with his job and the people he worked with. They loved him as part of their group, and they were from the same area on that side of town. He never cultivated deep relationships in the office, but in this setting he could find himself as a member of the gay community regardless of status or race, just an acceptance and appreciation of each other.

On his way home that night with a little juice in his system, the thoughts of the time difference in various areas of the country rested heavily in this mind. He could not understand the anomaly in the system, and he realized this idea had to be checked out. His constant thoughts were about what would happen if there was a delay in the system, and he wondered whether that half an hour would affect the game.

As he lay in his bed that night, he was unable to sleep. He tossed and turned, and then suddenly it came to him – the time difference of an hour between both towns could be a window of opportunity for a customer to use the extra hour to get a ticket. Then he thought it would not really be dishonest, but the closing off on the time was crucial to tallying numbers and the proper closure of the game.

His thoughts continued to trouble him, and if it were not for the betterment of the game, it may have been for selfish reasons or intrigue, but he could see if the plan would work, and then not cash the ticket. This would allow more funds to stay in the jackpot for the education of the children.

All employees of the lottery company had a wonderful Christmas that year, and spirits were high along, with their bonuses. Weighing heavily on Jason's mind was how to continue to manipulate the game. He knew as it grew bigger, the more complicated it would be, so he had to make preparations for this expansion each step along the way.

It was now January and the big expansion into the new state was the big talk. All the marketing and television appearances were to be put into action, and the company on the whole was excited for the day. Andrew met with Jason and decided that week there would not be a winner. The jackpot would again increase and this would increase excitement in the game.

Andrew said to Jason, "Can you imagine if the jackpot grows to over $60,000,000? Can you imagine in another week it could be $100,000,000?"

That Friday might Jason was out as usual with his friends off-loading. In his mind he had put together a plan he knew was not all honest, but since no one knew he was involved in manipulating the game, so what? It would not cause him much damage, he thought. His personality under the influence was interrupted with spurts of seriousness as he contemplated his next moves. His distant mood was felt by the others in the group who brought him back to earth many times during the night. That night he made his decision that early next morning he would make a call to his mother.

"Good morning, mummy," he said, as he affectionately called her all his life. "How are you?"

This affection was an incurably close bond which had never weakened over the years; it was stronger now than ever. His mother had raised him as a single parent struggling during his early years. Then she met her husband together with whom they had a hands-on approach in raising him. They were exceptionally close, and Jason never worried about public opinion; he loved his mother deeply.

"I am doing just fine, my darling," said his mother. "Why are you calling me so early? It's not like you. Are still in my bed?" she said.

Jason replied, "Our company will be making our first lottery draw to include your city and state. Have you been buying your numbers at the corner store?" he asked.

She responded, "Sometimes, I place a few numbers at the Orbit Store, but you know I cannot afford much more than a few."

He then said, "Hold on one minute, so I can see if they are one of the retailers." After a few minutes thinking it through, he said, "Yes, they are one of the retail outlets. I would like you to do something for me later this evening. Our company is doing a survey, and I would like you to check on the flow of the game."

She interrupted, "I know you are always thinking of me; love you for that."

Jason went on, "We want to test the system, and we think there is a loop hole. If it exists, we will have to close the lottery and correct the problem." He added, "It should be no big deal, but let's see."

His mother not knowing what he was referring to said, "I would like to understand what the point is, but I'll leave it to you guys to correct the problem."

Jason continued, "I am going to need your help tonight." He paused for a while. "Are you hearing me all right and do you still have the cellular phone I gave you?"

And, she responded in the affirmative, "Yes, very clearly."

"Well," he continued, "you have to be very precise in your timing. I need for you to be in the store at 9:15 precisely, no later, maybe earlier if anything. Can you make it?" he asked.

"Of course," she replied.

Then Jason told her to have a pencil and paper ready to take down some numbers and to buy a single ticket.

She then interrupted, "Can you buy one for me also?"

Jason laughed. "Yes, but you can by one for yourself, but only one. We don't want it to take too long."

"Thanks," she said.

Jason said, concluding, "You must keep the ticket safely in your handbag and I will call you on Sunday to cancel the ticket from our system."

Her first thoughts were that these instructions were so simple, but she then added, "I wish I could someday understand your job, but I am very proud of you and your dedication to keeping the company on the right path." She said this with admiration and pride.

This response caught Jason off guard because his thought patterns were going in the the opposite direction of her comment. Who knows, he thought, she may just be right. I might just be doing the program on behalf of the company.

As soon as he hung up, he hurriedly called her back. "Mummy, what time did I tell you to be at the Orbit Store?" he quickly asked.

"You told me 9:15. You thought I would forget?"

"No," replied Jason. "The time is really 8:15 your time and not 9:15. Will this be all right for you?" Jason had just realized the time difference was the reason this plan was being put together. How could he have made such a mistake?!

The week was filled with pleasurable excitement in anticipation of the massive expansion of the game. The marketing would take on the label of a once in a lifetime opportunity for the customers in both states if this worked, Andrew knew the next step would be nationwide; he admired himself for taking baby steps all for the growth of the game.

As Jason entered the building that Saturday night shortly after seven in the evening, he went straight to his computer desk. He saw a message from Andrew: "Good luck make it happen." On reading it at first glance he smiled. They both knew what was at stake and this week, with the addition of a greater number of customers, they had decided to manipulate the game, so that without a winner the next jackpot would be so high that the energy in the market would be substantial, maybe an increase to over a quarter of a billion dollars.

As Andrew entered the corridor to his office, he realized Jason's lights were on, so he pushed his head inside and said, "Hi. I'll be waiting on my end."

Jason smiled and nodded "As usual." They both knew that when pressure was about to be introduced into the environment, the fewer words, the better.

After Andrew had pulled back and shut the door gently. Jason felt his body tighten; his adoring smile changed to business mode. He knew that what he was about to try tonight was nothing near what he was taught when growing up, but he thought what the hell? It was an adventure to be harnessed. The adrenaline rush was about to explode; he felt the stimulation tickle his entire body.

All the equipment was working marvelously. The time approached 9 o'clock, and he started cross-referencing all the numbers, remembering the increase in the numbers was greater, but this would be compensated by having more powerful equipment. He and he alone knew the program, inside out, from the initial password to the firewall he had placed at intermittent stages.

At exactly 9 o'clock the main server shut down the game from all the outlets. "Game over" appeared on every screen. At this point Jason could start his cross-referencing. The numbers flashed across the screen, and he could feel his confidence in the program as he knew his ability to do his job. In the midst of putting on the final touches, he got his cellular phone and dialed his mother's number so that by the time he was through cross-referencing, he could tell her the numbers to play.

The phone rang, and after the third ring, Jason pulled himself up a bit since he knew the importance of the call. He felt his mother also knew how important this was, but truly to her it was just another call from her son. By the fourth ring, he started wondering if he had fully stressed the importance of timing to the process; sweat dripped on his nose.

On this fifth ring, his heart skipped a beat; a loving voice said, "My darling son, how are you?"

All Jason could do at this point was smile and think, my mother dearest. He then tried to keep his cool. "Are you ready to place the numbers?" he asked her gently, pronouncing each word accurately.

"I am on my way, only I few blocks left." Jason could not believe it, and he was about to get furious with her when in the most loving way she said, "I am just about to pass the gas station only a few blocks away, but I will make it."

She was truly walking fast to help her son's company; she had her son's interest truly at heart. Jason knew she might not make it to the Orbit Store in time. He then thought to himself, gas station? We should have these all tied up also.

He then asked her, "Mommy, stop a minute and look at the window of the gas station. Do you see a lottery sign?" By then he was shouting.

"Yes," she said. "There is a big sign saying lottery sold here." Jason knew that all the outlets that previously sold the city lottery had also transferred to sell Amalta Lottery, so he instructed her to go inside the gas station and buy the ticket there.

"No," she insisted. "I know my Orbit Store gives more luck than that dumb gas station store."

Disagreeing by now Jason was about to shout, but he pulled himself back, taking deep breaths calmly while the sweat by now was pouring down his forehead. "Please go into the gas station, and I will give the numbers, okay? Go fast, mommy." As she moved closer to the door, a customer got into line just before she could come to the ticket counter, taking a little time to decide which game he wanted to play.

Jason said, "Are you ready to buy?"

His mother by now was also becoming impatient with the customer. Jason had started shouting as he knew the minutes were counting down. It was soon going to be now or never. At that instant Jason's mother shouted to the cashier, "Can you please place my numbers before closing time?" she said angrily.

The cashier looking at the driver asked if he was ready. He again hesitated, so the cashier turned to Jason's mother. "What are your numbers? Do you have them on the betting sheet?" Jason told her no, but he would tell them from the phone.

She then said, "Jason what are the numbers?"

Jason quickly shouted 9. She repeated the number to the cashier. The cashier punched the number into the machine. Then Jason told her 16, and the operation was repeated 5 times through each number: 22, 34, 48. The cashier then gave her the ticket. With all the confusion she forgot to buy one for herself.

In the meanwhile the man ahead secretly had memorized her numbers and tried to play them, but the screen said, "Game over." The customer who was originally ahead of her was so angry at losing his chance to buy his ticket that he grabbed hers and shouted, "This is mine." He was about to run off with it when the sight of a cop patrol car entering the gas station stopped him. "I just wanted to see what you would have done, but anyway good luck," he said as he handed it back to her. With that he left her there, scared out of her wits.

By then Jason's mother had exited the building and was making her way across the road. As the customer from the gas station drove up past her in his vehicle, he gave her the middle finger. Not realizing what had just happened, she waved nicely to the driver, giving him the most encouraging wave.

On reaching the other side of the road she was exhausted but happy, happy to help her son. She did not even realize that the phone was still on; she still clutched the phone in the palm of her hand only to hear Jason shouting,

"Mommy, mommy answer the phone, answer the phone!"

She placed it to her ears. "I'm sorry. I forgot you were still there," she said.

"Did you get it?" Jason asked.

"Yes," she said. "This whole thing is exhausting. I prefer to call you back when I reach home."

Jason agreed. "I am sorry to put you through that, but thanks, love you."

At the lottery head office just as calculated, the balls predicted were played. Andrew replaced the balls and returned the six balls to their respective trays. "We had a good night; everything worked well," he continued. "Incidentally, I won't be in tomorrow. I will be going to my daughter's graduation."

What a relief that is, Jason thought to himself. I will not have to explain anything.

CHAPTER

ON THE DAY Andrew Cole and his two sons arrived for his daughter's graduation he felt he had accomplished all his dreams. He was very successful in his business, and better than this was his figure as a father for all three children. Today his little girl was placing herself on the path every parent would want to see their child take.

The years had passed by so quickly, and as he glanced at the boys, he knew they, too, would soon be their own path, hopefully in the same direction. He felt proud as their parent. As they went to sit down in their seats, David shouted, "There is Nadia!"

She was beginning to take her position in the front row of the graduating class. She was there for the sole reason to be called first, being number one in her class. The ceremony began with Nadia being presented with Summa Cum Laude. Andrew was a proud man. Tears came to his eyes, remembering his deceased wife, who he knew would have enjoyed seeing their little girl become such a spectacular woman. Using his index finger, he wiped away the slender streak of tears before anyone could see his emotions. After the ceremony, Nadia came over to meet with them in the joy of the moment when they embraced as a family, for all of the hope and love.

"Nadia, I am proud of you. I love you, but remember, we all love you," he said to her as they all embraced. She knew he meant those words which had resonated daily throughout her life.

"Dad, this is for you and my family," she added, sharing the events of the day.

Nigel walked up with his mother and father and the introductions were done. Nigel introduced Nadia as his best friend as they both looked at each other and smiled.

After the sharing of greetings, Nadia made a special mention to her dad of Nigel being the person of interest who could fit the role in his corporate search. This resounded with Andrew who said, "Nadia made mention of my company needing a management trainee?"

This made Nigel's eyes widen, and he quickly grabbed the opportunity. Andrew liked his seriousness and he sensed the desire to make a good impression.

Before they parted company, Nigel said, "Before you depart, I will have a profile package ready for you to look over. I hope you find it favorable."

And as they shook hands to leave, Andrew said, "It is a pleasure meeting you and your parents." He then reminded Nadia not to forget the parcel from Nigel.

Both families went their own way, but before they parted, Nadia and Nigel gave each other a big hug with Nigel whispering in her ear, "We may not be able to meet tonight, but I am all yours tomorrow."

That night Andrew took his family to dinner at Blancos, a 5-star restaurant. Still hungry as they walked along the boardwalk, the boys munched on local finger licking wings sold along the walkway with her brother David taking hundreds of pictures.

The next morning both families arrived at the airport nearly simultaneously, obviously planned ahead of time by the two "best friends." Again, they greeted with much affection. As planned Andrew received Nigel's package with his resume.

"It was a pleasure meeting you and your family. You should hear from my office within the coming weeks," Andrew assured Nigel.

Both families bade farewell, leaving Nigel and Nadia once again alone which they certainly didn't mind. However, there were some curious speculation by both fathers about this close relationship. They wondered if it could be more than what they were saying. As the families left, Nadia and Nigel both looked at each other and laughed and hugged all the way home.

As for Jason, his Sunday felt somewhat scary and uncertain as to what would happen as a result of having the winning ticket, and not even the purchaser knew she was the winner. That morning Lidia had awakened with the lottery far from her thoughts until the phone rang.

"HI, mom. How are you feeling after last night?"

She was still drowsy; her bones ached from all of the walking and so late at night. She was never out at such late hours, especially rushing to buy a lottery ticket. "Thank you for the excitement last night. If this is what you call nightlife, then you can keep it. It was exhausting too. How did it end?"

Jason hesitated. "Maybe worth a few dollars, but it gave the company the results they were looking for," he said in a calm tone. "Maybe we will invite you to Amalta," he added, "to visit our head offices in appreciation for your help."

In an instant, she replied, "That sounds great; whenever you are ready." She had so much confidence in her son there was no need for her to look at the draw or even know what the winning numbers were. If this were to help his company, it would ultimately benefit him, were her thoughts.

Monday morning found everyone in good spirits as Andrew arrived at the office for the scheduled 10 o'clock meeting. Discussion centered around growth and expansion. He reminded everyone that there was a winner on Saturday night, so the game would begin all over again. Jason was the only quiet individual in the entire room. His prowess was yet to be recognized. Jason himself did not know the final figure of the lottery at drawing time although he knew he was the winner of a prize.

As the meeting ended, Andrew made an announcement. "Before everyone leaves, I will be hiring an assistant for the beginning of the month. I have interviewed the person, and I am confident he will do a good job."

Frank and Jason glanced at each other in surprise, each had felt they would be the choice one day for the top post, and now there was someone else in the wings.

Andrew called Jason into his office. "How do we have a winner? What the hell happened?"

Jason by now was worried about the decision to hire an assistant, but he would never to say this to Andrew. "I guess one slipped through at the last moment. The game was well received, and you do not have to worry. It will continue to grow."

They both knew the growth was positive, so worrying wasn't necessary. Nothing further was said about the new hire.

Nigel received the call from the Human Resources Department of the Amalta Lottery company offering him the post and requiring him to make a visit to the company by the end of that week.

Jason previously had a plan in mind, but now within these pending changes he decided not to share them. He called his mother that same evening as soon as he left the office. "Mommy, how are you? How would you like to come over for a few days visit?" he asked. "Like, I would love you to come. What do you think?" She replied that she would come with delight. "Leave everything to my planning. Call you later," he said.

Jason's mother was surprised, and she wondered why things were so abrupt, but again she thought that it was just an example of her son being a business person. The next day Lidia went shopping for the proposed trip to meet her son.

A call was made by Jason to the Fostheim Hotel, the most exclusive hotel on the other side of town from the lottery head office. He selected this hotel, knowing very well it was the destination for the rich and famous who visited the city.

"I am calling on behalf of our company president, Mrs. Lidia Payne, and I would like to reserve the presidential suite for her. She will be requesting room service from time to time and a personal assistant." He gave the receptionist the required information. The grand royal suite was now reserved. After the booking, the receptionist promptly told her manager who instructed her to inform him when Mrs. Payne arrived. Next Jason called the airlines to book a first class ticket, and he arranged a stretch limousine with all the perks for pickup.

Later that afternoon, he called his mother, with the information and asked his mother if she could be ready. "I'll be ready. I am ready right now," she laughed. She was relieved that transportation to the airport was included in the arrangements to the airport, parking being so expensive.

At that point Jason said, "See you tomorrow. You will be picked up on arrival. Look out for your name on a sign carried by the driver assigned to you."

Jason, knowing how naïve his mother was, so he tried to eliminate and reduce the anxiety level.

The flight was wonderful, and Lidia made friends with the flight attendant who chatted with her all through the flight giving her anything she desired. On arrival the sign held by the chauffeur was bold and it said: Lidia Payne. On identifying herself, she was driven in style to the hotel.

On arrival at the Hotel Fostheim, Mrs. Payne felt like royalty just as Jason felt his mother deserved. He knew this hotel's good reputation, and he was sure she would respond with elegance and graciousness. The manager was summoned when she was about to register. "There is no need for registration, Mrs. Payne," the manager interrupted. "Your assistant Danny will get the particulars. Welcome to our hotel. We hope you will have a pleasant stay." They parted as Danny showed her to her suite, taking her luggage with him.

Jason arrived later at the front desk, having given his mother enough time to settle in. He introduced himself as her son.

"I can see the absolute resemblance," the receptionist replied.

After a short wait, Lidia's assistant Danny escorted him to her suite.

Mother and son greeted each other with hugs and kisses, having not seen each other for a while. "What a reception! I realize your company must be doing very well. Look at this room. I feel like I am in heaven," she said excitedly, looking at him with absolute admiration and hugging him some more.

"Are they making you comfortable, mom? This is going to be your week." He continued, "And what a week I have in store for you; tomorrow you have a tour of the city and you'll see the many changes. Today we will enjoy a wonderful dinner and share an evening together."

After she had freshened up and gotten ready for the evening on the town, they strolled through the reception area toward the limousine, and all employees' eyes were on her – this elegantly dressed woman. Rumors as to her position and wealth had already started. Her natural elegance added to the aura. The manager Mr. Potts was introduced to Jason as they passed.

Jason and his mother dined at the city's finest restaurant, relishing the escargot, caviar with champagne, the best the menu had to offer. They dined with the city's wealthiest. After a most wonderful night, both sat, reminisced, and made plans for the rest of the visit which included a trip to the lottery office on Friday evening.

Returning to the privacy of the hotel suite, Jason for the first time carefully shared the news of the winning numbers which afforded them this celebratory experience. It took some time and effort to make Lidia understand the structuring of the lottery business and how her purchasing the numbers helped them in streamlining the process to make it more customer friendly. In her mind there were lingering questions, but she felt sure her son knew what he was doing.

Up to this point Lidia, being naïve, was not aware of the value of the winnings. "Friday afternoon we will take the ticket to the lottery and collect the check and then go straight to the bank."

Jason wanted to instruct his mother on the visit to the lottery office to submit the ticket without any fanfare. They appreciated the anonymity of their customers. "Just to show your identification." Jason asked, "What name is on your ID? Is it your married name?"

"Yes," she said. "Mrs. Lidia Payne."

She had kept the name Payne after her husband died, but she never entered into conversation about why her husband never wanted to adopt Jason as his son although he treated him so kindly and was a great stepfather. This also suited Jason because he never wanted any connection to her as the winner of the lottery. Lidia accepted the sequence of events without question; she was having a great time. Sometimes she wanted to ask a question, but to hell with it, she thought. Jason was in charge and everything was all right.

She said, "I am all right. I am leaving everything in your hands."

They both shared a poignant good night, Jason telling her to expect her ride at 11 o'clock the next day.

At 11 o'clock, the limousine was there to take Lidia on the tour of the city, which extended into the countryside. The tour was customized by Jason even to her being escorted into the restaurant at Applebee's for lunch. The table was set with her favorite dish, the most tender sirloin steak. The tour ended at 5 o'clock, at which point she was joined by Jason back at the hotel.

"It was an exciting, relaxing day. I felt as if I was in heaven, being chauffer driven and enjoying all the limousine perks. Thank you, darling," she said. As they walked to her room, she recalled the day's events. "The city certainly has grown and it's good to be back, but give me the smaller city of Speightstown. That's now home for me." She told him her likes and dislikes of the growth of the city over the years.

His mother had a nap while Jason relaxed watching television. He nervously waited to give her instructions on the next day's activities, but he wanted her to rest first; it was a long day for her. After a well-deserved sleep, his mother entered the entertainment area.

"Did you rest well?" he asked.

"Yes," she replied while adding, "the tour took a lot out of me but I had a great time." The evening was comfortable, Jason setting up plans for the next day.

"First, pickup at 11 o'clock and a little shopping for you before meeting me for lunch."

The limousine was on time to pick her up the next morning. She had dressed modestly, and after shopping in the city, Lidia met up with Jason during his lunch period at 1 o'clock. Jason tried to hide his nervousness while eating, while Lidia was as cool as a cucumber.

Jason looked over at her and thought, there is no change in her personality. He guessed it was because she didn't know. She would never be nervous, but he thought some instructions were necessary.

"When you present your ticket with your ID, tell the receptionist you do not need any excitement; you just want to collect, that's all, and make yourself quite clear the customer's request is always honored." Jason had chosen a time of the day which was close to closing time. On Friday the office closed at 4 o'clock, so Lidia's request for anonymity would be less difficult and easily honored.

It was about 3:30 pm when Lidia Payne stepped into Amalta Lottery Head Quarters and presented her ticket, but before arrangements could be put in place for an official presentation. A security guard was holding the door as was a customary service provided near closing time every evening. Lidia Payne had collected her check and was seated in the back of her limousine, being taken to wait for Jason at the First National Bank of Amalta. Jason was with Andrew on the third floor during this time. The cashier was reprimanded by Frank for not making an official presentation to the first prize winner. This was a lost marketing event!!! Jason and Andrew looked on. Jason had a sardonic smile on his face but said nothing.

At 4 o'clock, Jason was out of the office and raced to meet his mother at the bank, the limousine was parked at the entrance. The chauffeur opened the door for Lidia who met up with Jason as he arrived. They both walked toward the bank door, which the guard opened as was customary near closing time every evening.

Jason tried his utmost to conceal his nervousness; he felt his heart skip a beat. Jason slowly composed himself by taking quiet, deep breaths. Jason had previously made an appointment for a Mrs. Lidia Payne to meet with the Vice President for Customer Affairs, Mr. Charles Steinburg. They were directed to his office.

On reaching his office after being seated, Mr. Steinburg said, "What can I do for you?"

"We are looking around at investment possibilities, with a special interest in real estate. We would like to start with this deposit in an interim account to be later moved to a business account," said Jason in a very confident voice, even surprising his mother, who smiled at her son's business acumen.

"For the time being, we would like a checking account for Mrs. Payne." Obviously, Jason knew that it was impossible to have his name on the account; it might have drawn too much attention.

"It will be a pleasure to open this account." Mr. Steinburg held out his hand and collected the check. When he saw the figure, he nearly fell off his chair. From that moment on, the treatment by the vice president was above that of royalty. They were invited to the suite of the president of the bank, where an assistant met them there to sign the necessary documents. Drinks were an option but rejected by both Jason and his mother.

The three papers were completed and signed accompanied by the pretax check in the amount of sixty-four million dollars. Lidia was asked to sign the last page, then passing the form back to Mr. Steinburg, his eyes again bulged seeing the total deposit.

He asked, "Do you want it all in a checking account?"

"Yes," said Jason. "It's only for an interim period."

Even at this point, Lidia paid no attention to the face amount on the check being deposited. Jason collected the check card for the account which he gave to his mother, asking her to always keep it in a safe place, and then they bid good evening to Mr. Steinburg, who opened every door for them on the way to the main exit, where he said, "Whatever advice you may need in starting your investment company, I am at your service. Good evening to you, sir," he said as Jason left the building and entered the limousine with his mother.

Then he said to his mother, "Thanks for your help." She looked puzzled and uncertain, but she knew it was all to help the company.

"Remember, this is why I am here," she replied.

The next stop was the lawyer's office. Jason had previously contacted the legal office of Johnson and Martin, who specialized in corporate law. He made an appointment for an influential lady who needed advice on offshore banking and real estate investment.

His preliminary conversations laid the background for half of the funds to be held in an investment off-shore bank in the Bahamas, a quarter to be invested in commercial property and the remainder in her private checking account to cover fees, taxes and corporate allowances. That evening Mr. Johnson, the senior partner, met with them in the board room. Jason knew beforehand from their preliminary conversations that the legal papers needed to be signed and that Lidia would be there only for the purpose of signing.

As Mr. Johnson's greeted them and explained the legal procedures, his voice was professional and compelling mainly because he knew there was a percentage there for his company's efforts. This law company was the best in the city and highly confidential. After signing, all parties shook hands, with Jason saying, "We will be leaving all transactions and negotiations with your office, beginning with property investments."

Jason felt it was a productive and successful day as they drove to the hotel exhausted. Lidia said to Jason, "Will you get any of that check or will I be getting any?" She laughed.

Breaking out laughing, Jason said, "I wish. Thanks for your help."

They hugged, tired but happy – Lidia for helping her son's company, Jason for pulling it off with no questions asked. They had an early dinner in the room at the hotel that night.

"One day I would love to take you on a trip to Jamaica or the Barbados," Jason said, looking at his mother.

"You promise," she said, looking at him expectant for a date.

"I mean it, when I get a break from the work," he said. "Now I must meet with my friends as we do every Friday evening. Remember your flight is at noon. You should be picked up at 10:30." They kissed and Jason was on his way to meet his friends at The Watering Hole, the only gay bar on that side of town. He had had an eventful day, actually what a week.

No one would ever imagine that this lanky individual, a gay guy was a multi-millionaire. He felt smart that he had actually outsmarted the system.

64

8

CHAPTER

AFTER A WONDERFUL night out with Nigel, Nadia made her usual weekend call. "Hi, family I am coming home today. Who is picking me up at the airport?" she asked with the joy in her voice beaming through the earpiece.

"I will be there at 2:40 to pick up my little girl," said Andrew.

They both laughed. "Incidentally, Dad, Nigel is coming in on the same flight. He will be staying at The Wake Inn. Can he be dropped off on our way home?" she asked.

"That's quite OK, at your service" Andrew replied.

It was Monday morning at the meeting, and Nigel was introduced to the team. Jason's first impression of Nigel was one of self-assurance and confidence, a go-getter who has to be watched. It was early, but he thought he had better keep an eye on him. As Andrew's assistant he was able to learn the ins and outs of the business, and Nigel was enjoying his first experience in the corporate world, especially in the boss's office. He admired Andrew's ability to command and dictate the direction of the company; he found it intriguing.

Jason had to work closely with Nigel in an effort to develop a real friendship, eliminate any jealousy and foster a comfortable working relationship, so they spent time getting to know each other. Jason invited him to have a drink after work at his regular Friday night get-together. Nigel accepted and saw it as an opportunity to meet new friends.

Nigel felt a bit uncomfortable from the start and asked Jason, "Is this a gay club?"

Jason smiled. "Do you feel uncomfortable?"

"No, but I have a certain feeling although everybody is trying to make me feel comfortable," Nigel said quietly.

With a few drinks under his belt, Jason told Nigel of his life and his preferences which frightened Nigel somewhat. When Jason realized that Nigel was becoming uncomfortable, he said, "Gays are misunderstood by others; you do your thing, but remember we're also happy in our space, so be yourself."

This cleared the air so the evening continued with a more relaxed atmosphere. The togetherness was great, and as they parted, Jason said, "See you back at work on Monday. By the way, what are you doing tomorrow?"

"Just relaxing indoors," Nigel replied.

Jason, unknown to most, worked every Saturday night, but this was known to those who knew he was a dedicated employee.

During the successive weeks, the relationship between Jason and Nigel grew better with Nigel saying to Jason after his second paycheck, "I am thinking of putting a down payment on a car. I may need your technical expertise in checking it out."

Jason felt elated with Nigel's confidence in him. "No problem. We can leave from here and go directly after work," Jason said.

That evening after work they both went to AB's Car Sales, where Nigel fell in love with a small blue two-door, two-seater Audi. Because there was a slight dent on the right door, Nigel was able to negotiate a five percent discount. The car was cleaned and prepared for Nigel that same evening, so he was able to drive Jason back to his apartment. As they drove, Jason said, "Look at this crack on the dashboard; we might have received another five percent discount." They laughed because they both knew he had already gotten a good deal on the price.

Nadia spent every Saturday with Nigel, unknown to Andrew, who still considered her his little girl. However, this weekend would be her last before going off to Paris for the next twelve months. When two people find true compatibility, there is the feeling of togetherness that bonds their hearts together even though they are young. They become one through the stimulation of touch and sharing similar thoughts and feelings so deep it penetrates into the inner being of the two people. This must be love.

Walking home, they passed a group of men standing and talking by the yogurt stand.

One made a subtle remark. "The world has certainly changed."

They knew it was meant for their ears but continued walking on their romantic stroll, looking at each other and smiling. They knew one day they would have to confront this issue. As they continued, Nigel stopped, held her, caressed her gently and kissed her in the most passionate way. This showed his feelings, and Nadia felt loved; she smiled without saying a word.

They sat on a seat along the sidewalk as they cuddled in the night air. Nigel said, "You know, darling, we will be hearing lots of these remarks in your lifetime; are you ready for them?"

She looked puzzled. "What remarks?" she asked.

"While passing those guys earlier, did you hear when one said, 'The world has changed'? Those remarks were for us."

As he tried to explain further, she looked at him. "All my life remarks have always come my way. I cannot change who I am. When I was a little girl and a bright little girl," – they both giggled – "one day my mama who died soon after told me, 'The world spins at a steady speed day in and day out; never try jumping off because it's going too fast or too slow; enjoy the ride all you can every day. Remember, as the sun comes up, today's goal is to be better than you were yesterday. So, always prepare yourself for the next day. Never walk in the company of those who want to stay in yesterday. It's a must; tomorrow should build on yesterday; do not be afraid to face it.'"

Nigel looked at her in admiration and thought how those words have helped to make her into the woman she is. The preparation was phenomenal. He felt proud she had prepared herself for who she was and she was his forever.

Nadia continued, "I cannot make others pull me down; I must move forward. I have no time for those who want to stay behind; I have no time for them; the world is not waiting –"

Nigel interrupted her. "Remember, I have never been exposed to people of other races. This is why coming on campus, color meant no difference as I saw each person as the same. I guess there are those who see things differently."

Nadia asked Nigel, "Can you deal with it?"

He looked at her amazed. "How could you ask me that? I love you and everything that goes with it. I will always deal with it."

She wanted to take it further with a smile. She said, "Are you truly certain? It is going to take a man with big balls to handle this throughout our lives together."

Nigel hesitated as he just realized that he had just experienced his first bout with color problems, and he never knew he would have to have a second thought on the matter of race. This was the first time she saw his face turn pale; his lips trembled and he said, "Darling, it was the farthest thing from my mind."

Nadia replied, "If you love me, it will always be an uphill journey together; never leave me. I have saved myself for a man like you. I thank God for sending you to me. I love you, Nigel Eckers." Nadia sat quietly on the bench, reflecting as they shared a silent thought. They both knew there was much to think about now and for the future. Both were deep in thought which remained private and personal.

They knew the twelve month interruption would be helpful in giving them the space they needed, and, if they could survive, then they would have a strong bond between them.

During the week leading to her departure, Nadia asked her father, "Are you taking me to the airport on Saturday?"

"What time is the flight?" he asked.

"In the evening, all flights from here are overnight," she replied.

"Sure," Andrew replied. Immediately, Andrew looked bewildered. His eyes opened wide in confusion. He had just realized it was a Saturday night when he usually did nothing but visit the office.

Then Nadia sheepishly said, "Nigel has asked to take me to the airport."

This took a weight off Andrew's shoulders. "Did you have this planned?" He looked at her through the corner of his eye. "Is there something happening that I do not know about?" They both had a peculiar smirk on their faces.

"We are just great friends and that's what friends are for." Nadia felt like leaving it at that and simply walked off, leaving the conversation at that point.

That Saturday night as Nigel came by to collect Nadia, she led him into the study while she gathered her things together. Andrew entered. "My, you are early. I am happy for these moments with my little girl, and now here you come to take her away."

This shocked Nigel and he thought, did Andrew find out about them?

Andrew said, "I have always been her chauffeur, but thanks to your help, I can be in the office to get the balls from the vault."

At that moment, Nigel realized what Andrew really meant. They laughed and enjoyed the few moments before Nadia's departure.

Andrew sensed something but left the thoughts unuttered: these two thought they were smarter than my old head.

"Drive carefully," he said, bidding them a safe journey and knowing he would not see her for twelve months. He hugged her. "Remember, whatever happens, we love you." Then the boys added their piece and they were off.

While getting into the car for the airport, Nigel said to Nadia as he closed her door, "He is such a dedicated boss; he works every Saturday night."

"Yes," said Nadia, "that has been his life and it is all he knows."

"Yes, I know the respect he gathers from the staff. I do enjoy working with him, but let's go. We do not want to be late."

Her Dad and both brothers stood at the front door waving.

Monday morning meeting with the team identified a problem with the equipment due to the expansion and a need for the company to plan ahead for even further expansion of the machine. The one presently being used had to be upgraded way ahead.

Then Andrew announced, "This project is to be headed by Jason Paye."

When Nigel heard this, he turned red with anger. As Andrew's assistant, he thought heading the project was the reason he was employed. Later that day he confronted Andrew. This was a quality Andrew admired in him but not every time.

He asked Andrew, "Why is Jason getting the responsibility? I can handle this. It should be handled by me."

Andrew looked at him, and seeing the ambitions that he himself had on his ascension to his position, pointed to the chair, asking Nigel to have a seat.

"Technology is Jason's forte. He is extremely proficient in this area, don't you agree?" he asked.

"Yes, I know," said Nigel. "But –"

Then Andrew interrupted him with his finger halting him. Andrew then continued, "Do you know that Jason was a marine in the Middle East and in charge of technical aspects of the drones division? He single-handedly outfitted the computers with his developed software to counter any insurgents monitoring their movements. Trust me, he is extremely good."

"I know he is," replied Nigel, "but I could have overseen the operations and he would still be part of the team."

Andrew added, "But not the leader of the team."

Andrew realized he had a power struggle brewing. He also knew Jason's importance to the operation in ways that Nigel would never know. He had to keep Jason satisfied; he meant more to the team at this moment in time than Nigel.

He continued, "He might look simple and feeble, but do you know he runs ten miles every morning before coming to work with the exception of Saturdays? Do not underestimate him. Despite his weird demeanor, he has a great practical mind. Remember, you will have time to prove yourself. Your turn will come to learn to use the people you have. You do not have to do everything yourself."

Andrew knew that anything involving computer technology would give Jason first preference as shown with his Saturday night activities.

The change over was highly successful, and again Jason was praised for his success in the Monday morning meeting. These accolades over time angered Nigel, who felt he was unable to be recognized by the company. He, however, handled it very professionally as Andrew had asked of him. He always remembered that he had time on his side.

The weeks seemed longer and lonelier without Nadia. Nigel felt that the job was great, but there was something lacking. He was comfortably blending into the team; he had all the qualities Andrew was looking for – ambition and responsibility. He, however, wanted to achieve too much too quickly, and as a result, Nigel's relationship with Jason boiled over at times. Jason was the one to cool the situation and, of course. he would always end the week by inviting him to The Watering Hole, even at times inviting him to private parties held at the houses of the guys.

One day while passing Nigel in the corridor, Jason called out to him, "I have always invited you to our parties and you never show up. I know your hesitation, but come over to my house this weekend. I am having a few friends over and would like you to come."

Jason knew he might not take up the invitation, but it certainly would soften the brewing hostility between them.

"You know the group and we are just hanging out together"

Nigel knew he always promised but never showed up. He also knew he had to play up to Jason's generosity. "Let's see what happens this weekend," Nigel replied with a slight twist of his head as a compromise, and then he continued on his walk down the corridor.

Nigel always felt bad not going out with Jason's friends, but now he knew all the guys in the group and this Saturday he had nothing doing, so why not? he thought to himself. That Saturday when he turned up at Jason's house and Jason answered the door, Nigel did not recognize him, this being a side of Jason he didn't know.

"Hi, is Jason in? I am here for the get-together."

Jason was a cross-dresser and was not recognized by Nigel. Jason burst out laughing at the surprise on Nigel's face.

"Should I have worn my badge halter top?" They both laughed.

"No, I certainly wouldn't," quickly replied Nigel.

"Come in. You know all the others here. This is just a fun evening," Jason said to smooth over their initial meeting. "Some other guest have on little or nothing." When he said that and saw Nigel's face drop further, he immediately said, "I am joking."

Nigel was now able to step in with a little more confidence as he said hello to the others in the group. The group was loud, but the discussions were serious yet playful. Interestingly, politics was one of the loudly disputed areas, and of course lifestyles were highlights of much laughter. They were all drinking and having a good time when Jason quietly disappeared. This seemed to happen every time Jason and the group got together, and they all accepted it and always laughed at his discreet departure. This was Jason's Saturday night office time. After visiting the restroom, changing and returning to the office, he headed off to complete his usual Saturday night assignment.

After submitting his numbers to Andrew, he went straight back to his apartment as if nothing was done. It was now becoming second nature to fix those numbers and to enjoy the ease of using the program he intimately called NOSAJ 12, his name spelled backwards. It was about ten o'clock, and because it was early, he decided to stop and buy chicken and pizza. At least if asked, he would have an excuse for his absence.

The group was having a good time when he walked in. He realized some of the members were gradually pairing off into different areas. Nigel lingered and became very comfortable with the small group which sat on the carpet engrossed in conversation, drinking and socializing. Jason was the joy of the group because he was a consummate host and with his charisma always set the amicable atmosphere. This Nigel also noticed in the workplace. It was just an inborn personality, an innate gift not acquired but a blessing to have.

Jason was the evening's joy of the group with his performance of The Wiggle, which had become his unique dance. He was the only person capable of performing this dance where he placed his index finger on his forehead while wiggling his entire body in a slow fashion. With a big smile he made the wiggle faster, stretching out his hand and suddenly, with an abrupt stop, it was finished.

The group loved it and everyone laughed at this novel, unusual dance and with a few drinks in tow it became funnier. The conversations continued late into the night, and the liquor glasses were refilled continuously through the night. Nigel, by now, was in his happiest state. He was constantly refilling his glass, not realizing there were only two other friends remaining, Jesse a pilot with aviation jokes and his flight attendant friend, Theo. Nigel felt comfortable and drank freely, enjoying Jason's endless jokes and his dancing which accompanied them.

Turning to Jesse, he said, "You could write a book." In no time they were all prostrate on the floor, falling off to sleep.

The next morning as Nigel awoke and as he looked around, he saw there were three persons spread out in the area; two were completely naked. As he inspected himself, he realized he had no shirt on, and he had absolutely no knowledge of taking it off or what had happened. He jumped to his feet in amazement trying to think back on the night's happenings. He had no recollection, but for the jokes by Jesse and the wiggles by Jason, but obviously something else went down. He quickly got dressed and went over to Jason, who had on only a pair of red silk undies patterned with white bunnies seemingly kissing each other – female panties!!

Jason was on the sofa snuggled up with Theo, startled by the desperate pat on his back. He opened his eyes and focused on Nigel, whose thoughts he knew right away, so to calm the moment he burst out, "What a night!" As he moved Theo's hand from around his waist and stood on his feet, he said, "Don't be overly concerned. We all had a great night. Look at them; they are tired and will be sleeping all day."

As Jason got to his feet, Nigel was concerned and embarrassed as he was still unclear as to his participation in the night's activities. To seem calm and inclusive he looked at Jason and could not allow the underwear he was wearing to go without a comment. "Where the hell did you get those from?" making reference to what he was wearing; they both laughed

"These are my kissing bunnies in red. You should see the new pair I got recently." They both laughed.

"I had better be going," Nigel said quite embarrassed and trying to hide it.

Jason following Nigel to the door and while thanking him for coming, promised, "I am going to get a new pair of those for you," referring to the underwear.

Nigel replied, "Thanks for an interesting evening. I am not clear about everything that occurred, but from what I remember it was great." They both smiled and embraced.

Nigel made it home that Sunday morning in a grossly confused state. It was an experience he never thought he would be a part of. Many questions remained on his mind as he wasn't clear of what had taken place. He decided to block all thoughts before it made him crazy. Not knowing what took place was better than finding out and not wanting to face up to the embarrassment of the event.

Later that night feeling guilty, he called Nadia. "How are you, darling? I am missing you more than I ever realized I would. How is France at this time of the year?"

She could not wait to respond. "Yes, you're trying to make frivolous conversation. Where were you all last night? I tried calling you numerous times."

Nigel had turned off his phone on reaching Jason's apartment, knowing that it was a party and getting away without interruption meant freedom without accountability.

He replied, "I was invited to a party by Jason as he was having a few friends over. I didn't mention it to you since it was a last minute decision." He paused. "You know him and how his friends are, so there is nothing to worry about."

After some hesitation, she asked, "So how was your evening? Were there any new girls in the group?" They both giggled, knowing what the answer to her question would be without him saying it.

He knew she had no worries on that score, but if she found out what really happened, things would be different. He had no explanation for himself, much less for her. They continued their conversation on other matters late into the night, he mindful not to mention any more about the previous night's party.

The Monday morning meeting began as per usual including the compliments given to Jason on the previous week's success. Jason already aware of this and not knowing how others were reacting to the special treatment replied, "We are happy with the smoother running of all operations including staying within budget keeping projections. Plans are in place to introduce a new software and upgrade the computer capabilities to meet changing demands, thus giving the company the ability to gather much more information from the market, eliminating possible errors while making sure there is no dishonesty in the system."

Andrew said as he looked at Jason, "Keep up the good work."

The staff accepted these projections as explained in the name of progress.

Jason and Andrew, however, had their own ambitions to better manipulate the outcome of each game.

Andrew continued by saying, "The mayor seems to be pleased with our effort, and in his election manifesto he has promised to double the number of student scholarships available." The staff applauded, complimenting their own effort as a team more so than the mayor's plan.

At the end of the meeting Jason and Nigel were exiting through the corridor. Nigel turned to Jason. "You were given some great accolades earlier. Congrats on the great work." In that compliment Jason could sense a sniff of jealousy; he, however, was gracious enough to accept it with a smile and a thank you.

Then Nigel continued, "Please, one day you must tell me what transpired at your party." Jason gave Nigel a cynical smile and walked on. This smile would always haunt Nigel as the uncertainty of the night's events made him feel Jason always had something over him.

Later that week Andrew called Nigel to this office. "You know I have been waiting for the right project for you to oversee. With the planned upgrades to the technological aspects of the game, I need you to collaborate with Jason on improvements to include the customers watching the draw on television to feel more a part of the play-by-play process."

Nigel agreed to do so and immediately called Jason for a meeting in the conference room. After going through the many alternatives to get the new program working, Jason realized if the meeting progressed, then the present working of the draw may be interrupted. After the meeting he went straight to Andrew's office, and being granted permission to enter, he confronted Andrew. "Why would you want to change the operating procedure of the game and not improve on what we presently have? Do you know what would happen if these changes were made?"

Looking straight at Andrew he said, "We would go back to the old system of small turnovers, small winnings and eventually smaller amounts of customers and smaller profits." He concluded, "It's dangerous to do so. It would be suicidal."

On realizing how concerned Jason was, Andrew consoled him. "Don't worry. I am depending on you to delay these improvements. The board is expecting improvements but has not assigned a deadline on the project. With all the profits generated there is no need to set indicators that might upset the smooth flowing of the game. So, try to extend the time line for implementation of changes, so the effects of the improvement on income will not be drastic."

He thought he was able to convince Jason, but he also knew Jason's thinking and it would take a lot more explanation to make him comfortable. After the meeting, Jason was confused as to how to handle this situation, especially with Nigel, who seemed suspicious of his every move. He realized that there was no alternative but to work with this assignment as best as he could.

The very next day Nigel and Jason met to plan their strategy. The atmosphere had some element of competition as each tried to show they were worthy of the position. They continued their meetings every day for the remainder of the week getting absolutely no-where. This was Nigel's moment to shine if this assignment was accomplished, but he found that Jason was not compromising when he expected him to be. Although Nigel had grown frustrated, realizing that each new idea met a push back from Jason. "Can we increase the number of balls, making the odds a bit more difficult?" asked Nigel.

Jason responded, "This would mean printing millions of coupons to check off numbers, also changing the advertising."

This type of thinking frustrated Nigel, who shouted, "No, it cannot affect the advertising. Why can't you get it into your skull this will not affect our marketing program?"

Jason knew that such a minor change of this kind would not have an impact on the marketing program, but his opposition was essential. He said, "Remember cost also has to be considered. Can you imagine the cost of adding those numbers to the coupon?"

Nigel jumped to his feet. "Remember, Andrew always said cost is of little consideration if we can make millions."

Jason then replied, "You don't want to scare the customers away." He knew very well this was a no-brainer, but he had to try it for what it was worth and those insinuations irritated Nigel even more to the point where he rose to his feet in frustration.

Jason, seeing what was about to occur, quietly said, "Ok, let's add this as a possibility if it can make millions." This simple act quelled the situation.

Nigel, seeking a conciliatory handshake, said, "I think that is enough for the day. I am tired, but before I go, I was going to ask you, "Why do you cross-dress?"

Jason looked absolutely surprised since this was the first time their private lives were ever discussed in the office. "Because I feel comfortable." Then he simply smiled and added, "Do you know when I use make-up, I look even better?" This added a small air of calm. Then Jason, who was enjoying the sudden mood change, said, "When I use make-up, I can disguise myself and my features. I want for that night changes to my personality and also my sexual feelings." By now he was looking straight at Nigel. "You can have that feeling also if you want to continue enjoying the good life like you did on Saturday night."

Nigel was caught off guard. "No, I was just curious. I don't want to ever go there." They were smiling as they both left the room. As Nigel walked out, he thought to himself that he would never want Jason to ever comment on the events of that night. He was afraid he would always worry that Jason would hold this over his head forever.

The regular meetings continued, but both parties involved could feel they were not making enough headway, so it was normal to be frustrated after the meetings. Since there was no deadline given to implement changes to the game, both Jason and Nigel knew this would not continue forever, but since to date there was nothing to show, it made Nigel experience a growing feeling of inadequacy.

That night on his daily call to Nadia he lamented about his frustrations. "I feel like Jason is stalling. Because he is technologically advanced, we can't even agree on modernizing non-technical items. It's frustrating."

Nadia could hear it in his voice, the sad feeling of knowing, the willingness of wanting to improve the structure of an entity, she knew it quite well, and she understood the frustration when the company did not recognize it. She tried comforting him. "Don't worry. Take your time. I have all the confidence in you to do the right thing." She didn't want to tell him how to do the job because she knew Nigel had little tolerance for interference and what he wanted was just to off-load those frustrations. How macho, she thought, never wanting to show how vulnerable he could be, but she continued to listen, knowing how and when to add her thoughts.

Nigel then responded, "I know I can; I know I can," he repeated. "I still have to convince the team I am capable of making the required changes since it's been over a month and I have nothing to show for it. I have the feeling sometimes Jason is my obstacle, and he can be a real shit bag sometimes." The conversation as always continued late into the night; it was all about Jason's growing behavior and work.

In parting Nadia requested, "The next time we speak, can we discuss us for a change? Love you."

The tension between Jason and Nigel was felt throughout the team and it was affecting performance. Both men were so uncomfortable with each other's presence that it hampered the discussions they were having. Jason could hold back no longer, and he went to Andrew. Unable to hide his frustration, he shouted, "There are difficulties in making changes, do you realize this? I have a feeling I can make some changes to the structure of the game. By increasing the odds of the customer winning, I can satisfy Nigel."

Andrew sat back and allowed Jason to continue. "If we increase the number of balls, this will decrease the odds of winning, and also decrease the chances of your balls dropping you know what that means. To do so, we will also need a new bin."

At that point Andrew had to interrupt. "We can increase the air pressure, causing the duration of spin in the air to be a little longer. What do you think?"

Andrew looked at Jason, who quickly said, "This whole thing can change the dynamics of our involvement. Another option can be to suction the balls upward instead of them falling."

Andrew, who had become familiar with the machine operations, said, "That's no problem. We will make the heavier balls settle at the bottom allowing the lighter ones to float to the top, but for this, the air pressure has to be worked out properly." Then Andrew smiled. "I realize both of you are diligently working on the project and I share your desire in wanting to make it seems to be favoring the customer winning, but at the same time we cannot lose our control of who wins and when. We need more time to make trial runs on any proposed changes, so keep

Nigel pacified and occupied while we look for the method that satisfies all we want. I can't afford to have any failures due to improvements. Truthfully, I don't think we have to make changes to the game that is already going great."

The following weeks the tension in the office continued to build between Jason and Nigel with Nigel wanting to go ahead with the changes, only to be held back by Jason, who was seemingly nonchalant about getting things done. The friendship was souring.

That night Nigel felt drained and anxious. He had to call Nadia to share his frustrations. When she heard his voice, she knew the situation at work was having a negative impact. He went on and on about having such hatred for Jason that he could kill him or make him disappear from the face of the earth.

At that point she had to stop him. "You can't go there. I know how frustrated you may feel, but take your mind off such dangerous thoughts and please don't ever mention those words again."

He apologized and promised never to get so wrapped up in his work that he would feel such animosity towards another person. He passionately said to his darling, "I must learn to separate my work from my personal life and so be able to think through situations properly before reacting."

"Why don't you speak to my father about what is happening?" she asked.

"I want him to know that I am capable of handling a supposedly simple project, which now is lasting longer than we originally planned. I can't see why this is happening," Nigel quickly said. "Anyway, you have a quiet night. I'll call tomorrow."

As they ended the call, the phone rang. It was his cousin John. "Hi Nigel, I am in town for the weekend, so I got your number from your mother. How are you doing?"

Nigel was taken by surprise, instantly forgetting all his work horrors. "How are you?" It was such a relief to hear a welcoming voice. "This town can be so lonely. We must get together as soon as possible."

John heard the excitement in Nigel's voice, but he also sensed something worrisome and could not wait, so he said, "Let's meet for drinks tonight. I know it's late, but so what the hell?"

Nigel was willing, but he knew he was in no condition to meet. The way he felt might make him drink too much and he may not be ready for work in the morning. "That's a good idea but it is a bit rushed. Let's make it tomorrow evening. The office closes early, and it would be great spending the entire evening catching up on old times." With this they made arrangements to meet at John's hotel the next evening.

Next morning in the office there was a knocked on Nigel's door and in entered Jason. He also was feeling the growing tension developing between them. "I was thinking that the proposals you suggested for this new system will have to go through a trial stage, and if successful, we have to get the accounts department to do the projections on the cost of changing tickets and vouchers.

The game can be played with six balls dropping instead of five. How do you feel about that?"

Jason knew this would make the game more difficult and, therefore, have fewer winners, thus interrupting the perceived success of the game. Nigel knew Andrew would never accept this proposal, so he wondered what Jason was up to. This proposal was ridiculous and would bring more attention to their inability to complete a simple assignment.

These thoughts infuriated Nigel as he tried to figure out why Jason should be making these frustrating suggestions even if eventually they would be for the betterment of the game. Nigel could not understand what was happening and the feelings of anger were overwhelming. "Are you here to frustrate me? These options were never discussed, and I did not want to increase the number of balls by two. I mentioned one not two."

Jason replied, "I thought you wanted to go to seven. I am sorry."

Nigel's composure belied his true feelings for the sake of his own ambitions. He replied, "How can you be thinking this way? It's so against what we have been discussing. Have we wasted all these weeks? You are pathetic."

Jason now realized he had to back off. He realized the approach inspired by Andrew to prolong implementing any meaningful suggestions for changes while not causing animosity with fellow workers was clearly not working.

Nigel was miserable for the entire day wondering how could he continue working with Jason.

9

CHAPTER

THAT EVENING AS Nigel entered the restaurant adjoining the hotel, he found John waiting for him at the bar at his hotel. As they embraced, John said in a welcoming tone, "Cuz, what have you been up to?" This showed the closeness between them.

Immediately, Nigel said to the bartender, "I want a double Jack Daniels." They then settled onto the bar stools.

John remarked, "You must have had a hard day."

Nigel shook his head. "That's an understatement in this town. I feel so isolated. I came here due to a job and my girlfriend, and this is what makes things so difficult. She went to study in France, and I am facing so much pressure at work."

The bartender then interrupted with small talk after he brought their drinks while welcoming them. John kept silent as he realized Nigel wanted to talk.

"I am having particular difficulties with my teammate whose name is Jason Paye. He is such a shit. If you want to go right, he would want to go left, and that son of a bitch will not budge from his stance. He could well be my nemesis." Jason's frustrations were palpable.

These frustrations were heard and felt by John as he stood up from his stool. He was a true redneck, unsympathetic to anything that interrupted his way of life, and he let nothing stand in his way. "Why do you stand for such obstructions? Just kick the guy in his ass, make him know you will not be pushed around. Who is the boss here?"

Nigel explained they were both on the same level. "He is the computer wiz. Seems that a lot is expected of him, so he continues to discount my suggestions. This guy drives me nuts and for no good reason."

The bar tender realizing Nigel's voice was getting louder recommended them taking a seat in the back where it was more private.

"Thank you," – Nigel smiled – "we need that, didn't think of it."

The conversation continued into late evening. Becoming quite hungry, they ordered dinner and as they dined the conversation went to calmer topics, the family back home and how they were doing.

Nigel who wanted to off-load on a familiar shoulder said, "Getting back to our conversation with work. It's frustrating. I am trying to make a name for myself, and I can't even get started because of this ass." At this point the waiter came over offering a refill. He was totally neglected as both men stayed engrossed in conversation, so he moved right along.

Nigel, however, felt as if the interruptions were overwhelming and said to John, "Let's go to a real bar so that you can have a clearer picture of what I am up against and of the people involved in this saga."

They paid and exited the restaurant and took a stroll towards The Watering Hole, where once inside, they tried to shun the regular clients as they moved towards a discreet spot. The action here was different and more high spirited than the previous restaurant and although not the best for conversation because of the nosiness, there were fewer interruptions. Nigel continued the conversation.

At that moment an elegant figure entered the bar. John immediately took notice of the person while still speaking to Nigel. Then while passing, the person said, "Hi Nigel." Nigel was blown out of his seat as he recognized the person as Jason. He had never seen Jason fully cross dressed and out in the public.

After catching himself, Nigel said, "John I would like you to meet a friend who works with me." But, as he was about to say his name Jason, he thought better of it. There was a pause and Jason sensed the hesitation. He smiled while stretching out his hand and introducing himself as Jesse.

John smiled while accepting the welcome. "Pleasure meeting you," he said in the most seductive voice.

Jason knew how to handle situations, so he kept moving right along saying, "You guys, have a great evening. I am going to have one."

Nigel and John continued drinking, while John kept looking around at the customers. You could the quizzical look on his face followed by his comment: "There is something different with this place. Although the place is great, the people are strange." He kept looking around.

Nigel was waiting for this and promptly said, "Don't worry. This is one of those places where everybody gets along." He paused for a while. "Whites gays, browns, blacks, everybody. No wonder it is named The Watering Hole. It caters to all." He paused, giving John time for that to settle and then continued, "Do you remember the person I introduced to you earlier as Jesse?" How could John forget.

"Yes," he replied. "Well, that Jesse is really Jason, the same person who continues to give me grief at work."

John was shocked. "You mean that cocksucker is not Jesse? I now want to kick his ass for you." John was a bit louder.

So to keep the lid on things, Nigel said, "Keep your cool. Not everyone here is like that. Jason's case is just his after work personality." John, being from a small rural area down south, had difficulties in comprehending.

After a few more drinks, Nigel realized John was getting louder and may not be handling to situation properly, so he decided they had had a good introductory evening, but it was time to go.

While John was leaving, he looked over at Jason and his friends having a great time with such openness. It irked him somewhat when trying to understand; he turned to Nigel and said, "I am sorry, I know the world is more tolerable of this new path, but I am from the old school and a little frustrated by all this acceptance."

Nigel smiled without saying a thing. His plan had worked and he knew John would now realize the true extent of his frustrations. Now he might understand why he needed his help. While Nigel walked John back to his hotel, he thanked John for listening, thinking how having a good listener helps in relieving some of the frustrations.

Monday morning found both Jason and Nigel trying to find common ground before the meeting. They hoped there might have been a truce, but within a half an hour of the meeting, there was no way a compromise seemed possible, so once again they would enter the Monday staff meeting without anything to present. Nigel's anger made his blood boil. Would this week be a repeat of the usual? He knew he could not handle this type of conflict. Out from their meeting Nigel saw Jason going into Andrew's office. He could not understand the relationship, and wondered why Andrew should be so open to Jason? Was Jason getting Andrew prepared for the meeting or was he throwing the blame on him for not being able to make the changes? He felt uncomfortable with them meeting privately and not involving him.

Andrew's meeting with Jason to discuss their actions for the weekend was something that happened all the time, and Nigel was never allowed to attend these early week meetings. He always wondered what the reason for these meetings was.

Andrew and Jason were unaware of Nigel's suspicions and continued their private meeting. "The lottery prize is eighty-two million this week. Should we allow it to ride another week?" Andrew asked.

"Yes," Jason replied. "The longer it stays running the more the activity and the bigger the pot. The only thing is if Nigel continues on his course to change things, the quicker we will have to act."

Then Andrew asked, "Do you really think I will allow him to change a good thing?"

Jason quickly responded, "He is becoming very frustrated on not being able to make changes."

Andrew immediately shouted, "I don't give a damn! Those changes will never be made."

Jason replied, "You don't have to deal with him. I do, and it's increasingly difficult."

Their meeting ended on this note.

The frustration deepened for Nigel, who now doubted Andrew's intentions. Could it be Jason who was doubling crossing him, taking wrong news to Andrew? And why the private meetings?

Their lack of trust in each other started to undermine the daily performance of the team and the overall dissatisfaction was felt. This upset the rhythm and upbeat spirit that had existed prior. Things seemed upside-down and unsettled.

That Friday evening Andrew got wind of the turmoil in the office and called Jason and Nigel for a conference. He well knew the cause but wanted to make it seem like a troubleshooting and resolution effort.

He began, "What the hell is happening with both of you? I need an explanation. As discussed, we need a change in the structure of the game, but your proposed changes are not forthcoming."

Jason had the same feeling as Andrew – leave things as is even if on the surface he made it seem as if he bought into Nigel's proposals.

At this point Nigel spoke up in defense of his position. "Whatever changes we are making, we will have more customers participating and increase the pool because of fewer winners."

Andrew knew Nigel's point was valid, so he looked over to Jason for a response, knowing the project came out of the mayor's request for more revenue from the game.

Jason understood Andrew's dilemma, but he also had to cover his ass with Andrew. "We have been running this game for a few years, and it is performing above expectations. What dramatic changes are now necessary and why?"

This surprised Nigel, who now thought Jason's actions in working with him on the project belied how he felt. "So, what have you been working on for weeks, if this was your thinking?" Nigel asked. "Why didn't you tell me this was how you felt all along?" Then looking at Andrew shaking his head, he said, "I think I am reaching a breaking point with this project." He asked to be excused as he had the urge to grab Jason in a choke hold he was so angry. "I have had enough," he politely said to them both before slamming the door shut.

With Nigel leaving, Andrew turned to Jason, "You know we are treading on dangerous ground, and we do not want the mayor's office getting wind of the happenings here and investigating our office. I might have to implement one aspect of his plan so as to appease him and not raise suspicions."

On hearing this Jason knew this would be the start to the end of their involvement in manipulating the game, and he so wanted to have a hand in its outcome.

Andrew then said to Jason, "If we have to look at increasing the number of balls, that will be easy to put in place. Look into that aspect and tell me the time frame required for implementation. Don't say anything to Nigel as yet. I have to quietly order the necessary items and first try them out while making the adjustments." Andrew knew that vertical suction might not work; things were now becoming too technical for the simple process they had started.

On leaving Andrew's office, Jason returned to his desk. He knew his control of the game was coming to an end, so first he had to place the program on his personal laptop, making it accessible from anywhere he was, while making provisions for an additional number. This exercise took him late into the night after all the staff had left.

Concerns about his honesty and integrity rested heavily on Jason's conscience, but with his growing dislike for Nigel and what might be the outcome of the game, he couldn't care less. He wondered how he might once again buy the winning numbers before the changes can be made. His conflicting thoughts interrupted his thinking at times, but he finally made the changes late into the night, eventually saving the newly revised program to his laptop. These conflicting thoughts bore heavily on mind. Unfortunately, he might have to involve his mother once again. Why not hit it one more time, not really for the millions but for the feeling of power it gave him? On his way out of the office Jason's attention was hell bent on the ease with which it could be done again. He was confident he could repeat the event successfully.

On the other hand, Nigel was in no mood to socialize. He went straight home and poured himself a double shot of whiskey, calling Nadia in France.

"Hi, darling," she said affectionately. "No after work drinks with the gang tonight?"

There was a pause, then he said, "I am sorry for being such an annoying bastard recently. It's that things in the office are not working out as I would want them."

Nadia felt relieved this conversation may be different than those previously with the emphasis on the goings on in the office.

"Jason has tried his best to shit me up again. He makes me look incapable in front of the team, and I am not able to implement my ideas to improve the running of the game. I hate him."

Nadia at that point took a deep breath, seeking relief because she knew where this conversation was heading again.

He continued, "I wish I could castrate that revivalist wiggler." They both giggled, hoping for a softer tone.

She asked, "What do you mean by a revivalist wiggler?"

Nigel thought for a moment saying, "An idiot." They both laughed again, but although he laughed he knew very well that he could not expose his complete displeasure because of his concern about his unknown behaviors at Jason's party.

He was gradually developing a hatred for Jason, now verbalizing his true inner feeling to her and his disdain for Jason finally surfaced without any restraints. He went into the workings at the office, describing the incidents that made him uncomfortable and suspicious. Nadia analytical in nature tried to offer objective advice, but Nigel confided he was ready to leave the company as he was sure there were other career opportunities awaiting him. Nadia suggested Nigel speak to her father and explain his dilemma because she could not offer much help from where she was.

The next morning Jason confidently started his mission to repeat the manipulation of the lottery drawing to his benefit, but this time remotely from his laptop. He called Andrew and explained what he wanted to try.

Andrew knew Jason was the computer expert and had already agreed a trial was necessary, but he had some reservations as to the outcome. "Please don't put all the progress in jeopardy."

Jason convinced him the trial was a "simple change" in the program and he would only place passwords to build the numerous firewalls protecting the program; he knew better than to do anything to jeopardize the lottery's future.

After getting the go ahead from Andrew, he made a call to his mother.

"Hello," she answered. He loved to hear her voice; this passionate and welcoming voice could warm your heart. When the going was challenging, all he wanted to hear was his mother.

"Hi, mommy. How are you doing?" he asked.

"Very well and glad to be hearing from you," she replied. "Thanks for the extra funds your company sends me each month, thanks."

Smiling to himself he thought, little did she know it was all hers.

He continued, "Mommy, we will be needing your help again later this evening. Do you remember what you did last time?"

She interrupted. "This evening, today?"

He quickly asked, "Can you manage it? Yes, today."

Before he could finish, she asked, "Will I be coming to Amalta again and can I stay at the same hotel? I enjoyed my stay."

He had to cut her off quickly. "I know you had a great time, but this time all you have to do is purchase the ticket and keep it in a safe place for me." Jason was clear and precise while trying not to make things difficult with his instructions.

"Please be in the Orkit store this time at 8:15, and I will call you with the numbers. Isn't that easier this time?" he asked.

She then replied, "You know, my son, I will be there at 8:15. Anything to help. Are you sure you don't need me in the city? It would be a timely break."

Jason smiled when he realized his mother was on the verge of playing hardball. He began to laugh and she joined him in response.

"Please, mom, this time just buy the ticket and keep it in a safe place, OK?" Then he added, "We want to see how long the market responds to unsubmitted tickets. Will this be all right for you?"

"Yes," she repeated.

Jason again reminded her of the time as they ended the conversation. Jason underestimated his mother's ability to analyze and decipher irregularities when they surfaced, yet she silently allowed his experience to dictate his methods.

That night at the appropriate time Jason made the call to his mother, giving her the numbers which she immediately wrote on the coupon and gave them to the cashier. Little did she know those numbers won the lottery that night.

Jason contained his invincible feeling but felt he had kicked Nigel's ass. So what if the game was on its final track? He had quietly benefited and no one would ever know.

Monday's meeting commenced as usual in high spirits. This happens when there is a winner and the pot is large. Things would rewind and start all over again. Andrew began, "With a winner last weekend the ticket sales will gain momentum, the start of hopefully another large pot." He smiled at the team with admiration. "This is usually the most strenuous period, but once it starts to move along, the excitement builds."

He then looked towards Nigel. "I know you have been working on the operating procedure to improve the game, and you know I have been somewhat disappointed with the slow roll out of the improvements. However, after analyzing the initial aspect you have presented, I may implement the change gradually."

For the first time in weeks Nigel felt a positive vibe. A few minutes earlier he had felt as if everything was going downhill, so he tried a smile as Andrew continued, "I was not impressed with the length of time taken to implement this initial part, so I will be adding another member to the implementing team for the second phase."

This caught everyone off guard as they all thought Nigel would be in charge of the entire implementation. Andrew continued, "At our next meeting I will say who will be responsible for the launch." The team was not certain of Andrew's plan. Could it be that Jason would lose the responsibility? Throughout the meeting Nigel maintained his composure and was silent although he was boiling over inside with venom for Jason, who was the one opposing each suggestion.

After the meeting ended Nigel was the first to leave the room. He went straight to his office and took a deep breath to collect all his faculties. As he sat, he reflected on all the efforts he had given to the project, yet he was not given the opportunity to demonstrate his true ability where it counted most just because of that ass Jason.

While Nigel was deep in thought, the phone rang disturbing the trend of this thinking.

"Hi, cuz. How are you doing? It's John." Immediately Nigel exhaled with relief just hearing a friendly voice who was on his side was all he needed.

"Hi, John. Great to hear your voice."

John, however, picked up on Nigel's unenthusiastic tone. "What's happening, man? You sound so down. Come on, is it the job getting to you again? Don't let this happen to you," he continued. "I am calling to tell you I'll be back in your town this weekend. We must meet up again."

It took a while for Nigel to respond, then an idea hit him. Immediately, he said, "John I am sorry for the tone, but my problems continue. Can you call me tonight? I have an idea I would like to discuss with you."

John, without skipping a beat, responded, "Of course, remember this is family. I'll call later."

On putting the phone down Nigel became very serious and somewhat nervous. He knew he was entering unknown territory that could ruin everything he ever stood for and maybe his entire life. Then he thought, so what? Jason has been ruining everything lately for me. So what if I do what I am thinking?

Nigel sat in his apartment that evening awaiting his much anticipated call. Then the phone rang.

"Hi, cuz," – as it came from the other side of the call—"I want to hear an upbeat tone. You have to learn how to keep those negative tones in the office," he said to Nigel hoping for mutual feedback.

"I am sorry I can't find it in myself to be happy anymore. This guy Jason I have told you about is a real shit. I wish I could get rid of him once and for all. He is trying to get the boss to get rid of me by constantly misleading the direction of the project."

John then said, "Why is he continuing to give you a fight? Is it your qualifications or the chemistry between you or both? Can you identify why he hates you so much?"

Nigel was happy that John was reacting to the situation at the level where he wanted him to. "Do you remember the good times we always had swimming by the river and hunting wild boars? Those were great days. It's such a pity life is now so serious and vindictive. Where has the love gone? No one wants to share and help each other. Jason exposes every ounce of dislike I have ever had for another human being. I hate that devil," said Nigel, who by now was receiving John's attention.

John then asked, "How much do you want to get rid of him?"

Without hesitation Nigel said, "Bad, bad… so bad. I don't care or have a drop of respect or love for that lowlife." Nigel knew he had John earned John's loyalty, and he wanted him to say what he was afraid of asking him.

At that point John said, "YOKING!"

"Let's make plans here and now. If you get him to me, I'll take care of the rest, ask no questions."

Nigel was gradually becoming excited. "Yes, I will get him to you on a Friday night. That would be the best evening." Both cousins spent the next two hours making plans.

"I'll be there anyway, this weekend. We'll have a lot to put in place. See you then. Keep your cool."

Jason, on the other-hand, was Mr. Cool. Nothing could diminish his composure, and he was floating with confidence without a care about Andrew's or Nigel's impression of his new found confidence. Later that day he called his mother. "Hi, my darling mother," he said.

She realized it was Jason's voice. "Wow. You are in high spirits today. When you were a child, the only time you called me was when you wanted pocket money or when it was something special. Ok, what is it?" she said, smiling.

"No, Mummy. I have been having a good day and wanted to call you with instructions about the ticket."

"Yes," she replied, "did any of the numbers play?"

In response Jason had to come up with something quickly. Fortunately, he had rehearsed earlier just in case this question was asked. He knew his mother. "We want to collect all tickets from each region we had asked to get tickets," he said without skipping a beat. Then he thought to himself, if she ever knew the value of that small piece of paper, she might certainly have a heart attack.

"What we want you to do is send it to a special address. Can you get a pen and paper?" He waited for a while. She then came back on the phone. "Go ahead," he continued, "place it in a sealed envelope and send it to the Forsheim Hotel, P.O Box 2821, Amalta, Indiana 61281. Please address it to your name, Mrs. Lidia Payne, as if it were coming for you. That's all right. We have made arrangements with the hotel for mail to come there and they are expecting it. Send it today by special overnight, so it should reach here sometime tomorrow. Can you manage that?" he asked politely.

"What do you mean, if I can? Do I look old and like I can't manage? Yes, I can." She loved her son so much she would do everything she could to help out in difficult situations like this.

"Thanks. I'll check the hotel tomorrow."

10

CHAPTER

WEDNESDAY EVENING JASON called the Forsheim Hotel to enquire if Mrs. Payne had arrived or if there was any mail there in her box. The receptionist said, "Mrs. Payne has not arrived as yet, but there is a letter in her mailbox. Incidentally, there seems to no booking registered for Mrs. Payne. When is she expected?" The receptionist asked this, knowing who Mrs. Payne was, and she realized she had to contact the manager immediately after the conversation because the presidential suite was occupied.

"She will be coming in on Friday morning." There was a sigh of relief from the receptionist since she knew the customer in the suite was registered to leave on Thursday.

"That will be OK," she said. Mrs. Payne's influence somehow had begun to spread throughout the hotel.

The next few days Nigel stayed out of Jason's way, not knowing Jason was also trying desperately to stay out of his way as he worked on his transformation. He had a picture of his mother posted by his bathroom mirror, and for the entire week he had been applying make-up and making the transformation look exactly like Lidia. To do this he purchased a wig, bought eyelashes, and from his own collection, he took varying lipstick and eyebrow pencils. After many attempts, he got better with the image, closer and closer to the picture. Then when he felt he had mastered the transformation, he knew he had to repeat it again on Friday, so he everything washed off and repeated the application all over just to perfect the procedure. This time again it came out perfect. No one would ever know the difference, he thought to himself as he compared the picture to the mirror's image. That night he was more than satisfied, thinking to himself, this is so good that if I am not successful in the computer craft, I might pursue a career in makeup application.

It was Friday morning when Jason called Andrew's office and spoke to his secretary. "Can you relay a message to Andrew for me? Tell him I will not be in today."

She was surprised to hear Jason would be absent, having never heard of him being ill. "Are you feeling all right? What's wrong?" she asked.

"I am a little under the weather and need to rest. Please pass on the message. Thanks," he said as he hung up.

He had spent the morning transforming himself into Lidia as he compared his image to the picture. He was satisfied when he finally put the wig on as he looked at the contours of his face in the large mirror in the bedroom.

He said, "Lidia, meet Lidia."

It was about three o'clock when there was a knock on the front door. It was the limousine driver. "Well, hello again, Mrs. Payne. Welcome back," said the driver upon recognizing the face. At this point Jason knew he had done a good job with his make-up and he smiled.

Jason said in a quiet voice trying to sound like Lidia, "I am fine but having a sore throat." The driver understood as he escorted her to the car.

Lidia felt very comfortable in her dress; even her shoes were easy to walk in. She had been selective in purchasing the right shoes, remembering the many years practice as a cross-dresser. She sat quickly in the back of the limousine as the driver closed the door.

There will not be much conversation today, he thought, knowing the throat problem Lidia had. He smiled. "Where will be our first stop?" inquired the driver.

"The Forsheim Hotel," instructed Lidia. "I'll be picking up a parcel and you can wait for me at the front."

On reaching the hotel Lidia disembarked and went straight to the front desk. As the receptionist saw her, she said, "Mrs. Payne, welcome back. Nice seeing you again."

Lidia greeted her also and asked for Mr. Potts. "Is there anything in my letter box 2821?"

As the receptionist went off to check, coming back, she asked, "Are you certain it's 2821?"

"Yes," Lidia said now puzzled while the receptionist went off again to check once again.

By now Lidia was questioning why he hadn't sent the letter by registered mail. This receptionist didn't know the value of what was in that envelope,

She then walked back in. "It's not there. I've checked all the boxes and it's not there."

By now Lidia was sinking through the floor. "I specifically posted it to box 2821. What could have happened?"

On hearing the commotion outside, the manager Mr. Potts came out of his office to inquire about what was happening. On seeing Lidia, he said, "Mrs. Payne, is everything all right?"

Lidia was getting upset. "Absolutely not. I sent some information here and it's not in my box."

Mr. Potts immediately raised his head. "I sincerely apologize. I must take full responsibility for this, but when I saw you were going to be a guest, I sent your mail along with a bottle of champagne to the presidential suite."

Lidia took a deep breath of relief, then smiled and said, "I will be checking later, but I need that information now to take to a meeting." The manager offered to send someone to collect the envelope and deliver it to Lidia as she waited in the lobby. As she was leaving, the manager looked so remorseful and apologetic to have caused an inconvenience while trying to make his customer comfortable. Lidia said, "This was just a misunderstanding, I will be back in town in a few weeks. I love your hotel. Please think nothing of the incident." She smiled shaking his hand, making the manager feel comfortable.

"Madam, we will always be here at your service." As Lidia walked to the limousine, she liked the feeling of being called madam and she smiled.

As the driver opened the door, he asked for her next destination.

With growing confidence Lidia said, "The Lottery Capital building."

This timing had to be precise in order to catch the staff off guard as if they were about to leave, there would be no fanfare over the winning ticket. The limousine pulled up outside the entrance of the building, and Lidia calmly walked inside, straight up to the cashier's window, and presented the ticket.

When the cashier took the ticket and matched the numbers, she smiled and said, "Welcome, winner. Whose name should I make out the check to? Lidia Payne?" Then she spelled each letter so as not to make any mistakes.

The cashier then said, "I now have to make a big deal on presenting you with this check. I have to call our Chief Operating Officer, Andrew Cole."

At that very moment, just as she was about to make the call, Andrew passed by and heard about the presentation of the ticket. As Lidia saw Andrew approaching, she quickly decided to take the initiative. "I heard you are the chief here, but I have to catch the bank." She then stretched out her hand in greeting, catching Andrew off guard, as the cashier explained who she was.

"Congratulations to the lucky lady."

Lidia accepted with her face a bit lowered and in a subdued voice, she said, "Forgive me. My throat is sore, but it was a pleasure meeting you." Lidia, offering all the appropriate pleasantries, knew her movements had to be quick but polite as she moved towards the exit. Andrew, since he too was on his break out of the office, did not insist; however, the lady's face seemed familiar. Could it be someone from his past, he wondered. It remained a recurring thought in his mind for the rest of the evening.

After exiting the building, "Lidia's" steps hastened towards the car. The driver opened the door for her and asked, "Our next stop will be?"

"She" could not contain herself, and a broad but nervous smile burst out across her face. She could not believe she had survived that introduction. She caught her breath saying, as she wiped the sweat from her brow, "The First National Bank will be our next stop."

Due to the unexpected delays at the lottery building, the driver explained he had to drive extra fast to reach the bank on time. As they made their last turn approaching the bank, the traffic brought them to a standstill.

Lidia knew she had five minutes to reach into the bank, so she shouted to the driver, "Stop here. I can't wait in this traffic. I am getting out." As she exited the car, she decided not to go on the crowded sidewalk, and she started running through the traffic that way being quicker. She was making good ground, but with only two minutes to spare, she started trotting, and with a minute left, it was an all-out run. Onlookers marveled at the sight of this person holding her dress up above her knees completing each stride with no time for gentle female struts but rather displaying typical masculine strides dodging traffic as she burst full speed up to the bank door. The doors were locked and the electronic barrier was lowered preventing entry – her long male strides did not save the day! Lidia was so exhausted she slumped into the iron seat adjacent to the door awaiting her driver.

As Lidia sat, she knew her plans had to change remembering the laborious task of changing her appearance, the make-up, the applications, etc. "Someone read my thoughts," she said as she heard the electronic barriers lifting and out came Mr. Steinburg.

"I was monitoring the entrance on the security camera and saw you just missing being able to enter, Mrs. Payne. You are one of our valued customers. Please come on inside." She was astonished, but elated.

"Thank you. You're a life saver." Lidia entered the bank that day and as she did, she felt like the vice president – she was somebody.

The limousine delivered Lidia to the apartment that evening, and the driver escorted her to the door asking if she would need him later. She explained her son would be taking her to the hotel later and she would not need him until she returned to town in a couple of weeks.

"My son will call and make the arrangements." They parted company as she closed the door behind her.

When Lidia closed the door, she was completely exhausted and sat in the small chair beside the door completely overwhelmed as she caught herself with tears gently trickling down her cheeks. How easy it is to cheat, she thought. Although the feeling of success was somehow stimulating, there was that feeling of displeasure followed by a feeling of the shame of dishonesty.

What the hell, she thought, the intrigue was sweeter and that adrenalin rush made everything possible. "Imagine, Andrew was right in my face and he didn't know it was me," Jason said to himself with a giggle.

He then went to the bathroom to wash off the disguise and he stretched out over the bed resting. He knew if there was one night he had to go to The Watering Hole, it was tonight.

Nigel's phone rang, and as he cautiously picked up the call, it was his cousin John. "Hi, cuz. I am in your town. How have you been?" As usual John was in high spirits.

"I am glad you called. I would like to make some changes to our meeting."

John sensed Nigel wanted to back out. "You getting cold feet so early?"

Nigel continued. "No nothing like that. When you reach to the bar, park as close to my car as possible to my car. Remember, don't be late."

John agreed that he would be there on time while wondering what was going on with Nigel and what his thinking could be.

That night Nigel pulled up in front of The Watering Hole and quietly sat in the car deciding on the most strategic spot for him to take Jason. He then moved his car into that spot. From outside, he could hear the music in the bar and he knew it would set the tone for much excitement tonight. Nervousness was his companion until he reached the door where the buzz of The Watering Hole took over and calmed his spirit.

The entire gang was there, including Jason's friends Theo and Jessie, the two most feared guys who Nigel thought had something on him. Jason entered later and immediately got into his element, with Nigel being very helpful in maintaining that high spirit of the activities in the bar. Unknown to all present, Jason had his reasons to celebrate. He was as usual doing the Wiggle after each joke, making the room come alive with laughter especially when he placed his finger on his nose.

Jason and Nigel were in a happy mood for a change. The drinks were flowing especially heavily. In Jason's glass he had red wine and vodka, the drink of the night. Laughing at one point, he said to Nigel, "This is a night of happiness and inner reflection, so put on your x-ray glasses." Everyone burst out laughing. Jason felt at peace with his life.

Nigel had received some good news that evening from Andrew, who was allowing most of the new modifications to the game giving him more responsibility. He soon set these fleeting thoughts aside as he needed to complete the bigger plans for the night.

As Jason was enjoying the evening, he thought, all these friends… if they ever knew who the real Jason was. He laughed even louder as tonight he would drink and celebrate this wonderful feeling. As the celebration continued into the night Jason, started stumbling from all the alcohol he was drinking.

"I am sorry I didn't mean to bounce into you. Did I spill your drink?" he said to a stranger next to him. The stranger laughed as he realized Jason was in high spirits saying.

"It doesn't matter." This was the common feeling throughout the room, and nothing mattered. It was a fun evening; everyone was happy. The celebratory laughs continued way after eleven o'clock. This was a little early for Jason, but his intake this particular night was different.

He was celebrating. As his head began nodding while suddenly leaning his head on Theo's shoulder, Jason was on the verge of succumbing to the night's activity.

Nigel quietly took something from his pocket and held it in his hand waiting for the right opportunity to drop it into Jason's drink. That was the final blow. As that was done, Nigel offered to take Jason home as he was the only one there not drinking to the level to be considered over the limit.

As he walked Nigel outside and placed him in the driver's seat, he flashed his headlights as planned with John. By now, seeing Jason had passed out, Nigel then started his to the bar.

Nigel stopped at the door as the red truck came over as planned and two large figures came from the truck quickly lifting Jason from the seat and placing him in the truck. As he was placed in the truck, he was about to vomit up all the alcohol in his stomach, making it very uncomfortable for the other occupants who quickly stuck his head through the opened door to disperse the solids.

Nigel was not aware of this excitement as he turned and went back into the bar.

Theo stumbled over, asking Nigel how it went with Jason. "I placed him in a taxi with his address."

Theo, unconcerned due to the spirits of the evening and taking another sip of his drink, said, "Seems good to me." This pleased Nigel as the evening's operation went so easily.

11

CHAPTER

JASON HAD REMAINED passed out during the entire two hour trip out of the city as the bright lights moved further and further away into a sea of darkness. The car suddenly drove off the main road, and just as they turned, there were the siren and blue lights of a police car coming in also behind the truck. John told the others in the vehicle to keep cool.

Emerging from his patrol vehicle, the officer asked, "Why are you turning into this desolate area at this time of the night?"

John quickly replied, "Our drunk partner started vomiting and we wanted to come off the road to allow him to finish his business. These single lane roads can be dangerous when pulling off."

The police looked at Jason passed out on the seat while the clean-up was being done. After checking John's documents, he was allowed to continue just as Jason was started to squirm in the seat. If Jason woke up, that would blow everything, so John hurriedly drove away.

Time was now crucial. John had to go as fast as he could to reach the designated point Nigel had suggested. It was now one o'clock in the morning when John reached a spot he thought would be ideal for the event. He pulled over, and they unloaded their belongings, throwing Jason into the back of the truck. The sudden impact caused Jason to open his eyes, immediately closing them again. He realized the surface he was lying on felt completely unfamiliar. He thought it was a dream and trying to recognize his surroundings, he asked what was happening.

He said, "Hello." No answers were given, and as he wiped his eyes and used his hands to wipe his face, he shouted again, "What's going on here?" He stretched to relieve the discomfort of the hard ground.

At that moment someone climbed into the back of the truck and it sounded as if he was loosening a bolt. The person then stepped past him. He tried sitting up only to be pushed forcibly backward onto the hard surface by that someone, whoever he was. His head collided with the floor of the truck bed and as he tried regrouping his senses and becoming quite still, he thought something was wrong.

As if to provide reassurance, someone said, "You are in our care and we will be taking good care of you. Don't worry."

For a moment with the intense darkness, mental confusion, and the insecurities he felt, he thought he was back in combat. The complexity of the situation was difficult to understand. He knew from his training that until he got his bearings and his vision adjusted, he should lie there and compose himself before acting. His position on the hard ground was uncomfortable, and it was at that point that he realized his hands were bound. He was able to recognize three separate and distinct voices as they conversed unloading things from the truck. The area was dark, and he thought if he sat up, he might be able to recognize the people.

As he lifted his head, he came face to face with the ugliest dog that gave the nastiest growl, so he decided to lie there quietly. He could hear the conversation. Two of the men were comparing their exploits in The Middle East War. He could not believe they spoke English, meaning they were not the enemy, so why were they doing this? They fought the same war on the same side, so how were they now enemies? The situation for Jason was confusing.

He decided to make the individuals know he was awake and explain there might be a misunderstanding this time. He quietly asked, "What's happening?" Continuing not to move while speaking, he said, "Why am I here? Who are you?" Again, no one answered.

Someone jumped up into the back of the truck and shouted, "Shut-up!" kicking him in the head to illustrate who was in charge. At this point Jason knew something was really wrong. He decided to keep quiet until he was completely out of his drowsiness and aware of everything around him.

He decided this was not a combat situation. As Jason gathered his thoughts, he wondered what was happening. Was someone after him for his winnings in the lottery? I have told no one about it. Could it be my mother had spoken to her friend about her winning? It couldn't be. She didn't even know she won.

These thoughts went through his head as he lay there. He thought of every scenario possible as to why this was happening. The area was pitch black and there were no other cars around, no one to help. Is this my end? Jason thought to himself. Why are they doing this? What could be the reason? I have always tried to live a peaceful life with everyone around me. I always offered jokes to keep the crowd happy. What have I done to deserve this treatment?

One thing that came to mind was the money in the bank. Only the bank manager was familiar with my mother and why didn't they trouble her? Why me? In that case they might have taken us both; he began to worry for his mother. He was the one who got her involved in this scheme. Oh God, forgive me if that is what is happening.

Jason's thoughts continued to race through his mind. He questioned everything – all his meetings in the past, all his relationships, everyone he came in contact with over the past months. But his thoughts always came back to his deceitfulness at the lottery, playing them out of millions so that the winnings would be higher. He felt sorry for his behavior and prayed if he got out of this situation, he would give it all to charity realizing that thoughts and actions are willed in tragedy.

If this situation was one of his first preferences, he would prefer never to be placed in anything as dangerous as this. Also, he thought, how easy it was as an insider to manipulate the numbers the first time and easier the second time through his greed. He questioned why he could allow himself to be caught up in the world of dishonesty.

He heard the men walking around the truck offloading their belongings. These things sounded heavy as he could hear them being pulled over the surface of the truck bed. Then someone jumped into the back. He pulled Jason by his shirt dragging him from the truck throwing him onto the cold surface of the ground in the most inhumane manner. This was the scariest moment and he knew this may be his end. As he hit the ground, he felt the grip of his assailant pulling him to the clearing to the front of the truck. He was then placed in a sitting position as if a meeting was about to start, and he knew this was not a decent meeting. With the treatment he was receiving it could never be anything good.

As soon as he corrected himself into this position, Jason asked, "Why am I here? What do you want?"

He was immediately pushed back to the floor by the one who pulled him over shouting, "Be quiet! Not a word from you. We'll do all the talking. Just shut up!" His voice was mean and abrupt.

Of all the voices Jason picked up while on the back of the truck, this voice sounded like he would be the leader of the group. Jason suspected they knew what they were about to do, and he could hear them working out details. He recognized this was something they were accustomed to doing and this was certainly not the first time these men were doing this job.

Jason wondered, are they going to kill me now or is it a practical joke? But with such rough treatment, Jason knew it was otherwise. Lying there he could hear the dogs being released from their cages as they were taken off the truck, and they seemed to be on their leashes. As they were brought over to Jason, his blood ran cold as the dogs started smelling him all over.

One of the voices said, "I hope this is going to go as well or the same way as last time." Jason didn't know what conclusions to be drawn from what was said, but he knew it could be nothing good.

As the dogs sniffed him, the three gathered around him. Jason picked up on the clothing they all wore – hunting gear. These guys were dressed for hunting with their camouflage uniforms and their hunting boots and hats with attached masks for cold conditions. And, of course, their rifles. That's why they were offloading their equipment from the truck, not wanting to travel with that gear on.

Jason got accustomed to the dark and could now pick up distinct images, but faces were masked. Then the one who was presumably the leader said with a cold firm voice that had no remorse or sympathy, "Welcome, Jason." Jason gradually moved his head looking in the direction of the voice, trying to see the person.

"You are here to be the main event for our hunt." Jason looked astonished. He thought, what hunt? I don't even know these guys. I have never met these roughnecks in all my life to even know me by name. Yet he kept quiet as not to agitate anyone, but he could not keep it in any longer.

"Something is wrong. There must be a misunderstanding."

The commander interrupted, "I told you to shut up." His voice was loud and commanding; Jason was speechless. "You don't ever have to speak. You are about to hear what is going to happen to you."

Jason's thoughts switched into gear at that moment becoming limp. In his mind he knew this was going to be a battle of survival. From his time in the army he knew he must think straight and analyze the situation, the enemy, and the imminent danger.

I must have been brought here for one purpose, he thought. So I must put my mind in full survival mode.

"You have angered my family and disrespected a blood member. You have been judged by us. Sorry, you can't escape the wrath of our punishment." An eerie laughter filled the air. "No one has ever escaped the hunt of the YOKE."

This surprised Jason, who thought to himself, what the hell they are talking about? What yoke? They must be a set of madmen. Is the yoke something to chase me that I will not escape? What are they talking about and what family member did I disrespect or was it Andrew's family? He tried to gather his thoughts, amidst the confusion.

The commander said this time calmly, "Our rules of the yoke are simple. We will give you a fair start to go in any direction you prefer, but when started we will be coming for you. We will be hunting you to your death." These words brought shivers to Jason's skin. He continued, "We promise you we will find you and you will be buried on the same spot where we kill you. Not many people know where they will be buried, but in your case, you will know ahead." He smiled. "Prepare to meet thy God. It lasts about two hours after we start. One I know lasted a little longer than that. A daytime operation is a lot shorter, but at night it is a real test for us." He laughed and repeated, "In the end we will kill you."

On hearing this Jason started weeping; he could not hold back the tears while thinking, I don't deserve this. There must be a misunderstanding.

"Incidentally," continued the leader, "you will be wearing a yoke during the hunt."

Jason did not understand what he meant. Was it a type of clothing for easy detection or to slow him down? What the hell, he thought. Who the hell cares? I just know I have to run for my life and I will.

For the next few minutes a small fire was started in the middle of the group. Jason laid amidst his captors whose intentions were evil. The warmth of the flames brought some type of sensibility to the situation as he cuddled on the ground awaiting the next stage of this insane event.

As they sat around and calmly chatted, sometimes bragging, Jason heard them outline their upcoming venture and their past experiences with other "creatures" as they were called. Obviously, this was to drive fear into Jason and he knew it, yet he tried to concentrate. He tried looking to see where the moon was, then gradually turning he found the north star as this would give him a reference point and serve as a compass. Up to this point Jason felt this was a practical joke, that if it suddenly ended at this moment, someone would get, at worst, a work over, but as time went by, it began to seem to more real and dangerous, and he was the one on the shitty end of the stick. The ensuing interval gave him time to think of the hell he had gone through during his army days. He decided that he had no time for negative thoughts, and so the army training moved him to survival mode.

He surmised he wouldn't be able to see much looking at the thick undergrowth which would make the going slow, even for the dogs. The only drawback was they had his scent, and with this in mind he checked the direction of the wind. It came from south to north. He lay there in silence, his brain turning over with the reality of the ominous future; then, he started to tremble in fear.

One of the other two men came over and pulled Jason to his feet, saying, "You will soon be on your feet for your last journey, so get used to the upright position. It will feel like forever, and you can go anywhere, but I can assure you it will only last about two hours. The world is at your feet." With that, he gave Jason an evil look.

Then he offered him water from a plastic canister. At first Jason was about to refuse, but he knew water was important, so he began drinking only to have it pulled away after a few gulps.

In an instant the third assailant came from behind and quickly placed something heavy around Jason's neck with the leader clamping together the two ends and finally placing a padlock to make it permanent. They then pushed him onto the ground as he tried tugging at the neck frame.

The leader said, "That's the yoke you will take to your death. Get used to it."

This thing is heavy, thought Jason as he felt its weight on his shoulders. How the hell am I going to run with this frame thing around my neck? As he turned his head, he heard the sound of bells that were attached to the yoke. The dogs got very agitated with the sound of the bells, and they were growling aggressively more than just barking. They had to be held back by the two handlers. It seemed as if they were trained to attack the yoke.

Jason was about to object to the yoke around his neck, but just as he was about to open his mouth and ask the reason for it, he refrained knowing it might bring another kick or beating. He preferred to reserve whatever strength he had against these hunters.

The leader realized the significance of the bells and laughed. "You are gradually finding out what is going to happen to you. Well, you have on a piece of armory our forefathers used and we have been using it since childhood, This is the yoke." He continued, "It's very valuable in many ways, and it has the most musical bells attached around it. Unfortunately for you, the dogs are trained to recognize their sound miles away, so along with your scent we'll find you easily. Incidentally, the yoke will expand as your body heat increases, and it will wrap onto itself and get tighter. It might eventually choke you to death." They all snickered, knowing the dogs would find him well before this happened.

Continuing they said, "When you drop dead and your body gets cold, it may slip off easily although at that time you won't need it to." To this they laughed loudly. "It took the two of us to clip the yolk on, so it is not possible for you to remove or open it. Don't run too fast. It might heat up too quickly. Wait for us." By now they were killing themselves with laughter.

Jason knew this demonstration was to break down what courage he had, so he never reacted to their insults. As Jason lay on the ground awaiting his demise, one of the hunters said to him, "How lucky you are. Years ago each end of the yoke would be melted and fused by the local blacksmith before each race." He said smiling, "You see how good we are in these modern times with mechanisms and clips. The yoke is modified just for you to make it easy for us to find you quicker."

With this the laughter was uncontrollable. Under the influence of their alcoholic drinks, they were ridiculously stupid. It seemed to Jason that this celebration was necessary to block out the cruelty that was about to begin.

They then started ripping off Jason's clothes removing his pants and shirt using their large hunting knives, cutting his laces and removing his shoes and socks. The knives were used so aggressively as a method of intimidation that it scared Jason seeing how close the knife came to his neck and to the middle of his chest. He was stripped down to his underwear. The leader knew Jason was lucky being hunted at night. The victim is usually stripped naked, but when they saw Jason's underwear, they all had to laugh.

"What kind of shit do you have on? You thought you were going to a carnival?" They mocked him. "Red underwear with matching opposite teddy-bears!" They laughed louder. The dogs were brought closer again to smell him. Upon seeing them so close, Jason knew he dared not move a muscle with the dogs so close to his body.

When the dogs were pulled away, he felt relieved, but he also felt the cool of the evening on his bare body. He was fit, but that was no match for the dogs, the guns, and the cool weather.

The leader then stood up and shouted, "Time for the hunt to begin! Untie his feet."

Jason thought to himself this was the most opportune time to strike at his captives, but he knew it was not worth it. He was not only outnumbered but also the bells would attract the attack dogs. He would just take their insults and physical abuse and find a way to survive.

As soon as he was untied, just as he had thought, the one who had kicked him earlier was waiting for him to retaliate. Jason smiled as if to disarm him knowing they thought he was an ass, but that smile made them uneasy as they then pushed him over to the area to be used as the starting point.

The leader pushing Jason forward said, "It's now passed two o'clock. We will give you a head start and it will add some excitement for us, so make good use of the time and put some distance between us. You you'll need it. You are on your own. GO! See you in hell."

For an instant Jason was confused. Everything was happening so fast he looked around puzzled. Then, he took off running for his life. Glimpsing upward at the north star, he ran towards that direction as fast as he could realizing this was not a joke; it was real.

As he sprinted into the thick forest, he could see absolutely nothing but soon became accustomed to the complete darkness. The lighter areas meant nothing was in front of him, and he could gradually make out the outline of the large trees and instead of colliding into their trunks or tripping over the roots, he gradually made forward progress.

He initially ran at full speed; then he thought of preserving his energy. But again he realized this would be counterproductive as the dogs and men would soon be in fast pursuit.

He had checked before starting, and as he knew the wind was blowing from south to north, running towards the north star would make it more difficult to detect his scent if only he could get rid of those damn bells. He still could not make out outlines of houses if they were here in these isolated woods and shouting would only provide clues to locate him quicker.

Jason felt alone wondering if God had forsaken him. He felt the tears starting, but he just kept moving. His military training helped

111

him to keep focused on his goal of survival. The thick undergrowth slowed him down and made the going difficult. The thorns from the vines ripped into his skin as he ran for his life. These hunters would soon be coming and he had to keep going regardless of the cuts and bruises. His bare feet were hurting. These feet that were used to pedicures were, instead, now were pounding against the roots and stones emerging from the ground.

He stepped on sticks with thorns. Then he was crashing into the low branches, not seeing them fast enough and having to constantly bend over. The large ones would knock him down but for a moment, only to have to be up again running.

He kept wiping the blood from his forehead and continued as if nothing happened. It was obvious there was no cut pathway for him, so ditches and bumps were surmounted with the same strenuous effort as dodging tree trunks and branches. As he continued, he thought, God, free me from this ordeal. while he ran hoping heaven would do something to make him free of the moment. He didn't expect an answer but he would welcome the favor. He had to hold back the tears that blinded him, though it was no time for tears, so with a deep breath and tons of resolve he stopped feeling sorry for himself.

He suddenly heard a different sound as he moved forward. Getting closer he could hear the sound of water and it seemed to be close by. As he moved in the direction of the sound, a tree branch swiped his cheek, bruising the side of his face and tearing into his flesh, causing a deep gash. This new injury with the added weight of the yoke became unbearable. When the yoke was first placed on his neck, he felt as if he could run with it, but the weight was now cutting into the flesh of his collar bone. Even with this pain he continued. There was no alternative, and he was not sure if the blood came from the pressure of the yoke on his neck or his face.

By now the sound of water flowing seem closer. It seemed as it was crashing onto rocks below, and he surmised there was a waterfall. He needed to see if it was a possible escape route, but as he tried to make sense out of the looming outline, he lost his footing, grabbing the vines layered onto the branches of the tree close by. This did not help as the tree got pulled halfway over into the ravine with him hanging on. He used every ounce of strength and jumped upward going after the next tree branch he could feel. This branch too gave way, but the vines he had previously held onto were tangled in the yoke and that kept him suspended for the moment.

The thorns on the vine punctured his skin, but he refused to let go of the branch. Holding on with one hand, he felt himself moving lower into the ravine and falling, so he tried anchoring his toes into the rocky edge refusing to let go of the branch. He had no idea how far the drop could be, but if he let go of the branch, the vines wrapped around the yoke and his neck would serve as a noose causing certain strangulation.

As he tried to reposition himself, he could feel the edge where he had tried to anchor his toes crumbling and giving way, and he was slowly and certainly slipping. He hitched the free end of the yoke onto something jutting out and with the other hand, he held on to what he presumed was a branch thankfully free of thorny vines. This gave him instant stability, and he knew this may not hold for long, but he prayed for time to regain his footing while feeling the ledge and desperately searching for some sort of stability in the darkness.

The same yoke that intended to kill me assisted in saving my life. What an irony, he thought. He refused to move as he savored the feeling of stability even if for a moment and whispered in case the hounds and their masters could hear. "Thank you, God."

He caught his footing once again and gradually inch by inch moved across the ledge. The going was tough, and then he heard the sound of something tingling as it fell. The vine had broken off one of the bells it had entangled. As he continued moving along the edge of this presumed waterfall, he realized he did not hear the bell anymore and he thought, one small victory for "Jasonkind."

He realized this ravine could be deeper than he thought, but regardless of that, he kept holding on to the branches for support constantly anchoring his toes into the sides until he could find a ledge suitable to pull himself back up onto the brim. He looked over his shoulder, and as his eyes adjusted, he could see the glitter of the reflection on the surface of the water far down. His military training kicked in as he estimated the ravine could be over a hundred feet deep. He felt confident now as he tried to work his body over the edge, but during a moment when he lost concentration paying attention to his bruises, bleeding, and the yoke, he almost lost his grip and started slipping downwards.

He tried not to panic as he thought of his two choices – falling to his death or the alternative of being hunted by the dogs and being shot and buried on the very spot where he was caught. There seemed to be no hope for him. As he held on, he knew his anchor was about to give away as he could feel the entire tree and roots easing from their position.

Reflecting on his life, he knew he had been the master of his fate in many aspects. If his luck held, dying would be on his terms and not the decision of strangers with dogs. As the tree eased from its support, in desperation he tried to "dive" with all the strength in his body, carrying the vines and the branch with him trying to estimate the middle of the ravine and the deepest part of the water. He pulled his feet close to his body and hoped for the best. On the descent he steered the branch to hit the water, and he would then allow the leaves on the branch to cushion the impact. It was frightening as he kept falling faster and faster. Then came the impact as his body hit the water. It felt as if his whole body had exploded on the surface, and he was momentarily dazed but quickly became fully aware of his aquatic surroundings. He knew he was alive yet still frightened out of his wits. He thanked God again.

The water immediately started moving him in the direction of its flow as he lay on the branch resting after the ordeal. He knew he was alive and that was all. He rode the surface for a while checking out his head, neck, hands, and back. He could not believe he was bruised and battered, but alive. There was a large gash under his chin from the yoke when he made contact with the water but despite that, miraculously everything was in working condition as he pulled himself to the side of the river breaking himself away from this branch leaving the vine still wrapped around his neck. All his body ached as he lay on the bank of the river catching his breath as he pulled himself up while wrapping the vines around his neck to dampen the tinkling sound of the bells. The thorns he had now gotten accustomed to were like company to him.

Those daily morning runs along with his military training kept his body in good condition to withstand such a fall. Jason just wanted to lay down and rest. He knew he had to continue; the chase was not over and the dogs were still coming followed by men with guns. As he pulled himself up, kneeling first then standing and stretching, he needed to find the areas of injury on his body. He massaged where needed, but the short rest would have to take care of anything hurting.

He starting walking along the banks of the river on the opposite side of where the chase began, he surmised. Movement was slow he knew, but he could go no faster. As he moved, he knew his scent might not be easily detectable on that side of the river. This knowledge gave him some strength that helped him to start moving faster and faster as much as his aches and injuries would allow.

He had lost track of time and was unable to estimate, but he was certain it was over an hour into the hunt. He felt they were now definitely on his heels, so he must keep moving. Luckily, he didn't hear barking and that was good. He checked the wind, which was continuing to blow northerly and that was also good. The movement was difficult with thick undergrowth due to the fertile soil around the river, so he decided to move away from the river making the journey away from the banks and taking to the slopes.

As he moved through the bushes, the thick undergrowth and the branches continued to attack his body. His face felt it most, and the bloody bruises when mixed with perspiration burned like living hell. This concoction drained into the side of his mouth, and as he ran, the bloody taste and the other discomfort and pain irritated him and made him so angry it fuelled his movement as he ran faster and faster.

He had to overcome the hurting in his body and soul physically and emotionally. He had to survive as he needed answers for this night of hell. His eyes were so inflamed from all the assaults on his face that he could barely see but a few steps ahead.

Running now involved placing one hand over his eyes to protect them while he peeped through the slit between his fingers while dodging low branches. This slowed him down a bit, but protecting his eyes was most important. He was in survival mode at any cost. Certain thoughts lingered with him continuously as he remembered his army staff sergeant saying, "Bare feet on the ground not only toughens the soul but also hardens the resolve." Jason had proved this over many times in the past few hours of this fateful night.

Escape plans were foremost in his mind, and if he could escape the fall from the ravine or the waterfall – he was not quite sure which—he felt he would survive anything. His best revenge was staying alive, he thought. The military prepared you for attack, not retreat, but now fleeing was needed for survival.

The yoke around his neck was cutting deeper into his skin, the milk from the vines entangled in the yoke draining into the wounds while the heat from his body tightened the yoke all aggravating the situation. He stopped to reassess how best to deal with the encumbrances to his neck, including silencing the sound of the bells. The vines may as well serve some other purpose, he thought, as he tried to rearrange them to dull the sound.

The hunters' dogs usually by this time would pick up the scent or they would hear the sound of the bells. Neither was happening, so the leader realizing this started to speed up the pace pushing the dogs harder. They had to find him before sunrise which gave them a window of one and a half hours. Although it was enough time to reach the goal, he was getting anxious to end this hunt. Too much was at stake if that man managed to escape and word got out. That would be dangerous for many.

Over the years he was involved in three yoking episodes, but this was the first one he had organized and led. He was nervous and did not want to fail. He knew it had never happened in the known history of yoking. To cover more area he told both handlers of the dogs to spread out. One would go to the right and the other to the left. He would stay in the middle about twenty-five feet on each side. In that way the dogs might pick up a scent or hear something within the fifty-foot spread. Also, he said, "Keep your guns ready at all times and your ears and eyes open at all times. I know it's dark, but you shouldn't have to worry about the little man. He is a homo, so he should be a softie. We will soon catch this bastard and when you find him, automatically shoot him. Little did they know Jason was miles ahead and out of their area.

Jason knew he had lost track of time and longed for daybreak, just to be able to see where he was going. He kept running while rearranging the vines around the bells whenever he heard a bell making the slightest tingle. Preoccupied, he fell into a ditch, this time tumbling forward nearly ten feet hurting his left leg. As he lay there exhausted and hurting all over, he listened intently but there was no sound of dogs or their leaders, which was enough reason to continue in spite of his leg injury. He was never going to give up.

The stream turned away from the northerly track, but Jason wanted to continue in the direction that was working for him, so once again he had to climb a slope to make it to the highlands. As he ran, he started making out images – dawn was breaking making his running path more visible. This also worried the leader of the hunters, who was now pushing the group to find Jason, creating a nervous and anxious atmosphere. Then suddenly the dog on the left broke direction and went directly towards the left, meaning he had picked up the scent. One of the men yelled, "We have something."

The leader responded immediately to the other hunter to his right, "To the left, to the left." As all followed moving towards the left, they were moving faster with excitement when the lead dog came to an abrupt stop, causing total confusion for the others following. The group had to hold on to whatever they could to halt their momentum, realizing they were on the edge of a deep canyon. They could actually see how deep it was because it was near daybreak.

He shouted to the others, "Be careful. We are on the edge of a cliff. Don't move." This was a command the dogs had sensed well before he said it, and they were not moving a muscle.

As they looked over the edge, it was obvious some part of a tree had broken away leaving the roots exposed. There was a lot of activity along the side of the ledge where it was clear someone had been struggling. At this point he then told the others to take the dogs to see if they could pick up a scent nearby. After doing this, the dogs came back to the same point. The leader then said to the group, "Well, he must have gone over at this point because he could not have climbed down." While checking the area, it seemed as if there was extra activity in one area, but the dogs' response indicated Jason had not moved from that spot.

With the morning getting brighter one could see clearly over the edge and there was no way for anyone going over to climb back up. Whoever went over would be dead. "It seemed as if he tried holding on to the thorny bush and went over the side. Can you see anything?" They went closer making sure to keep their footing. "You see how deep this place is? If any one falls over here, they could never survive and he went no further up here. If he did, the dogs would have picked up his scent," the leader continued, "and they didn't." He sounded desperate and worried questioning his statements and answers.

It had never happened that there was no body to bury. "We have to find the body. We have to continue walking along the sides of the cliff. If there is a scent, the dogs will pick it up, but we have to make it to the bottom of the cliff and inspect the river."

There was no time for a consensus. They had to go down to the river and find that body. Those were the rules of the hunt. A body was evidence of success. They were now running against time and with morning breaking, a body had to be found. As they ran, the hunters did not realize the dogs were on to something going in the direction of Jason earlier, but since the humans' intentions were focused on reaching back to the spot where Jason fell, they weren't paying attention to the dogs. They had lost focus; the handlers were so intent on reaching the supposed end to Jason's run they stopped paying attention to the dog's lead along the river.

The hunters continued to concentrate on the ravine and finding Jason's body. In the meantime, Jason was seeing better and moving at his fastest pace since the fall. He looked to his right and in the distance he could make out the outline of something round. With this sighting he had an adrenalin rush running at his maximum speed towards the structure. As he ran closer, he realized it was an elevated water tank with markings which were not immediately legible, but with renewed hope, he moved with determination. Those structures usually signified a town nearby.

While moving towards the tank, he became aware of his being almost nude, knowing he would be conspicuous and suspicious looking to anyone who saw him. He kept running, trying not to lose sight of the structure he saw in the distance. He didn't see the deep hole obscured by vegetation in his path, and he fell head first into the five-foot deep hole. The fall displaced the yoke, which ripped into the old wound deepening the cut under his chin. His blood was now flowing, and again his military training surfaced. He used some of the leaves and applied pressure hoping to control and slow the bleeding. Pulling himself out of the hole, he felt such severe pain in his left leg that he had to actually drag the leg as he moved forward. He did not want this to stop him. He knew help was ahead. Looking up, he saw the round outline ahead take the form of a large fifty-thousand-gallon water tank with large markings reading: YELLOWSTOHE. He saw there was another house in front of the tank, and he knew for certain someone must live there as there was a garden patch with cabbages and tomatoes. The short garden hose was left lying attached to a pipe.

Yes! he thought, someone must be here. He started shouting, "HELP, HELP, HELP" as he drew nearer to the building, but as he shouted louder and louder, he realized it was a tire fixing station not a dwelling. He read the sign at the side of the building: CHEAP GAS AND TIRE FIX. He ran to the back of the building, and while at the back, he saw lights approaching. A vehicle was coming up the road. He was of two minds as he thought it might be his hunters. So, he cautiously ran to the front of the building because he was unsure who was coming. Being overly cautious, he took some time to reach the front, and in so doing, he missed out on possible help. He watched them as the car sped by oblivious to his dire need.

He made a quick inspection of the building to see if could get inside. It was impossible because it was so well protected from theft, possibly due to its location. Remembering the hunters were on his heels, he had to make a plan. He decided to keep running as his scent would be picked up by the dogs if he stayed there, so he decided to move on. He was about to leave although he was so tired and he knew he could not go much further with the pain all over his body, especially his left leg which was now swollen and painful.

As he was about to run off, he looked up at the water tower. He knew his body could not make it any further and since he was about to collapse in pain and exhaustion, he was willing to try anything. In his hasty run not paying attention, he kicked over the garbage can at the front door; a loud noise with an echo ensued. The plastic bag spilled its contents of decaying food. Looking once again at the water tank, willing to try anything at this point, an idea struck him. On seeing the large garbage bag, he remembered his underpants had been a source of embarrassment, so he thought that later he would cut out a place for his feet, thus fitting inside to hide his beautiful red underpants. Throwing the remainder of garbage out, he emptied the garbage bin with its contents onto the floor. There was food, ends of cakes, and biscuits, all kinds of food that make one hungry, but that was for later.

Then another idea struck. He ran back to the vegetable garden he had seen earlier. He grabbed the garden hose lying on the ground and ran towards the tank. Before mounting the ladder attached to the tank, he pulled the end of cake from the plastic bag and pushed it in his mouth. While eating he fitted the plastic bag over this foot and tied the ends. He then ate the biscuit ends using the bag to cover his other foot, tying the ends firmly over his foot trying to eliminate any scent for the dogs. While doing this, he thought of the delicious meals he once ate and now these scraps had to suffice.

While he was climbing to the top of the tank, the hunters had gone to the spot where they assumed Jason had fallen, but they did not find a body. The dogs had also located the bell that had broken off the yoke. Finding this, they were positive he had fallen and was washed away by the rough flowing water. He could never have withstood a fall from that height, and being convinced of this, they hurried back to the ledge where he had fallen.

Moving forward the dogs became increasingly agitated, and the leader knew the dogs were their guide and they must be followed. They kept going until they reached a bridge, and to their surprise the dogs made a dash to cross the bridge. The hunters followed pushing hard while the morning brightened as they moved forward.

As Jason climbed up the tank, he felt the weight of the yoke bearing down on his neck; with the blood from the wounds now clotted around the metal it helped in slowing the bleeding. The climb was taking a toll on his body as he passed the halfway mark, but despite the difficulties of the climb, he was happy there was no stress from the hunters being close. At that height he could hear sounds from a distance, so he tried keeping an ear out for the hunters but the climb was now at a snail's pace. As he was making it onto the top rail where the tank flattened, he heard a barking in the distance and he knew they had found him. Was this a good idea coming up here? he thought to himself, though it was too late now to go back down. One thing was for certain; the dogs could not climb up the rail to the top of the tank.

He then tried pulling the lever to open the top of the hatch. It refused to budge, so he pulled it again hoping to get it released. It was in vain due to years of rust and neglect. Then the idea came to him. He removed one of the small plastic bags and urinated into it. Then with some of the urine, he was able to remove the rust continuing to tug on the lever back and forward until it started releasing. He knew he could climb in and hide hoping not to be found.

Using the remainder of the urine in the bag, he distributed its contents into the air far and away from the circumference of the tank. He lifted the hatch only to find it was nearly half filled with water. He shook his head as he had thought in an isolated area such as this the tank would be empty and he would have used the hose to lower himself to the bottom. Now if this was not possible and he could not make it back to the ground in time to continue running, he was dumbstruck, not knowing what to do. He remembered never to give up; he had to think it through. He could hear the barking of the dogs getting closer; he knew something must be tried even if it didn't work.

Realizing there were rails on the inside of the tank, he had to change his original plan, so he took one end of the hose and hooked it into the top rail on the inside of the tank. Taking the other empty plastic hose, he started lowering himself by the railings along the sides into the tank. At the water level he used the biscuit bag to tie the end of the hose onto the side of the railing.

It was inconspicuously placed, and one would have to look closely to see the opening. He then placed the large garbage bag over his head while placing the hose under the garbage bag. Jason wanted to make a trial dive placing his head in the bag and lowering himself under the water, but the water filled the hose so that did not work. He then drained the end of the hose and bent the end holding it from the side inside the bag. At that moment he heard footsteps on the outside of the tank; someone was climbing up the tank.

Jason knew there was no time for trial and error, so he placed the large plastic bag over his head again, wrapped the end of the plastic bag tightly around his neck, holding the bent end of the hose inside the bag and allowing him to breathe while wrapping the smaller bag around his neck to prevent water from entering. He lowered himself into the water one rail at a time downward as far down as he could. He then hooked his foot into the last rail to have some type of stability as he settled into the best position possible. At that very moment the hatch started opening as someone started inspecting the inside.

He could hear it as the person stepped off the ladder onto the platform. Then trying to open the hatch and have some light illuminate the area, he looked inside. The inside of the tank was dark; however, as he looked in and peered from different angles, he could see, even with the rising sun casting shadows, there no one hiding there. Jason heard the hatch door shut, but he remained in position and the yoke assisted in keeping him under as its weight pulled him towards the bottom.

Suddenly there was light again. The hatch opened; the hunter had come back! Jason had not heard him this time, but he took out his hand gun and fired a couple of shots onto the water's surface, hoping to get some movement.

These shots made Jason squirm, while he continued holding on tightly to the railing and concentrating on the improvised diving gear his only source of oxygen. All he could do was to hope the shots would not come in his direction.

Jason could hear the footsteps disappearing as the hunter descended. After making it back down to the ground, all three hunters stood with their dogs under the tank thinking of their next plan. A car approached. It was the owner of the tire repair store arriving to open his business.

On parking, the owner inquired, "Hi. Good morning. What can I do for you?" He spoke in a jolly way. He had retired from his automobile sales job and planned to enjoy his retirement in peace and quiet. He enjoyed opening up his little business each morning and having a quiet productive day in the isolated location sharing the time between tending his vegetable garden and fixing tires; the retail aspect of the goods in the store was minor.

The hunter replied, "We were tracking wild boars when the dogs lost the scent leading us right to this point. We are now deciding who is to go back to collect our vehicle."

At that point one was selected while the other two waited with the dogs. "Don't worry. This is the only building in the entire area. We pump gas here and have a little general store inside, just right for a retired man," the storekeeper stated and smiled as he moved towards the building.

The hunters could not understand why the hounds were so restless. Although they were waiting outside the tire shop in the cool of the morning, they would not settle down, so the men decided to check the area under and around the tank while they were waiting. As they spread out, the dogs were agitated but not focused on one object or one direction. Individually they came to the conclusion the dogs were tired and hungry.

The other hunter who did not initially go up to the tank suggested since it was now bright and they were waiting on the truck, he would climb up the tank and look around again. "Can you look after my dog? I am going to the top instead of sitting here waiting for the truck."

Jason continued to listen closely to sounds coming from the ladder again. He knew he could hear the steps on the ladder only when they were near the top, so he surfaced quietly listening. As soon as the steps could be heard, he closed the plastic bag, tucking the end of the hose into the bag while wrapping the end of the bag tightly around his neck.

He breathed heavily a few times to make sure the hose was working and submerged himself, locking his foot again into the last rail.

Once again the surroundings were lit up as the latch was opened. This time it was for a longer period since the hunter left it open while he walked around the outside, scoping the forest with a pair of binoculars looking for signs of his prey. This time Jason had been careless while fixing the head gear and it started taking in water. Suddenly Jason's body started to move – his hold on the rail was slipping, his feet started moving upwards. At that moment the hunter peered into the tank again. When Jason saw the shadow, he allowed his body to float outwards so as not to create ripples in the water. Unfortunately, this also bent the hose making breathing difficult.

The hunter kept looking shouting as he closed the hatch, "I am coming down. No one up here."

Jason heard his footsteps descending the ladder for the last time hopefully. Jason's ordeal continued in silence. By now the large bag was stuck around his face, and he knew he had only a few seconds of air remaining, so he tried quietly to reverse his position immediately swinging the hose trying to straighten it. It worked! Air was again coming into the bag from above; he could breathe. It was the best breath he had ever taken in all his life, and he felt his chest expand as the air entered his lungs. His position was awkward, but it allowed a patent hose the upside-down position was well worth it. It was a tiring experience with one hand holding the rail with the other keeping the wrapped plastic bag with the hose around his neck. He had to keep this position for the next few hours. He tried correcting his position from time to time. The water was taking a toll on his body as it was depleting his strength, yet he refused to give in. After about two more hours had passed, he got extremely tired and quietly made it to the top rail where he could release bag from his neck and breathe normally. He rested in that position, not daring to open the hatch. He had now been the hunted for an estimated seven hours, maybe less. Jason had lost track of time.

With the vehicle back the hunters packed up their belongings inside, still lingering and wondering if this was truly how the hunt would end. With some uncertainty the leader told his two counterparts, "Let's drive around as far as we can. I want to be certain that we covered all bases." His voice was no longer commanding but nervous and disappointed.

As they went off, the old man was constantly watching through the store window; he was not accustomed to having so much excitement. He dialed 911: the police station

"I have some hunters knocking around my property at YELLOWSTOHE. I would like someone to come out and investigate."

The dispatcher replied, "Do you mean Tire Service along Highway 147? Is this correct?"

The old man replied, "Yes, and it's not hunting season yet."

The dispatcher replied, "OK. We will be sending someone, but remember it will take a while to get to your location, and this is the reason we have been asking you for years to close your shop… because it's too isolated"

The old man responded, "This station is the furthest point from civilization. We have assisted many stranded motorists. In addition, if you had to stay home all day around my wife, you would understand."

The dispatcher knew she could not take on this old guy and said, "Look out for the police car," and hung up.

The leader and his two hunters had doubled back to the starting point and had now made it to the ledge overlooking the ravine where Jason's fall had taken place. As they looked around, they were even more convinced as the leader mumbled, "I am sure he went over the ledge here. Look at the dogs. They did not have a scent after this point and look at the broken tree. No one could withstand a fall from here." They were looking at the spot now in broad daylight, and it was truly too dangerous and precarious for anyone to survive a fall.

All three agreed that Jason was dead. As they stood there observing the river for any movements or signs of life, nothing could be detected. They had a clear view from above and there was no way Jason could be alive if he had fallen in and they were sure he had.

The leader looked at the others for dissenting opinions but all were in agreement. They said, "This is what we will tell cousin Nigel... that we finished the hunt." Still as they were leaving not fully convinced, they continued looking for any signs or evidence of Jason being alive. They decided to drive in the direction of the tire shop, and as they turned in, they realized a police car was parked outside. The owner and the police were in deep conversation; it was too late to spin around and drive off as that would only raise suspicion.

They greeted the officer waiting in front of the tire store. "You guys are back again? So what's going on?" said the old man who felt uncomfortable at this continued interruption; his idyllic location was being transgressed. He never knew hunters to backtrack.

The leader now had to dig deep for an explanation. We are amateurs and not professionals who want to have a good weekend hunting. Our dogs picked up the scent and lost it, so when we came here this morning and saw the garbage bin overturned, we assumed it was a wild animal that may have remained in this vicinity. We decided to come back here to buy some food for ourselves and the dogs." The explanation was believable and he continued, "We saw that you had a phone here and we wanted to call home. Can I use your phone?"

The police understood the situation and asked the old man how he felt to which he answered with a smile.

The phone in Nigel's apartment rang. He quickly grabbed it and without seeing who was on the line said, "It's about time. I have been waiting for this call all morning. I am certain I had only two hours of sleep last night waiting for this call. How did it go?"

The leader replied, "Not as planned but the same end result."

Nigel was puzzled. "What do you mean by that?" he asked.

"Well, it seems that he fell off the cliff while trying to get away from us and was washed away by the river."

Nigel immediately interrupted. "How do you mean washed away? Did you find his body? Did you see his body?"

The leader paused. "No, but the river was flowing so quickly that by the time we could make our way down, the river had carried off the body."

By now Nigel sensed things had gone wrong. "So you don't have a body, you didn't see a body? So why are you convinced he is dead? The rules of the hunt dictate you carry out the instructions to the end, remember?" Nigel was adamant about how the hunt should be done. "Remember the only way to end the hunt is by burial? No other way, and those are the rules."

The leader, knowing what they had gone through during the last nearly twelve hours, understood how Nigel felt. "I understand how you feel but all three guys are convinced he is dead. The dogs sensed no scent after the point of the fall. Consider the hunt closed."

To which Nigel shouted, "Hell no! We have always covered our tracks and I have to be certain he is dead. We have to go back to the cliff where he fell."

The leader now becoming short with Nigel's reaction asked, "So why can't you go with our observation?"

Nigel replied, "I have to be convinced everything you tell me can't be challenged by anyone. I have to look at it from all angles. We are dealing with murder." The leader for the first time began looking at the hunt from another perspective as Nigel stated, "We have to go back there today. Can that be arranged?"

Knowing the urgency of the situation for closure he replied, "It can be done, but the guys need to sleep or rest." He continued, "When can you make it out here?"

Nigel responded, "I'll try to reach you before night fall. That should give you guys sometime to rest. Will that be all right?"

The leader thought through the time given and replied, "That should be all right. Remember the quickest route from town will be Highway147. Look out for the water tank at YELLOWSTOHE. You can't miss it. We'll be here waiting for you nearby. By the way, bring two hundred feet of climbing rope and two big bags of dog food."

Nigel knew the guys were tired, so he wished them and the dogs a good rest, letting them know he would be there as soon as he could. The hunters purchased as much as they could eat from the old man and went on their way only to park in the forest nearby to have a well needed sleep.

While all this was going on Jason was struggling to keep holding on to the top railing. He was exhausted and hungry. He drank water constantly only to urinate in the surrounding water and drink again when he felt thirsty. He would do anything to hold on for dear life. Sleeping was his major concern, and he found himself dozing off as he locked his arms through the rail to stabilize himself.

There was a crack or hole in at the side of the hatch producing a single ray of light on the water's surface. Jason was able to watch the movement of this ray guessing the approximate time of the day. Earlier the ray was to the left, then as it was in the middle, he assumed it was midday. Now it was to his right; it was a challenge that had to be met to survive.

When he wanted to urinate, it was not a problem in the water but when his stomach started to hurt due to the stale food he had eaten, he had to rub his stomach then grab back the railing each time. Then the inevitable happened. He had some serious stomach pain, so he had to relieve himself right there in his underpants; the weight of the underpants with its contents and the water stretching the elastic waist caused them to sink to his ankles. He shook them off and was now completely naked.

How do I explain this to any one? was his first thought. But who the hell is out here in this isolated area? No one.

The time seemed to take forever to pass as he tried to understand why someone wanted to kill him in this manner. They could just shoot me after leaving the bar, he thought. He questioned everything. Could it be because I am gay? He could not put it all together thinking confusedly, I am not gay because of my choice. This is just my feeling towards another person not because I want that feeling to happen at that moment. It is only my feeling towards another individual even if it's for the same sex. I go along a path to make everyone around me feel comfortable and happy. What's wrong with that?

Then he thought of his treatment of Nigel. He knew he was somewhat harsh, but Andrew was instrumental in delaying the implementation of the lottery. It was not all his fault. Could it be Nigel? No, he told himself, we shared drinks. Remembering the evening together that night, he smiled. He remembered Nigel getting even drunker that night than he was. I hope he got home all right, he thought.

This was the longest day in his life waiting and looking at the inner metal walls of the tank while trying to hold onto the rails. His body was cramped having to tread water and exercising only the lower part of his body, and he felt worn out and hungry. He needed to put something in his stomach. The water was his menu, yet he knew he had changed its constitution with excrement and he could not bring himself to drink it.

After a few hours had passed and with no alternative, he drank initially with difficulty then it tasted no different, so he filled his guts that being his only choice. The evening sun heated the metal tank making the air at the top above the water warm and uncomfortable. He treaded water to stay alive but even with growing frustration, he tried to take his mind off of everything. He watched the ray of sunlight going further and further to the left. By his approximation it was late evening.

He was waiting all day for this opportunity to lift the hatch and peep outside. He knew he had to be careful not knowing if the dogs or the hunters were still around or if any eyes from anywhere −there was no one in sight—were glued on the top waiting for signs of movement.

He was so tired holding on that he had to take a chance. He tied the other end of the hose to the top in case he needed to make a quick dive back in while he emptied the plastic bag and tied its ends to be free of water. He stuffed it under the first rail. He then moved to the hatch which he carefully pushed upward, and as it opened, he had to adjust to the dim evening light although it was getting dark. Coming from complete darkness, it was a strain on his eyesight.

Getting accustomed to the light, he pushed the hatch wider and wider until he could stick his head through and was able to see the area surrounding the building. There was a parked vehicle,] so he knew he had to wait a bit longer. He knew there was no sense going down not knowing who he would meet. He was not going to take the chance, and he felt safer here at the top, so he closed the hatch and waited until it got darker.

While waiting he knew there were plans to put in place. How not to be detected? How to find a change of clothes? How to escape the dogs? The tumbling thoughts brought the excitement of being able to escape the clutches of the hunters. His body drained from exhaustion yearned to just escape the water. If things continued as they seemed, he knew he didn't have much time left to be in the water. The anticipation of escape was enough to help him "calmly" wait for the right time to exit.

He pushed open the latch once again. As soon as he did, he saw car lights moving out of the area and all the shop lights were turned off. It seemed as if there was no one left in the area. He was elated and he realized he could soon confidently climb out of the tank. He was naked and exhausted as he dragged himself through the opening and lay down on the top platform to rest. He stretched out his limbs on the warm metal. It felt so good that now he could rest for a while as he decided his next move. With his arms outstretched and comfortable in the quiet wind of the night and finally being able to take a deep breath, Jason closed his eyes gently and he fell into a gentle sleep.

He slept undisturbed catching up on a well needed rest. Suddenly, there was the sound of dogs barking and lights coming from vehicles below. He was awakened by these sounds and he could hear the commotion of men arguing and dogs barking. As he quietly moved his head to the side, he was reminded that he was still wearing the yoke which may attract the dogs; he slowly peeped down below.

The men arguing had hats on and no masks. He could recognize the truck. It was the same one used in the hunt the night before, and although alarmed he remained on the top of the water tank. As he continued peeping over the side, he realized there was a fourth person he knew. If they were coming towards the water tank, he could make it back underwater before they made it to the top, so he continued to wait and watch.

The voices were inaudible from that distance, but the men seemed to be arguing while putting on their gear as if they were going for another hunt. He could not hear it as Nigel voiced his displeasure with the hunt and he made quite clear to all three hunters.

Nigel said, "I can't believe you guys left without cleaning up the job completely."

This angered the leader. "I am telling you he is dead. Believe me, the dogs could not pick up a scent in the entire area and if he went over that cliff, he is certainly dead. There is no other alternative for him, so stop worrying. This is why we wanted you to see for yourself."

Jason strained to hear and could sense these conversations were about him although the distance was too far to hear clearly.

Nigel asked the hunters, "How far from here is the cliff where he fell? Can we drive there?"

They responded, "Not into the forest."

Jason could hear the disgust in their voices.

"It is approximately forty-five minutes to an hour walking distance," they replied. Then they asked, "Did you bring the rope with you?"

"Yes," he responded, "over three hundred feet along with hooks and climbing gadgets. It's in the back of the car."

He also reminded them that what they were there for was to see the job through to completion. That meant finding the body. That was what he was there for and nothing short of that. As soon as they were geared up with the dogs leading the way, they were off to the spot on the cliff. Jason could only watch from the distance seeing everything going on but not knowing their intentions. He assumed it was nothing good.

After they had left, he decided to give them some time to clear the area waiting for over fifteen minutes. Then Jason started making the journey down the outside of the tank. Remembering his nakedness, he didn't know whether to go fast or slow to be undetected. He then thought, detected by who? There was absolutely no one around for miles. He hurried down mainly to hide his nakedness.

With each step he made he pushed the entire apparatus of bags and bells away from the ladder so as not to make loud sounds, thinking as he descended that this was a lot easier than what he had gone through in the past twenty hours. This was easy going which meant he had to be closely attentive to his surroundings. He found the experience so overwhelming that he cried all the way down not knowing if it was due to the sadness of being hunted, being so close to death, or simply the joy of reaching the ground. When he reached the third tier of steps from the bottom, the weight had become so unbearable he fell to the ground. He quickly wrapped his hands around the yoke decreasing the sound of the bells hitting the ground with a feeling of total exhaustion mixed with total exuberance. He didn't feel a thing; even if he was hurt there was that feeling that he had escaped.

As he made it across the road and onto the veranda of the store, he knew he had no time to waste. The vehicles were parked and the men could return at any time. However, he enjoyed his new freedom and no one would ever humiliate or dehumanize him again.

He thought to look around the building but decided to get out of the vicinity remembering the building was completely burglar proof, and it would be impossible to break into. He preferred to get as far away as possible from the entire area; all the time he kept stuffing the plastic bags around the yoke making it as sound proof as possible.

Instinctively, he looked around with anger and ever-present frustration; revenge and escape were on his mind not necessarily in that order of importance. Looking at the truck, the truck that transported him to this situation, he focused on a stone to disfigure the appearance of the vehicle just like he was disfigured.

He found a stone and after deciding where to start the destruction just before it left his hand, he thought that he needed to be rational and concentrate on doing something that could help with his escape.

So, walking over, he threw the stone into the driver side window shattering the glass. His training in the military taught him how to hotwire any and everything that had a motor. The military training came into use; unfortunately, there was no light to see properly, but he knew what to try to find.

Quickly he found the wire compartment under the dashboard. Pulling the wires he referenced the correct wires and started the truck without a hitch. Getting out of there was foremost on his mind, so he drove around the building towards the back and turned on the lights to see better. Then without a second thought he rammed into the side of the building, choosing the easiest point under the window. With lights assisting him he quickly jumped out and broke open the window.

Entering the building, he found the food aisle and started to stuff himself with pastries for quick energy. Then he threw the excess snacks and juices into the truck. As he moved, he realized the yoke didn't bother him as much as before. How easy is it to get accustomed to things weighing you down, he thought, but sometime, somehow it would have to go. As he walked the aisles, he found wire cutters and pliers, the implement he wanted most to find. He grabbed three along with a handful of the cutting tools and threw them into the truck. He also found a thick pair of overalls hanging on the back wall, maybe belonging to a worker. At this point a designer suit would not have looked better. He tried it on while holding his genitals, just in case there were any critters in the pants as he had no underwear protection and would hate being bitten in a critical place. It seemed as if the owner's belly was extra, extra large, but it didn't matter as his body was finally covered. Everything looked even more hopeful when he saw water boots like three sizes larger, but it was something for his feet. He added hydration to the foods packing juices and water into the truck. Jumping back into the truck while reversing, he spotted the extensive damage to the building, but it was necessary as it helped his quest for escape and survival. He hoped the owner had insurance and comforted himself that he was not responsible for the owner's predicament.

Driving quickly from the back of the building, he passed the other parked car, a small sports car. He could not immediately make out the make or color, but it looked like a car he knew. It looked like Nigel's car, this seemed to him to be a coincidence. But, after slowing down he took a closer look. The blue color and the large dent on the right side could be no coincidence. His eyes popped out when he saw this. With this sudden "awakening" he had to gasp for breath as the whole scenario became clearer.

While looking over his shoulder for the hunters, Jason jumped from the truck focusing the lights on the car to be sure it was blue and had the dent. He inspected the entire car to be certain. He knew the car but had to be certain, and after inspection he was convinced – it was Nigel's car.

He felt betrayed and in a dash of anger he fired his fist through the driver's window shattering the glass. He then walked back to the truck, placed the truck in reverse, braked up, and in the forward motion slammed into the front of the car with the large truck. He slammed it once again, smiling with satisfaction. After inspecting his handiwork as he circled the vehicle on his way out, he wished the car could never be driven again unless the tire shop got involved. Exiting he headed north bearing the pain in his fist after shattering the car window and not realizing he had also cut himself.

Angry and disappointed with the person he considered a friend, he questioned himself, the voice was that of his captor, John, who he had introduced to me at the Watering Hole. Did he hate me so much that he wanted me killed? He was still reluctant to associate the name with the deed. Jason felt betrayed now knowing Nigel was connected. Shocked, disappointed, angry, after a couple miles he slowed his erratic driving and self-preservation prevailed.

Understanding that people are not always who they seem to be and his thoughts in turmoil, he wondered as he drove north how he could release his emotions?! Tears welled up but they only clouded his vision more and not being able to navigate the unfamiliar roads would be suicide.

Work with a successful goal in mind always relaxed him, so he concentrated on using the cutting implement to start working on releasing the yoke from his neck.

As Jason drove himself north, Nigel and his hunting party were about reaching the spot on the cliff where they were convinced Jason had plunged to his death. They took out their high-powered, hand-held lights to survey the area including the sides of the cliff.

"Are you certain this is the place?" Nigel asked.

All the others agreed this was the place showing Nigel the broken tree and explaining the broken away area. Then they beamed the lights into the deep ravine below. Nigel seeing this evidence almost agreed but still wanted to go down to inspect for himself. The rope was securely tied to the trunk of the large tree nearby and the bag with lights and other implements were lowered into the ravine with Nigel and the leader climbing down the rope. The other two hunters would travel back to the water tank checking for more evidence as they went on their way.

Nigel knew this type of outdoor activity was not his first choice, but he had to show the other hunters he had the capacity to lead this "factfinding and conclusive mission." Too many things did not fit into place, but he had to see for himself that the evidence did fit the conclusions. When he was maneuvering, he saw something stuck between the rocks – a bell. This was the place the yoke had held firm for Jason before his final fall ripping the bell off causing it to be left stuck in the groove.

Finding this on his way down, Nigel shouted to the leader, "What is this I found? It was embedded in this groove. Does this look familiar to you?"

The leader looked at Nigel and said, "Yes, that's one of the bells from the yoke. I told you he fell here and plunged to his death. Now what do you think?"

Nigel placed the bell into his pocket continuing to the bottom. The sides were steep causing the men to bump into the rocks, bruising their elbows, and sometimes losing their footing and crashing into the side of the cliff. They continued to the bottom, where they spent three hours surveying the area shining the light in every corner looking for more evidence as they walked along both banks of the river searching.

Nigel finally said, "Well, there is absolutely no need going any further. I am convinced." While walking along the bank, they continued looking for Jason's remains.

Nigel said, "The evidence is here, but I am still uncomfortable. If this didn't happen as we think it did, we will be on shit street." He paused but continued, "I would have preferred seeing some evidence. I know finding the bell is proof and you are right he must be dead, but I wanted to see a dead body."

They knew there would be trouble without evidence of a body or blood trails. Absence of these left the hunt open to anything. If Jason had gotten away, it meant the story would come out into the open. In over a century of Yoking, the secret had never been leaked. The secret was always able to be contained within a select group of friends and family.

The end result was always the same because no one had ever escaped. The victim was always buried with the evidence. He literally felt his feet tremble in his boots with the fear of being discovered. The search of the ravine concluded and they walked back the usual route along the bank as they ascended the gradual slope towards the water tank.

Nigel continued to be uneasy and troubled. If evidence of past hunts were ever to surface, many families and friends would be in serious trouble dating back to decades, even centuries. His thoughts reflected on his grandfather telling him of using Yoking as a means of entertainment. It was the getting together of real men who never told the women when and what they were going out to do. This secret was the main bond; it was an important secret keeping the clique together. It was an unbroken bond strengthening the individuals from childhood on, to be made better men and ultimately a stronger family, or so they thought. Failure of the act was so serious. It had to end in the burial of the hunted. This belief gave the participants the work ethic that whatever they did, it had to be done correctly and carried through to completion even in their everyday lives. This concept was genuinely considered by the men involved as justification for the act, a type of validation of the concept of commitment.

These thoughts tugged at Nigel's conscience as he knew something was wrong with the whole exercise – there was a human being involved. Why did he choose to seek revenge through his cousin John this way? Could it be an innate and inherited trait from their forefathers that they shared? So, how would John feel if anything went wrong in this operation and he was exposed? Would he want Nigel to protect him or seek to avenge? Would this need for righting a wrong follow through? Would John want him to intervene? And how? Seemingly, times had changed in terms of method, but attitudes had not. However, at this point and time he was too otherwise deeply involved in the situation as leader of this dastardly act which had gone wrong from all historic accounts. Enough time spent on that aspect, Nigel had no time to consider its legality or morality. His reputation and future were at stake and protecting that was the priority.

As they approached the water tank, the dogs were barking, and from a distance in the dark they could not see what was happening, but they knew something was awry.

As they got closer the other two hunters shouted, "The truck is not here. I am sure this is where we left it." As they started the search, one of them saw the damage to the back of the building and shouted, "You guys, come here now!" They all ran to the side of the building thinking the truck was there, only to realize someone had taken the truck and rammed the building destroying a major section. They shined their lights at each other in amazement.

"Holy shit! We have to get out of here before someone passes by and thinks we did this."

In the get-away move they all ran towards Nigel's car, only to see it too was damaged. There was no time for questions; they had to get as far away from this building as possible. Nigel jumped into the driver's seat and tried starting the car. As he turned the key, there was no sound coming from the engine; he tried again and again – nothing. Panic which now gripped the group manifested itself in different ways. John started to sweat profusely as if he were having a heart attack. One hunter could be heard praying loudly while the other shouted profanities. The dogs hungry and agitated would not stop growling.

"What the hell are we going to do?" John barked, sweat still streaming down his face. "Fly the hood." As the light shone on the engine, just as he hoped was the problem, the impact had shifted the battery and its connections. He immediately made the reconnections and put the battery back in position. "We will try it again," he shouted, getting back into the driver's seat himself and trying once more. It worked; the car started.

"We all can fit in this small car," said Nigel, who was already in the driver's seat as under no circumstances would he let anyone drive his car. "We have to. I am not leaving anyone or anything here to answer questions, not even the dogs. Do you know the trouble if anyone found us here? Let's start packing in." The two front seats easily occupied two persons, but the single back seat was very small, so he held his heavy hunting jacket on the inside of the back glass and with a stone hit the glass until it was completely shattered. Then throwing the excess glass from the jacket through the opening he was able to fit the other two hunters and the dogs in the back seat all with their heads sticking out through the missing rear glass space.

John was anxious to leave. As soon as all six occupants were packed in the car and the bag with the rope was dumped into the trunk, Nigel drove off turning right to go south along the road thinking how stupid they looked with the four heads sticking out – two belonging to the men, the other two to the dogs. If he were ever to be stopped by the police, what would be the explanation?

There was not a single word for the first hour. No one dared to think it was Jason. After all he had drowned in the ravine. This was proven by the bell from the yoke, the broken tree, and the sheer drop, all enough to seal his fate. The truck which could be traced back to John was missing. Who had it? What crime would it be used to commit? Different thoughts and concerns were in everyone's mind, including visions of their comfortable beds at home.

Nigel finding his voice stated, "We have to report the theft to the police. It will be reported missing from my apartment." There was absolutely no response from anyone. The dog and two men exhausted from the previous two nights' hunt were fast asleep on top of each other – man and dog in the cramped space. Nigel knew this would be done early Sunday morning when they returned home.

12

CHAPTER

JASON PROCEEDED IN a northerly direction without any money. He was determined to run the tank dry, then abandon the truck wherever he reached. He continued cutting away at the yoke. Sometimes the cutting tool would slip and cut into his flesh, but Jason did not care as it had to be done. He reminded himself that he had been through worse pain remembering the fall preceded by the other cuts, lacerations, and bruises.

He realized the hunters made the yoke especially strong so as not to be easily removed. He guessed when the hunt was over and the person was dead, they could just as easily cut the victim's head off, as easy as that without any feeling. Well, he thought, this is one head they wouldn't have to bother about. I can remove this yoke without their assistance. This time he smiled. He was determined he would be the one to escape the claws of the ruthless hunters. With this in mind he continued driving even faster, knowing he had a task to complete. Then he felt the yoke shift. He had cut through the first bend in the yoke but there was another bend, so he started on that one, hoping it could be finished before the truck ran out of gas since he would not know when or where that would be.

His immediate goal was getting rid of the yoke before the end of the drive. Eliminating the first bend in the yoke brought tears to his eyes thinking of how people treated each other and how someone could kill another human being trying to survive being chased by hounds and carrying this weight on his neck.

His thoughts then turned to Nigel. He could not imagine how he could have upset him to the point where he made him a target for such a gruesome death. Hate was infectious and now mutual, he thought, with tears flowing freely as he analyzed his predicament. I am here in the wilderness with no money, stolen ill-fitting attire, no identification running for my life all to satisfy your ego and feelings of non-achievement. Jason felt unsure of his direction but once he could stay ahead of those hunters, he had a chance to stay alive to one day get even with Nigel.

He read the road signs forever staying on this one road, hoping it would lead to a major highway. There was one place he knew he could always find help and he hoped there was a link for The Association for Friends of the Heart in the first town or city he reached.

The sun was now rising on the horizon, showing acres and acres of farm land ahead. He could go faster as he was able to see further ahead. There was a sign ahead showing directions to the town of Cherpin twenty miles to the west. When he reached the highway, he turned left on his way to Cherpin, and he felt relieved. At least there would be some form of civilization.

He could see the city in the distance and it seemed to be a small town, so he drove a half mile off the highway and parked in a cluster of trees to cut away at the yoke. It didn't take long to complete the job, and as he realized the last cut, he grabbed both sides and bent the yoke away from his neck. He took a good look at its construction before he started to dig a hole in the ground using the curved end. It was as if he could feel the heavy body weight of many who had worn this evil piece of metal but did not survive.

As he furiously dug the hole, the bells made the sound of feet running. The faster he dug, the louder the sound of the bells making it easier to be picked up by the dogs. The hole was now deep enough to fit the yoke; he placed it in the ground, making sure to cut off one of the bells as his souvenir. Then he decided to keep two bells just in case. He made a ceremony of it shouting, crying, and singing "never again" as he covered the object with the dirt and stomped it flat. He wiped his face removing the sweat and dirt and using the leaves from the trees to wipe the sore on his neck left by the yoke. The leaves wiped his physical wounds and stale blood while the hurt felt inside eased as he continued crying. He was now free of everything the evil hunters had contrived as a burden for him to carry. He felt free; it was a true catharsis.

At that moment he realized the purpose of tears and prayed that he would never have to cry again like this. Hope engulfed his being as he thought a better tomorrow was in store.

Jason climbed back into the truck, pushed the seat back, and rested while making his plans for the coming days. He knew he had no money, no identification, and no one to call on, but if he could find The Association for Friends of the Heart, it would be a start. He knew their policy was to ask no questions as they provided shelter, allowed you to work for your meals, and if you got an outside job, you paid twenty-five percent of your salary to contribute in helping with chores and cooking. This would do as he hoped to be on his own before the three months they allowed expired. If he abandoned the truck, no one would know if he went into the town or continued on his journey, so he decided to abandon the truck, leaving it in the cluster of trees and walking into the town.

On reaching Cherpin he immediately realized the town was small. Everyone seemed to be in church. He started by asking questions only to hear there was no organization called the Friends of the Heart in the town. He was told he would have to go the larger city seventy-five miles away. He decided to hitchhike his way west to Evancora which took him the entire day but Jason was determined. He had to make it. Reaching Evancora in time for supper, he did his first dishwashing and wiping chores in exchange for lodging. He didn't know how long he would stay there. When he first walked in, all eyes were on his attire and water boots, yet no questions were asked.

He assumed the name Junior Hoply. He was at peace for the night. He had a bed and was protected and comfortable with his plan to reach his mother's house. This could take him a couple of weeks, but for now it was important to place some new perspectives in his life, working out the direction and timing to properly avenge the person who planned his demise.

While Jason was comfortably settling in to Evancora, it was a long night for Nigel, who was going through the evening and into the night nervous and wondering what was next. All the time he kept asking himself how he ever got into this mess. All he could envision was the cliff and the river area; he barely got two hours sleep.

Sunrise found him in no condition for work, but he had to go to see if Jason would turn up at his job. His rollercoaster thoughts jumped from one conscience-searching ride to another, to justify his actions. He wanted to believe that arrogant Jason deserved what happened to him, but wasn't extinction too drastic a move to punish arrogance?

After dressing he decided to leave the partially wrecked car and decided to take the bus to work. When Nigel reached the office that Monday morning, he inquired at the front desk if Jason was in yet.

To his surprise the security stared him straight in the eye saying, "Good morning." This caught Nigel off guard.

"I am sorry my thoughts are roaming today. I usually see him in the car-park. That's why I am asking."

The guard replied, "Don't worry. I am waking you up. No, he is not in as yet."

The usual members were present at the Monday morning meeting with the exception of Jason, whose absence was out of character. This was noted as Andrew started the meeting.

"Where is Jason? He knows I prefer everyone to be here to report on their department. Let's get started. He must be caught up in traffic." Andrew was ready to get going and anticipated Jason opening the door and walking in.

On the other hand, Nigel was on edge and nervous throughout the meeting. Each time someone left the room, he turned his head and kept turning towards the door.

Then Andrew noticing his uneasiness asked him, "How is the project going? I know it's been drawn out. What's the latest report?"

This was the first time Nigel was drawn into reporting as this was Jason's role. He quickly composed himself and forced a smile. "Everything is in place. All that's left is its implementation and waiting for Jason to complete the programming. Then it is a go." Nigel realized without Jason's opposition his job was easier. This is what he had yearned for. Nigel felt he could now confidently chart his own course. Smiling, it felt good when he thought, goodbye, Jason. I hope you are dead.

Andrew knew without Jason present he had to give the go ahead. "Well, let's get started with the change over. The ball is now in your court," he said reluctantly to Nigel, still hoping Jason would make an entrance through the door. With that he adjourned the meeting, the first one without Jason since the good times.

Later that day Andrew was still inquiring about Jason, asking Frank to put a check on Jason. There were no calls and this he found strange since he knew the importance of the Monday morning meetings. For Jason to miss it with no excuse caused him to wonder if something was wrong.

Frank came back the next morning reporting that Jason's phone kept ringing with no one answering.

By Wednesday Andrew's concern grew as to Jason's whereabouts. They had grown very close while on" the lottery project," and he even considered the collaboration like a father and son affair. By this Saturday coming he would need his involvement as Jason handled the computer aspect of things.

Andrew knew one draw was not important, so he could do without Jason for this week, but the future depended heavily on him. He also knew the information Jason had given him might be enough for him to figure out the inner running of the software, but he needed Jason's expertise.

He picked up the phone and called Frank for an update as he did every day. "Any word from Jason?"

Frank replied, "No."

"Did anyone go over to his apartment to find out anything or are there any signs of him in the community?" Andrew added, "We have a responsibility if our staff is missing. We have to report it to the police, so please file an official police report today."

For Nigel that week was a good week. His confidence grew each day and things got better at work. In addition, no word meant Jason had died from the fall, and it was becoming a reality that he was gone forever. The silence was reassuring.

As the week closed, Andrew worked on the program quietly from his office. He taught himself to manipulate the numbers waiting for Saturday's draw. The problem he saw was from Nigel changing the system and Jason not being there to manipulate the new program. Andrew tried fixing the game but it didn't work. He knew he needed Jason. That week there were two winners sharing twenty-eight million dollars. Andrew was getting worried.

At the Monday morning meeting Andrew's secretary interrupted the meeting. Police officers were in the lobby waiting to speak with Andrew Cole. He immediately adjourned the meeting going off to meet the officers.

"Good morning, officer. Please come into my office." With the usual pleasantries and affirmations, he led the procession into his office. As they entered, they formally identified themselves and stated their intentions.

"I am Detective Dunn and this is officer Gore from the Amalta Police Department. We received a report regarding a missing employee." Dunn took the lead. "We will be handling the case and we wanted to know what your impression might be of what has happened to your employee. Sorry, could you tell me his name?"

Andrew realized there was no frivolous conversation with police. They were direct and to the point. Andrew answered, "His name is

Jason Paye and after leaving work on Friday last week approximately ten days ago, he has not been seen by anyone and no one has heard from him since."

After the usual questions directed at gaining information, the detective asked, "Did anyone check his desk for any notes or messages? Did anyone go to his home?"

This surprised Andrew because it never occurred to him to invade Jason's privacy. He told the detective the neighbors at his apartment complex had not seen him and no one had checked his desk as they figured he would soon return to work.

"You can come with us to check his desk. I will personally accompany you," Andrew urged. The police having completed their search and finding nothing left to obtain a search warrant to search his apartment. They asked Andrew for contact information, so his next of kin could be notified.

Three weeks had now passed and Jason had not turned up for work. The lottery business was having winners every week causing the prizes to be lower never going above twenty million.

Andrew knew when this happened, the betting public would become disinterested cutting back on the amount spent to buy tickets while looking at other betting interests. His concerns were not only for Jason's disappearance, but Jason was also an integral part of keeping the game at its highest level. Without him profits would spiral downward over time. He had to get into Jason's program and understand it before Nigel could implement the new program as he knew that when it started, there was no way of manipulating that program. If he could not fix this one, he had to find Jason.

Andrew spent Sunday in the office examining the program. He worked on it feverishly trying to penetrate the program. He now understood why Jason was so important to his organization to pull in those tickets, analyzing them and coming up with the unsold ticket numbers. He now appreciated Jason's efforts.

He worked way into the night analyzing how Jason could have taken the numbers from the night before the draw and seeing how he could have found numbers that weren't played. After many tries, he found a way to have drawn a single number that was not played. When he found this, he realized he had rewritten Jason's program.

Andrew was confident this would work for the next draw; however, his ultimate demise would be Nigel. Andrew knew that with him introducing the new changes, Andrew would have no way of manipulating the win. Still he left the office that night in the best spirits he had felt for the last three weeks.

In his nightly conversation Nigel told Nadia, "I am worried that with all the activities in the office, it is interrupting the proper flow of operations in the company. The investigations with the police are affecting the growth of the lottery and, therefore, the morale of the staff. It is about to reach rock bottom. No one knows what happened to Jason, but it is the attitude of your dad that is surprising. I can't understand why he relied on Jason so much. Remember that son of a bitch who tried to screw me? Not literally, but you understand."

They both laughed, but for Nigel there was more to his laugh remembering his experience at Jason's apartment, the experience that always kept him wondering. Their conversation went on for hours and Nadia felt the personal improvement on Nigel's part since he had informally taken over for Jason. He was now in an improved frame of mind in which they could think about making personal future plans for themselves as he finally saw himself with a future.

Monday morning meetings were never the same without Jason. It was now the fourth week since his disappearance and his laughter and antics were missed. They always laughed at how he was dressed or his amusing battles with Nigel when they all knew Jason would always have the upper hand in the end.

The marketing team's performance was now in question for the first time in months. Andrew told the meeting of decreased sales so changes were imminent. Other funds would be diverted to advertising for marketing to stay effective and entice customers once again although

Andrew secretly knew that without Jason things may never improve. Andrew was aware his computer abilities were not capable of handling the technical changes. Frank was given the responsibility to have a comprehensive survey done of the market. His responsibility was to find out: 1. where the heaviest betting took place; 2. where the winners were buying their tickets on average; 3. how much was spent on each bet. This information was to be gathered for the change over to the new system in two weeks.

Later that afternoon there was a call from the front desk security to Andrew's office. "There is someone here to see you. Her name is Lidia Payne."

Andrew responded while looking at his appointment diary, "I am sorry I don't have her down on my calendar and with so much going on it's impossible to see anyone else today."

The front desk added, "It regards Jason Paye."

Immediately Andrew put the pieces together as at first the name Lidia Payne had not rung a bell. "Oh," – he gave in – "yes, please send her up."

This caught Andrew off guard, but he knew sooner or later Jason's family would be contacting his office and he had made arrangements with his secretary to expect visitors on this behalf.

There was a rap on Andrew's office door, and he quickly opened it and welcomed his guest. She smiled immediately, and Andrew was taken aback as he somehow knew that smile. She took her seat.

"It has certainly been a long time."

He looked at her in doubt, not recognizing the aging face at first; then it came to him. He shouted, "Lidia Payne!" She smiled in return, realizing that she was just a memory like all friends of the past. "It's been a long time. How have you been?" he asked.

For a fleeting moment they exchanged admiring glances as they looked at each other smiling and guessing at each other's memory of their former acquaintance, wondering if it was the same.

"The years have passed, but things around here haven't changed," Lidia said softly. "The only thing different is I don't know the whereabouts of my son." The glitter in her eyes turned to sadness as the whole episode from before conception to this moment raced through her mind.

Andrew tried tiptoeing softly around the delicate situation as he surmised it was. "I don't know. We don't know." He knew he had to console her. "Jason is a great fellow and we all love him. We can't understand why he would quit his job and go off without telling anyone... which reminds me of someone else."

Andrew expected a response, but Lidia kept to the issue. "I was contacted by the police, a Detective Dunn, who told me what was happening but I needed to hear from you personally." She hesitated asking, "Was he in any trouble?"

Andrew immediately corrected her. "Not at all. He was a great employee. Jason left work that Friday evening as usual, and no one has heard from him since. There were reports of him going for drinks at his favorite bar after which he was never seen again."

Then she asked, "Did the police question his friends at the bar?"

Andrew replied, "I guess so. If anything came up, Detective Dunn would have told us. We have built a good understanding due to the disappearance -"

She interrupted, "Please, he is my only child. He is my heart and soul. Please help me find him." The atmosphere had become tense and she was hoping Andrew had better news for her.

To lift her spirits Andrew began telling her some admirable qualities Jason exhibited on the job as he reminisced about their good times working together. From the tone of the conversation she could feel the closeness of the two.

Then Lidia suddenly stopped speaking and got very serious. "I have been keeping a secret in my heart for many years, and I must tell you now because of what is happening."

Andrew unable to anticipate what she was going to say replied, "Yes, for years I have wondered why you left this job so abruptly."

Lidia smiled. "I know you never knew I was leaving or why I left." Andrew now listened attentively as she continued, "You and I had something very special, at least for me it was."

Andrew tried adding his appeal, but she halted him using two upwardly spread index fingers as she continued, "I loved you and you loved your family. I would have done nothing to interfere with your family." Andrew kept silent. He knew Lidia was a good and honest woman.

"But you didn't have to leave the job," he prompted her.

She continued, "Yes, you may not think so, but I left the job because I was pregnant with your child."

Andrew's eyes widened. He nearly fell off his chair in disbelief. Words could not come out of his mouth, but Lidia remained calm and continued, "Do you know the problems we could have had if the word got out? Well, I was not having that, so I made my way to the furthest place I knew."

Andrew could barely get the words out. "You mean, I have been working with my son all this time and did not know?" He felt hurt, but she knew his reaction was too calm to be true. So she braced herself for the storm to follow.

"Shit! You kept this secret from me all these years? That's unfair. I could have helped both of you. How did you manage over the years?"

There was a concern in his voice, so she decided to tell him about her life after leaving the job. "It was simple and orderly after I left here and settled in a small town called Speightstown, about thirty miles from Campbellville." She smiled. "I know you don't even know where that is and that's just what I wanted." She knew how to calm him. Her secret was to keep him interested and involved. If he was listening, he might keep quiet. "I found a job and met a wonderful man who took us in. We got married although he never adopted Jason, so it was not necessary to change his name, but he always treated him like his son. So, our lives just continued until a couple of years ago. He passed away and that was our life. This is why I need my son. Please help me to find him."

Andrew for the first time since Jason's disappearance felt broken. The connection grieved his inner soul to know this was his son. Jason was now more than his employee or valuable business partner. Every fiber of Andrew's being ached; finding Jason was now more important than ever. He prayed he was alive to give him the opportunity to accept him as a son and for him to meet his siblings.

They had a reconnecting chat trying to explain events of the past many years. Now the reason for meeting paled into second place for a moment.

Abruptly, she decided it was time to go. As she stood up, he held her hand caressing it and with a compassionate feeling he said, "We will make every effort to find him and we will keep you abreast of everything we are doing."

She rose from her seat as he refused to let go of her hand. He gently embraced her saying, "It could have been so wonderful."

She thought to herself, he hasn't grown up, still playing the same old game, but she hid all feelings and with poise she smiled gracefully. "You haven't changed! At a time like this when I am off to my son's apartment to collect his things? You must be joking." She moved to the door.

As he opened the door to see her out, she said, "I hope my assistance to the company was valuable."

Andrew, thinking she meant her past involvement with the company, said, "Your assistance was so valuable. Look around at the company. It shows success, thank you." This was Andrew's downfall. He always arrogantly portrayed the essence of success.

Lidia was past that and had no interest in hearing his accomplishments. She graciously stepped out saying goodbye, but ending with, "Please, find our son." They both parted secretly hoping and praying that Jason would be found and soon, with so much more to make it worthwhile.

While everyone was working out plans to find Jason, he had preferred to remain underground until the dust settled and his bruises physically and emotionally mended. He needed to be psychologically prepared to face everyone, including his mother, the latter being the motivator for his plan to return to the only place he felt totally safe – his mother's house. He knew there would be many questions asked and he was prepared to tell her everything, in short the truth, the whole truth.

13

CHAPTER

ON THE SATURDAY eight weeks after his life made the dramatic change, it was time for Jason to leave the Friends of the Heart and make his way back into the arena where people and friends could not be trusted. The limited funds he made during his stay would be enough to take him home. He thanked his new friends for their compassion and understanding, and he promised himself to anonymously send the organization an annual gift to help them continue the tremendous work they were doing. He remembered the first day after finding them. He felt very much "at home." They did not ask questions; they just kindly met his needs. He bade them goodbye and made his way to the bus station.

Ironically, the bus station in Speightstown was across the street from the Orkit store, and Jason on seeing the sign smiled at the coincidence and kept on walking to his mother's house.

On approaching the door he exhaled and taking another deep breath he pushed his finger into the groove of the familiar object carved by his step-father and pressed the button, he could hear the doorbell chime and remembered it did so through the entire house. The chorus to the "Little Drummer Boy" brought back wonderful memories of this house.

He stood awaiting the beautiful face of the one person he knew loved him unconditionally then the door knob started moving. The chain on the door held it slightly open as the person inside checked who was on the outside; then there was a shout.

"Thank you, God!" The door then burst open to accommodate mother and son embracing each other.

They were both openly crying. Jason was quiet while his mother continued repeating uncontrollably, "Thank you, God." They were stuck in one position swinging forward and backward and could not move from the entrance. The greeting seemed to go on forever until Jason asked to be invited in. They both laughed excitedly his mother still looking at him to make sure he was real.

"I missed you. Where were you?" Holding hands as they entered, she repeated, "God, thank you. You answered my prayers. You sent my son home. You gave me back my son. Thank you." They hugged again until it hurt as Jason still had some bruises healing around his neck.

Lidia sensed something was wrong and asked, "What's wrong with your neck?"

Jason, not wanting to go there right away, said, "It's a long story. We will get there. I am home and that's the most important thing. We have all night."

Lidia wondered, but not allowing that to dampen this feeling, she left it alone for later. As he stepped into the house, the familiar smell of the surroundings rekindled his affection for his mother as well as the recollections of all the happenings in the household.

Her next question was "Are you hungry?" This was his mother's trademark greeting. He remembered her asking this of all his friends whenever they visited the house. This made Jason one of the most popular boys at school and as for his stepfather who he called Pops, his football and baseball friends got the same greeting. This socially friendly atmosphere growing up may have carved his personality. Then in later years the computer club meetings were held at the house. All the comforts of his mother's hospitality and cooking were extended to all who passed through these doors.

"Why ask, mom? You know I am always hungry for your food."

Sitting at the kitchen table the chatter and catching up began. Soon all topics of the family and friends' births, deaths, divorces were covered except for his disappearance. After satisfying his empty stomach with his mother's food, they continued sitting at the table way past midnight, which for his mother was a record. He had to tell her about everything including the bruises on his neck and his disappearance. He held nothing back; nothing was left out. Her reaction was motherly as expected and she was very enraged.

He spoke about his job, his failures and his successes. He even revealed his sexual preferences. Somehow, he did not feel it necessary to reveal the details of her being a winner on two of the many occasions he manipulated the lottery game. He figured she would not approve or even understand its significance. He knew he may have to tell her one day, but for now there was a lot for her to absorb.

His most recent ordeal made her very angry as she thought of her son running through the night hiding from dogs in the bushes and in the water tank. The ordeal he must have gone through was beyond her imagination. She wanted everything to sink in overnight; she would leave all the questions for tomorrow.

Finally, they admitted they were tired and sleepy, and they decided to go to bed. Tomorrow they would pick up where they left off. It was enough that they knew they had each other again.

The next morning at daybreak Jason lay awake in his old, bumpy single bed. As he stretched, many happy and some terrible memories flashed across his mind. He gradually pulled himself up, pushing the memories deep into the recesses of his brain. Smelling the aroma of coffee, he knew his mother was up. The sun brightened the room and the air had a freshness to it.

The happier memories of his youth were allowed to surface as he walked into the kitchen. "Good morning." He gave her the usual smack on the cheek.

"This is like old times," she said as they began their day at the kitchen table. She reached over, bowing her head while grasping his hand. "Dear God, thank you for bringing my son safely home." With that she was finished. It was important to her just to have her son home and safe.

Jason had always enjoyed his mother's company, and he felt protected and loved in her presence. "What's for breakfast?" he asked. She smiled in her usual motherly way and he then added, "Can we go for a walk after breakfast to celebrate this significant home coming?" She shook her head in agreement.

Jason did that deliberately because he wanted to experience an event which changed his life. He remembered his mother asking him to go for a walk with her when he was sixteen and failing at school mainly due to his popularity and preoccupation with all things besides academics. During that walk, she asked him what he wanted out of life. She was not commanding or authoritative. She became his true confidante that day as she shared the thoughts and viewpoints of a sixteen-year-old. After listening attentively, mother and son discussed that achieving his dreams was all left up to him, but there was one thing Lidia emphasized – failure was not an option. Re-enacting that walk was, in part, to reminisce and celebrate their reunion as another "rite of passage."

The walk lasted over two hours, interspersed with sitting by the river and then in the community center gardens, just as they had done twenty years ago. Not much had changed.

Jason kept saying to his mother, "Thank you for all the things you have done for me over the years I have lived in Amalta. I did not visit as much as I should, but always remember I love you. Never forget, I have always loved you and always will."

As they started on their return journey, she said, "By the way, last night I got so caught up in listening to your exploits I forgot to tell you that I visited your office in Amalta, trying to find your whereabouts. I spoke to my ex-boss Andrew Cole."

Jason was surprised. "What else did you discuss?"

"We discussed you and that was all."

He was not getting the information he wanted, so he had to push the question. "Any questions about you helping the company recently?" He wanted to be as vague as possible but he had to ask.

"No. Your disappearance was our main concern. He didn't even thank me for the recent help but commented on my past contribution working at the company. It's all right. At that time I did my best."

Jason felt a ton of weight removed from his shoulder. His mom's naivety did serve its purpose or was she playing a game? He looked at her puzzled, but there were no clues to go on.

As they approached the house, it was still quiet with only a few cars passing as people went to work. The sun brightened the atmosphere and the air was fresh, so they decided to sit on the verandah a while longer seeing the neighbors passing. They too remembered Jason as a boy living there. They knew Mrs. Payne's son, not knowing his name was Paye and not Payne.

Before entering the house, Jason could feel something important coming as she looked at him. Making eye contact, she asked, "Why are you gay? What happened?"

Jason was caught off guard with this question. No one had ever asked the question before. Those who knew just accepted it and moved on or out, but he knew his mother had a mixture of insight, intuition and innocence and one never knew which would surface.

After some hesitation he said, "It's nothing that started in my recent life or exploded overnight. It was a feeling there from my childhood. I found myself admiring the same sex as a young child; I remember this before I was seven. I was never attracted to the girls in my class. I preferred the company of the boys in my class and those who played football and it was not their ability to play football I was admiring, but their stature and built. I thought nothing of it since it was a natural feeling.

"Getting older into my teenage years and realizing something was different, I masked those feelings by being one of the most popular in the class – everybody's friend. The feelings continued into my adulthood when I could choose what would make me happy and comfortable. To me, it feels right."

All this was a lot for Lidia to absorb in one take, but she was captivated by the conversation. She had previously seen relationships like this as opportunistic or part of a fad; now she was hearing the true feelings from an individual, her son. And now she was truly interested in understanding how a person can have the desire and feeling for another of the same sex.

She had to draw closer as he hugged her in acceptance and respect. "I have never asked these questions of anyone who is gay, so this is an opportunity to get some answers and put some things in perspective." She then asked what gave him the inner strength to come to terms with his feelings.

Jason knew it must be difficult for her to understand and did not expect her to immediately accept his sexuality now that he had told her the truth. In her presence with the truth out, he felt helpless and alone. His pressed his lips against her cheek for a long time, his way of thanking her for her unconditional love.

Looking at her son and admiring his ability to survive, she knew he was a stronger person internally than his exterior portrayed. She was full of pride that he was such a strong young man. Still puzzled by his latest revelation, she again repeated, "So, why are you gay?" She tried to understand and find reasons for his sexuality and, like every mother, tried to figure out if there was any way she had contributed to this lifestyle. At the same time, she was equally disappointed knowing she would never have grandchildren to embrace, love, and spoil.

Jason could sense her unexpressed thoughts, so he said to her, "I will be fine being the person I am. It evolved over time after much soul searching and attempts at heterosexual alliances. He tried to educate her. "Everyone thinks homosexuality is only about the sex act, but it involves a feeling of enjoyment and comfort from another person of the same sex which is not felt with the opposite sex." As he looked at her, he repeated, "One can still interact with both sexes, but the preference for the same sex remains, not unlike a heterosexual relationship.

"The right person is your soul-mate with a commitment to share the other person's space. He provides love, affection, companionship…" He paused for a while then continued, "I once had a relationship that lasted over three years where sex was not a part. We were friends. It was beautiful."

His mother listened as she tried to really get to know her son and his lifestyle, but at the same time not wanting to intrude too much into his personal affairs. She cut him short. "These questions I ask because as a child growing up there were never signs of you playing with dolls or wanting to dress in dresses instead of pants." She wanted to know what contributed to this lifestyle. Jason sat back while rubbing his dry lips with his fingers so as to moisten them.

He knew he was delaying the inevitable and he wanted to be honest with his mother even though he had made a promise many years ago never to reveal that secret, but this conversation had to be the exception. Everything needed to be honest and she deserved the truth.

Lidia picked up on his reluctance to go much further with the conversation, so she quietly reassured him that honesty would not change the facts and they were too far into this revelation to be playing games.

After thinking of the best way to approach, he started, "As an only child while I was growing up, you had to work in the morning while Pops worked at night." She pleasantly remembered how things were as they tried to provide a comfortable family environment, and she nodded proudly in agreement. "When I was about six years old, I would come home from school and put on your hat, shoes, and hand bag. I would jokingly walk around without Pops seeing me. I admired you so much that I wanted to emulate you."

Her face started looking serious as she didn't know where she stood in the direction of this conversation. "Then one day when I was modeling, Pops came in and laughed with me as he shared my childhood prank. It was all laughter initially, but soon instead of me doing it for enjoyment, I did it for Pops' excitement. I moved from dressing to make-up and lipstick, all fun on my part and we enjoyed it together. As I grew older, I started to like how it felt." He knew his mother's feeling were now being affected, so he lightened the conversation as he tried to protect Pops' honor. He remembered the promise he made to Pops never to tell his mother, but if he did not continue with the truth, he knew his mother would feel responsible for his lifestyle.

Her mind was in a turmoil, wanting to stop Jason from continuing but knowing there was more to come. Yet she prayed that was all to the story.

Jason wanted to be gentle with his mother's feeling. "He introduced me to the life from his perspective. I never told you, true to my promise, but I grew older, and I realized what had happened. I didn't want Pops to leave us and for me to be blamed for splitting up the family, so I continued with our fun as he called it. He always said I was not his blood son so it was all right."

She listened experiencing a pain so strong she felt as if it surpassed the pain of Jason's birth.

Jason continued, "The closeness that developed between him and me was enjoyable. I actually looked forward to coming home to him after school. There was a genuine connection. It felt right and legitimate, and it lay the groundwork for my sexual development. This is the lifestyle I have known and I have enjoyed it without questions."

Lidia was shocked, never knowing the bisexual nature of her deceased husband; never once did she have the slightest inclination of her dearly departed husband's secret which he had carried to his grave. Her face was pale from shock and she said softly, "You can never read the heart of another person."

Jason felt the hurt and he wanted to be truthful to her but not to cause pain. As he hugged her, she continued, "I know it's too late for apologies, but if I knew this was going on, I would have helped you." Her gentle voice turned to tears.

Jason realized the breaking point was forthcoming and said, "Don't worry. You have nothing to apologize for. I am happy now and would not want to change this area of my life."

Grasping for breath and words, all she could say was, "Remember I always loved you." There was a slight embarrassment in the air as they hugged for a prolonged time, saying nothing. Sharing the truth in a strange unexplained way had made their bond stronger.

They sat a while longer – mother and son experiencing a new understanding of each other. Jason felt he should be the one to break the silence, thinking of another topic to offset the quietness. He decided to address his mother's desire for grandchildren, knowing he too wanted to share his thoughts on this matter.

"Mommy, I know you love children and would like to have grandchildren. Do you know same sex couples can adopt and raise kids sometimes even as well as or better than some heterosexual couples do? We are not here to influence their lives and their choices. We will certainly explain to them our chosen lifestyle and will show them love and respect for others as you have taught me." This being a good time to explain his thinking on matters dear to him, he decided to continue, "The world is full of abandoned children who need a stable home environment. There is no blueprint to raise children. You just have to give it your best shot and continue loving them. I know that's what you have done and for that I will continue loving you unconditionally."

His mother accepted his reasoning but had her reservations. "What worries me is how two same sex people can raise a child. This is not a family."

Jason already knew that for people who have developed a certain mindset, it is difficult to convince otherwise. He decided to express his opinions in an effort to make her see his point of view at another time. He felt exhausted wanting to come up for air. His mother, on the other hand, could have gone on as she needed to hear it if there was more to come.

Understanding the sympathetic side of her son, she looked at him and smiled, hugging him and telling him how much she loved him. "I am going to be all right and I want you to be also. You have a good heart." She was proud of the man she brought into the world and she was happy sharing everything with him.

After the long morning discussion, they moved from the living room naturally into the kitchen where conversations always concluded around the wooden kitchen table.

"We have been talking all morning about you. Now I'll tell you about my life." His mother was now ready to tell all. Jason realized he knew little about his mother's earlier life.   "Now remember, you can ask me questions at any time. Yes, this is a good time to tell you all about my life. Let me start from the beginning...when I was four years old, I was born out of wedlock and my family was ashamed of my mother, so I was sent to live with my aunt whose husband had fishing boats. He refused to have me join his family, so once again I was packed up and sent to some unknown relative to be sent to school. They found out I was cleaning her house and cooking while her kids went to school, so I was moved again to live with another aunt... Babsie." Jason by now was quite attentive hearing this for the first time.

"Can you imagine at 10 years old I was in a grade with six-year-old children? I had to learn faster than anyone I know to be on par with the other students by fourteen. This is why when you were small, I thought you were comfortable and protected—"

Jason interrupted her. "Don't worry. I had a wonderful childhood. Like we agreed earlier, don't blame yourself for what happened. I am contented and happy with who I am."

She then said, "There is also something I have to share with you. I had a doctor's appointment some months ago and my heart is not in the best condition. After my bypass operation, it has deteriorated somewhat, so I am delighted you are with me and we can cherish these moments together forgetting the past and looking forward together."

Her voice lit up the air and they were happy together remembering her bypass surgery and how he had reached her the day before the actual surgery to be with her. He did not know of her updated condition and he felt a bit worried, but for now at this moment he was enjoying the company of his darling mother.

He said a silent prayer for her. Please God don't take her away from me not just now as we have rekindled the affection I missed when I was a child. I know she loved me, but she was always tired and now I can give her all of what she never had.

They never spoke of illness any more for the rest of the day. Happiness, laughter, and positive energy filled every corner of the house.

At the lottery company office tensions remained high as police investigations were in full steam. Detective Dunn had interviewed all members of the staff, given access to all information deemed relevant to the case, and his report was near completion. At the Monday morning meeting Detective Dunn was invited to address the staff. He did so with an element of desperation, and his questions almost made one feel he expected someone to confess to knowing Jason's whereabouts.

Where is Jason Paye? Why did he disappear? Who wanted him out of sight? Who wanted him out or dead? Why should a jovial person employed in such a progressive company as this just opt to drop off the face of the earth? He questioned some more. Why would such an integral person in this organization just fall out into the unknown? Each question was followed by a pregnant pause for effect so that anyone who knew something would answer and expose something not yet discovered.

If it were not for a life being at stake, the whole affair could have been comical. It felt surreal but all were jolted back to reality with the next statement. "Hard to believe, but we have found out that his lifestyle may have something to do with his disappearance," said Detective Dunn.

Immediately Andrew, as the CEO of the company, jumped in. "What lifestyle? You are referring to fact that the guy was a little goofy and theatrical at times, but he was a good person?" Andrew in a moment of introspection thought, this is a father protecting his son; the instinct came with Lidia's recent revelation.

The entire table became silent, then Detective Dunn responded, "I am not attacking his personality or his demeanor. I am placing all the facts on the table. It is my job to investigate all the circumstances. Some people might be affected by his way of life."

Andrew jumped in once again to Jason's defense. "Here we go again. Why do we keep on making these inferences?"

Dunn then stated that because it was a criminal case, no further explanations would be given. The staff knowingly looked at Andrew and remained silent giving no clues as to what they knew or suspected. Everyone remained quieter as Detective Dunn pieced together a timeline of Jason's activities after leaving work that fateful Friday evening.

At this point Nigel became agitated and nervous. He never realized those details would have been uncovered. Still he said nothing and added no details to the conversation not wanting to incriminate himself.

Dunn continued, "No one remembered who the person was that he left the bar with. There are surveillance cameras in the area however."

Surprised, Nigel asked, "Did any of the cameras pick up any images?"

Dunn did not expect questions but replied, "Unfortunately, I can't comment on the specifics of the investigation."

After the meeting, Andrew met with Nigel giving him the assignment to look within the company for any activities Jason may have been involved in.

After Nigel left, Frank knocked at the door and entered. "I can't believe you didn't know about Jason. I always assumed you knew and since he was like that I never bothered to mention it since it was his way of life. Frank, wanting to get back to the safety of discussing company business with Andrew, said, "I have some concerns, so I did the investigation and found there are two large winners coming from the same area in Kentucky." He seemed so proud to have important investigated news for his boss. With Jason around, Frank felt jealous of the two men's relationship, so Frank preferred keeping his distance.

Andrew said, "This is no coincidence. This can happen easily and when it does, it stimulates the betting in the area creating more betting from the customers attempting to capitalize on the winning spirit."

Frank then added, "It can happen, but if you'd like, I'll investigate it further and see if anything fishy is going on. Jason was good at his job. I hope he returns." The latter statement was added to find favor.

Evening came and Nigel decided to drive past The Watering Hole to take a look at the positioning of the cameras in the surrounding area. He took a slow drive through the parking area while looking at the building across from the bar observing the direction the camera was pointing. He parked in the same spot he parked that particular night, and while sitting and looking around, he realized Detective Dunn was exiting the building. Nigel instantly started slowly sinking into his seat so as not to be recognized while he waited for Dunn to leave in his unmarked police car.

Nigel realized two of the cameras were directly monitoring where he had parked the Friday night in question and they may have picked up some images as he was leaving the walkway towards the bar. This fact disturbed him a lot, but as he did not know what the outcome would be, he hoped the odds were on his side. Nigel drove home that evening thinking he needed a foolproof story in case he got implicated now that Dunn had done his homework and was on top of everything.

Andrew decided to pull the team together the next day since the police investigation report had monopolized the Monday meeting. He wanted to address the lottery's recent poor performance and asked them for renewed effort in regaining the vibrancy of the organization. Displaying the readout, he commented, "We have slipped poorly over the past few months and we have to regain our position." Andrew knew the reason but had to try his best to keep the game going and now that the new system had been implemented, he knew things would never improve as he could not manipulate the outcome like Jason.

It puzzled Nigel why with Jason's disappearance the lottery business went downhill so rapidly. After Jason's disappearance, many in the company blamed the investigation by the police as the cause of the company's instability, never mind the poor performance.

Nigel would sometimes sit at Jason's computer to see if there was information that may benefit the company, but he could never penetrate the firewalls set by Jason to protect the files. Nigel enjoyed the challenge of trying to access Jason's computer and the anticipation of success became an obsession.

One day while meeting in Andrew's office Nigel asked, "What did Jason have as support documents in his files?"

Andrew replied, "I have absolutely no idea. He concentrated more on how and where to market to increase sales, using information from the previous week's betting patterns to make predictions like an actuary would."

Andrew knew this explanation was vague and full of useless jargon for Nigel to accept, knowing his inquiring personality, and he hoped it would keep Nigel quiet for a couple of days. This would give him time to plan a strategy for what he was not quite sure.

Nigel's brain went into overdrive as the answer intrigued him. Maybe the responsibility of the underperformance in the department could be blamed on Jason's absence and ultimately Andrew as he seemed not to know much. This would leave Nigel's reputation intact.

In another meeting later that week Nigel asked Andrew another of his fact-finding questions. "Why did Jason have to come into the office on Saturday nights?"

This caught Andrew totally off guard, but if there were questions to be answered, he had to be at his best and in the right tone at all times not to draw attention. Andrew confidently said, "Jason was able to gather all betting information after the closing of the game and somehow provide a security blanket for the auditors so that dishonesty would not creep into the system. You know how people like to try their hands to manipulate and skew results." Andrew was becoming increasingly weary and wary of Nigel and his questions. This was clearly not the time to be inquiring and he had no answers for Nigel or the police.

Nigel was gaining confidence daily; everything was coming together for him and as per usual he would call Nadia, this time to share with her his recent observation of Jason's involvement in each draw. In his discussions with her she felt the frustrations in his voice as he kept saying, "I cannot seem to find what Jason's involvement is. Apart from collecting information, I have a gut feeling there was more to what Jason did than is being told to us."

Nadia responded, "Have you checked all the angles?"

Nigel quickly replied, "And found nothing."

Nadia added, "So there may be no need to keep checking. Do you think with the current police investigation there is fear permeating throughout the company? Please don't get too wrapped up in your sleuthing. It scares me." Her love for him came before the job. She wanted him to be happy, but the job was stressing him and he knew it.

"You are not getting my point. The company profitability plunged as soon as Jason disappeared. There had to be some interference by Jason and the actual outcome of the results by him being there every

Saturday night." He said in his commanding voice, "If anyone was helping Andrew – sorry I know he is your dad – but he might know Jason's whereabouts. I am not implicating him in anything, but my mind is working overtime." He expected her to explode with his insinuations. Was she was so shocked she could not respond?

Then she quietly asked, "Are you implicating my dad in your fictional scheme? Be careful." She was growing angry. "What's going on with your thinking? You are becoming overzealous and it's beginning to hurt."

Nigel realized his position and tried to recoup, but he knew he had irritated her so to justify it, he replied, "I am not implicating anyone, least of all your father but as the pieces fall into place, I have to express my suspicions and if not to you, then who?"

Nadia already frustrated said, "You are suggesting my father had some involvement in the choice of winners? Please. I hope you are not also suggesting my father had anything to do with Jason's disappearance. Allow the police to do their job." By now she was angry, not hearing an apology or any denial of what she had said forthcoming. "I don't like what I am hearing."

Nigel tried softening the air. "Darling, I am thinking aloud and sharing my thoughts with you. Please forgive me. I have no reason to implicate anyone. It's just that I need answers." The tone of the conversation seemed strained, and there was underlying tension although the conversation continued for some time. Both could feel it.

His work issues were pushing them apart. Nadia was sad. She knew Nigel was so overwhelmed with his job that it was affecting their relationship. Maybe it was not a good idea to have him working so closely with her father.

Nadia was depressed after her conversations with Nigel as over the past couple of weeks it had gotten worse. Their relationship had taken second place to work issues. She knew the only person apart from her father where compassion and understanding would be found was her best friend Vern, who had remained close to her from the early days in university. Moving to Europe had forced their communication adrift; however, she knew the relationship was solid with Vern always available to talk. She grabbed the phone and called her. It rang for a while then went to voice mail and she left a message: "Please call me." That was all the message needed to say. She hung up the phone and lay prostrate on her bed, feeling deserted as Nigel was being stupid and unreachable and her best friend was either comfortable, asleep, or being laid by some bitch. Whatever, she thought, I am on my own. She felt as if no one had time for her.

While lying there feeling sorry for her unfortunate situation, the phone rang and it was Vern. "Nadia, why are you calling me so late in the night? You should have been sleeping for the last four hours. Why are you awake?" She was always the one chiding and although she pressured her, Nadia knew she would always be on her side and in her corner.

"I am fine, but why don't you answer your phone?" Nadia replied in a cool sarcastic voice as a tease for Vern.

"Do you know what time it is over here? If you don't, then I'll tell you. It's two o'clock and I was in court all day today," Vern responded in a tell-it-all voice with the affection Nadia picked up on. "I was so tired after reaching home I actually forgot to turn off the phone. You had to wake me, but I love you for it." They both laughed knowing each other's personality.

"Vern, you know I can depend on you and I value your opinion. I need your thoughts on a matter." This stimulated Vern's attention who was now wide awake.

"Fire away," she said as Nadia went directly to the point.

"Nigel called me last night—"

Immediately Vern interrupted her. "You called me at this time of the night to discuss Nigel?" Nadia smiled knowing Vern's displeasure of Nigel.

"Shut up and listen. You know you want to hear this, so just listen."

Vern in a quiet tone said, "OK, go ahead."

Knowing their mutual understanding, Nadia continued, "Nigel called me last night and I did not like the trend of his conversation. He always calls late in the night, but it was important for me to hear what is disturbing him. Sometimes, I can listen for hours to his problems with the company. I even sometimes miss early classes by him talking into the night as he does not honor the time difference. So I keep quiet and listen. It is important for me to hear." Nadia continued to vent giving Vern the entire background to the company and Nigel's involvement.

Nadia continued talking to the point where Vern had to stop her as Nadia said, "I know it is complicated but bear with me. The bottom line is Nigel is spinning out of control and unwittingly taking everyone with him."

Vern glanced at the clock and she could not believe the conversation was so interesting that the time had slipped by without her noticing. She knew she had to put a halt to it. "Nadia, I know there is so much for you to put together to make correct decisions, but don't rush into making them irrationally. Think it through properly. I am disappointed at Nigel's compulsion. I have to be in court early this morning, so we will have to talk again later. I need to think about all you told me, so I can make some sense of this."

Nadia was grateful and said, "Vern, thanks for sharing my problems. We will talk soon. Love you and thanks again." They both hung up knowing their friendship was still intact and the miles between them did not change anything.

On her way to court that morning Vern could not clear her mind of Nigel, making such suggestive statements as she tried to analyze the work situation. She never liked him, but she did not make her feelings known to Nadia. In short, she never wanted Nadia and Nigel to get together. Over the years her friendship with Nadia blossomed and she smiled as she remembered the past and how their friendship built on a foundation of trust and honesty had matured. They trusted each other explicitly. Her current case was important; she was an intern for the eminent lawyer John Bortrovitz Esq. and a senior partner in the law firm of Pitt, Pratt, and Bortrovitz. She had passed the bar exams on first try and wanted to prove herself capable of joining the legal fraternity soon. Bortrovitz was always tough on her as he was on all his assistants over the years. He wanted them to be assertive and confident. After a long day in court successfully defending their client, Vern felt determined to get to the bottom of the happenings at the lottery headquarters. Knowing it was late in the evening when she reached back to her office, she still called her in-house investigator Ray Long, who apparently lived out of his office

"Hello, Roy. Can you come to my office? I want to share something with you?"

Without hesitation, he responded. "On my way. You know you can call on me anytime and I will be there for you." He had always admired her intellect and looks. He also had a secret crush on her and she knew it, but being professional she kept her private life separate.

He was in her office as soon as she got off the phone.

Vern began, "I want you to check on the activities at the lottery headquarters in Amalta city. I am hearing the company is spiraling downward and not making profit, apart from that there was a strange disappearance recently of one of their key employees. Can you look into this for me? Remember now this is outside the scope of the office."

She winked at him. "I need this information for another matter." Ray understood what was required, nodding his head. "I need this information on a personal level" she finished off.

"How deep do you want me to get?" he asked.

"As deep as it gets and as far as you can," Vern replied. "All the way if possible. That would be good."

He being a man of few words smiled at the confidence she had entrusted in him. "I will spend all of my spare time to complete this for you. I am under lots of pressure as you know." He then glanced at her. "Anything for you." The grin turned to a huge laugh as he closed the door behind him. Vern understood well how to tap into the masculine gender as she herself shared similar traits.

The Monday morning meeting found Andrew discussing their continued dismal performance while another meeting was taking place at Vern's office as Vern met with Ray, who thought it important for them to meet first thing Monday morning.

"The investigation is intriguing. I will give you an overview of the situation. Remember this is Monday morning, our busiest time, but this is important. I'll place all the findings in a chronological order so we can address them." Vern settled in her seat to hear the report. "The business was highly successful until suddenly one person went missing. With his departure the business takes a nose dive and looks like it is going to go bust. They are both connected. This is an overall assessment; one does not need to be a rocket scientist to make this deduction. Give me another two weeks and I will be able to give you a factual report." Nadia readily agreed.

In the meeting at the lottery headquarters Nigel was showing his true colors now that everything "lay on his shoulders." The boss was about to acknowledge Nigel's progress on improving the staff moral when there was a loud knock on the door. This was unusual as no one was allowed to interrupt these meetings. Then there was another loud knock on the conference room door. Immediately all heads turned in that direction, as the door knob turned and Mayor Michael Orrett entered. It was unprecedented for anyone to interrupt the Monday morning, let alone the mayor himself.

He was recognized immediately by all present. Andrew did not understand what was happening, but he knew it could be nothing good for the mayor to come to his office without notice. At that moment there was a flurry of activity in Andrew's thoughts and there were many questions waiting to be answered.

Did someone find out about the manipulation of the game? Did the police get wind of what was happening? Then there was Jason's case. Were they here to arrest someone in the room? He started to sweat as he stood on his feet to address the mayor's presence.

"Good morning and welcome, Mr. Mayor, to our Monday morning meeting." Andrew tried to add a touch of professionalism as a response to the mayor's unceremonious entry.

The mayor said, "I know you all have been trying to get the game on its feet, but that's not working. What you have been doing is not good enough, Your company is losing its shirt and soon you will lose your pants."

They all knew this was coming, but somehow Andrew was trying to prolong the inevitable outcome. The mayor continued, "Some changes have to be made around here."

On hearing this Andrew said, "Mr. Mayor, can I meet with you in my office?"

The mayor turned to him in everybody's earshot and said, "This is no time for the usual protocol. Your team has one month to correct the decline. You have done it in the past and need to do it once again. I repeat, revitalize the industry."

He paused looking around at all the members of the team. They in turn expected the hammer to fall. They did not know where and when it would happen, but it was imminent. As he walked towards the door, he concluded, "If you can't get this thing working again, then heads will roll. Good morning to you all," he said, making his exit as unceremonious as his entrance.

Andrew was shocked at the mayor's handling of the matter. He knew the ultimatum was real. In turn the team had heard it and had a clear understanding of what was at stake. Facing the team, he said, "Did everyone hear clearly? You all now know what you have to do. If not, there will be job cuts, no department spared. Frank, get together with your team starting this afternoon to find new ideas. As we did in the past, we must find ways to stimulate the customers." Everyone could see the strain on Andrew's face as he said, "Have a good day all of you and think us out of this hole."

As he walked towards his office, past Jason's desk, many memories surfaced. Andrew knew how to save the game and ultimately his job. He had to find a replacement for Jason, someone who could share the secret of the manipulation and take up where Jason left off. He had resisted taking this action for a long time but it was inevitable. His thoughts wandered to who was as trustworthy as his son, Jason. He smiled with this acknowledgement.

He lovingly thought, I miss that son of a bitch. He was so good at his job and a pleasure to work with. He always got the job done."

As he walked into his office and sat at his desk, a feeling of disappointment over come him. Then he remembered Lidia had kept this secret from him and tears stung his eyes, but he kept them unshed. He sat with the thoughts of his son working with him, remembering the weird dressed guy in shorts and a pink shirt, coming down the corridor always thinking out of the box and making those thoughts a successful reality.

The happenings at the meeting rested on Andrew's mind so much that on reaching home he had to take a drink to calm his nerves. He had resisted the temptation for female company over the years, but now he wished he had someone to come home to, to share these depressing times. He had thought it better to concentrate on his family and the lottery business. Now after all this happening he questioned if it was worth all the sacrifice. In times like this he would call the only level-headed person he knew – his daughter.

"Hello," the person answered from the other side of the Atlantic.

"How is my daughter and firstly how are the studies?" he asked.

Nadia was pleased to hear her father. She knew he was going through trying times but would wait for him to tell. She would not let on about all she knew. "Dad, I miss you and the family so much, but all is well here. What have you been up to?"

"Working hard," he answered. With those few words she heard the stress in her father's voice. Her dad always had so much to say about life and how to live it, and he tried his best to keep work issues out of their conversation. He had no idea she knew everything about the happenings in the lottery office.

"Dad, I hear something in your voice that concerns me."

He thought about it and feeling a sense of recklessness, he replied, "I am having some problems." He paused, then confided, "I want to draw Nigel into my corner. Can he be trusted?" he asked as he thought, who else should know better than her?

There was a moment of silence on both sides of the phone. She felt torn between her father and the other love of her life.

Honesty dictating her reasoning she replied, "Nigel is an achiever who strives for perfection seeing things in black and white only. He also possesses a kind and willing soul, but he does not like to be guided and this is why he sometimes trips up." But she cautioned, "Take time to guide him, give him small steps to achieve. That will be your best yardstick."

Andrew read through what she was saying, and he knew she had to be careful with her answers.

Nadia's reply made good sense to her father. While she had her father's interest at heart, Nigel was the man she loved and she was not going to let him down either. He felt pride in her loyalty saying, "I must entrust someone with certain secrets of how the game operates, and he would be the only one I can think of." On hearing him say that, Nadia knew right away something unusual was happening at the lottery, and as if to confirm her suspicions, she recognized the importance of this call.

"Go ahead and involve him. If he understands early in the game his importance to the process, I know he will see it through to a successful end. I will also use my persuasive powers." Nadia was sorry she did not let her father in on the secret relationship she was having for the past eighteen months. She couldn't wait to call Vern and discuss this latest information. They continued with a father and daughter conversation, cementing the bond of deep respect and love for each other. Their talk today certainly fostered a better understanding of business and family affairs.

Minutes after the conversation ended, Nadia had a moment to reflect, recognizing there was something more to the lottery game than what meets the eye. Was this the missing link Nigel was suggesting? She was becoming confused with all the issues both stated and imagined. She hoped a full explanation would be forthcoming from either or both men. Then all the speculation would end, bringing her life back to the good times. So, this was adulthood facing the complexities of life. Many things were not what they seemed. She knew now she certainly had a lot to think about.

The next day Andrew was quite nervous when he called Nigel into his office. He was never comfortable with him as he seemed and behaved overly ambitious. That could cause a problem as the truth of the game was revealed to him, which was the plan. Andrew knew the job previously performed by Jason had to be continued for the future success of the game. His plan would be to have Nigel gradually take over Jason's responsibilities. In the meantime, he would watch his performance and get to know him with the goal of gaining his trust and so win him as a confidante.

As Nigel took his seat in Andrew's office, his facial expression alone confirmed Andrew's reluctance to confide in him, but if not him who else? "Nigel, I want to know why Jason was so successful in sustaining the profitability of the game. I wonder if he had a particular secret in his program. I am going to transfer his computer to your office and also give you total access to all his programs. Please see what you can find. See if you can decipher anything of importance and if you do, I want to be the first to know. Is that clear?"

Nigel nodded in agreement. Then Andrew continued, "Remember our ultimate responsibility is to the city board?" Andrew knew with Nigel he had to be cautious, although sometimes correct, he was inflexible. He continued, "Yes Nigel, the board will be informed of any irregularities we discover. Remember, do your best in the interest of the game."

Nigel left the office and Andrew was thinking how rewarding it would be if he could kick Nigel out of his darn office because he that knew Nigel would bypass him and that he would be the first to take any irregularity to the board without informing anyone in the company. This fact disturbed Andrew immensely.

That night Nigel took home Jason's computer to try to break down the firewalls set up to protect entry to the program. He started on the computer as soon as he entered his apartment. After dropping his shoes and briefcase at the door, he went towards the dining table to set up and find the pathway on the computer.

After many hours realizing midnight was approaching and he had made no progress, he went at it for another two hours. In his frustration he picked up the phone and called Nadia. "Darling," he whispered with little feeling; he needed the comfort of her voice but he had little to give tonight. All he wanted was an avenue to vent his frustrations. "I know our conversations have been starved of romance recently. I get so tied up in the job. Forgive me, but that's who I am," he tried to explain.

Nadia could only think back to the old romantic Nigel. Where had all the gentleness gone? she thought. She responded, "I still love you and miss your presence. Do you realize whatever you are going through takes a toll on you? It is affecting our relationship, and you are not the same person I once loved." She paused. "Please don't allow the job to come between us."

He didn't want to hear this truth and tried change the topic by saying, "I know a lot is happening and this is the latest – I now have in my possession Jason's computer. I have to decipher what he was doing to positively enhance the game. I have a gut feeling he manipulated the game, but I can't find out how. I need to know what he did to make the game such a success."

Nigel stayed adamant about this and no one could swing his opinion. "I have been up all night trying to break into his program. I don't know what else to do. I am tired and need your comforting shoulder."

Nadia felt a twinge of regret for her opening statement, but she was tired of his insensitivity and having to listen to his frustrations. She pounced on him. "This is what I am saying to you. Don't let this exercise totally consume you." She paused waiting for a reaction, but none was forthcoming. He must be really tired. It's not like him, she thought. She was asking for affection and not only a conversation about work. "You are becoming irrational and arrogant. Please can you chill and concentrate on us for a change?" For the first time ever she had to be firm with him.

This surprised Nigel, who somehow understood her position; however, he too was becoming frustrated. "You can sit in your comfortable place in France, but my job is at stake. If I can only prove how things are done, that would put me in line for another promotion. It would make the board pay attention to my presence."

At this point Nadia realized he was consumed by his own ambitions and he had not heard what she was asking for. This is the person she would one day call her husband. Was this the person who in his quest for upward mobility in the company was willing to surpass her father's position, all in the name of ambition?

There was a lot for her to think about in such short time, so she calmly asked, "Nigel, with all things happening where is the 'us' in all of this?"

Nigel finally woke up to the reality. It was a choice – save his relationship with her or allow work to dictate his future. He knew what he wanted. "I want you to understand our love for each other will be separate from our jobs. I want to do well in my job and to be successful."

Nadia too wanted this, but it needed to be put into practice and not be convenient cheap talk. She knew what it was like to have a father who loved his job but never let it cause neglect of the family. She also knew that without a mother's presence her father needed to find companionship but never allowed himself to become so consumed in the job or the pursuit of his love life that he neglected his responsibilities to her or her brothers.

Nigel seemed unable to make these distinctions in their relationship, not being able to split himself away from the job. She wondered if in the long run he might not be able to handle pressure that would certainly arise in their lives.

If this was so, she thought, this kind of life was not for her. He could be too self-centered. Did she want a future with someone like this? All these thoughts would have to be revisited and settled. She then quietly said, "When this challenging exercise is over and you need a rest, come to France for a few weeks." She wanted to believe otherwise, but she was convinced that her assessment of the situation was true.

The realization was beginning to hurt, so not being able to deal with any further discussions she said, "We will talk at another time. See you." With that she hung up the phone. While Nigel tried desperately to stop her from hanging up, he heard the click and dial tone.

Nigel tried calling back immediately, but it only rang. Nadia refused to answer as she got ready for her classes. Instead of the conversation being a chance for Nigel to reflect, his focus went back to analyzing the computer program. In his mind the relationship between Nadia and himself should not have priority over the most important challenge he had ever undertaken.

Nigel continued his search, and he realized Jason had deliberately made the program almost impenetrable. It was now all coming together. This finding was a big deal for Nigel, and he felt elated but did not want to risk losing information if he was ever going to be able to go further into the program. This finding confirmed his suspicions. Why would Jason have to protect the running of the program and prevent the possibility of others finding out how it operated? Things did not add up.

He could not wait to pass his findings on to Andrew and with only an hour of sleep, he was in his office first thing the next morning.

While Nigel was in his office waiting for Andrew to arrive at work, Jason in another city was taking his early morning walk along the dirt tracks that winded through the farmland in an effort to get his body back in condition. He also needed to plan his next move. After breakfast he decided to spend some time in the library researching the origins and history of yoking and other related incidences. As he sat searching the archives in the public library, he saw many accounts circa the early part of the twentieth century of individuals who simply disappeared from the face of the earth and were never heard from again.

Some in his search were probably men who simply ran away from their families who could not handle the responsibility and stressors of family or commitment and preferred the simple unencumbered life of hunting and fishing.

His search was extensive, but finally he stumbled upon a Friday night disappearance whose sketchy details seemed in no way similar to his. In the accounts they would all have vanished without a trace or a record of any search that was made.

As he probed further, it took him back to the days of slavery, men who were classified as runaways who went out and were never seen again. As he read further, some instances recorded were unreal because they were written from the different perspective of plantation owners, who saw themselves as wronged due to the loss of income and wanted to be absolved of any blame.

The more Jason found, the more he wanted to dig into the past. He spent the entire day reading and trying to get a better understanding of the era. At dinner that night his mother asked him how the search was going. "How is the research going? Are you finding any information against your perpetrators?"

Jason had to remind her, "As far as they are concerned, I am dead. Remember, I have their secret. My death means perpetual silence and protection from wrongdoing for them. We have to be careful. Not many people know I am here remembering."

She said, "Yes, I forgot that part, but you are compiling all the information to be used as evidence in your case. So, how is it going, what have you found out?"

Jason was proud his mother had moved away from her initial anger and could now handle the incident with empathy. He began to share with her his findings. "I went as far back as 1800 to all cases of disappearances. Those with the details of fatalities had significant undertones of yoking. In the southern states in excess of nine thousand persons had disappeared during the northern migration under what was then described as 'normal circumstances,' both white and black."

His mother looked surprised at the high number.

He continued, "I am taking on this project as my mission in life to possibly find which of these were victims of yoking or attempted yoking." She knew it would be difficult for him, but she knew his precision and compassionate heart was always a part of his character, and he would seek to find explanations for injustices committed against people. She wished she could be of greater assistance, but her health difficulties made her assistance minimal. She would continue to give moral support as long as her mind and body were functional.

Jason continued, "Further research revealed these acts were taking place under the nose of the law because law officials were part of groups organizing them. One could easily suspect yoking as the answer for someone who went missing whose movements were not sequential or properly accounted for. Rates of the practice differed by states. Our state showed the highest incidence. I guess the practice got embedded in the genes."

His mother asked, "In your research did you find out how this was started and by whom?"

Jason took time to think through the answer. "It seems that the genesis of yoking took its roots in the time of slavery when the rich white owners gave the power of running plantations to poor whites who were mostly expelled from the British Empire or came to the new continent in search of a new life. They were called Bushas/Backra Massas and were given the power to do as they pleased without consideration of morals."

Jason continued excitingly, as he felt he was now an expert on the subject, "In some areas they would be selective as to who to submit to this indignity as the plantation owners would never agree to use their young, virile slaves who served as collateral and as a valuable commodity even if they deserved the treatment. There were half whites or mullatos, half-breed sons of the owners with slave women, who might compete one day for the ownership of the plantation were spared. The practice continued through the eighteenth century when this gaming factor came into play. It was essentially for fun. Can you imagine a harmless individual who had no means of defending himself being subjected to this all for another's sick sense of pleasure?" As Jason was telling it, he thought, I may have been the only to survive the ordeal. I need to be in the records.

His mother asked, "Why didn't the authorities find out what was going on?"

Jason responded, "The closest the authorities came to exposing the practice was in 1853 with the disappearance of a young man in Tennessee who was a drifter, working odd jobs in a certain small town. He was liked in the community. Then one Friday night he disappeared. Later investigations found that he was yoked when the husband who had given him a job to mend the fence found out his wife had a liking for the drifter. The wife reported the incident, so an investigation was started. However, in these small towns the families were all somehow linked through blood or marriage and nothing came of the case. No one was ever arrested, but rumors circulated for years later. When the wife shot her husband, people felt the suspicion was validated.

Jason's mother by now was so intrigued by events of the past she said, "Did you find other cases that occurred in recent years?"

Jason had to remind her. "Remember, these incidences were never recorded as yoking, but all the circumstances led to the suspicion of yoking. There is the case of an Ananias Walker, who was drinking on a Friday night fifty yards from his house and never made it home."

Jason paused while thinking how agonizing it would have been to be hunted when intoxicated and totally confused. He refused to share the experience with his mother, but it could have happened to him that night. Fortunately for him, the winding, bumpy drive to the site helped him stay awake and the inherent fear made him sober quickly. The alcohol in his system seemed to have dissipated.

He continued, "The incident was recorded as a disappearance resulting from drunkenness. How stupid. I guess he did not fit into the privileged category. Jason was visibly angry. He felt someone should have made a stink but without evidence and impartial investigators the incident died a slow death, just as the victim had.

Then there was the incident of the only children of Mattie Samuels, the two brothers Jeremiah and Jobe, who disappeared never to be found. Rumors were heavy in this case."

His mother continued to ask, "What were the police investigating?"

Smiling, Jason continued, "In these cases there is no body found as evidence of a crime, so the case was left open and placed in the archives. That's where I found it. Someone had made notes on the side of the print saying hunters had found two decomposed bodies with metal things found around the neck. Unfortunately for them, these bodies were dug up by wild dogs in the area. The disappearance on a Friday night with connection to a hunt and a yoke made Jason conclude, "The hunt had to be completed early on a Saturday morning for the hunters to clean up everything by the end of the day in order to be in church on the Sunday morning, those hypocrites."

His mother realizing Jason's anger was building to hostility tried neutralizing the situation and said, "As you try to find answers, try not to get engulfed as you relive the experience. It will only make your mission unrealized."

Jason caught himself and taking a deep breath, he regrouped his thoughts with his mother's words, which helped him out of his agony, and he continued trying not to break his rhythm. There was also the disappearance of little fourteen-year-old John Wasnik, who disappeared on a Saturday morning while working on his family farm. I guess the gang could not find anyone on the Friday night, so early next morning on their way home, they had to satisfy their adrenalin rush. They found the first candidate in a youngster riding his horse. Can you imagine the hell a child went through running and no one to help? He must have felt rejected by his parents who were waiting to have breakfast with him. He must have asked why God would leave him for this to happen as they pursued him."

His mother now fighting back the tears said, "Can you imagine just fourteen and having to run for your life, those big dogs chasing you and then catching up with you?"

Jason heard the pain in her voice but didn't want to continue with the story about the completion of the job. They had to dismember the limbs leaving as little evidence as possible.

Drying her tears with the towel from the laundry basket, she could not understand why this activity continued into these modern days with the evidence right in front of them. They both looked at each other without a word being spoken.

After this period of silence Jason said, "This is like a brotherhood where secret bonds could never be broken. I might be the first one to break the cycle and I will do what I can to stop this madness."

She understood his desire to dig deeper to uncover the mysteries of this crime. She knew that whatever he went through with this horrific experience, due to the pain he had endured, someone should pay for this crime.

Fortunately, she had her son, but many parents or partners did not have this outcome.

She wondered if sharing with her son by telling him of her families' experiences would lessen his pain, and she gave him the option. He enjoyed the conversation, trying not to miss out on any important aspect of her life. She did not tell him anything about his father nor did he ask. He was satisfied with the fathering he had received, not wanting to know if it would have been different with his blood father and how his father would have loved him any differently.

She in turn remembered Jason entering the military at an early age. Was it to get away from the conditions at home or was it for the experience? Whatever, it was, it had left her with a void in her life, so these conversations could fill in these gaps and also provide an avenue to help Jason resolve some of his concerns.

The times now spent with each other were valuable and meaningful. They shared everything and went on walks. She also saw him never short of money using the check card she had received from the bank in Amalta. He bought conservatively, never extravagantly, everything she needed.

One day Jason asked her for one of her dresses, a wig, and a pair of her shoes. After dressing and putting on make-up, they then both stood in front of a mirror as she looked into the glass and there were absolutely no differences. They were both gorgeous and looked strikingly like twins. Jason suggested they go on the town together, but she could not bring herself to walk on the road with her son in this manner, so they hugged and laughed.

Soon after this enjoyable evening, his mother started coughing uncontrollably. She had to lie on the living room couch to rest and to catch her breath. Jason knew her condition was getting worse; he did not know how long a time he had remaining but he wanted to make every moment count.

After the bout of coughing, she developed chest pains. He immediately had to rush her to hospital, where she was diagnosed with heart disease. Investigations revealed her aortic valve was extremely weak, thus the cough and hunger for air. The hospital decided to keep her overnight to observe her condition.

The next morning she was released and informed a visiting nurse would be assigned to her at home to continue the observations. In the meanwhile she was confined to bed until told otherwise. Jason felt it was a blessing for him to be there in her life at this particular time as he could take over the chores and make life pleasant as best he could for her. It was a privilege to care for the love of his life.

While Jason was spending precious time with his mother, Andrew was "meeting" hell at the lottery headquarters. He was under pressure and it was coming from all directions. He had just received a call from Frank asking to meet with him. He said it was an emergency and wanted an immediate meeting.

As he waited he sat at his desk contemplating how to instruct Nigel on manipulating the game, he knew his choice of person to share the information with was not ideal, but the pressure of handling this by himself was too much.

There was a knock on the door and Frank entered with a worried look on his face. He was already a nervous character and could never handle pressure. "What's the problem?" Andrew asked Frank, who could not wait to offload.

"You had asked me to do an analysis on the drawings in the little area in south Kentucky. Well, I have found an anomaly in the time difference at our office and the venue. I think it is more than a coincidence and something is suspicious."

Frank was nervous the city council may find out and explode. He was also concerned the game may have been compromised. "When we close off the game here in Amalta at nine oclock the computer does not shut down the betting in that venue until ten o'clock." Frank was so nervous he was not talking straight and hurrying his facts.

Andrew shouted, "Slow down and explain once again what is happening! Do you mean when we close off the game, they are able to continue purchasing tickets up to the time of the draw?"

Frank responded, "Yes."

After thinking Andrew said, "But if the draw is at ten and usually the winning numbers are completed about ten minutes after the hour, then they would not know the winning numbers. I don't see a problem, am I correct?"

Andrew waited for Frank's opinion as he thought about the mechanics of the game. "Do you agree?" Andrew asked once again.

"Any person buying tickets would not see the numbers that are played after ten o'clock."

Frank by now was moving his head in agreement. "You may be right. So you think there is nothing to worry about since it doesn't affect us? I am going back to my desk to continue the analysis. We will talk later if anything irregular is found."

As soon as Frank left the office, Andrew called Nigel to his office. The time had come; either way it had to be done.

As soon as Nigel entered Andrew's office, Andrew asked, "How is the analysis going with deciphering Jason's information?"

Nigel knew this was the reason for his dilemma and for this reason he had stayed out of Andrew's way until he could finish the job. "Don't care how I attack this program. I am getting nothing to help the game," he said with full frustration. "When investigating the parameters, I can pull up how many bets were made and where they were made. I can pull information about how many times a certain number was played and even what numbers were played and the amount of funds sold each week, but I cannot find a way to find or predict any of the numbers playing for that particular draw."

At that point Andrew's face stiffened waiting to drop the big one on Nigel or was he going to drop the big one on him? Instead Nigel said, "I have come to the end of the line. I don't know what else to do."

Andrew knew Nigel was on to something but was stuck, somehow seeing it but not knowing how to pull it all together. If he could only help him to fit the last piece in the puzzle. Andrew wondered if Nigel was trustworthy and reliable enough to be given the last piece of information. As Andrew pondered these thoughts, he remembered Nadia's advice: Give him small portions at a time; allow the trust to be built.

Andrew then said to Nigel, "If you were to have all the numbers played and you are gathering no information from them, change your approach. Look for the numbers together that were not played and see what the results would be. Remember, combinations may be the key."

Nigel did not understand what Andrew was getting at, but he knew he had his work cut out for him. Thinking about this new idea, right away Nigel could see something positive. "You may be right, but you are still missing the point. There is no link between the draw and the computer."

Andrew could not believe what he was hearing. He had just given Nigel the package and he was not making good sense of it. He thought, what kind of idiot is this? I give up. He doesn't get it.

Andrew simmered in disgust while trying to be calm, saying, "I understand. Why don't you take an alternative approach? Remember, Jason always thinks outside the box. Consider what I told you and see it from another perspective."

He opened the door for Nigel to go and try the new outlook on the game.

As Nigel returned to his desk, somewhat skeptically energized to try to see it from another perspective, knowing that if he was to proceed down this new path, he had to let go of the hostility for Jason and Andrew and embrace a new outlook on the game. Thinking about it he decided to be broad-minded and try the new approach. This new way outlined by Andrew seemed so easily thought out. Did he know more than he was letting on? He provided this possibility so easily. I guess that's why he is the boss, he thought.

Nigel continued trying for the rest of the day but success remained elusive. That evening driving home in his newly fixed car his thoughts remained fixed on why was Jason so successful. Could it have been just luck or was there another explanation and was Andrew privy to it? How he wished he was as lucky as Jason, but was it luck? Why would a sucker like him have such a bad ending? "Jason Paye, I really hated you," he said aloud.

The hatred Nigel had built up for Jason grew out of jealousy; the harder Nigel worked on the project, the more Jason would always come out on top. This fact did not endear Jason to him any. Also, not being able to satisfy Andrew would nix the chance that one day he would be promoted to head the company.

On his arrival home it took no time for him again to be on his computer. Night came and found him busting his brain again trying to break the code from Jason's computer. He swore the computer provided the information for the successful functioning of the game, and although he knew he did not know what he was looking for, breaking the codes was clearly the first step.

He decided to run each number one to fifty realizing a pattern. Jason could have pulled up all the numbers played, then how many twos would be played. He continued this process for all fifty numbers, which told him how many times the possibility of that number being played would be. He wondered if Jason had used the probability theory to guess the possibility of the number playing. This would give the company better odds only if they knew what the balls for that particular draw were to be played. It was all confusing to him.

At about four o'clock in the morning he realized he had not slept or had anything to eat. Nigel finally gave up the quest and packed up his belongings, saying to himself it was an impossible promise to Andrew of breaking into Jason's files. As he lay in bed, he felt like a loser; he had tried everything and would report to Andrew the next morning that Jason's method had no specific system and that he was just lucky.

Next morning as Andrew entered his office, he had mixed feelings, knowing Nigel was staying away from the vicinity of his office. He wanted to see Nigel's ability to follow simple instructions, knowing Nigel would go into some upper level theory to solve a simple problem. As he settled into his chair, he hoped there would be no early knocks at his door.

Andrew grew anxious, so he walked out into the main offices passing Nigels's desk. As he walked past, he saw that Nigel was seated at his desk dutifully working on the computer. Nigel looked up and in disgust said quietly, "I can't come up with anything on Jason's computer."

This left Andrew in wonderment. Why is he trying so hard? I gave him the simple explanation. He thought Nigel would have grasped and run with the information he gave him instead of unnecessarily busting his brain. Then he understood that what he had in Jason proved he was a genius. This bright college kid was unable to see through the fog in front of him even with Andrew clearing it some.

Andrew could take it no more, so he looked Nigel straight in the face and said, "Using the information you have from the game played last week, find me the numbers that were not played. If you are wise enough to find these numbers, then place them in a sequence of five numbers that were never played together during the game."

Nigel was totally knocked over. Why would he want the numbers that were not played that had no bearing on the winning number? This speaking in parables was one of the things Nigel hated; he preferred a straight and direct instruction. "I will start right away; that may be another angle to consider."

Andrew walked away thinking of Nadia's instruction: Small pieces at a time. She was truly right.

As Andrew walked away, he knew pulling Nigel into his confidential loop meant he must have his trust and loyalty. These were big items to ask anyone for, but he needed to have someone trustworthy to work with him if he hoped ever to regain the success of the lottery.

Andrew waited all day for Nigel to come into his office until he was becoming restless. Then it happened. There was a knock on the door, and it was Nigel. As he entered, Andrew stood up from his desk, and smiling he asked, "Is it coming together now?"

He was totally floored when Nigel said, "No."

Andrew by now was growing impatient. "Why not?" he asked.

Then Nigel said, "I have in my possession the five numbers that were not played. No one would have won the lottery if this was the winning number." He looked so disappointed as if he was stuck at that point not knowing where to take the project.

Andrew looked at him in amazement, thinking you dumb ass. You have the secret in the middle of your palm and don't realize it. He smiled keeping these thoughts to himself. Trying to keep his composure so Nigel could not read his thoughts and pick up on his exuberance, he tried to find a way to make Nigel feel as if he was responsible.

He said, "You are a genius and you don't know it. If we could find a way to have these numbers played in the last game, we would not have had a winner and the pot would have grown making betting popular once again. This is the beginning of another second run for the game."

Nigel's knees buckled and became weak. He had to sit asking Andrew, "You mean if you had these numbers and had a way of playing these numbers, then we would have winners only when we want them to win? This would allow the pot to grow until we want to have a winner?"

Andrew looked at him and said, "You have found a way to make the game successful once again. That's a brilliant strategy."

Then Nigel asked, "How do we get these numbers to play?"

Andrew replied, "I now leave that to you to come up with an idea. That's enough for one day. Now work on the second stage of the game. See you in the morning." With that Andrew escorted him to the door, bidding him off and reminding him of the confidential nature of his suggestion.

As Andrew closed the door, he knew this was a defining moment in his career. The role was changing from Jason to Nigel, and he knew the characters and methods were different. With Jason the intrigue and willingness to try new things may have been his delight in succeeding, while with Nigel on the other hand it was much more complicated more of gaining recognition and status. What a difference, Andrew thought. However it goes, Nigel would now be a part of the secret and as for Jason, wherever he was, he will forever keep the secret.

For the next few days Nigel ran the program using previous draws in order to get a feel of the game compiling the five numbers for the new game. After a couple tries he perfected the process, but he was concerned that he could not make the connection going from the computer application to the mechanical playing of the game. He could not find a way to get the balls falling as he wanted them to fall.

On reporting this to Andrew, he received his instructions. "Let's have a trial run seeing that today is Friday. If you are given all the numbers played in the game this week at nine o'clock tomorrow night, how long will it take you to give me the five rejected numbers that were not played?" he asked Nigel. "Take that as a project."

Nigel looked at him with confidence. "I can now give you those numbers in an hour."

Andrew looked at him seriously. "Make that half an hour; better yet make that fifteen minutes." Andrew knew he had only half an hour to prepare the balls and did not want to take any chances with Nigel's perfectionist methods.

Nigel with disappointment said, "That's impossible. I can't collect and categorize the numbers in such short a time."

"Then find a way to utilize Jason's program to assisting in filtering and sorting quickly."

Nigel now realized what Jason was doing each Saturday night. If this worked, then the game would be totally dependent on his acumen. He felt good about himself.

Andrew then instructed Nigel, saying, "Now go to your desk and connect to Jason's computer and at three o'clock I will have the audit department send to you last week's readout of all numbers. You will have fifteen minutes to compile and sort. Then give me the five numbers that were not played."

He looked to see if Nigel was up to the challenge. Nigel, who now was ready and feeling a part of the inner circle and gaining instant self-respect and job security, said, "All right. Let's go for it." He immediately went straight to the computer clearing all the unwanted files and waiting for his three o'clock posting.

Andrew cracked his office door only to see Nigel sitting at the computer awaiting the delivery of the files. He knew with confidence Nigel could do the job having all the pieces fitted into place for him. His problem now began as to how Nigel would handle what he now knew.

At three o'clock the revenue department redirected all the information to Nigel's computer. He maneuvered through the program remembering time was the most important factor and moving as fast as he could. He saw this as a test and, better yet, as a dry run to see if it was possible. After ten minutes seventy percent of the numbers were cross-matched. Could he make the deadline? He pushed himself.

Andrew was also watching from a distance quietly pleased to know there would be a resurgence of the game. He was at last also pleased at Nigel's effort and tenacity. He knew Nigel had no idea that if it was done in the time frame, this Saturday's draw would be tried as the real thing without him even knowing it was being done.

It took Nigel twenty-six minutes to come up with the five numbers. When he rushed to Andrew's office to present his findings, Andrew was disappointed. "Twenty-six minutes cannot work. Use the program to go faster to get below fifteen minutes."

Andrew knew it was his first time, but he had to get Nigel to work faster, so he preferred to push him for a better time. "If you can't meet the fifteen minute deadline, the process has no hope of succeeding and your theory will fail." He had to be firm with Nigel.

From the surface it needed to seem as if Andrew had given Nigel the benefit of thinking he was the one who had visualized the idea, so he would have the responsibility to see it through to fruition. Andrew knew Nigel's yearning for the spotlight was always there, so if he believed the process to be his, he might just keep his mouth shut and bathe in the glory of success. If Nigel could provide him with even four of the numbers within the given time, he could control the game by not having a winner.

Andrew then turned to him and said. "I want to see you here Saturday night for a dry run. This time we will be working on the numbers only."

Nigel felt he had made it to the pinnacle in Andrew's eyes and to the inner circle. He felt he had to prove himself. Nigel smiled with a feeling of accomplishment, and although short of the deadline, he knew it was his last try. Things and times will get better, he thought. He spent the next few hours improving the program to cross-match faster and more reliably.

As Andrew left his office that evening, Nigel was still at his desk working on the second phase of selecting the ball to drop.

In Speightstown Jason and his mother continued reminiscing about old times and enjoying the moments together. He knew she was ailing, so he spent each earthly moment he could with her. Those moments were joyous and memorable times. He dearly loved his mother and she also believed in him and was happy he was there now when she needed him most.

Although Jason loved her and told her most everything, he never once let her know he had such a big bank account. With all that money he could not replace his mother, so all he could do was to make her comfortable and earnestly tend to all her needs. She was proud of him.

The next morning the doorbell rang. Jason answered the door expecting the nurse. As he opened the door, he stood facing the most beautiful female specimen he had ever seen. For the first time in his life a female was able ruffle his feathers; he was dumbstruck and unable to move or speak. All he could do was to stare in amazement of her beauty. As he gradually recovered from the catalytic moment, all the blood in his brain rushed downward to his heart and feet, making any movement impossible and his brain functionless.

He could only mutter the word, "Nus..."

She smiled with affection, replying, "No, nurse," making fun of his lapse in sanity. "Yes, I am Nurse Smith. Can I come in?"

Jason then caught himself opening the door for the nurse. "I am sorry. Good morning. I am Jason, Lidia's son." The blood was now flowing correctly as he showed the nurse to the living room where his mother sat waiting. He could not get over that initial meeting, such a feeling he had never before experienced. He liked how it felt – novel and sincere, genuine and primal.

After introducing herself to Mrs. Payne, the nurse went through the general procedure. Jason sat in awe not being able to keep his eyes off Nurse Smith. The nurse then whispered to Mrs. Payne, "I feel somewhat uncomfortable. I think your son does not think I am doing my job. Please tell him I am very competent and comfortable in what I do."

Jason's mother smiled. She knew it had nothing to do with competence as she looked over her shoulder towards Jason. She knew what that look meant, and this made her heart smile. "Is everything going all right?" his mother asked.

By now Jason was gradually coming out of his dreamy, transient state. "Yes, yes. I will be in the other room. Call me when you are through."

Jason knew he had to get out of there, and he hoped he didn't make a fool of himself. Instead of further embarrassing himself, he preferred to just move away to clear the air and also his head. As he sat in the adjoining room, he was beyond confused. His hormones were battling each other with the endorphins in his brain that were sending mixed messages through his body. He thought, could I be having feelings for a woman? Was it her attractive face or was it her physique? He tried putting the pieces together.

As he sat nervously in the adjoining room, he heard the nurse say, "I think I am through, but you have to continue with your rest and absolutely no harassment." She then called for Jason.

As he entered the room, the nurse in her compelling and charming, professional manner said, "Hello Mr. Jason. Please take care of her. She is delicate." As she documented her findings, she explained to Jason that his mother needed an evaluation with a cardiologist. "I will be making an appointment for her to see Dr. Mc Arthur, the best cardiologist in the area. The earlier the better."

Jason listened to the nurse while trying to make eye contact with her as she spoke. She realized what was happening and smiled, keeping the stare focused as she also felt something. "You will definitely hear from me about the appointment before the end of the day," she said with all attention on Jason and little on the patient. They both felt a common chemistry.

As he saw her to the door, she said, "Incidentally, the results showed your mother's heart is weakening. Over the years the disease has taken its toll, so continue to take good care of her."

Jason was very impressed with the nurse. He liked her compassion and honesty. He said to her, "Is there a name between Nurse and Smith? It would be easier to say."

As she was stepping through the door, she turned and gave him one of her special smiles and said, "Nurse Smith." They both laughed as she departed.

Jason walked back into the room with a broad smile which was picked up on immediately by his mother. He was so impressed with the nurse and could not hide his feelings from his mother. "What an impressive lady, I mean nurse."

His mother smiled. "You have been smitten by a woman; there is yet hope for you." They both laughed and she continued. "I don't understand you. Your head needs to be examined. You don't know what you want."

This question struck Jason. He also did not understand his feelings, and it was new and different. Was it the time taken off from the job and taking a rest that was making him able to investigate these new feelings? He decided to leave the introspection and let things fall where they may. This time was for his mother, so other things needed to wait for a more convenient time.

Looking over to his mother, he said, "From now on, you will be taking life a little easier." Although mother and son had just experienced an air of being visited by love, they both wanted to leave those thoughts to linger and to concentrate on the medical aspects of the situation. Everything else had to take second place. Little did Jason know, when the love bug bites, even itching feels good. His mother felt it and smiled at his naivety.

Jason spent the remainder of the evening sitting quietly in the living room uncertain about his feelings. He knew he was not supposed to have these feelings. The opposite sex had never excited him, and he was always indifferent to females. Why is this happening? he wondered, but he had more questions than answers.

His mother knew her son. "Jason, can you come in here?" she asked.

He entered her bedroom and she looked at him. "Why do you look so lost?"

Jason was wondering the same thing. She continued, "You know the reason, don't you? Love is a feeling. You will never know where it comes from, but when it hits you, it makes you unable to act rationally and makes you act stupid, as you are doing right now. I saw how you looked at her. You can fight it or accept it. You will never know how it will end, so enjoy the journey wherever it takes you." Despite the advice she hoped he was about to change.

Jason was embarrassed but excited. "I don't know what I am feeling. There is something about her, and I don't know what it is. I have never had this feeling for a lady," he said with the most compassionate expression on his face.

At this point, she felt so proud of her son, and he asked her. "Why is life so complicated? Why should a feeling of this kind come into my life to cause confusion at this time?"

His mother gave it some thought, knowing she had missed out on participating in this phase of his development as she had left that to her husband. She said, "In every person's early development there is that innate feeling for both sexes that brings the adventure and questionings of youth. It comes before we find our preferences, and by the time we have had all these various experiences, there is a pattern we find ourselves fitting into. It will feel right for us. We know when we have reached that point, it's usually the direction our lives will follow forever."

She looked at him, hoping he understood her thinking. Jason was surprised at his mother's thinking. She understood all along but wanted him to be certain he knew what he wanted.

He still wanted to explore this feeling, saying to her, "This feeling has consumed me. It is somewhat different. It's hard to explain my feelings."

She then tried to fill in the blanks for him. "Why? Do you think men and women have different feelings? Absolutely not. We may be psychologically different, but our individual feelings of love come from deep inside all of us. It's unstoppable. If it is to happen, embrace it and let love flow. You can't stop love."

Jason was amazed of his mother's depth of compassion and understanding. He replied, "I have never seen this lady before in all my life and at the first sight of her I went berserk. It must be love." They both laughed with excitement, he with apprehension and she with hope.

Talking to Nadia, Nigel tried explaining the working environment at the company while discussing the up-to-date happenings. "Well, some of the pressure has been lifted. We got closer to uncovering Jason's program secrets, which brought the lottery company success and I think your father gave his approval."

Nadia quickly asked, "How is that? What is really going on?"

Nigel responded, "I am not quite certain, but it's a matter of reverse positioning. It's not what number was played; it's a matter of what was not played."

By now Nadia was confused. "Isn't it the idea of winning that matters in the lottery game, not one of losing?" She did not understand. "You are saying you want people who play not to win. What are you trying to have happen?" More questions lingered in her head, and she tried to ask them in sequence, while trying not to initiate any information that would point to her father being complicit with any manipulation. She stuck with the format of the game.

"Put it this way," Nigel assured her, "by the end of the game, no one wins, if none of the numbers are played." He hoped now he would have answered Nadia's question. He too was realizing and seeing the whole picture coming together in his mind even in areas he had not thought of.

Nadia then asked, "How could Jason have predicted the numbers from the millions of numbers played?" As she questioned, she grew more curious.

"Simple. The power of technology and the complex high-powered computer, and if you have the right program available or you have Jason to write just the program you want." Nigel replied.

They both sighed simultaneously; for Nadia it left her father squeaky clean for now and threw blame squarely on Jason's shoulders.

Nadia went on to ask, "Since you have now found the first stage of the puzzle, how do you get the balls to fall in the desired order for that game?" Before he could answer, she added, "Why did you say my dad gave his approval?"

Nigel knew he had to be careful. He would not want to offend the boss of the company, also the father of his girlfriend. "This is why I said your father knows everything about the running of the game. He is the best. It was he who guided me to this point in finding out how it was configured, so he had to know what was happening." He shielded her father from blame, but somehow exposing him.

Nadia came on the defensive. "You are assuming. These are only assumptions," she said, getting hot under the collar.

"Yes," replied Nigel. "Let's wait and see what happens next. It's too early to choose sides."

By now Nadia was steaming. She knew anyone can make assumptions, but this was her father's integrity and not to be messed with. He was her guiding light over the years, the one she looked up to with admiration and respect and now the man she loved was implicating him in dishonest dealings. Careful, Nigel, she thought. You are treading on dangerous ground.

Was this a loss of respect or nonchalance? Was she now getting to know her man? His feelings were absent from the conversation, which seemed to be one of revenge or payback, but why? There was an uneasy coolness as the conversation continued. Nigel felt it, but he thought, what the hell? Let's wait and see how the game will play out. Meanwhile, Nadia felt betrayed, but by whom?

By now Nadia knew her decision to pursue her graduate studies in France was not the best idea knowing Nigel's personality, but he was an adult who had to take responsibility for all decisions while adjusting to the system. She sensed something was wrong.

Nadia was becoming uncomfortable with the situation, so she called her sounding board Vern, who was totally responsive to her depression. Vern never approved of the relationship between Nadia and Nigel. She, however, kept her feelings to herself, so even Nadia did not suspect. Vern listened to Nadia's uninterrupted rant for nearly fifteen minutes; then, her eyes rolled as she was unable to bear the name Nigel. She interrupted, "Can you hear yourself and the many times you have mentioned Nigel's name? Do you get ahead by helping him? How much does he appreciate you helping him in getting ahead? By this I mean all your energy is used in addressing his problem. Does he understand this? Has he ever said thanks for your advice and lending a positive ear? Does he stop the BS? That cry baby needs to 'man up.'" This was the first time she had interfered in her friend's private affairs and it scared her.

There was complete silence on Nadia's end. She knew how protective she was of Nigel's feelings, but Vern need not know. Skillfully changing the topic, she asked, "Well, incidentally, how are the investigations going in the company?"

Vern smiled to herself, knowing Nadia would eventually make the right decision, so she also decided to swing the conversation further away from Nigel and said, "While we are on the phone, I will call Ray and have a conference call to update us on the situation."

Vern dialed Ray's number, and he picked up on the other side. "Hello, Lee. This is Vern. I have Nadia on the conference line. Is there anything further on the investigations on the lottery headquarters?"

Ray responded, "Great meeting you, Nadia. Recently, I had to visit another customer at the adjacent building, so I decided to pay a visit to the lottery offices just to get a feel for the environment. The first thing I realized was the low morale of the staff. The courteousness was missing, and I got the feeling the operation was going through a bad period. After that, I got a call from my contact regarding a breakthrough in the case of the missing employee. More on this I will be able to tell you in the next week when I will be meeting with him."

Nadia had satisfied her curiosity on hearing the Ray's objective reporting of what was happening. At least he did not mention her dad's name. She exited the conversation with, "Thank you, Ray. I will be calling next Wednesday to hear more. Thank you, Vern. Bye."

Saturday night came and Nigel took his position, instead of Jason. It was his turn to carry out the Saturday night task. As soon as the game closed off, Nigel began working on the numbers. The practice he did leading up to tonight's draw made it better for him, so he completed the task in twelve minutes.

Andrew sitting at his desk smiled as Nigel gave four numbers to Andrew. "Why only four?" Andrew asked, testing his knowledge.

"All other numbers were played, but these were the only four that were not played together," Nigel explained, awaiting a rejection from Andrew.

He was pleasantly rewarded when Andrew said, "With four numbers together there will be no winner. Do you now understand how the game is played?" He again smiled at Nigel while showing him to the door.

Andrew never allowed Nigel to see him taking out the balls or changing out the weighted balls from the vault. When the numbers were announced and all four numbers presented to Andrew were played, this amazed Nigel as this was the missing link, and he was never told by Andrew of its existence.

Anyway, Nigel smiled at the outcome as he drove home.

As expected Jason's mother's next appointment by the visiting nurse was eagerly anticipated by Jason. Unknown to him the feeling was mutual. When the doorbell rang, both mother and son stood still with no one wanting to show their anxiety. "Jason, can you please answer the door?" she said with a smirk on her face.

"If you wish," he replied as he sprinted to the door stopping a footstep away to compose himself before releasing the lock. "Welcome again," he said looking into the nurse's beautiful eyes with the most affable smile.

She said, "Thank you." She felt so good that he was the one answering the door. She too had stood on the other side anxiously waiting at the door, pleasantly excited to see him again. However, her emotions were left at the door.

She stepped inside. "How is the patient doing today?" she asked in a professional tone.

"She is waiting for you in her bedroom." Jason and Allison engaged in small talk as they made it to the bedroom.

As they entered the bedroom Nurse Smith said, "How are you today, Mrs. Payne?"

Jason's mother looked at her, then she looked at Jason and said, "Looking forward to seeing you again." She then looked back towards the nurse and smiled as if she was speaking through Jason. She knew women have this inner ability to reach each other on the same thought level; in short, both knew Jason's feelings with little said.

After the examination was completed, Jason wanted to know if his mother ever got worse, could he get the nurse's number to contact her directly, she smiled knowing very well where he was going and said softly, "Call 911 for emergencies."

Jason loved her sarcasm and it intrigued him. "I know that's an alternative, but I may need your expertise since you are familiar with the patient and I may have to contact you for advice. At least tell me your first name."

Trying to keep it professional and to send a message to Jason she said, "Nurse."

They both laughed but she sensed his feeling of rejection and gave him her business card.

On her way through the front door Jason whispered to her, "Can we have dinner one day after work?" She expected this next move and was smiling when he said, "What about Thursday ... Juddie's Seafood?" A well known restaurant to everyone.

She shook her head. "Sounds good, eight o'clock?"

Jason nodded in the affirmative as they parted as he closed the door exulting in his latest success.

Making it to the sofa in the corner of the living room, he sat down trying to understand all the happenings of the day. Taking it all in was his mother watching from her bedroom. She maintained a smile on her face, knowing all too good what Jason was going through but pleased to know he had a passion for her preferences. The interaction seemed natural. She was elated as she hoped her son would remain traditional.

On Thursday evening as Jason was getting ready, his mother brought into his room a bottle of cologne. "This is to attract all the girls to you tonight," she said as she passed it to him with pride and satisfaction in her face thinking to herself, he is trying so hard to understand himself. May God give him understanding, and hopefully with this he will know where he stands. While in the meanwhile, I'll give him all the ammunition to succeed in the role society delegates.

Jason arrived at Juddie's on time and waited in the assigned waiting area for customers. He waited for ten minutes which seemed forever. He wondered if the nurse had changed her mind. This new assumed role and the waiting caused him anxiety. After fifteen minutes in walked Nurse Allison. She was radiantly beautiful. Jason got up to welcome her, then summoning the waiter for them to be seated, he chose the seat near the window with a view of the outdoors.

On taking their seats she bent over towards Jason and said, "It's Tisha." Jason smiled then laughed in amazement; he found her so fascinating. Tisha felt proud being out with a strong man who got what he wanted, and she admired his qualities. He seemed compassionate and caring, and she enjoyed the banter. They sat and chatted, enjoying the meal and each other's company, while getting to know each other. Time slipped quickly away as they engaged in conversation, and they soon realized they were the only ones left in the restaurant. The waiter drew this fact to their attention. "My, you are the last in the entire restaurant."

As they walked to her car, he asked her, "Did you enjoy the evening?"

She smiled. "Yes, I enjoyed the company. It was a wonderful evening and thanks for inviting me." They both felt the evening was enjoyable; he was hoping it would go on forever.

He drove with her to her apartment after realizing she lived within walking distance to his house. As he walked to her door, he embraced her tightly and they could feel the mutual attraction. He kissed her goodnight and as they embraced, Jason did not want to release her. "I hoped I could hold you forever," he whispered into her ear.

"Give time a chance," she said. "My roommate will be out for the weekend. She leaves on Friday night for Miami."

"Would you like to spend the weekend together? Let's see where it goes."

She knew she wanted to see him again and soon. She hoped he also felt the same. "I would love that. Can't wait."

He again kissed her gently on the cheek as she slipped through to the inside of the door, throwing a kiss for him while closing the door. She remained at the back of the door contemplating whether to invite him in, but she knew she was not alone and that was not possible. She liked him a lot. While for him walking felt more like floating all the way home.

On reaching home he entered and went straight to the living room and sat down reflecting on the evening's events. He was thinking at his age this was his first date with a female; he had never felt so excited. Was it because it was something new and different?

He was ready to sleep, but he didn't want to move from the living room. He just lay there reminiscing about the evening's event and the person who caused this new experience. Why where there were so many positive emotions? he wondered. If in this upside down world, if love is possible for him, then why can God, whomever God is, make everything flow in such a positive way making all persons have such a feeling of belonging and happiness? He thought the world is a beautiful place if seen through the eyes of one who is in love. He felt spiritual and closer to God as he fell asleep on the couch.

An evening like this could only result in a comfortable night's sleep.

The next morning his mother got up earlier than usual as she did not hear him when he came home last night. She found him peacefully asleep in the living room, and as she stood above him gazing, remembering when he was a baby, it seemed as if only yesterday he was comfortably curled up in his crib. She wondered, why did you have to grow up so soon? Why didn't you conform with what society considered normal? She knew she was thinking as any mother would if faced with a similar situation as hers. She wanted only the best for the offspring she had delivered to the world. "I love you whatever decision you make. All I want is for you to be happy," she said softly. She continued to look at him with admiration, and she did not require an answer from him and decided her happiness was dependent on him being happy. She remained a while longer looking at him, knowing her health was deteriorating, and said quietly, "I love you." Then she kissed him on his cheek and as the tears stung her eyes, she slowly walked away leaving him in his dreamy, sleeping state.

The day passed quickly in the Jason/Lidia household with Jason silently planning his evening while carrying a smile all day. Then he had his bath and carefully dressed himself in anticipation of his evening. His mother stood at a distance watching in silence. Nothing was discussed about the previous night's outcome and she appreciated his privacy, but his ready smiles and seeming contentment meant something good was happening in his life. She left him alone to find himself; she was not going to interfere.

As he dressed and got ready to leave, she looked at him with pride and love knowing he was trying to chart his course. He was not one to satisfy her or society's dictates, but he wanted to explore this new experience. She hugged him as he departed confidently with a skip in each step.

Earlier that afternoon at the lottery headquarters things seemed brighter with interest improving as the jackpot started to climb upward. Nigel's involvement went unnoticed although it had somehow enhanced the game. This significant incident was important for his ego and he expected recognition, but in this case it was not forthcoming. He felt slighted, a feeling he would need to get used to.

There was an uncertain strain between Andrew and Nigel. There was limited communication as Andrew was allowing Nigel to come to terms with his involvement in the manipulation of the numbers, while Nigel felt Andrew knew all along how to fix the game but was unwilling to come clean.

Later that day Detective Dunn came into the office requesting a meeting with Andrew. This request was agreed to within minutes as Andrew wanted answers to the disappearance of Jason. The detective was ushered into his office.

"Well, we meet again, detective," Andrew said as they shook hands and sat down for a discussion. "Do you have any good news for us?"

"Not at all. What I would like to do is interview all persons on your staff who are directly associated with Jason on the job. I am not getting the information fast enough for my investigation, and I need to collect information while memories are still warm."

Andrew agreed, "When do you want to begin?"

Dunn happily said, "Immediately, if possible."

Andrew knew right away it was possible. "You can use the conference room. I will inform all department heads for them to choose all staff who worked directly with Jason to start rotating through. We will start with the IT department which was Jason's department. We will start with Nigel, who now runs the department."

Andrew took Dunn to the conference room. "Please have a seat. Nigel's office is next door. Let me tell him we are ready." They shook hands as Andrew left to get Nigel.

On reaching Nigel's desk Andrew said, "Detective Dunn is in the conference room and he would like to speak to all staff members. You will be first. Remember, stick to the Jason issue. These investigations have nothing to do with the running of the game." That was sufficient to tell Nigel the manipulation of the game stayed with both of them only and no one else.

Dunn was known for his thoroughness when investigating. As Nigel entered, he offered him a seat and immediately asked him, "Do you know what happened to Jason?" It was a direct question. Dunn always used this line of questioning straight to the point as it always surprised the person being interviewed.

"No." It was like a stand-off. "Like everyone here, I don't know whatever happened to him," Nigel said confidently.

"Have you ever contacted him or made contact with him after the weekend of his disappearance?" Dunn asked.

Again Nigel answered, "No. As I have said before, I have not been contacted by him nor do I know of his whereabouts."

Then Dunn asked, "Do you own a blue sports car that was damaged due to an accident?"

This time the question caught Nigel by surprise and completely off guard. He had always thought this was his Achilles tendon hoping it would never come back to haunt him. He now had to face the inevitable, but he would try to make his answers simple.

"Yes. Some weeks ago I damaged my car."

Dunn continued, "Why didn't you report it?"

Nigel was surprised. Did Dunn know more than he was saying? "Since I was the only one involved in the accident, I thought it was not necessary to report it. Also, I paid for the damages because I did not want the insurance company to get involved as it might hike my premiums."

Dunn then asked, "Are you sure no one else was involved in the accident?"

Nigel could not believe his ears. He was not willing to be cornered by this line of questioning, and he knew if he kept his composure, everything would be accepted. As far as he knew, they had not found a body, so these may be leading questions and should be thought through carefully before answering.

The next question was, "Were there others in the car?"

Nigel knew John and his two counterparts were in town at the time, and they had returned to the apartment with him under the shade of darkness, so that question was not a matter of importance.

"No. I was alone at the time of the accident."

Dunn then asked Nigel to write his address on the sheet attached to his name. When Nigel picked up the sheet, he realized there was much more information gathered on him, but he could not quickly read even the first page.

Dunn recorded Nigel's answers and assumed he was truthful and credible. He then asked him to call the next witness. Dunn was not one hundred percent satisfied with Nigel but understood his answers to be quite in order.

The questioning had shaken up Nigel, who went directly to his favorite restaurant after work where he had dined with John. He needed a drink to soothe his nerves. He felt alone sitting there by himself. There was no other member of the family or close companion to share his thoughts with. He knew there was one person who he could call to share his thoughts and concerns, but with his discontentment with Andrew he was in no mood to place Nadia in the middle of these problems.

While Dunn was interviewing Nigel, Frank was in a huff speaking with Andrew in his office. He could not understand Andrew not taking the initiative to change the time for the game in the Kentucky town, where it may cause some difficulties if there ever was a winner. "The changes should be made immediately. If not, we stand the risk of a recurrence of irregularities," he stated.

Andrew responded, "I showed you last time it was coincidence when that happened. There is no need to worry. I will act on this matter next week, I promise."

Jason knew he was early to Tisha's apartment, but he could not hold back his anxiety. He wanted to see her again. It was six o'clock when he reached the door where he waited for a while before ringing the doorbell. He was trying to waste time or was it to settle his nerves? In the meanwhile he took out his pocket comb fixing his hair and then tucking his shirt into his pants; he then brushed off his shoes with his bare fingers, and as he was rising from his final task, the door opened.

Standing before him was another elegant beautiful female smiling. He quickly stood up and stuttered, "Is Tisha in?" Both people were shocked at the sudden appearance of the other, neither knowing the other one was waiting. He repeated his question. As the air settled both understood the situation and smiled at each other.

It was at that moment Tisha appeared and laughed at these two immovable objects saying, "Dawn, this is Jason and Jason this is Dawn."

Dawn was a good sport and quite an adorable roommate. She then said, "Pleasure meeting you, Jason, but I am late for my flight, so I'll see you next time. See you guys." She was through the door and off.

"Come in. You are early," said Tisha as she welcomed him into her home.

"Yes," Jason replied not telling her how anxious he was to see her again. He said, "I had a wonderful time the last evening we were out. I have never been so fulfilled in another person's company as I was with you." She felt the same way but did not express it.

"What can I get for you to drink?" Seeing the drink cupboard, he was amazed at the large variety of liquors to choose from.

"Are you guys heavy drinkers? You have certainly surprised me. You don't look the type to have so much liquor in your home. There are still things I have to learn about you," he said.

She looked at him. "There is a lot you don't know about me and I you, give it time."

The evening went along wonderfully starting with drinks and lot of conversation; they spoke of their lives and their future plans. Jason asked her which from her collection of movies was her all-time favorite. She told him it was "Sounder" because it had pain, sorrow, and joy all wrapped up in one film.

While she said all this, Jason looked puzzled. "I have never heard of this movie or seen this film."

She happily said, "So, let's watch it together and while you are watching it, I will fix something for us to eat. Is that all right with you?"

Jason could not believe how comfortable he felt in her company. Looking over at her while she prepared the food for them, he saw what a special lady she was and he kept falling for her.

She returned in about half an hour with an assortment of wings, each with different seasonings and other finger foods specially prepared for her guest. Both cuddled up enjoying the food and the movie.

Jason raised his glass to her. "Compliments to the chef. Compliments for the tasty food."

"Yes, compliments to Captain Nik's Wings at the end of the street," she said laughing. Jason was thrilled with her sarcasm. They enjoyed each other's company and the movie, hugging and laughing with each other. It was the beginning of a passionate embrace as Jason drew her in closer and kissed her gently on the lips. He adored her.

He never wanted to stop the kiss. This was the first true kiss he had ever received from a female and it felt good. He wanted this woman and he sensed she wanted him. He stood up and hugged her gently, and he then lifted her and carried her into the bedroom. He laid her onto the bed removing her blouse. Her breasts were firm and responsive as he gently licked her nipples and circled her breast with his tongue. This action made her body squirm in ecstasy as she turned her body toward him. He removed his shirt and she felt the hair on his chest, which turned her on even more. The feeling in the air was full of sensuality; both people liked the feeling when touching each other. As he removed her skirt and as she pulled his pants to his knees while he pulled off her underwear, he looked at her body. Her skin was flawless; her shape other women would kill for. She was a true goddess of women.

They enjoyed touching each other. He excited her and she obviously loved his erotic technique. This drove her crazy; it made her feel like a real woman.

"I want you to first experience me in bed touching you. I want you to enjoy every moment of our first experience." He wanted to find a way to show her love because he was not becoming aroused.

The experience felt good, and his satisfaction came from experiencing her arousal. He was gentle and she loved everything about him, but she wanted sex. As she cooled down and returned to earth's orbit, Jason embraced her and lovingly he kissed her as the sweat rolled off her forehead. She wanted him and although his feelings were intense, he could not be aroused. He actually preferred the pleasurable feeling of rolling in bed satisfying her without him being sexually satisfied.

The load on his head grew heavier as he could not satisfy her the way she wanted. He then said as he hugged her affectionately, "I need to tell you something."

In her tired state she smiled at him and said, "Is there a problem with me?" His face was one of surprise.

"No." Jason repeated, "No, it's nothing to do with you. I have never been so stimulated by a female in all my life. You are the most sensuous woman on the face of the earth, but I am a little different."

She stopped him. "Please go straight to the point. I care deeply for you so be honest with me."

He turned to face and said, "I have never been with a woman. I have never had such a feeling for a woman in all my life."

She again interrupted him. "Nonsense. The man who just made me feel so good is a virgin?" She cocked her head to the side. "The man who turned on every sexual connection in my body has never done it with another woman?" She then looked at him and asked, "Are you gay?"

With little hesitation he said, "Yes, I am gay." For a moment there was complete silence in the room. Then all of a sudden she exploded into loud laughter. She could not contain herself and she laughed uncontrollably.

Jason by now felt embarrassed and ashamed. He felt like a small rat.

In the midst of her laughter she controlled herself and stopped, realizing Jason's masculinity was being affected. She took a deep breath and said, "So am I."

This immediately puzzled Jason, and he did not know how to respond. He did not know if he was hearing correctly. "What did you say?" he asked.

"Yes, I am and like you. I am trying to find myself." She paused. "Remember Dawn, who you met when you were entering the apartment and she was leaving at the front door? She is my lover and well, like you, she is giving me space to explore this feeling. It started when I met you at your mother's house."

Jason felt relieved and less confused as she hugged him embracing him with a feeling born of mutual understanding.

"I find that liberating that she could allow you to explore your feelings. Tell her I love her also," Jason added.

She then continued to tell Jason about herself. "We have been friends since elementary school." Jason continued looking at her and he embraced her passionately. They both still felt a strange emotion, yet they burst out laughing with the happiness that comes from deep mutual understanding.

"When I found I had these feelings, I discussed it with Dawn. She thought I should find myself and explore these feelings, so here we are, both of us still not truly knowing why these feelings exist. One thing is obvious; we know now who we truly are."

She felt so relaxed and comfortable with Jason even though they were spending time together on a conversational level while on an emotional level they were uncertain how to proceed, so that was left to nature. For the rest of the night they chatted enjoying each other's company. It was a special night for both.

Tisha said, "It's five o'clock and I have to be at work early." Neither wanted to leave each other. It was so easy and comfortable to exist in this cocoon of mutual admiration, making no demands yet knowing it must come to an end.

They hugged feeling the finality of it. Jason said soberly, "I have enjoyed your company. My heart hurts to know, it could be the only time this experience may happen, but I think I deserve this at least once in my life. Thank you. I will always remember you and our time together – short, eventful, enlightening. Tisha, I will forever love you, always. I have now experienced the fact that there are many loves in life and no two are the same."

Jason got home after six o'clock that morning. As he turned the key in the door he quietly entered knowing his mother would be up early as usual and even moreso awaiting the outcome of the night's events. Or, she would just be looking for a reaction from which she would draw her own conclusions, which were usually correct.

As he walked into the living room, he said In a low tone, "Mummy," but there was no answer. As he moved towards her the flooring squeaked and she opened her eyes. He took a deep breath delighted to see her response, and he felt the burden in his heart lifted as he was filled with joy, amazement, and gratitude.

He said, "Mum, I love you." It was an unconscious response and he truly meant it.

She smiled. "I love you too my son. Where have you been all night?

He was so glad to see her and said, "Before all that, it is time for breakfast for you. What do you want on this special day?"

She picked up on the special treatment. "Why am I being treated so specially?"

Jason wanted to keep it simple not making a big deal of his frightening thoughts when he entered the house. "This is nothing special. It's like every other morning. Now what special food do you want?" He knew he was lying. He was glad to see her that morning, and he felt alive and grateful that as she was. He knew he wanted to be there for her the rest of her life.

That morning was special for him. As he served her breakfast, she said, "That was a breakfast to die for." Looking at her. he smiled.

After eating her breakfast, she then hit him with the question she wanted to ask all morning. "Where were you all night? And then you come home this morning like you were in Smilie Land." She laughed knowing asking about his private life was complicated; however, she could not hold it any longer. It was up to him either to be willing to talk about it or be silent.

He smiled knowing it was coming; she could not keep it in. She was so proud of him which encouraged his willingness to satisfy her curiosity. "I know you want to know everything but nothing from these sealed stiff lips." Those words sounded familiar but funnier.

She felt something happened, and whatever it was, she felt proud to know there was another experience he now knew and the choice was his.

They spent the entire day reminiscing about their lives and experiences. Jason knew they were treasured moments. Knowing he had the funds in the bank, he asked her, "Have you ever thought of having a larger and more elegant house in an upscale neighborhood? With our resources it is entirely possible."

She turned and look at him. "Never," she said emphatically. "I love this neighborhood. I love my neighbors. If I moved, I would have to drive everywhere and I am in no condition to drive. I can walk to the market and to the bakery, and the exercise has always kept me in good health. My health may be down now, but it will be up tomorrow." They both knew she was satisfied with the simple life. She went to her room and came back with a small black draw-string bag which she opened taking out the contents one by one.

She said, "I want to share these with you. You see this button? It was from your first baby shirt." She laid it on the dresser. She then took out a small silver spoon. "You used this for you first for your first taste of solid food." She then took out a small yellow item. "This was you first tooth lost. It was one of your front teeth." Although it may strike others as silly, it was touching to see she had kept these small items from his childhood to adulthood. It had meant so much to her.

He felt the love as she shared the story and associations pertaining to each item. Only a mother could understand. Each item was a symbolic of the memories she had in her heart knowing very well her years of hardship, struggling, laughter, and accomplishments. These were all just to show appreciation for life, and he would never know how much love was locked in that small black bag of memories. All he could do was to hug her tightly as his expression of his love for her.

Jason got up and started taking down the groceries from the cupboard. "I am going to cook the finest dinner this evening for you," he promised as she nodded her head in agreement. She thought, what a wonderful human being. Why should a group of gangsters try to end his life, this beautiful creature God has given to the world?

"I am proud to be your mother," she said looking at him with pride. After dinner they spent the evening watching television and he watched the lottery draw.

"I hope Andrew is doing what is necessary to keep the game alive," he said to his mother, who could not understand why he took this position after all the terrible things they did to him. "How can you still love those cruel people? Look what they have put you through."

He quickly corrected her. "It was not the company; it was one individual, Nigel."

While Jason and his mom watched the draw, Nigel was at his desk compiling his numbers. He knew by now what was required of him, so he went ahead finding his numbers and then passing them on to Andrew. The numbers 11, 26, 31, 43 and 57 were the numbers not played together that week.

Before he could pass the numbers to Andrew, he made it quite clear. "I am not particularly in favor of this type of manipulation of the game." Nigel wanted to be clear about his position, and by making Andrew aware of this, he was letting him know that he did not want to be part of such a scheme. It was unethical and immoral.

Andrew turned to him. "This makes our company successful. As long as you do your job, you will be a part of the experience and successful." Andrew was cut and dry and one to play around; he shot the facts straight from the hip telling Nigel what mattered. As Nigel walked out of Andrew's office, Andrew knew he had a problem on his hands with Nigel, but tonight the game would come first.

The phone rang. Andrew's younger son was on the line. Andrew asked, "Have you reached the lottery and are you at the cashier?"

His son replied, "Yes. You told us to call you at this time, before we bought the ticket." His son did not understand where the conversation was going, so he arbitrarily said, "We have stopped at the gas station and had a bite to eat. What next do you want us to do?"

Andrew asked him to buy a lottery ticket. "Are you ready to write down the numbers?" With that said, he started calling the numbers – 11, 26, 31. At that moment Nigel knocked at Andrews door and entered just to hear Andrew say, "43 and 57. I will call you later." He quickly hung up.

Nigel had heard him but never said anything to Andrew, who also remained silent. Nigel was unusually quiet as the balls were rolled out and the draw done.

The boys bought the numbers without questioning their father. They bought the numbers thinking it was a company project and feeling important to be part of the process.

Jason and his mom watched the draw from home after which they wished each other goodnight. What a wonderful day in my life, she thought to herself. "I still want to know what happened last night," she muttered and smiled as he kissed her smiling. "Good night. I love you always." They parted for the night.

Nigel's apartment that night saw him pacing the floor. He was disturbed and troubled knowing the police were investigating his office while he and his boss were twisting the rules of the lottery by manipulating the game. Again he was hesitant in making calls to his girlfriend in France. He did not want to make her choose between her father and him. It would not be fair involving her, but with who the hell else could he share such thoughts?

He decided would call her but would stay away from conversations of the running of the game. He poured himself a long drink of coconut rum which relaxed his nerves; then, late into the night he gave into his stubbornness and he called Nadia.

"Hi." He sounded like a mouse seeking forgiveness. She picked up on his mood knowing this guy had a lot on his plate. "I know I have not been calling as frequently as in the past. I have been under pressure from work recently with the police investigation. They are now questioning staff members, and incidentally, they knew of my accident."

She inquired, "What accident?"

He caught himself. "I thought I told you I damaged my car in a slight accident recently. I guess it was so simple I did not mention it to you. Don't worry. No one was injured, and I repaired it out of pocket."

After pausing she replied, "I think you are beginning to take me for granted, which concerns me. Recently, I have not liked the tone of our conversations. For me there is feeling of mistrust."

To which Nigel said, "I need to share time with you and for you to help me through this." His voice was one of despair.

To which Nadia replied, "Nigel, I don't want to be a whiner, but you want me only when you are down. Why don't you want me all the time?"

Nigel tried to explain in seemingly order of importance. "The pressures from figuring out Jason's computer and dealing with the police questioning has worn me down, and I feel as if I am carrying so much more than I originally agreed to carry. I have become short tempered even with your father, for whom I have a lot of respect. I just don't understand why he made me work so hard on the project when he could have made it easier for me."

Nadia with understanding asked, "So why did you react so negatively to something you did well? I guess he expected the opposite reaction from you."

Nigel, wondering if her father may have spoken to her about the events at the lottery headquarters, retorted, "So you are taking sides? I knew you would take his side."

Nadia interrupted. "I am not taking a particular side. I love both persons involved. He might have had an unseen plan for you and you came through with flying colors."

Nigel, who felt patronized, replied, "These past weeks' exercises have been stressful and taken a toll on my emotions. With righteous indignation he stated, "Do you know there is another aspect to the procedure of the game? I find it to be inappropriate and somewhat illegal." He then blurted out, "I don't want to be a part of this scenario. It scares the hell out of me."

Nadia felt his frustration and knew his sense of confidence had been undermined, so she proposed, "I have two months remaining to complete my course. I think it's best for me to take a leave of absence and come home."

To which he replied, "That's not necessary. I can handle what's about to happen."

"Nonsense. You are handling it but not coping very well it seems." She did not want him to feel perceived as weak and incapable of handling his own affairs.

He shouted, "Nadia, I don't need a babysitter or one to guide my actions. All I need from you is a listening ear and some understanding to help me through this period."

Nadia paused and then replied, "I see." She gave Nigel the leeway to further vent his frustration.

"I would like to leave this job despite the career potential it affords, but the investigations make it an inappropriate time to leave." Nigel continued, "With what has unfolded I do not want to be a part of this operation. It's not the environment I want for myself, but if it were not for this job, I don't know if we would be together, and I value that aspect dearly."

Nadia had always wondered if Nigel felt trapped due to the family inter connection with work and their intimate relationship. She so wanted to separate the two, but as Nigel kept the conversations directed towards the business end with little emphasis on their relationship, she realized which one had taken precedence.

It would take a lot of maturity for either of them to separate both aspects, so she said quietly, "Don't get mixed up. My love for you is not tied to your success in business. Never lose sight of that. In this instance if you are going to base our love on one day becoming chief executive officer of a big fancy business, then take your love and roll it with the lottery balls and flush them. I have listened to enough for the night. Please let's end this conversation before someone says the wrong thing. Good night." She hung up the phone. Nadia placed the phone in her lap as she tried to place matters in perspective. They both knew the relationship had become strained under the circumstances.

This "sweet thing" was now becoming a burden, she thought. If only one could have seen ahead. She had tried her best to separate her loyalties and be objective, but that was not working out. It had taken its toll.

One cannot foresee the challenges early in a relationship. It seemed listening to Nigel's problems and providing advice as best as she could had not been enough. What kind of man was he? she questioned. After all, she only knew the kind of woman she was.

While one world was in turmoil, Jason's was not. He had slept very well after spending a memorable evening reminiscing with his mother. He awoke this Sunday morning feeling relieved and free of the conflict evoked by Tisha. He made his coffee and as usual made a cup also for his mother since she stayed in bed longer hours in the morning, and she liked the service. She was still asleep, so he rested it on her bedside table. As he looked at her, she looked so peaceful that he didn't want to wake her, but he also didn't want her coffee to get cold. So he gently kissed her on her cheek and whispered,

"Wake up, my darling mother. The sun is rising and it's a beautiful morning. Come make yourself shine."

He realized she did not respond. He also realized her face felt unusually cold when he kissed her on her cheek. At that moment it struck him something was wrong as there was no stirring or effort to wake up on her part.

He held her and shook her gently. "Mom, time to wake up." Her entire body was cold and he wondered what had happened. He shook her vigorously, still no response. His training kicked in; he realized she had made her transition.

Sitting on the side of her bed, he raised her head into his lap hugging her and kissing her on both cold cheeks, telling her how much he loved her, and thanking her for all she had done. He also thanked God for granting them the quality time they had spent together, the exquisite outcome of a horrendous experience.

Jason followed procedure and called emergency 911 and also Dr. Williams, her primary care doctor over the years. Remaining calm during the entire time knowing the past weeks were the best in his life and in hers also, he was sorry he didn't get to say last goodbyes, but he was comforted by the fact that she was especially happy for the time they had recently spent together.

Dr. Williams arrived soon after the ambulance. When writing the death certificate, he reminded the doctor her name was spelled incorrectly on the medication bottles. The doctor quietly made the changes, making a mental note to correct her medical records also, and he called the undertaker to take the body.

While Dr. Williams was performing his duties, Jason saw on the bed side table the little black drawstring bag with her memorabilia. He took a moment sitting at the dinner table to remember her pleasant thoughts. As he opened the bag taking out each item, he could not remember the significance of every item to her. Their particular interest to his mother were her treasures. Disappointed with his lack of recall, he replaced all the items into the bag and decided he would give them to the undertaker to be placed with the body.

As he reminisced, it struck him then that the things of interest we gather during our lifetime that fill us with such beautiful memories, these things have no significance to another person regardless of the close relationship. Each person has his or her own treasures. They are ours and ours alone until due to death we part from them. No one else can appreciate their value.

The undertaker asked, "Have you decided how you are going to treat the body?"

Jason knew due to earlier discussions with his mother and replied, "Yes. Cremation. I would like to take her ashes with me to the falls to be scattered." He then asked, "When is the earliest you can complete cremation?"

The undertaker replied, "Within three days the urn will be available for you to pick up. The cost will be will be discussed at that time. We knew your mother so well in this community and that can be dealt with later."

He paused to see Jason's reaction and since there seemed to be an agreement, he continued, "We will be ready around midday on Wednesday." And with that they took the body.

Jason closed the front door turning and around to an empty house where only a few days ago there was joy and laughter. Now there was palpable silence. He sat at the table lost and lonely at the thought he would never see his mother again and it hurt. Jason wanted everything finalized quickly not to have too many eyes on his situation. The spelling of her name had to be incorrect on the death certificate, so theoretically even for some time until the situation could be cleared, she was still alive in the city's registry, but among her friends she had passed.

He now had time to plan.

14

C H A P T E R

THE FOLLOWING WEEK the lottery headquarters had a renewed energy and vigor while relations between Andrew and Nigel remained tense and strained. They had limited interaction. The situation concerned Frank, who being an executive of the company, felt it necessary to address.

He said to Nigel, "Why are you in such a bad mood? Is everything all right with you? If you ever need my help, you know where you can find me."

Nigel shrugged his shoulders saying nothing to Frank, who accepting his mood, moved away. He was thinking something was certainly causing concern. Was it business or personal? Frank conveyed his feelings to Andrew, who immediately called Nigel to his office. He needed Nigel now more than ever, and he knew he might need to use his fatherly instincts to mend their differences.

As Nigel entered Andrew's office, the tension in the air was felt. Andrew asked, "Why are you reacting so negatively to something that's positive as the lottery is performing well again? Or is this a reaction to Jason's disappearance and the investigation? Is there anything I should know?"

When Nigel heard this, his reaction was one of arrogance. "You are just like the police. Why do you think I had anything to do with Jason's disappearance?" he shouted. "He might not have been my favorite person but that was his life. It had nothing to do with me."

Andrew was surprised at the outburst. He could never interpret Nigel's reactions, and this was no exception.

Nigel continued, "I am having a hard time dealing with the operation of the lottery game. I am not comfortable with the game. It should not be manipulated." He paused. "I don't want to be part of this activity."

Andrew did not know how to respond. Apart from Jason and himself, Nigel was the only other person who knew the secret and he needed him for a smooth operation.

Looking at Nigel he said, "I am sorry you feel this way, but the success of the game – hence the future of the company—comes first. It is your choice; the ball is in your court."

Nigel was uncomfortable knowing his relationship with Nadia would become a part of this and things could permanently crumble, but he thought, what the hell? The relationship was going bad anyway, so what the hell?

Nigel knew if he brought to the forefront the inner operations of the game, it might provide the well needed cover for Jason's disappearance. "We have to stop it and find a legal way out."

Andrew was now angry. "Sorry. It's gone too far. What you do in an entire week is not as significant as what you spend half an hour each Saturday doing."

Nigel was completely surprised and disappointed. "You would like me for the rest of my life doing this every Saturday night in order to cover up this shady operation?" He was growing angrier by the minute.

In the midst of the conversation the phone rang. It was Andrew's secretary. "Detective Dunn is on the phone."

As she waited, he lifted the phone. "Hello, Detective. How are you?" Andrew was happy for the interruption from Nigel's conversation.

"Very well, thank you. The reason for me calling is I have been trying to contact the youngster Nigel and your secretary said he was with you. May I speak to him?" Dunn asked.

"Certainly, please hold." He passed the phone to Nigel while whispering, "Dunn."

On taking the phone Nigel spoke cordially. Andrew, remembering the arrogance of the recent conversation, thought to himself, who is this Nigel? Is he a Dr. Jekyll and Mr. Hyde? What a switch."

Nigel on the phone heard, "This is Detective Dunn. I would like to meet with you in my office. Do you know where it is?" he asked.

"Yes, I'll be there within the hour. Is that ok?"

Andrew had captured the trend of the conversation and again asked, "Is there anything you may want to discuss with me?"

In disgust Nigel said, "No... why can't everyone understand I know nothing about Jason's whereabouts?" He stood up and left Andrew's office for the police station.

Arriving at the station that afternoon, it was buzzing with activity. There were handcuffed people moving from one department to the other and a line of women along with men all handcuffed and yelling. It showed Nigel another side of life, one with little or no hope.

As he stood in the midst of this activity awaiting the detective, he reflected on his life after college. His desires were constructive, purposeful, and with direction. Was this over ambition that brought about the desires to eliminate Jason? Why didn't he think of Jason's mother's pain in losing her child? He was dismayed standing there watching the criminals around him not sure if soon he would be just like them.

He was now being escorted to Dunn's office. As he walked the corridors, he had never given much thought to the families of these perpetrators, families who had to cope without the financial or emotional support of those locked away. How would his own parents manage without him? His monthly check subsidized their expenses. Why did I ever get involved in such a crime? What was I thinking? I have a great job and a great girlfriend. The future looked great. What was I thinking? These thoughts lingered in Nigel's mind as he made it through the corridors towards Dunn's office.

He heard a sound and out of the corner of his eye he saw an elderly woman crying and begging for sympathy while the arresting officer held her tightly by the upper arm leading her presumably towards a holding cell. Nigel hoped this would never happen to him, realizing he had not considered these alternatives when making plans for Jason. He just wanted a permanent solution for the ever-continuing situation in the office.

He snapped out of these thoughts when his escort said, "This is Detective Dunn's office." As he entered, he saw the detective seated at his small desk overrun with files which obliterated the surface.

Dunn could hardly be recognized through the small opening left to accommodate the upper part of his head. There were no photos of family on the wall or other memorabilia. It seemed as if work was all he had.

"Please come right in. Welcome to my world. Hell, it is not as bad as it looks. I know it's nothing like the uptown corporate world you are accustomed to. Here we deal with everyone –the dregs to the white collar crooks. We have a package here for everyone."

Nigel suddenly felt the walls closing in. Was Dunn calling him in to trap him into saying something stupid?

Dunn then continued, "The accident you outlined to me does not add up. I need a proper explanation for the cause and particulars of the accident. You said it happened on Ration Street, which is less than two hundred feet long, and no one on this stretch remembers an accident on that day. You said the extent of the damages were small not necessary for reporting to the insurance company, yet we checked with Basil Garage and those damages were extensive, far worse than you led me to believe. How do you explain this?"

Nigel knew this trip was more ominous than it seemed. He replied, "The type of insurance I had was inadequate for the coverage of the damages, so I decided to do it on my own. It may now seem strange, but at the time I thought nothing about it. So, I just simply went ahead and fixed the vehicle."

Dunn was quietly listening to Nigel's explanation, and although it might be straightforward, he had to hear it for the records. After a short discussion mainly discussing the accident and matters at the lottery office with regard to Jason, Nigel's answers were noncommittal.

Dunn's invitation to his office had rattled Nigel and the unspoken question as to whether he had anything to do with Jason's disappearance hung over his head. On leaving Nigel felt Dunn had more information than he had shared. Nigel stayed moderately comfortable and satisfied with his explanations.

After leaving the police station he went directly to his apartment. He was finished with work for the day. Tired mentally and physically, he felt as if he was reaching the breaking point. There was too much going on, the pressure was becoming unbearable. Up until now he had survived the investigation up, unloaded on Andrew, and argued with Nadia. For him it was a completely uncomfortable day from start to finish.

The day-to-day activities at the lottery headquarters were filled with scandal. It became the talk of the town. There were rumors of insider fraud, theft, and the ultimate, the disappearance of a member of the staff. All these accusations reached the mayor's office, with the mayor himself growing tired of the poor publicity associated with this department. This worried the mayor and his popularity; he wanted the publicity stopped whoever got hurt along the way was not his responsibility.

He called his secretary. "Please set up an emergency meeting of the executive committee of the lottery company. We have to know what is going on there."

She was surprised at the urgency in his voice. "When do you want this meeting?"

He impatiently said to her, "Do you know what emergency mean? Right now. Today if possible." His face was changing color.

At that point she calmly said, "Yes, sir. Consider it done."

Her first call was to Andrew. "Mr. Cole, the mayor would like for you and your staff to attend an emergency meeting. How soon can that be arranged?"

Andrew considered. "Two days should be just right."

She responded, "He would prefer tomorrow at ten o'clock. Can I tell him you have agreed?"

Andrew immediately knew something was not right, but he agreed on the meeting time. Andrew got his team together that evening for a briefing in preparation for the mayor's meeting. All the facts were placed on the table.

He urged the managers to be as open as possible in the meeting. One key person absent from the meeting was Nigel, who Andrew apologized for, saying he was out on the company's errands.

Nigel was furious on learning of this meeting and rushed into Andrew's office. Still venting his frustrations Andrew said to him, "I am sorry you are not prepared, so don't speak. I will cover your portfolio. Leave things to me."

With that Nigel was happy because all the blame was now on Andrew's shoulders. Little did he know that Andrew preferred that Nigel not speak as he lacked the required confidence. Nigel knew no preparation was necessary but felt there was too much happening and didn't trust the players around him, including Andrew. He was thinking this was a set up between Andrew and Dunn, and he again spiraled downward into a depression. As he sat there, he decided to call to make sure of no recent developments he was unaware of. John was the person who he could always confide in.

He was just about to call as the phone rang. The person on the other end said, "Hi. This is John."

Nigel responded, "How you doing, cuz? I was about to call you. Great hearing you, been a while, but it's better for us the less communication, the better. I wanted to completely cover all remaining bases. I am having a meeting soon and I wanted to know if all is well is your area."

John replied, "You are the only person in your office who has the answers. All you have to do is keep your mouth shut. Stop worrying."

Nigel then said, "I think we had better protect our asses in the event something is left uncovered."

John interrupted, "Like what?" John knew there was nothing to connect them to the "murder" of Jason.

"I have no idea. Was the truck found?" John knew Nigel was struggling to find faults in his handling of the Yoking where the body could not be found.

"Yes I made the report and the next day and they found the vehicle. There was no suspicion of wrong doing, and if there was, it happened after the truck was stolen, so rest comfortably. There is no concern by the police on our end."

Nigel wanted to be open with John. "There is a meeting in a few minutes, and I am very suspicious when meetings are planned without my involvement. I think plans are being put together to entrap someone. It may be me. Who knows?"

John asked, "If there is a link to us, do you think they are putting the pieces together when I could not find a trace of him? I was convinced the river had taken and consumed the body. The news reports have mentioned nothing over the past three or four months of a body found in the entire vicinity. I bet the mangroves with those alligators have dealt with the corpse."

John's tone was now serious, but Nigel as usual had to air his fears. "You are of the opinion he died, but look at the alternative. The police might have him in hiding to bring him out at the right time to testify against us. Every time I am going to an impromptu meeting, it scares the life out of me. This is attempted murder if he is alive. It is thirty to fifty years, and I am not spending the rest of my life behind bars."

You could hear the concern and fear in Nigel's voice, and he had to vocalize the seriousness of the situation and its consequences. This amplified fear deliberately lingered for a moment.

John then asked, "Who are you meeting with, the police or the mayor? Try not to mix everything up."

Nigel replied with more confidence, "Bullshit. If they had anything on us, we would know by now. They want to see who cracks under pressure in our organization and individually." He continued, "We all have to stand firm, including Andrew if he knows what's good for him."

John then interrupted, "Is there more going on in the company?"

Nigel surprised himself. His tongue had slipped, and he could not let John know about the dishonest manipulation occurring with the game. If John ever knew, he would have one more thing over his head. This was Nigel's alone to keep, to be used against Andrew as needed. No one else should know.

Nigel then replied, "No. Business continues here as usual. You just concentrate on the action we have to put in place while hoping nothing comes up." Both parties were quietly understanding each other's concern.

Nigel then said, "We will speak another time. I have to go off to the meeting."

Andrew and his management team entered the conference room at the mayor's office with an air of suspense. They knew the game was once again on the upward momentum, so why a meeting now? Nigel too walked hesitantly with the group. He knew there was nothing they could link him to. One thing he knew for sure – he would not be "going down" alone if anyone came after him in the meeting. These thoughts persisted as he took his seat awaiting the start of the emergency meeting.

It was ten o'clock when all parties finally took their seats. The difference with this meeting was that there were no usual greetings by anyone. The side table with coffee and snacks were absent; only a large jug of water with glasses was provided.

The mayor entered and took his seat at the head of the table. "Good morning. Are we all here?" There was silence. "Let's get started. Anyway you all should be here before ten o'clock," he said in a firm and assertive voice.

He was certainly not the same person I met at the airport some months ago, thought Andrew. This is pure hostility.

"Let's cut to the chase and go directly to the rumors circulating. It is embarrassing coming from a gambling concern. You all should know how society looks at companies who move so much cash weekly. There is always the suspicion of swindling." He looked at Andrew while he was making the comment.

Being the chief executive officer of the company, Andrew understood the mayor's concern. As Andrew was about to respond, the mayor asked, "Is there theft occurring within our walls, and if so, let's address it first." Andrew could relax for a moment as he now knew if this was the emphasis of the meeting, then was no knowledge of manipulation of the winnings.

He then addressed the issue. "No, Mr. Mayor. There is no evidence of theft in the company. Our internal audit shows absolutely no signs of misappropriation of funds."

"Well," said the mayor, "that's good for starters. Then next, what about the disappearance of this employee?"

Andrew replied, "Well, problems began with the disappearance of Jason Paye, a member of our staff. He left work one Friday evening and never returned. We are of the opinion he got another job offer and moved on. Meanwhile, the police are investigating the disappearance."

With such an explanation Nigel was not going to add to Andrew's statement, nor was the rest of his group.

The mayor shook his head, seemingly understanding the situation, then asked, "So why was there such a departure from profitability after his disappearance? Was he such an integral part of the game?" With that question hearts started pounding as he looked around for answers, while all members of the team were calm without an answer. Andrew and Nigel were the only faces with sweaty noses both thinking, did the mayor know more than he was letting on? Was a trap being set?

Nigel was about to make his presence felt. As he was about to stand up unconsciously to cover his ass, he raised his hand to speak. Andrew, on seeing this all unfolding, was about to stand in order to outplay any move by Nigel, but on second thought he allowed him to proceed. If he wanted to hang himself, he thought, let him go right ahead. He allowed him the floor. "I would like to introduce myself. I am Nigel Eckers, and I am the computer and Information manager. I took over this department after Jason left unceremoniously. To date we have not found any irregularities with our accounts, but the moment he disappeared the rumors began."

Then the mayor looked at Nigel. "Did you find any discrepancies at all which could be linked to his disappearance?"

Sheepishly Nigel looked to Andrew for answers, then said, "No, Mr. Mayor." He answered with little conviction.

The mayor picked up on Nigel's insecurity and grilled him further. "Is there anything deeper in the department we should know?" This time there was distinctly more probing in his tone.

Nigel felt the intimidation but also knew if the secret was exposed, shit would hit the fan. He again looked in the direction of Andrew as if he required his consent. What he saw looking back at him was an inscrutable expression. To Nigel it said: "Sail your own boat. You wanted to be the center of attraction, so you are on your own."

Looking towards the mayor, Nigel repeated, "Sir, I must repeat, no." He said this with more confidence than previously, but he was believable.

After a grueling two-hour meeting, the mayor was convinced there was no indication of wrongdoing and the rumors were false. He had his reservations about Nigel. He liked him, but his gut feelings told him there was more to Nigel's story. His mannerisms were not convincing and though it was just a hunch, he stayed with the impression. In the end the mayor expressed a renewed confidence in the work being done by the team and indicated giving the necessary support, so the lottery company could look to better days ahead.

After the meeting was adjourned, the mayor felt a whole lot better about the running of the lottery office and decided to mingle with the team before they left the room. He deliberately moved in Nigel's direction wanting to have a word with him. Quietly he said, "If you ever have anything else to report, you can always give me a call directly. We are always looking for those with top management qualities and you may have what is necessary." With that said the mayor moved on to the next person.

Nigel felt elated and excited with such an endorsement. He felt rediscovered, and it boosted his confidence. He had covered his ass and Andrew's also. He now had the backing of the mayor and, hence, the Board. He envisioned new horizons, and he felt like the kid in "The King's Pajamas."

Things seemed to be heading in the right direction, but his thoughts were always on the manipulation of the game and what effect it could have on his future advancement if the truth was known. He also realized his newly formed closeness with the mayor mandated that he keep up all appearances, not laying any of his dealings open to suspicion. His future depended on maintaining the right connections.

The mayor called a press conference later that day where he outlined the benefits derived from having a lottery. He stressed the benefits to education and in closing explained that after an intensive internal investigation, there was no need for an inquiry into the running and performance of the lottery company.

Ray, the investigator in Vern's law office, had kept Nadia abreast of all the happenings in the lottery office. He knew about the meeting at the mayor's office and the outcome was not as straightforward as it seemed. The political climate was far from what the mayor was letting on to the staff of the lottery office.

That department was still his main target in order to take the mounting pressure off his office. The mayor's plan involved making changes in the management hierarchy, which was an effort to relieve himself of pressures from rumors and speculation. He would wait for the opportune time, continue the inquiry, and make the outcome to remove blame from his office and place it solely on the Lottery Department.

These findings were delivered in a three-way conversation with Vern and Nadia.

On hearing this Nadia said, "It's time for me to go back home. I have been contemplating this for a while, and whenever my father seems to be under suspicion, I have to give him my support. I was the one who recommended Nigel."

Vern saw it differently. "There is no need for you to interrupt your studies. I know your father can handle himself, so your proposed move will not make him perform better."

Nadia then responded, "You wouldn't understand. From my last conversation there may be more to the activities at the lottery office." She paused for a moment remembering Ray was still present on the call. She then continued, "Let me call you back later. I have to start making preparations."

The next morning Nigel was again complaining in Andrew's office. "I would like you to seriously understand my feelings. I am not comfortable with the activities with the game, and I am thinking of leaving. I will not be a part of the biggest hoax of the century in this town. I have no intention of letting the secret out, but I am uncomfortable with my role, and I have no intention of working under these conditions." Nigel poured his heart out to Andrew, who somehow listened to his concerns.

Andrew thought he was a coward and replied, "I hear your fears and concerns, but I thought you were made out of the right stuff to handle this. Guess I was wrong."

Nigel was prepared for Andrew's reaction, so he kept his calm as Andrew continued, "I understand your inability to handle pressure that comes with management experience. In addition, you are handling and overseeing the operations worth millions of dollars. The community involved is expecting you to deal fairly with them. You are new to this arena, but you will one day learn to satisfy all parties involved and that the end will justify the means. So, do not be so self-righteous. There is much more to this than meets the eye. You may want to give up but think of the thousands of families you are helping, which makes it all worthwhile."

Suddenly there was a knock at the door. His secretary interrupted the exchange and left Nigel to wonder if Andrew knew more about Jason's disappearance than he was letting on.

"I seem to be the one who is always interrupting. Forgive me, but Detective Dunn is here to see you and he says it's urgent." Andrew was not done with Nigel, but Dunn had to be seen. "Show him in," he instructed.

Dunn walked in realizing Nigel was also present. "I am glad to see you again. This is a continuation of our previous meeting, and I would like to speak to Nigel in private."

Nigel without hesitation said, "Whatever is happening, it can be said in Andrew's presence."

Then Dunn indicated Andrew was welcome to stay if he cared to, and with a show of his hand the go-ahead was given.

Dunn proceeded, "As part of our investigation we took the opportunity without your permission to give your car a good check-over while it was in the garage."

Nigel questioned, "Why without my permission? Am I a suspect? Why was this necessary?"

Dunn explained, "It is all a part of our investigations. All angles have to be covered."

Andrew then added, "Do you guys still want me to be here?" Dunn looked at Nigel who indicated yes.

"Do you have a dog?" Dunn asked Nigel, who shook his head indicating he did not.

Dunn continued, "The forensic report showed all types of DNA present, human and animal to be specific. There is evidence of dogs being in the car. Are you into any activities involving dogs?" After collecting the DNA, we exported the files through the FBI data base only to find there were matches with DNA found in a stolen vehicle found in another state miles away. "Is there a connection with you and that truck?" Immediately Nigel denied the connection. He kept his calm knowing the importance of the connection.

Dunn continued, "We have requested Jason's DNA from the military, which may be difficult due to confidentiality, but we are working on it. We are still making our investigations, so I am asking, "Is there anything you would like to share in helping the investigations forward?"

By now Nigel was sorry he agreed for Andrew to sit in on the meeting, but it was too late to change his mind. As he continued he felt the intensity of Dunn's work realizing how thorough he was in his investigations and with the truck coming into the picture things had taken another direction. He knew there would be more to come.

In an effort to cover himself he said, "I am sorry. I don't know how that could be. Maybe someone sat in my car when it was in the garage or the guard dog at the garage slept in my car. I really can't help you with the connection."

Andrew kept his cool just sitting and listening. He was attentive mostly to Nigel's reactions to the questionings. He also had his own secrets and had to keep quiet. In fact, he could have contributed to Jason's DNA for matching, but he knew there were consequences.

Then Dunn pulled a bombshell. "Well, since there is a disappearance of an individual with no trace, I know the district attorney will have to convene a grand jury to inquire into the disappearance and all coincidences will have to be explained with a thorough investigation." He paused, then loftily stated, "With respect to the persons present, my goodly gentlemen, I wanted to deliver this latest information personally. I have a feeling there is more to this than meets the eye. Anyway have a good day."

As Dunn was about to leave, Andrew asked Nigel to see him out. Nigel was hesitant thinking he would escort him only to the office door. Dunn then requested that Nigel accompany him to the front door, and out of diplomacy Nigel agreed.

As they both walked towards the elevator, Dunn said to Nigel, "Things are not adding up when it comes to your explanation and the damages to the car. Something is puzzling."

Nigel chose not to comment, then Dunn said, "In cases like this there are persons who can cover you from all sides. I want you to get in touch with a group of associates call Stefan Gambani." He passed a small piece of paper with the name and telephone number as he exited the building.

Nigel could not understand why the sudden change in Dunn's opinion of the situation. He was convinced Dunn had evidence he was holding back. Unfortunately, he knew he had to return to Andrew's office where he had left his notepad. He also knew, with all the information passed during the meeting with Dunn, that Andrew would be asking questions.

As Nigel knocked on the door and entered, Andrew was ready for him asking, "I want the honest answer. Do you have anything to do with Jason's disappearance?"

Nigel without a flinch answered, "Never." This was enough for Andrew, who said, "I accept your answer as a man, an understanding man. I will put a stop to any more questioning. In the meanwhile we must get back to our original conversation. I want you to guide me through the NOSAJ12 program. I have no intentions of giving up what we have started. It's the only way to keep the company successful.

You have no need to worry. I will do all the cross- referencing of the numbers and gather the numbers. It will all be on me and there will be no implications of your involvement."

This absolutely satisfied Nigel, who would wanted to get himself out of the clutches of this "unlawful act." He agreed with Andrew's suggestion saying, "That's the best news for the day. I will start downloading the files to your desk immediately. The training will be done in here, your office where it's more private."

Andrew agreed as he said good-bye to Nigel, who returned to his desk to start the process. As Nigel worked on sending the files to Andrew, he decided to check on the name passed to him from Dunn. As he typed the name into the computer, he felt confident Dunn was fishing for information, thinking this name was someone who he mentioned arbitrarily, but when the information came onto the screen, Nigel was emotionless. His eyes could not believe what he saw. This person was investigated by the Federal Bureau of Investigation. Although he was acquitted for the matter, he was aligned to the local mafia in the South Eastern states. Nigel took a deep breath trying to understand what he had gotten himself into – this for sure he wanted no part of.

It was Saturday morning when Vern and Ray decided to meet and discuss the latest findings at the lottery head office.

"Ray what do you have for me?" that was all needed to start Ray off.

"Well, there is always something happening at the lottery headquarters, apart from the latest upbeat in the game. The assistant to the top guy, I think his name is Nigel, is dissatisfied with the company and wants out. Unfortunately, he was questioned on the disappearance of Jason, the computer wiz genius in the company. He tried to gather his points together." All these parameters are the making of something special. I can feel it in my bones that there is more happening in this office."

Vern stopped him, asking, "Is the press on to the story as yet?"

Ray told her, "No. To push a story out there we can get the press involved, but do you really want the story out there for the public?"

Vern, who knew Nigel's love for sensationalism, knew he also had limits and did not want to be involved in negative publicity. This thinking reflected the disdain Vern had for Nigel. "Let's see if the press can dig up more dirt. Use your sources, throw it out to the press, and let them run with it. Anywhere the wind blows it, then that's the direction; leave it to settle naturally." She sounded excited. "This way we will get to the bottom of the situation at the office." She knew very well if Nigel was involved in anything fishy, it would take him down forever. Ray began making his phone calls.

Saturday night in the lottery office saw Nigel working with Andrew to manipulate the numbers resulting in a winless evening for the customers. It was also an eventful evening for Andrew, who handled the complete manipulating operation from start to finish. He had separated the numbers, then pulled out the numbers that were not played together, and finally selected those numbers from his batch of specially weighted balls.

Andrew felt as if he had accomplished greatness. He knew with this power he could rule the outcome of every draw, and he felt invincible. Driving home that night from the office, he knew this was not the way he wanted the game to go, but it worked and benefited the public, so he saw nothing wrong with doing this.

By the following morning all the Sunday newspapers in Amalta had lead stories about the lottery business, some so outrageous others subtle, but the overall underlying story centered around Jason Paye, who seemed to have disappeared taking down the lottery business with him. The stories told of all the confusion, lack of organization, and mayhem surrounding the management of the company since Jason's disappearance.

The phone rang in Nigel's apartment. It was Dunn. He asked, "Did you give the story to the press?"

Nigel said emphatically, "No! Why what is going on? Is there new information on the disappearance?"

Dunn was boiling and he was trying to understand the situation. "Well, the press has gotten hold of the story and is bending it in all directions, making insinuations which are not good for business. It makes our investigation seem worthless. We need to meet first thing in the morning, nine o'clock in your office."

Nigel hesitantly agreed.

Before he could hang up, Andrew called. "Do you see what is happening to our office? We are the laughingstock of the city. I want to see you first thing in the morning in my office. I might take you up on your request." Despite his angry words, Andrew knew this was not the appropriate time for Nigel to leave the company. The attention would cause more speculation about activities. He, however, hung up abruptly for effect.

Nigel did not have time to inform him of Dunn's earlier call, that he too wanted a meeting. The rest of the morning was spent purchasing every edition of newspaper to see each opinion and report. Fortunately for Nigel, not one linked him to Jason's disappearance. He spent the day trying to think through the many scenarios and directions his life had taken. This made him very uncomfortable in his position with the company knowing how to manipulate the game and the fear of being caught, not to mention his involvement in Jason's disappearance.

The many options haunted him. Should he come clean or leave the chips to fall where they may? At this point no one was pointing fingers at him, and all the blame seemed to be mounting in Andrew's direction. The questions were heavy on his head – the thought Jason may still be out there, the unexplained damage of his car that could be his undoing. He would never come forward and admit to anything. The promotions within the company were not worth it; it left him raw and exposed.

Attempted murder, manipulation of the lottery – his reward for all this would be prison time. He knew he was not coping well. Ambition was a demon; it had taken over his mind controlling his emotions and eroding his values. Despite these negative feelings he remembered the offer from the mayor and thought this may be his road to escape and his saving grace. His innate ambitious drive made him for a moment insensitive to how much trouble he was in and the thoughts of still being able to rise to the top seat in another company despite the other negativity gave him momentary and short-lived pleasure. Reality soon set in, and nothing could erase where he was at this point in his life. He had committed beastly acts and now there was karma.

Andrew's phone was constantly ringing, and he had to take it off the receiver. He felt disappointed that, after all he had contributed to the company's growth and success, this negative news in the press was what his department might be remembered for. To name a few of the good things the company provided in the community – the giving of scholarships to deserving students, providing employment opportunities, and thus improving the livelihoods of many families – all these put Amalta in the limelight as a successful city.

The press had given no positive coverage. It only concentrated on the negative and scandalous aspects of the story, many of which were fabricated even the suspicion of murder. (Where was Jason anyway? There were no clues, no body.) He genuinely feared for his future all tied up in this stinking job, becoming more smelly as the days passed. Jason's disappearance had initiated this public scrutiny; however, he was proud of their accomplishments, like father, like son. Would I be disappearing soon? he wondered. Annoyance was replaced by fear. He had reservations about some personnel appointments over the years. Nigel, who was the benefactor of Andrew's desire to help youngsters just leaving college, headed the list. He had thought young people were easier to mold over the seasoned workplace employees who were set in their ways. What an exception! He vowed never again to solely employ on compassionate grounds, and he wished Nadia had never met him.

The lottery headquarters was alive on that Monday morning with the press occupying the steps waiting for executives as they came to work. No questions were left unasked. Were they in league with the investigators? There were no answers in return to satisfy their thirst for sensible leads, as no one knew what to say.

As Dunn approached, the members of the press deferred their onslaught of questions out of ingrained respect for the police. Dunn made his way to Andrew's secretary to have Nigel summoned. Andrew was also informed. Dunn approached Nigel with an air of calmness, Nigel thought, but as usual he went straight to the point. "The district attorney would like to have a meeting with you. The recent publicity by the press has surely led us to believe there is more happening here than you are telling us." He then pushed the ultimate question. "Is there any connection with the lottery and Jason's disappearance?"

Nigel's response was just as arrogant belying his nervousness on hearing about the district attorney's involvement, thus indicating how serious the situation was becoming. "Why ask me? I don't know. I have a job here and it is done to the best of my ability to earn a decent living."

Dunn's calmness had dissipated, and he said icily, "Your car keeps on turning up valuable clues. There is a disconnect between what you say and what we see. I am going to find out. I hope that you will not be implicated."

With the last insinuation Nigel lost his cool. "My car accident has nothing to do with Jason. Wherever Jason went has nothing to do with me. Both situations have absolutely no connection."

There was the usual knock on the door. This time an unfamiliar face was ushered in. "Nigel, let me introduce the assistant District Attorney, Mr. Clifton Weeks."

The well-dressed gentleman went over to Nigel and shook his hand saying, "Good morning and how are you today?" He sounded so polite Nigel thought, but he remained wary knowing a warm greeting could bely a trap.

Weeks, on the other hand, wanted Nigel to feel comfortable with him. He wanted him to feel as if he was there to help him and relinquish any animosity built up towards Dunn in his investigations. The DA began, "We have been following the inquiries closely and now the press has picked up on it adding their usual flair. This is not good for our investigation." He paused for a while making sure Nigel understood his inferences. "The press never cares about the correct story. They prefer the one that is exciting and will provide more readership, so before this story goes in the wrong direction, what really is going on at lottery headquarters?"

The DA looked at Nigel for answers. He replied, "I had an accident and my insurance was a Liability policy, so I decided to pay out of pocket for the repairs. While the car was in the garage, someone sat in my car, some animal. Maybe the guard dog or pet slept in my car and I am being asked questions for which I have no answers. That's all I can surmise and contribute to the entire situation. I have nothing else to report."

Turning to Dunn he said, "I have told you this on numerous occasions. I have nothing more to contribute to your case. I feel like I'm being accused of something, and I am tired of it." Nigel knew of his constitutional rights and wanted to put a stop to the harassment.

The DA recognized the puzzled look on Dunn's face. The detective was thinking these adamant denials and logical explanations made Nigel's reactions appear like that of a caged animal. Book smart he may be, but guilty as sin he was.

Belying his gut feelings Dunn replied, "We are not accusing you or even implicating you, but the strange damages to your car and the way it was handled aroused suspicion. We have many years of investigative experience, and there is a new piece of evidence also." This got Nigel's attention. "DNA was found on a piece of shattered window glass which is different from those found in the car. When it's analyzed, we hope we will not have to come back to you for clarification. Furthermore, if it's Jason Paye's, there will be reason for more doubt, do you understand?"

Nigel was left dumbstruck. All he could mumble was, "Yes."

Weeks added, "We are finished for today." To Dunn he said, "Let's get back to the office." They then turned and left.

In the meanwhile Nigel was thinking that he needed to stop talking or risk betraying the brotherhood.

These country folks would not be allowed to outsmart the city slickers. Weeks was effective in leaving his "victims" uneasy and guessing after they were cross-examined. This was no exception. It was not unusual for confessions to be made after these cross-examinations, but not today. Dunn had set up this shake down, so he had solicited Weeks' help in interviewing Nigel to see if he would break or add more insight. Weeks sometimes before leaving would present the option of a plea deal, but this time with so many doubts and no body of proof, he decided to leave it up to the judge and jury to come to conclusions. In this case he thought Nigel's story was dubious and with too much bravado, but he left without giving that impression.

Nigel was scared beyond belief. He could feel the hammer falling fast and felt they were giving him a chance to come clean. He had to do something and soon. If the blood sample had Jason's DNA, then there would be a certain link to Jason's disappearance and although there was no body that could finish him off, he also remembered telling Dunn that Jason had not been in his car. Recent findings of DNA was enough to incriminate him. The thought of prison worried him; however, he sought comfort from the fact that without a body it would be hard to prove any wrongdoing, DNA or not.

Everything was happening so fast that morning. As soon as Dunn and Weeks stepped out, Andrew's secretary informed Nigel he should report to Andrew's office as soon as the meeting was over. Nigel knew Andrew would want to discuss the reports in the press with him. As he stepped into Andrew's office, he could feel the tension and he braced for the attack.

"Well, it took you a mighty long time to get here. I sent a message to you. Why the hell have you kept me waiting? Don't you understand what is taking place in the community? We are being portrayed as the villains on many counts, including robbery, people disappearing, and even murder. We are defenseless and effectively burying ourselves in it. We could do without this unnecessary attention. I am expecting a call at any moment from the mayor. It's unusual for him not to have called already. I guess he is working on something bigger for us."

Nigel had to defend himself. "Firstly, I must start by saying I did not contact the press or have anything to do with anyone outside these walls apart from your daughter." Pausing to allow Andrew to understand his position he continued, "The police were here this morning with their inquiries. I am tired of their questions as I have always said I have nothing to do with this disappearance"

Andrew went on to tell Nigel of his disappointment in his approach to the job, and he did not hold back. He also told him of his deficient interpersonal skills. Andrew wanted to tell him more of what was on his mind but stayed restrained knowing how sensitive Nigel could be and remembering the "shared secret." He did not want to gamble. Nigel, however, sensed the unspoken sentiments.

Nigel spent the rest of the day at the computer interacting with no one. The staff suspicious of his recent behavior kept their distance.

Later that evening there was a call coming through to Nigel's desk. "Hello, Nigel. This is Clifton Weeks. I hope you remember me from the meeting earlier with Detective Dunn."

Nigel replied, "How could I forget you?"

Weeks continued, "Well, there have been some developments in the case. We have made contact with Jason's father and he has provided us with a blood sample for DNA testing and the lab thinks there is a positive match." Weeks was bluffing, but as a lawyer he knew he had to use the word think, in order to cover himself making it legally correct.

Jason never spoke to Nigel about his relatives, so this new development heightened his concern about being under suspicion of being directly involved in Jason's disappearance.

Weeks had no DNA from Jason's father but felt Nigel was somehow involved and had to try something even if it was dishonest. He had no other evidence, but by scaring Nigel into believing he did, this new evidence might lead to a confession. Weeks had to play his hand carefully, realizing the sensitive nature of the case and the person he was dealing with.

Nigel then asked, "How can that be? We need to meet to discuss this development as it makes no sense whatsoever. Can I come down to the station?" He was becoming nervous thinking if he met with them it might cool the situation and at the same time convince them he had nothing to do with the disappearance.

Weeks would not give Nigel time to think out a story saying, "Let's meet right now."

Nigel agreed but after quick consideration said, "I have had a hard day. Too many things are happening, and I would prefer we make it first thing in the morning." What Nigel did not know was that Weeks and Dunn had together planned this scheme to catch him off guard. They were both disappointed at not having an immediate meeting, even knowing it was not truthful they could not force Nigel into a meeting.

"OK," Weeks reluctantly replied. "The results remain the same today as they will tomorrow. Will nine o'clock tomorrow suit you?" With that the agreement was set.

Nigel felt his world crumbling, and the lack of confidence from his fellow employees was obvious. As he looked around the office, he saw employees looking so somber and uncomfortable. He felt responsible for disturbing the upbeat flow in the office. This feeling of worthlessness had become his demeanor. He felt as if the world was pushing him into an inescapable corner. Then he thought that it he had no one to blame, for he had done wrong and he was paying the price. He got up from his desk and walked into Andrew's office and not remembering to request permission from the secretary, he knocked and went right in.

"Andrew, I want to speak to you." Fortunately, Andrew was alone.

Being surprised and seeing the disoriented look on Nigel's face he said, "Please sit down. What is so urgent?" He knew Nigel could be irrational at times. Perhaps this was one of those times. He wanted to sit him down and bring him back to earth, and he could see the person entering his office was in need of help. "All right, tell me what this is all about. I was expecting this melt down from you for some time. Why don't you learn to handle pressure? Now I am not chastising you; I can only say what I see and I could see it coming for a long time."

Nigel sat down and began, "Please hear me out. You have been hard on me in the past, as Nadia says it is your method of training me from the ground up. I may have resented your approach, but I understand why you found it necessary for me to start from scratch in deciphering Jason's program." He braced himself for a while as he didn't want to lean too heavily on Jason's disappearance. "At the time I was doing the unraveling, it was harassingly difficult when you knew all along you could have shortened my efforts. Unfortunately, I cannot work with your approach. Nothing against you personally. It's your management style that is not compatible with my approach."

Andrew knew where this was going and for the first time felt no compulsion to put a stop to it. He was fed up with the childish behavior. Nigel continued, "The best thing for me to do is to resign." He passed an envelope to Andrew, who somehow expected it, attack being the best form of defense. Wasn't he using the same tactics?

Nigel continued, "My reason for resigning is basically a matter of stressors brought on and compounded by working here. You can do whatever you want with the game, but I will not be a part of it. It's left up to you." Andrew sat back allowing Nigel to spill his guts. "Something did go down between Jason and myself, but it was all mental not physical. One thing I don't know is where he is, I can tell you that much. I have not seen him."

Andrew by now was tired of listening and decided to just go for it, so he asked, "Nigel, what the hell have you done to the youngster? Did you kill him because he was better than you?"

By now Nigel was trembling in his seat as he heard Andrew react for the first in this conversation. "Whatever happened between us was personal. Believe me, I did not touch or lay a hand on him," Nigel said in a plaintive voice. "Adding to the pressure was a call from the district attorney's office saying they had collected a DNA sample from Jason's family and there was a match from a piece of glass found in my car. They have made contact with Jason's father, who gave them a sample for cross-matching."

When Andrew heard this, he only smiled and knowing the truth he could only shake his head. He also knew if Nigel resigned at this sensitive time, it would attract unnecessary attention to the company and he had to protect the secret.

Andrew was moved to see that what he had considered a game had brought so much disillusionment between working partners. He was surprised that what he had considered a great pastime activity would have resulted in such a serious outcome. He had not considered nor did he know that much about the players. He could not give up what he had built over the years making it the success it had become, so he played his bluff.

Nigel seeing Andrew's concern said, "I am hoping these investigations do not cause an embarrassment for the company, so the best thing for me is to exit before it interferes with the company.

Andrew said calmly, "Why can't you see how the disappearance of a fellow employee would have had devastating effects on the company? Even if you leave now, this will travel with you, so you had better stay and see it through to the end. You will need a reference and I will not give you one. Two can play nasty. At this time we are all under suspicion, and I will not accept this letter. Go home Nigel for the rest of the day and think of the consequences of leaving. I trust all around common sense will prevail. I hope that nothing comes of Jason's disappearance and that he will reappear. Many people could get hurt. Remember, no one can squeeze information out of you unless you want them to do so. I am older and more experienced than you. Give me some credit."

When Nigel left his office, Andrew had a good laugh but had to keep the secret. At that point he knew the police were bluffing. They didn't have anything on Nigel but were only suspicious of his actions. So with Nigel submitting his resignation, he would have been nailed, Andrew for the first time wondered if Nigel might have been involved in Jason's disappearance. He was his son, after all. He now sat at his desk trying to come to terms with what was happening around him.

Andrew was fully aware of his jeopardized position in the company as he tried to think of all the options and reflecting on these extraordinary day's events, he knew that he was at the crossroads of his professional career. Either it would be the start of his coming failures or the start of something special. His the inner feelings made the latter feel quite unattainable. These feelings were the result of the many calls on his cell phone from the mayor himself, something which no one else knew about. Were they getting ready to "throw him under the bus?" He would not go down quietly.

The next morning Nigel reported to the DA's office, where Weeks and Dunn were waiting for him. "Good morning, Nigel. How are you? We want to continue our conversation regarding the blood-stained glass found in your car."

Weeks spoke to Nigel with a smirk on his face as if to say I have one on you and I am about to tell you. "The results link Jason to your car, so we are looking for answers." Nigel became restless in the chair and stood up.

Weeks reading his nervousness pushed harder for answers. "What's up? Did you actually give Jason a drive that night or did he steal the car and meet with in an accident? And you were angry and hit him too hard? Explain what happened." There was a deafening silence as everyone waited for someone to respond.

Nigel replied sarcastically, "Since you know it all, why don't you continue and tell us the end of your remarkable story?"

Nigel always thought blood from Jason was farfetched. At no time did Jason entered his car bleeding, much less to leave blood stains. Was there a possibility these guys were trying to trick him into a confession? He could not be quite sure if it was all a game, so he decided to bluff his way through the questioning and interjected irrelevant personal feelings.

"I don't care for your line of questioning, so before I say anything more to you, I need an attorney."

With that the DA and the detective, knowing they had nothing on Nigel, decided to quit that line of questioning. The intended exercise to squeeze as much information out of him was aborted.

Disappointed Weeks reminded Nigel that the same questions would be asked at the inquest next week. "I hope you will be ready for them. Since you refuse our questioning now, this could serve as a trial run. Nonetheless, all you said so far has been recorded. The questions will be much more intense. Please leave the "I" out of it. This is more about investigating a missing person report, the same as you would expect us to do if it were your kinfolk." Nigel got up ready to go, but Weeks was not finished with him.

"I wish you luck, but I still have the feeling you were involved in something shady. We will be taking all the evidence we have collected, and we will continue in front of the inquiry to extract the information including the results using Jason's father's DNA." Weeks was continuously working on Nigel's psyche, and he wanted to break Nigel using his skill and experience, usually intended for persons who ran afoul of the law, even though he was not certain if Nigel had anything to do with Jason's disappearance.

He wanted to gain Nigel's confidence, for Nigel to trust him and give up any valuable information, but his line of questioning seemed to have had the opposite effect. Little did he know Nigel had gone to the edge but found some comfort in the fact that he himself did not know what eventually happened to Jason. He held on to the possibility that Jason may still be alive and if he was, there was no way he would be implicated for murder. He preferred to believe that Jason had died and had left no trace or clues for anyone to follow.

The following morning Nigel's phone rang off the hook. Somehow the press had found a way of finding his direct phone number and were calling for information on hearing of his resignation at the lottery company. All wondered, some more quietly than others, if the disappearance of a coworker had anything to do with it, was he running scared or was he involved in a crime? Curiosity and excitement were in full pitch.

Nigel was about to take the phone off the hook when it rang once again. He angrily grabbed the receiver about to give them a piece of his mind when the person said, "Hi, Nigel. This is Andrew. How are you doing?"

Taking a deep breath, Nigel said, "Hi. It has been like hell this morning, I am glad you called."

Andrew knowing how the Nigel could crumble under pressure said, "You have to stay strong during these trying times."

Nigel was happy to share his thoughts with someone he knew, even if it was Andrew. "The press is all over the building. It is truly hell here today."

Andrew added, "Don't mind. They are at our building milling around, but thankfully they can't pass the guards. Like I foresaw, the big question I am having to answer is, why you resigned at this critical period. Keep your focus and don't give too much information. Watch what you say."

Nigel knew Andrew required his silence to save his own neck for other reasons. He was not sure what he would do if cornered. He knew that he would not be taking the fall alone for any wrongdoings with the lottery game and that he would spill everything to save his neck.

The stories in the newspapers kept coming with the release of the car accident information. They published all types of scenarios including Jason being seen at the steering wheel and that he ran from the accident and was eliminated later. The stories became absurd, and Nigel knew it was common for the press to assume a variety of scenarios to explain an incident when no facts were available. Somehow he seemed to be closely linked to Jason's disappearance. It scared him as all three newspapers he bought on a daily basis had that one certain fact, that of his involvement in Jason's disappearance. He tried to keep abreast of the news circulating to see how current they were on developments, and he felt sure they had inside information. The days were long and uneventful except for this pesky case.

Nigel remained restless drinking a bottle of whiskey each day as he wandered aimlessly through the apartment when not at work. The wait for the inquest so his name could be cleared seemed relentless, and his mental capacity to deal with murder, illegal tampering with the lottery, and prison were too much for him to deal with. He kept thinking of Andrew's role is nurturing the unnecessary hostility between Jason and himself. If only he knew then what he now knew now, he would not have asked John to get rid of Jason, and to think John did not even call him. He guessed by now he knew of the mess Jason was in.

As he lingered in bed trying to stay away from the press, his doorbell rang. He answered it cautiously, and it was a pizza man. Realizing he had not eaten in two days, he was tempted to take the wrongly delivered pizza, but instead Nigel said, "I am sorry but you may have the wrong door."

The pizza man replied, "Aren't you Nigel? This is a delivery from Nadia." He made sure Nigel saw the short note: "Stay strong." The pizza man then brazenly asked, "Do you have a moment to discuss unusual occurrences at the lottery office? Can you give me some information? Were you forced to resign because you wouldn't play their game?"

Nigel, who was taken aback realizing a reporter had intercepted the delivery, was furious and shouted, "How dare you invade my private space? Who is Nadia? I have nothing to say. Are you guys are so desperate to sink to this low, disguising yourself as a pizza man? I have a right to call the police and charge you with impersonation and attempted burglary."

He grabbed him by the collar and threw him out of his apartment. The reporter shouted, "When the inquiry begins, it will be a tell-all. Everything will come out, all the secrets." He hastily tried to make his escape, just barely avoiding a kick to the cheek, still he fell prostrate on the ground.

Nigel suddenly realized how hungry the activity and anger had made him as he ate six of the eight slices of pizza before getting a drink. Then he went to sleep wondering how they knew about Nadia.

Awakening, Nigel was facing a feeling of mounting frustration – no contact with Nadia, no job, and he had lost his new found influence in the mayor's office. Thinking back, he had felt comfortable talking to Dunn and Weeks, who initially behaved as if they believed him; then, they seemed to lose confidence in his accounts becoming accusatory. All these factors made it look as if his world was closing in on him.

The thought of having to testify at the inquest was in its own category. If it ever came to the point where that blood sample linked him to Jason's disappearance, he decided he would spill all the information on the manipulation within the lottery business. Revenge felt sweet but how would that help him? He knew this decision would hurt many people, but why should he care for others and leave himself exposed to suffer the consequences of murder while they sat in their big offices earning large salaries from swindling a community? They would all go down, even if for different reasons. He knew the day of the inquiry was fast approaching. He felt like a bowl of gelatin – he was restless, nervous, and shaking. Even he knew was not handling this well.

Making the situation worse was the Sunday newspaper story which became the talk of the town. Its caption, "Amalta Lottery The Killing Field," had everybody's attention. People now had their suspicions confirmed. There were insinuations being made without pointing fingers at any specific person while still implicating everyone from the mayor down to the auditors regulating the lottery. There were calls for the resignation of the mayor, the entire gambling board, and all the executives of the lottery company. The only ones spared were the regular workers the lowest on the hierarchy. Blame landed squarely on the management staff.

Many individuals expressed disappointment with Andrew's inability to hold the company together even though he had done so well up to this point. A section of the article even surmised the disappearance of Jason was associated with the mayor's ticket not winning the jackpot. Another wrote Jason was against dishonesty in the lottery games. The article went on to say he was fired and paid off never to return or be seen or heard from again. It also offered the explanation of the possibility of the lottery being manipulated to generate the winning numbers. The manager of the bank in Amalta read and wondered and read again, but although unable to connect the dots, he was left wondering.

On reading the various articles, Nigel became deep in thought and he realized that he was no different from Jason. He realized he was given some unprecedented insight into human nature. He even experienced some stirrings of conscience although he had no name for the emotion. Stranger yet was the fact that he felt uncomfortable with the press getting insight into the inner workings of the game, which was a secret for two people only. The stories in the newspapers had no end. All avenues were perused and pursued. Monday morning the inquest was to start.

Jason was in Spieghstown following the progress of the investigation from the confines of his home and enjoying every revelation. This was the moment of humiliation for all the "evil persons" at the lottery office. He was glad not to be a part of it!!!!! It was a great work environment before Nigel came onboard. Then the work place changed to one of aggression and envy, leading to attempted murder, if it were not for his physical prowess.

Jason knew Andrew, instead of Nigel, was unfortunately seen as the perpetrator by the press, who would never have all the facts. The way he interpreted the case when following the reports, he saw Nigel serving as a witness against Andrew and the lottery company. He promised himself he could never allow Nigel to get away with what he did, causing another person to take the rap and eventually leading to the downfall of the lottery business. Then Nigel would come away "smelling good." NO WAY.

For Nigel this was the longest night of his life, surpassing that of not knowing how the hunt went that Saturday night. He was unable to sleep, and he tossed and turned all night into the wee hours of the morning. Unable to bear the nervousness any longer, he decided to think of the questions Weeks would be asking.

The questions could span the period from Jason's presence in the car on the night at the bar. He knew he could not lie with the cameras providing proof. But the presence of blood on the broken glass found in the car – how did the blood get there and on the driver side? How and where did they find Jason's father? There were so many questions, enough to make him feel as if he would lose his mind, and he was scared of any possible true stories held in secret by the DA to be used as evidence.

These uncontrollable thoughts fed a nervous stomach causing him to run off to the toilet again and again; it was his third time in the last two hours. How would he survive cross-examination? Getting back to bed, he refused to go through the agony alone, so he called John, who had not been in touch but he had no other form of support.

"Do you know what time it is?" John shouted.

"Yes," stated Nigel, who understand John's position but cared nothing about it. "The case starts in the morning and I have to talk to someone. If not, I'll go crazy."

John, who by now was stretching and coming out of his comfortable position, said, "Go and sleep. I'll be coming to the inquest tomorrow. In fact, it's actually in a few hours. Go and get some sleep. You are going to need a straight head to handle the questions. Prepare yourself and don't go crazy thinking too much. Get some sleep."

Nigel knew John wanted to hang up the phone and continue his comfortable sleep, so he quickly interrupted so as to prolong the conversation. "If they corner me tomorrow, I'll be spilling everything and saving no one. I will not be taking the fall for anyone."

John on hearing this hung up the phone in disgust.

Nigel, in turn, got some comfort knowing John would be there in the courtroom. He continued to pace the room reflecting on the good times with Nadia. How he wished he could call her to help him through these bad times. He knew she had always there for him. How could he be so stupid to have given up on such a fantastic person? It was times like these when the genuine qualities in a person are needed. Nigel knew he had made a mistake where she was concerned and felt he was being punished for it. He remembered all the good times they had together. He knew he was her first love, so they would forever share that bond, together or apart, and the memories would live on. Why hadn't they chosen to live in a small house in the suburbs and start a family, instead of trying to build a career?

Some events cannot be recaptured if not captured at that particular moment, just as the ripple seen in the river as the water is running can never be seen again. What is gone is gone. There can be many similar repetitions, but not that precise one. He felt they had lost the moment.

He could see the sun rising as he lay in his bed. If only he had the power to force it back on to the horizon and beyond. He needed some more time; he was not yet ready for the dawning of Monday. The sun still kept rising and it was a new morning, a morning he deeply feared. It was the Monday when all the stuff would hit the fan, and he dreaded the moment. As he got up, he knew it may be the beginning of the end for all.

15

CHAPTER

AT THE COURTHOUSE the media were out in full force, and the major networks from all over the country had descended on sleepy Amalta to cover the event. It was an opportunity for entrepreneurship. There were persons selling T-shirts with the mayor and Andrew smiling under the caption: "I love the lottery." There were also mugs with winning lottery numbers engraved, and other cartoon references to the whole gang of three, not excluding Nigel.

The atmosphere mimicked a circus; people filled the streets jeering everyone as they walked into the courthouse. The crowd yearned for a glimpse of the "lottery demons," as they were called, the culprits who subverted the normal win or lose process. The rumors circulated by the press coverage were imprinted on the minds of the public now convinced that swindling activities were a part of the lottery, albeit with no clear understanding of how this was done.

As Nigel made his way to the steps of the courthouse, someone shouted, "Stool pigeon," the name given to informers. He hoped no one thought he had given up information, but he knew there were those who hated backstabbers even if it is done for their benefit.

Then one person shouted, "You thought your resignation would help. Now the courts will find out what you were up to." There were some shouting, "Tell them what happened to our money." Nervous and shaking, Nigel heard these shouts as he made his way into the building.

The crowd became angrier when Andrew reached the steps. They regarded him as the leader of the operation, the person responsible to protect the public's interest, but in their eyes it seemed as if he had not represented them responsibly. The police had to escort him by forming a barrier around him; the loudest jeers, chants and expletives were saved for him.

The mayor used a back entrance to the building, so he was spared similar treatment. From the mood of the crowd, it was obvious these were the three principal villains who they were interested in confronting. When other officers of the lottery entered, there was no uproar. The crowd was happy they had expressed their opinions to all the concerned parties responsible for the problems.

Inside the courtroom Nigel was nervously seated towards the back. Andrew entered, accompanied by Nadia. When Nigel saw her, his stomach churned knowing the outcome of this inquiry may make them enemies for life.

As she passed his row, he stood up to greet her and, to his surprise, she stopped and quietly asked, "How are you doing"? Her voice captivated him; it brought back such memories. Oh, how he missed her company. Stepping over the person sitting beside him, he moved towards her, then held her not wanting to let go. He was reminded of how much he was missing and missed this stabilizing person in his life.

As he hugged her, he whispered, "I was stupid. I miss you." Not wanting to be conspicuous, she returned the hug ever so slightly and then walked off to her seat leaving him to reminisce, and for a while all the anxiety and nervousness related to the issue of the day dissipated.

But soon it was back to reality and all were seated. Nigel started looking around the courtroom. The mayor was seated up front with Andrew a few seats behind him. Both were intent on staring ahead; neither acknowledged the other. Behind them were others from the lottery office, and Nigel wondered why they were not at work but decided they came early to hear every word so they could put all the pieces of the story together. Then he guessed they would decide whether to stay or go to work, depending on what they heard.

Behind them sat everyday citizens who just wanted the lottery business to continue as it was a source of income for them. At this point, the goings on were more a source of entertainment as the excitement and scandal at the lottery had customers getting together to gossip on the latest rumors, true or false. Bets and numbers were assigned to dates and events that had meaning, and these would be played for the next draw. All wanted the lottery to continue; even if its current chaos brought about excitement and small-town buzz, it did not make up for the income lost.

There were also those who wanted the mayor to pay by the worst means possible for allowing such problems to enter into the closely scrutinized gambling fraternity bringing bad publicity to the heavily regulated gambling business. There were also others, unidentified but seemingly important people. No one wanted not to miss out being a part of this historical event.

An elderly lady was one of the last to enter. Leaning on her cane, she made her way all the way down to the front row of seats and stepped into the row. She seated herself in the tight space, thanking both people beside her for allowing her the space that previously was not there. There she sat quite insignificantly.

The judge entered, at which point the bailiff summoned all present to stand, this being customary for the start of all court proceedings. As the judge sat, he beckoned all present to be seated, then continued with his instructions.

"Good morning. My name is Judge Muir. Firstly, I must remind all persons giving testimony here today that this is an inquest and not a trial. We are here first to investigate the disappearance of Jason Paye. However, I am going to have to address and investigate the situation at the lottery company to determine if one has a bearing on the other in order to get a better understanding of the case and put to rest all the speculations. Although this is not a trial, certain legal requirements have to be met with each witness taking the oath to protect the honesty of their testimony or else face dire consequences."

The bailiff stood to call the first witness. "The court calls its first witness, Frank Rhoadz." Frank made his way to the witness box to take the oath. Passing Andrew's row, he looked in Andrew's direction acknowledging him with a fleeting smile which oozed confidence. Andrew acknowledged Frank, giving him an imperceptible thumbs up to signify he had his back even though he had not been not aware that Frank was summoned to testify. It was never mentioned in conversation, and he knew their relationship over the years was close, so Andrew had nothing to fear.

Frank was questioned by District Attorney Weeks, who started by asking Frank,

"I would first like to establish the characters of the individuals in your company. What is the relationship between yourself and Andrew Cole?"

Frank comfortably answered, "He is my boss and we have known each other for many years."

The DA continued the questioning to establish the relationship between both men personally and professionally, which Frank handled very professionally. Then the DA asked, "What happened on Saturday night at the lottery offices?"

The question was short and very direct, but it left Andrew and Nigel unnerved. Andrew wondered if Weeks was setting the tone for the inquest and if this was going to be the direction of his questioning. Where did Weeks get his information? Did Frank leak secrets to the police? How could they have possibly found out and how much did they know?

Frank started, "Well we always found it strange that every Saturday night Andrew and Jason, who was gay, would meet in his office to have drinks after every draw. There was certainly something going on between them. I don't know what it was and I never asked." Andrew's tension eased immediately as he laughed loudly, and he quickly apologized but kept the smile on especially for Frank, while shaking his head.

Weeks then asked, "What happened recently about winners within a certain time zone?" With this question Andrew knew right away Frank had been speaking to the DA's office without him knowing and that caught him off guard not knowing what to expect next.

Frank continued, "When we expanded the game into other states and therefore changed time zones, a certain aspect was overlooked by our operations department. So that area continued placing bets after the game was closed. I brought the situation to Andrew's attention and nothing happened."

Weeks then asked, "Would these customers know the numbers drawn?"

Frank answered, "No, because the drawing would have been done after those machines also closed down." Andrew knew Frank's answer cleared him of any suspicion. As usual, Frank was protecting himself, appearing to be a saint in front of these proceedings.

Weeks realized his line of questioning was not getting answers he had hoped. The one thing it showed was Andrew's poor management style, but he wanted something substantial from Frank so he continued, "In your opinion, do you think there was something underhanded happening at the lottery headquarters?"

Frank answered, "The everyday struggle between Nigel and Jason was concerning everyone in the office. They began meeting on Friday nights to build an understanding and hopefully a friendship between them at our "office meeting" at The Watering Hole. But in Monday meetings at the office they were at it again, their getting together did nothing to improve their relationship."

Frank realized Weeks was painting a picture of succession for Andrew's post with the introduction of the two youngsters Jason and Nigel to the company, which completely excluded himself from possible consideration for promotion.

Weeks then asked him, "How was Andrew Cole's friendship towards you? He certainly didn't have your interest at heart while preparing the two youngsters for his post." Weeks knew very well a question such as this showed Andrew as having no regard for Frank's advancement, which hurt Frank's feelings to the core. He was embarrassed in front of all these people, and although he knew Andrew tried to bypass him, by saying it in front of all these people, he felt belittled and angry. After his years of loyalty, commitment, and friendship, at that point he lost it.

He looked over at Andrew and said, "You don't know the first thing about friendship. I don't know what your relationship with Jason was, but you never know you might even have been his father. Who knows? The way you went about living with little moral consideration for your own behavior, he might have been your son."

If the ground could have opened, it would have been a safer place for Andrew. He wondered if Frank knew that he was Jason's father, and he braced himself for Frank's next statements. After all these years Frank wanted to get everything off his chest, all the pent-up feelings of envy and suppression. He thought Andrew's self-interest had to be exposed without care or favor.

Then Frank, with a sardonic smile towards Andrew, who was getting scared not knowing what was coming next, looked his boss straight in the eyes and said, "I know you didn't expect to hear such evidence coming from me, but you betrayed our friendship. The loyalty we had for each other was destroyed by you years ago." Frank began to choke up. "You hurt me and you destroyed my family."

Nadia, sitting beside her father, compassionately held his hand so as to provide confidence and to comfort him. As the buildup of her own inner anger towards Frank had become too overwhelming, she too needed some comfort. She knew the relationship had declined over the years, but she thought they had remained good working companions.

Frank continued, "I know you didn't think you would hear such evidence coming from me, but you betrayed our friendship. I have delayed a DNA test for my child because I don't want to know who the father of my son is. How could I have walked away from him after all these years? Sorry, it's a story I must tell. I have had it pent up inside for too long, but now the story is out. I hope the relationship between me and my child will be stronger than the outcome with you his godfather." Frank by now was extremely emotional.

Andrew's lawyer, on hearing the outburst, jumped to his feet declaring,

"Your honor, this is a personal vendetta and has no bearing on the proceedings—"

The judge interrupting asked, "Is this pertaining to the case?"

Weeks replied, "Your honor, we are trying to establish the credibility and honor of the person at the head of the lottery business. As we try to go deeper into the running of the company and its management, it also involves the disappearance of one of its employees, who may have been murdered. I ask your honor for us to hear the remainder of this witness' testimony as it will establish what led up to the disappearance or murder."

With this the judge agreed to proceed. Although it was allowed, it gave Nigel chills when he heard the word murder, not knowing what other surprises Weeks may have had coming for him.

Frank was ready and could not wait to continue to further embarrass Andrew. Looking across at Andrew, who lowered his head in anticipation, he continued, "I dislike you. You made my life a living horror and I wish no less for you than what you have put me through. I have held it back waiting for the right time to let you know. Strange that this is it. As kids growing up together we had each other's back, but time changes everything. The night before I got married you took me to see my other girlfriend to spend the last night with her. You dropped me off and after four hours, you picked me up. Unfortunately, my mother-in-law said the wrong thing one day, asking me why I allowed you to stay with my wife to be that night."

By now Andrew's face showed his guilt and astonishment at the revelations he thought only he was aware of, He held his daughter's hand tighter, anticipating a bombshell.

Frank continued, "I watched the affair from a distance, but it came to light the night you knew I was travelling to Cayman on business when you turned up late in the night not knowing I had missed my flight and was at home. That night was the turning point in my life. I hated my wife thereafter, yet she never knew. When my son was born. I made you the godfather. Unknown to my wife and you, the year before I had completed a series of test with Dr. Kumpt, who after testing told me I knew I would never father a child. I was completely sterile due to the effects of a childhood infection."

Frank's face contorted with emotion as he finally told his story. "I had a choice of killing you both or accepting the situation knowing very well I would never have the chance again of fathering a child. I kept my mouth shut and enjoyed my son. When she became pregnant the second time, I went through the mental torture born from betrayal, but God knows best. When they both died at delivery due to complications, I got a strange comfort as I thought it was a shame that caused her high blood pressure to lead to her stroke. I should have asked for a sample of the child's DNA to see if it was the same as my son's."

During the testimony Nadia's grasp on Andrew's hand slackened to the point where she held both her hands in prayer. Andrew recognized Nadia's withdrawal, and he felt the hurt portrayed through the watering of her eyes. He had hurt the most important person in his life.

Frank was about to continue when the opposing attorney stood up in annoyance to make an interjection. The judge realizing this calmly asked,

"Attorney, please remind me of your name."

The attorney answered, "Charles S. Campbell."

The judge added, "Mr. Campbell, this is an inquest. It is not a trial." Looking at Frank, he said, "Please continue."

Frank was glad for the permission to continue. "I want you to know the psychological pressure you caused me over the years nurturing someone else's child, but I love my son dearly. You can't take away the bond we have created; he may not have my blood but he has my heart."

By now the entire court was against Andrew. If there were a jury, he would certainly lose the case, but this was an inquest and there was no jury. Frank continued, "You are so evil. I was sorry when your wife took the bullet for you—"

Frank could not finish the sentence as Andrew jumped to his feet shouting, "So that third shadow I saw was yours. I always told the police there was a third person. My God, it was you." This caused an uproar in the court.

Judge Muir now annoyed shouted, "There will be order in the court. I repeat there will be order in the court." The court orderlies tried to maintain order with some of the reporters starting to become restless with the salacious story being interrupted.

Frank looked at Andrew shaking his head. "That's something you can never prove."

Detective Dunn, who was seated next to Weeks, said, "It seems we have something here bigger than we thought."

The inquest continued for the rest of the day except for a lunch recess. Frank gave his testimony on the lottery business, which truthfully showed Andrew's inability to run the business. At the end of the first day's inquisition, The press reporters were in a hurry vying for who would get the story to print first. Andrew watched Weeks making his way to Mayor Orrett's seat before detaining him for an animated discussion, thinking to himself, they must be planning my downfall.

For Andrew, leaving the courthouse was more dramatic than his entering. There were photographers and reporters asking questions. It was embarrassing for a CEO of such a large company to be described in such terms, but he finally made it to the car. The two occupants in the car that evening were silent all the way home. Andrew did not know what to say to his daughter while Nadia did not have anything to say her father; the disappointment weighed heavily throughout the entire trip home. Andrew thought he would say something when the car was parked in the driveway, but Nadia had different plans. On reaching home Nadia disembarked the vehicle as soon as the engine was turned off and went straight to her room.

Andrew understood her feelings. How would he approach her after hearing today's revelations which he could not prove untrue? He did not know how to approach her, so he decided to see if time would mellow things and make the approach easier or if she would come around. He made himself a drink and went outside to sit in his garden.

Later that evening he heard the room door open and as Nadia emerged Andrew, seized the opportunity to explain. He walked over and tried to meet her halfway, but Nadia stopped him in his tracks. "Could I have something to eat? I am hungry and exhausted. In fact,

I am truly disgusted," she said as she walked to the kitchen to prepare her meal. Andrew knew this was not the time and place to rehash any part of the day, so he gave her space and left things alone. He knew his daughter and she was hurting so he retraced his steps to his garden seat.

Later that night Nadia's phone rang. Recognizing the incoming number as Nigel's, she allowed it to ring and then turned it off completely wishing herself a good night's sleep. As for Andrew he tossed and turned in his bed the entire night questioning his past and wondering what Nigel would be relating in court the following day.

The next morning in a packed courtroom, Detective Dunn took the stand as he had done on numerous occasions. After taking the oath, he sat down in the witness chair. DA Weeks asked, "Where are we with the disappearance of Jason Paye?" The detective wasted no time in starting his line of questioning.

"I will start at the beginning of our investigation. Jason disappeared the same weekend Nigel Eckers' car was reported stolen. Human blood was found on the front floor mat. The lottery business started deteriorating after Jason's disappearance until just recently when it has regained some momentum."

Weeks then asked Dunn about the latest evidence gathered. Dunn replied, "The blood stain seems to be our only hope. If can we establish it comes from Jason Paye, then we would have something to work on. The individual's car was involved in quite a serious accident without a witness to back up the story. Then there is the blood on the glass on the car mat. Was he barefooted or was he bleeding so hard as he reached the mat?"

Weeks seized the momentum and asked, "Have you established this blood is Jason Paye's blood?"

Dunn smiled. He had to remain non-committal with his answers. "Yes, seated in this court is Jason Paye's father who has provided us with a cross match." At that moment all the heads started spinning looking for a face that resembled the newspaper picture of Jason. As this continued for a while, the only person who didn't have to look around was Andrew. Nadia recognized her father's non-reaction to the alarm and picked up on this immediately. She wondered if Frank was right.

The court settled down. Weeks wanted to leave the matter open to speculation, so he asked the judge's permission to call the next witness. The entire court waited in anticipation for Jason's father to be called knowing this would bring everything together with the possibility of murder lurking in the wings. Nigel started sweating. He was so nervous his stomach hurt. He want to go to the restroom, but he tried holding it.

Weeks then shouted.

"I will call our next witness, Nigel Eckers, who may be able to give critical clues leading to the outcome of this case, He needs to have a chance to give his side of the story."

Dunn immediately returned to his seat. He and Weeks had worked out this plan, hoping that the sudden call for Nigel would have caught him off guard. In addition with all the evidence building around him, he might crumble. The entire court waited with great anticipation of Nigel's testimony as he walked to the witness box to be seated. Weeks stood waiting; he knew he had no known father for Jason waiting to give evidence, but he had to present the case this way hopefully scaring Nigel into telling the truth.

As Nigel made it to the box, the old lady with the cane from the previous days hearings entered the courthouse again making her way to the front. This time she was noticed by everyone including Nigel as he was taking the oath. Nadia felt an ominous air to this old lady's presence.

As he sat down, the old lady gave Nigel a broad smile. Then, in an instant she immediately changed to a stare down coupled with a serious face. You could never miss her attention focused on Nigel. This was again picked up by Nadia, who was curious about this lady.

Weeks wanted all the all the information gathered on Nigel to be known and documented by the court. He asked him immediately as he took his seat to state his name and position in the company.

Nigel began, "My name is Nigel Eckers. My last post held was head of Information at the lottery company of Amalta.

Weeks then asked him, "Were you an assistant to the CEO Andrew Cole?" Nigel replied, "Yes."

Weeks wanted this line of questioning because he wanted to implicate Andrew in anything Nigel was involved in. If Nigel wanted to protect his boss, that was his choice. At this point they were both under suspicion. Weeks really didn't know how to tackle Nigel, but he was going to bluff him all the way. Little did he know Nigel was out for himself and himself alone. To hell with Andrew Cole and others.

Weeks continued, "When Jason disappeared, there is evidence to show you worked conscientiously to dig deeper into the goings on in the company. Why were you so suspicious of the functioning of the company?" as he asked.

Nigel was gathering himself together but scared as hell as he began,

"With what I was able to research and learn the lottery company has held itself together for many years. It provided hundreds of young people with education assistance not available otherwise. Plus, it gave many a perceived access to small fortunes. For unknown reasons, its popularity started dwindling as fewer people were playing. The directive from the Board requested a re-energized game to regain its appeal. Then entered Jason Paye with his team working feverously to re-energize the game with success. He disappears!!!! The game again lost its appeal. Did the game depend on Jason's charisma? Something strange was happening. This should not have happened because a team was in place." Nigel by now was stuttering in his delivery. Andrew grew nervous knowing Nigel's low stress tolerance.

Weeks then asked in a firm voice, "What do you mean and what do you think happened to Jason? What was his part in the success of the game?" He was now rushing Nigel for answers not giving him time to change direction. He had also recognized Nigel's nervousness and wanted to capitalize on the moment.

Nigel was ready to spill his guts. He knew if he could swing things at this point, he could slant the proceedings in Andrew's direction and make him the person responsible for Jason's disappearance. If he could get out of this web, he might still be able to position himself to take over the lottery after getting rid of Andrew. If this became a reality, there would be no future with Nadia and he reminded himself of how lately things were strained. She would not even return phone calls, so it didn't matter. He knew she would never trust him again. Nadia had relied on Nigel's discretion in the past and she knew he was honest, but sometimes hard-nosed and inflexible. This time she saw these qualities destroying her father's legacy.

Nadia had many thoughts during Nigel's testimony. Could it be real that her father was destroyed by her lover, the one she helped to get the job? The rumors circulating for the last couple of months pointed fingers at Andrew, hence removing him would be easy. The next question jolted her back from her reverie.

Weeks asked, "Do you know the blood sample showed a match with Jason Paye's blood?"

Nigel was now unprotected and he knew he had murder hanging over his head. Weeks made a last-minute attempt to hold Nigel accountable. He could see the surprise on Nigel's face at the direct inferences. In desperation Nigel was about to turn the entire proceedings into turmoil, but he did not care. He was about to bring Andrew down with him.

As Nigel was about to start answering Weeks' question, there was complete silence in the court in anticipation of something special. The old lady seated in the front row stood up to exit the row. Moving toward the middle walking aisle, she was disruptive when passing the others seated in the row. As she exited the row, she passed a note to the elderly gentleman sitting at the end. She said to him, "Give that to the man on the stand if you get a chance. I feel faint so I must leave." She thanked him for his help. He asked her if she was all right and she nodded. "I'll be all right."

All this activity from the old lady caused a restlessness throughout the crowd; she somehow had that effect and aura. The judge trying to control the disturbance had to use his gavel to jolt all into silence while calling for order. The crowd was again focused on Nigel, who could not take his eyes off the old lady. There was something strange about her step as she made it towards the door. She made it to the landing in front of the exit door and at the top of the aisle she turned around to face Nigel. She looked him straight in the eyes, and he could not get a word out as the crowd waited. As he sat looking at her, he saw the old lady place her index finger on her forehead and wiggle around twice singing a little song. Then, she abruptly stopped the routine, placed her index finger on her lips which was the international signal for "shut-up, say no more." Then she pointed at Nigel meaning I am directing this to you. "SHUT-UP" The finger then moved and she moved that same finger across her throat to say, "This will be your downfall."

The old lady then held a small object between her fingers, so Nigel could see it. She gently placed it on the ground to roll down the sloping aisle. It jingled as it moved towards the witness box, and as if predestined, it stopped at the row where the elderly gentleman bearer of the note sat. He picked it up, and turning to Nigel, he shook it so it made a distinctive sound. He thought, how sinister things had become.

Nigel, on hearing the sound knew that this, along with the old lady's actions, could be no coincidence. Nigel experienced the revelation. This is Jason in drag, his favorite pastime. She was telling him to shut up. Could this be providence?"

The old lady continued on her way out, but just before she exited the door, she turned 180 degrees and placed her finger on her lips and with the famous wiggle she left smiling. Nigel was now certain it was Jason.

Shocked, Nigel stood up forgetting all protocol. He pointed to the door. Looking at the judge and needing help from the people in the court to stop her from escaping, he managed to shout some unintelligible words, he tried jumping over podium and fell to the floor.

Was he having a seizure? It was a complete shocker for the court, but with all attention focused on Nigel the old lady easily made her escape.

Nigel in the meantime was held by the guard, coming to his senses but not realizing how much time had elapsed, he tried to reach the door, shouting, "Stop her." But the old lady was gone. The guards grabbing Nigel thinking he was going crazy or trying to escape questioning.

By now the court was in an uproar and no one understood what was happening. The judge in the meantime was beating his gavel continuously while other guards tried sealing off the doors from the inside, all in an effort to restore order and decorum.

Nigel was initially scared since Jason was the only one who knew what he had done and was warning him to shut up. He certainly didn't not want to be charged with attempted murder. Nigel was unable to run after the old lady while being restrained by the guards, and the secrets to every aspect of his recent life just went through that door. It was only a few feet in front of him and he yet he was unable grab onto it for answers he needed so urgently. As usual that bastard Jason got the upper hand.

As the old lady was approaching her limousine waiting for her, she saw a figure she recognized. It was Nigel's cousin John coming up the steps.

Seeing the old lady trying to move quickly, he said, "May I help you?" The old lady faced the instantaneous decision of the moment and agreed to submit to John's offer of help to the car. As he opened the rear door, she acted as if she was slipping and looking him straight in the eye, she kicked him straight in his groin. He buckled in pain, slowly curling to the ground.

She said, "I am sorry. Let me help you until you can help yourself." So the old lady helped him to sit on the bottom step of the courthouse nursing his mid section and wondering what kind of old woman that was. Some things about her did not add up.

Opening the door herself while John, despite his pain, offered a hand- shake sticking his hand into the door of the limousine. She slammed the door, and there was a crunch as his fingers were locked into the door frame. She quickly opened the door and seeing him pulling back at least three bent and broken fingers, she said to the chauffeur, "Please, driver, that man tried to get my purse. I had to defend myself." As she closed the door, she looked back with a satisfied smile. She put her hand through the window giving him the finger – that chapter of her life was behind her and was now closed.

The chauffeur then asked, "Where to madam?" she gently replied.

"Take me to the Hotel Forsheim. I am having a signing, and my lawyers are waiting. Then tomorrow please pick me up early in the morning for the airport."

Back in the court Nigel quickly weighed out his odds. With the old lady signaling him to keep his mouth shut, not telling the court what he knew about manipulation of the game was outweighed by a case of attempted murder. He immediately knew what to do. On being released by the guards, he asked the judge permission to quickly walk to the window to see if the old lady was still there. The judge was at first reluctant, but he also wanted to fulfill his curiosity and asked the guard to accompany him up the aisle. On reaching the window and looking out there was no old lady to be seen. She was gone, leaving only a man sitting on the sidewalk holding his groin.

On his way back down the aisle as he reached the first row, an old gentleman at the end of a row gave him a note, saying it was left by the old lady. He also passed a small metal bell to him, which Nigel cautiously took. He knew for sure it was Jason and he was confused.

On reaching the witness box he unwrapped the note. It read: 'What will a man who places a yoke on another be willing to change to fulfill his own ambitions?" There was no signature, but he knew who left it, the same old lady person who signaled for him to shut up.

As the court settled back into a sense of order, Nigel again approached the witness stand, and as he took his seat his stomach was hurting. With all the excitement the urge to use the toilet had intensified. He wondered why Jason would want to warn him to save his hide. Maybe he was not as bad as Nigel thought.

Nigel's stomach became so unbearable he had to ask the judge's permission to urgently use the restroom. There was laughter throughout the crowd. Nigel had not evoked anyone's sympathy. The judge said, "Due to the previous incident, we will have a half an hour recess for us to settle back with some well needed decorum."

With that Nigel quickly made his way out of the courtroom asking for directions to the nearest restroom. As he burst open the door, he saw the toilet door at the back was closed. The only other object was a urinal and face basin. Seeing this was a small restroom for emergencies, he turned the latch to open the door only to realize it was locked and in use. Nigel's growling bowels made him realize time was of the essence. He started pounding on the unyielding door. He looked at the urinal and decided, what the hell? As he released everything relieving himself of all his burdens while holding this posture, the father and son came out. They could not believe their eyes as the father lifted his child trying to keep the child's face away from the shameful sight as they exited through the main door.

Nigel was so embarrassed he stretched his hand and latched the main door then limped into the toilet. Sitting there, he felt demoralized and belittled for the things happening recently in his life. How far downhill had he allowed himself to sink? He thought of his misdeeds – trying to commit murder topped the list. He thought these were paybacks for his wickedness, and he felt less than a person. He was so ashamed of himself; he had betrayed those who helped him to rise in the company those who had so much confidence in his ability, only to lose their trust. Later on his way back to the courtroom, he stopped at the door peeping through the hinge space before entering, he saw Nadia seated there. He remembered their loving days together, the kindness and love from a loving girlfriend who gave him the encouragement he needed in the different aspects of his life. He questioned why he had become a self-centered animal losing sight of kindness in the name of ambition.

The limousine had pulled up at the Hotel Forsheim, and Mrs. Payne was greeted in suitable fashion from the front desk staff who remembered her. She asked if the Presidential Suite was available for her to freshen up and for an overnight stay. On hearing the excitement outside, the manager Mr. Potts came out quickly from his office. Seeing who the guest was he said, "Welcome back, Mrs. Payne. I overheard the conversation, but the Presidential Suite is occupied. I know this is your favorite suite, but we are having an important signing here this morning by the new owners and its being held in the Presidential Suite. Can I offer a comparable suite, The Caribbean?"

Mrs. Payne turned to him and said calmly, "Mr. Potts, this is why we are here. I am here for the signing and will be leaving early in the morning."

He then connected the name. He wondered how he could be so daft. This was no way to start with new owner of the hotel. Penitently he countered, "Madam, I am terribly sorry. I will personally escort you to your meeting. The lawyers have been waiting. Again, please accept my apology."

Mrs. Payne was driven early next morning directly to the private airport to her private jet, The YELLOWSTOHE. Waiting for her were her pilot Jesse and flight attendant, Theo. The three were making their way to the newly acquired house on the Caribbean island of Barbados.

As Nigel now relieved of his burden sitting pondering his next move, there was a knock on the entrance door. He hurriedly wiped his entrails the best he could. On opening the door, he realized the person entering was the cleaning crew. He immediately lowered his head in a sheepish manner to avoid recognition.

As he journeyed back to the witness stand, he made many in the court grow increasingly nervous anticipating the outcome because no one understood the situation and what was happening. As he took his seat, he looked at the people seated before him. He saw Andrew, who knew Nigel's testimony could destroy all he had built up over the years. He looked at Frank, who had nothing to hide, knew how angry Nigel was in his last days and was excited with the upcoming explosion. Then there was the love of his life, Nadia, who was angry with him for wanting to destroy the person who meant more to her, her father. Also, before him sat the office staff who had decided things were more interesting here than at work. They awaited the scoop behind the running of the lottery company wondering if all these years they were working under the umbrella of dishonesty and if Nigel had a secret to tell.

As Nigel settled into the witness chair, DA Weeks could not wait to resume questioning and asked, "What were the irregularities found at the lottery office?"

Nigel said confidently, "In all my time spent there, the game was performed with the highest degree of honesty and with a management of the highest caliber. It was a pleasure to work with such a group. I resigned from the company to return to help my family and their business. I tried the corporate world, but I think small town living is best for me. As for Jason's disappearance, you need to look more into his background and you may find clues there.

Dunn and Weeks looked at each other disappointed knowing their strategy had imploded. They had failed to extract the evidence to destroy Andrew and the lottery business. The press reporters present were also unhappy with the outcome. You could feel the discontent and disappointment in the room after Nigel was asked to step down. The star witness had become "tame." Had he taken a hit to the head when he fell?

The judge then asked for the results from the cross-matching of the DNA and for the father of Jason Paye to come forward. At this point D.A Weeks knew he had to take the embarrassment of the moment and face the criticism.

"Your honor, that relative did not fully cooperate with us."

When the judge heard this, he knew right away what was going on, and he asked both Dunn and Weeks to meet him in his chambers after the inquest.

Weeks asked the judge for an adjournment of the proceedings stating the need for other witnesses was unnecessary. On this basis the judge agreed for adjournment with the final sounding of the gavel.

16

CHAPTER

NIGEL SEEMED HAPPY as he stepped down looking over towards Nadia and smiling as if he had experienced the greatest achievement of his life. His smile was not reciprocated. As the court house was clearing, Nigel signaled to Nadia that he would call her later. Her response was nonchalant.

On the way out, the mayor met up with Andrew as they were exiting. They were both cordial and polite when the mayor said to Andrew, "I would like you to meet Stefan Gambani. He will be taking over the running of the lottery company as of next week."

He did not expect Andrew's reaction when Andrew proffered an envelope saying, "That will not be necessary. Please accept my resignation. It is effective immediately." Then Andrew walked off, to the surprise of both men.

Later that night Nigel called Nadia at home. He was cautious with his conversation. He wanted to know if there was something still between them worth reactivating.

Nadia said to him calmly, "I don't have to ask how you are doing. I could have seen that from your performance this morning."

He was happy to hear her voice. "How did you like the outcome? I guess I handled it quite well?" he asked.

Nadia paused. "You handled yourself admirably."

Nigel interjected, "Thank you."

While Nadia trying to continue and not wanting to break her trend of conversation said, "You have become an inductee of the corporate world, one that is selfish and self-centered. You are now a part of the "I" club. Congratulations. You have lost the part of you I once loved. You have not seen me for many months and your conversation is about you and the business, as usual."

She waited patiently for him to interject, but he was taken aback and speechless so she continued. "I have a disdain for greed. It tells me your journey does not include anyone but yourself, so you will do whatever it takes to get you there by fair or foul means. You have no need for me on this journey; I will not be a part of your program. I have absolutely no desire anymore to be in your world. Good-bye." She hung up leaving him to think through what she had just said.

He sat speechless his last breath meant nothing, his world was gone, he felt helpless. There were decisions to be made, so Nigel spent the next couple of hours packing all his belongings. The next morning he fitted them into his little blue car before the press could take up their position to ask questions and start another day of harassment. He had had enough of the city and its fast life. He had lost his lover and his ambitions in the corporate world had brought him close to losing his freedom, almost to be considered a murderer. He felt this was not one of the things he had considered when moving to the bright lights of the city.

As he drove off, he reminisced about the good times at The Watering Hole, the fun he preferred to leave behind as he drove cross-country. He wanted to travel Highway Route 147, where Jason disappeared.

On reaching the area, he slowed down to take a last glimpse of the general store and maybe Jason's shadow. He gave himself a smile. What he saw on reaching the general store was an unusual sight of many people gathered, so he pulled into the parking area to see what was going on.

Asking the first person he met, he was told the old man who ran the store had passed away so the store is being auctioned.

"How did he die?"

A person replied, "He was climbing up the rail on the tank and fell. The stupid tank was blocked for weeks. He thought he could fix it and fell. Bad decision."

In the background the auctioneer shouted, "Two thousand!"

Someone in the crowd said, "Three thousand."

There was silence for a while, then another call. "Four thousand." Then there was silence again.

Nigel thought to himself, I could live out here far from everyone, build a house, and do some farming while expanding on the shop. It might be just what I need.

The auctioneer shouted, "Going once..."

Nigel raised his hand and shouted, "Five thousand."

Again there was silence as the auctioneer shouted, "Going once, going twice... Sold to the gentleman standing by the blue car."

Just as the auction formalities were ending, there was a shout from the top of the tank holding something. "I found what was blocking the water. It was this piece of cloth." A man threw it down from the top of the tank, and it landed with a splash.

On the ground splattered open were the red underpants with the kissing bears pattern. Nigel recognized it immediately, but all he could do is laugh as he looked up at the water tower. That's where Jason was hiding. There was instant admiration for his ex-friend who he was truly convinced was not dead.

You bastard. You are truly out of this world. Yes, my friend, you survived. I don't know how you did it, but you survived, he thought to himself. Despite all the chaos, no one died; no murder was committed, thank God. This was a great source of relief for Nigel as he looked up one more time shaking his head, appreciating Jason even more as he looked up at the water tank one more time and laughed.

Flying overhead was a private jet with Jason and his crew laughing at the coincidence of both the name of the airplane and that of the water tank–both misspelled–named YELLOWSTOHN.

How ironic, all were laughing from the ground to the air.

THE END

Printed in the United States
by Baker & Taylor Publisher Services